HUNGER

Mika pressed Bailey against the wall of her bedroom.

His hands skimmed up her back, his hips easing forward so she could feel the heavy thrust of his arousal. Sweet passion sang through her blood, the intoxicating sensation making her head spin like she was drunk.

"Tell me that you missed me."

She leaned forward to press a kiss to the pulse that beat at the base of his neck.

"Every minute of every day."

"Yes." He trembled, his silky hair brushing her shoulder as he leaned down to whisper directly into her ear. "Damn, but I need you. . . ."

from *On the Hunt* by Alexandra Ivy

ON THE HUNT

ALEXANDRA IVY

REBECCA ZANETTI

DIANNE DUVALL

HANNAH JAYNE

ZEBRA BOOKS
KENSINGTON PUBLISHING CORP.
http://www.kensingtonbooks.com

ZEBRA BOOKS are published by

Kensington Publishing Corp.
119 West 40th Street
New York, NY 10018

All Kensington titles, imprints, and distributed lines are available at
special quantity discounts for bulk purchases for sales promotion, pre-
miums, fund-raising, educational, or institutional use.

Special book excerpts or customized printings can also be created to fit
specific needs. For details, write or phone the office of the Kensington
Sales Manager: Attn.: Sales Department. Kensington Publishing Corp.,
119 West 40th Street, New York, NY 10018. Phone: 1-800-221-2647.

Zebra and the Z logo Reg. U.S. Pat. & TM Off.

First Printing: September 2015
ISBN-13: 978-1-4201-2513-9
ISBN-10: 1-4201-2513-3

eISBN-13: 978-1-4201-4141-2
eISBN-10: 1-4201-4141-4

10 9 8 7 6 5 4 3 2

Printed in the United States of America

Contents

On the Hunt

Alexandra Ivy

Prologue

It was no surprise that the history of the high-bloods had been lost in the midst of time.

Although they'd been worshipped as gods in ancient times, their powers had eventually caused an overwhelming fear and envy among the humans. They went from being revered to being hunted as if they were dangerous beasts.

In an attempt to save their people, they'd gone into hiding.

For centuries they remained in the shadows, still using their powers, but keeping them secret from the world.

Then, with a slow caution, they began to band together, creating communities where they could help to defend one another. Witches, necromancers, healers, psychics, clairvoyants, and a dozen other types of high-bloods all living together.

The largest of the communities was Valhalla, a sprawling compound in the Midwest that was protected by a dome of impenetrable magic. It was also defended by Sentinels, the monk-trained warriors who were defenders of the high-bloods.

The Sentinels were divided into two groups.

Those warriors born with magic who were chosen to be the personal guards to the high-bloods. They were marked with tattoos that protected them from magic or any attempt to manipulate their minds.

Then there were the hunters. Although they didn't have magic they were faster, stronger, and far more lethal than a mere human. And without the distinctive tattoos of their brothers, they were able to move through the world without attracting attention.

They were the enforcement for their people. They tracked down renegades and those high-bloods who were a danger to themselves or others.

No one, no matter how powerful they might be, wanted to attract the attention of a hunter.

There was no place you could hide. . . .

Chapter One

The location of Valhalla, the main home of the high-bloods, wasn't a secret.

Even with a magical dome of protection, it was tough to hide several thousand acres of land smack dab in the middle of the United States with two-dozen structures that included living quarters, workshops, garages, barns, and a school.

Of course, very few "norms" were allowed through the magical barriers to visit the central building that was constructed in the shape of a pentagon with an inner courtyard that was famed for its gardens. And those who were permitted to enter found themselves confined to the upper floor that was reserved for official offices and formal reception rooms, plus a small number of guest rooms if the visitors were expected to stay more than a few hours.

Only high-bloods were allowed into the nine lower levels that contained private quarters and secret labs that were dug deep into the earth.

And only Sentinels were allowed on the bottom floor that was reserved exclusively for their use.

With a central room that was dominated by a state-of-the-art computer system and heavy wooden furniture, it looked like something out of a James Bond movie.

Two walls were lined with monitors that were connected to dozens of satellites and surveillance equipment spread throughout the world. On another wall were several doors that were closed and monitored with motion and heat sensors. The weapons that they kept inside were not only lethal, but many were magically enhanced to create enormous damage.

Standing in the attached private office, the two Sentinels stood face-to-face.

At a distance, the warriors were remarkably similar.

Both had long, dark hair that framed narrow faces with copper-toned skin and eyes as black as polished ebony. Both had the lean, chiseled muscles of trained warriors. And both were wearing casual jeans and T-shirts that did nothing to disguise their lethal power.

A closer glance, however, revealed that Wolfe, the leader of the Sentinels, had a streak of white in his hair at his right temple and that his features had been hewn in the deserts of the Middle East.

Mika Tanner, on the other hand, shared the chiseled features of his Native American ancestors.

Over the years, his stark beauty had attracted the notice of women. A *lot* of women. But none had managed to capture his aloof attention.

Of course, his lack of interest only made them more determined to be the one to claim him.

Not that Mika noticed.

It wasn't that he didn't like women.

Hell, that was the problem.

In one spectacular case he'd loved a woman.

Deeply and irrevocably.

Now he was dedicated to his duty as a hunter Sentinel. Nothing was allowed to distract him.

Which was why he'd abruptly walked away from the pretty witch who'd been trying to convince him to join her for dinner the second the text from Wolfe had hit his phone.

Folding his arms over his chest, he studied Wolfe with a stoic curiosity.

"You wanted to see me?"

"Here." Getting straight to the point, Wolfe shoved a file folder into Mika's hand. The Tagos (leader of the Sentinels) was never big on chitchat.

Thank God.

Mika hated wasting his time with worthless small talk.

Opening the file, he stared down at the photo of a young man who looked to be in his early twenties with short brown hair and a face that was remarkable only for the fact it was so completely average. The type of face that would never stand out in a crowd.

He read the name at the bottom of the photo.

"Jacob Benson. Is the name supposed to mean something to me?"

"Until yesterday morning, he was an acolyte at the monastery in Louisiana," Wolfe readily answered.

Mika lifted his gaze, not surprised to find that Wolfe's expression was unreadable.

The older man rarely gave away his inner thoughts.

"And now?"

"He's disappeared."

Mika arched a brow, waiting for the rest of the story.

Even for Wolfe, that was vague.

"What happened?" he prompted.

The leader shrugged. "According to Brother Noland, the young man was a quiet, diligent student who'd never caused trouble until he unexpectedly snuck into the garage and stole one of the cars used by the monks."

All Sentinels were trained by the monks, whether they were to become guardians or hunters. It was a tradition that had started in ancient times.

And while a few of the methods had changed to include

the latest weapons and technology, the basics had remained the same throughout the centuries.

How to kill as swiftly and efficiently as possible.

"It's not that uncommon for an acolyte to decide to go for a joyride," Mika pointed out.

Boys would be boys regardless of their special powers.

And since Sentinels lived several hundred years, they were still considered juveniles until they reached their late thirties.

"On his way out of the garage he hit one of the monks," Wolfe said.

Shit. Mika scowled. "How bad?"

"He's on the mend, but Jacob never stopped or even slowed to check on the man he'd injured." Wolfe leaned against the corner of the desk. "His complete lack of concern is so out of character that the monks are certain something is wrong."

"And no one has seen him since then?"

"No, they checked with his family and friends, but he hasn't contacted any of them."

Mika understood their concern if the acolyte was acting out of character, but there were a number of fairly obvious explanations for his impulsive behavior.

"What about a girlfriend?" He named the obvious. "When a young man is doing something idiotic, it can usually be traced to his belief that he's in love."

Wolfe sent him a wry smile. "You sound as if you have personal experience."

A familiar ache twisted his gut at the memory of a young girl with white-gold curls and huge green eyes set in a heart-shaped face.

Bailey Morrell was a healer who'd stolen his heart when her parents had traveled to the reservation in Oklahoma to teach.

Odd, really.

The two couldn't have been more different.

Where Mika was quiet and reserved, Bailey had possessed an infectious spirit and a joy for life that instantly captivated him. She'd been like a brilliant butterfly who'd fluttered into his life, dazzling him with her charm and generous heart.

Of course, it was those same qualities that had ripped them apart.

While Mika had gone to the monastery to be trained as a Sentinel, Bailey had traveled to Valhalla to hone her skills as a healer.

He'd thrived among the other warriors, perhaps for the first time in his life feeling as if he truly belonged. There was no need to disguise his superior powers or to feel as if he was a freak. The Sentinels became his family.

Bailey, on the other hand, had felt stifled by the rules demanded by her trainers. She'd inherited her parents' disdain for authority and constantly rebelled by sneaking away to heal those high-bloods who were afraid to travel to Valhalla or were hiding from the authorities.

"Bailey's strays" became a constant source of irritation to her teachers as well as the Mave, the powerful witch who was the ultimate ruler of Valhalla.

By the time Mika felt in the position to turn their passionate love affair into a more permanent arrangement, Bailey had reached the end of her patience.

Instead of putting down roots at Valhalla, the beautiful healer wanted him to turn his back on his duty to follow her into a life of constant travel and uncertainty.

Bailey might call it freedom, but he couldn't walk away from the brothers who depended on him. Or the pledges he'd made to the monks.

So she'd left.

Without even saying good-bye.

Abruptly realizing that Wolfe was watching him with a knowing gaze, Mika cleared the lump from his throat.

"Don't we all have a past?" he demanded.

"Touché." Wolfe's expression hardened, as if he had his own painful memories. "What happened to yours?"

Mika grimaced. "She refused to be caged."

"I have no information on a girlfriend." Wolfe abruptly turned the conversation back to the reason he'd called Mika to his office. "But that might be an angle for you to investigate."

"Me?"

"I want you to track him."

"Why?" Mika frowned. Without false modesty he knew he was the best tracker in Valhalla. It seemed a waste of his skills to send him on a chase for one boy who would more than likely return from his mysterious journey within a day or two. "He isn't the first and he won't be the last acolyte to run away, for whatever reason."

"As I said, the Brother is convinced that there's more going on here than just the disappearance of one student," Wolfe said.

"What?"

"He doesn't know, but I trust his judgment." Wolfe's voice warned that he wasn't in the mood for a debate. Hell, the Tagos was never in the mood for debate. His word was law among the Sentinels. "We need to make sure that Jacob wasn't forced or intimidated into leaving the monastery."

Mika heaved a sigh. "Perfect."

Wolfe arched a brow. "Did you have other plans?"

"Would it matter if I did?"

"Nope."

Mika gave a short laugh. He liked the fact his leader was so predictable.

Besides, it'd been over a week since he'd last been on the hunt.

He had to remain active to keep his instincts sharp.

And to keep his thoughts occupied, a voice whispered in the back of his mind.

"I'll leave after lunch. I assume you'll have a guardian transport me?" he demanded, referring to the Sentinels who could travel from monastery to monastery through mystical pathways.

"Fane will meet you in the chapel."

Knowing the meeting was over, Mika turned to head out the door only to be halted when Wolfe cleared his throat. Swallowing a curse, he glanced over his shoulder.

"What?"

"When you do find the boy, leave the punishment to the monks."

Mika stiffened, instantly offended. "I wouldn't hurt a mere boy."

"I know, but you can be . . ." Wolfe searched for the appropriate word. "Intimidating."

"Me?"

"It's all that stoic silence," Wolfe informed him. "It makes people itchy."

Mika shrugged. He knew what people whispered behind his back.

He was aloof.

Unapproachable.

A cold, unfeeling bastard.

He really didn't give a shit.

"I speak when I have something to say."

"Good." Wolfe tossed him one of the disposable cell phones they always used when they were in the field. "Then you can call me when you find the boy."

It was difficult to decide what was more aggravating.

The swarm of bugs that attacked without warning.

The goopy mud that clung to her shoes.

Or the air that was so thick with humidity that breathing was an Olympic sport.

August in the swamps of Louisiana was a lesson in endurance.

Still, there were bonuses to choosing the area for a temporary home, Bailey Morrell reminded herself as she ran her fingers through her short mop of blond curls that were already clinging to her damp skin.

It was isolated. Dangerous for humans. And best of all, a local witch had wrapped her small cabin and the surrounding grounds in a powerful layer of magic that meant no one could enter without her allowing them through.

A perfect place to set up her tiny clinic to help those high-bloods who preferred to avoid the more formal healers.

Like the young man standing beside her.

She frowned as she glanced at Jacob, no last name given.

As a healer she possessed the rare talent of being able to sense when a high-blood was injured or sick in the local vicinity. Which was what had led her from her cottage yesterday morning to discover Jacob staggering along the deserted road that ran next to the bayou.

She'd been horrified to see his battered and bruised body. Although he was still young and hadn't yet received the tattoos that would offer him protection, he was a potential guardian Sentinel. Which meant that he could endure ten times the battering to his body than a normal human could.

For him to be so grievously injured meant he'd taken one hell of a beating.

Not that the acolyte would tell her what had happened.

And she hadn't probed.

That was her mantra.

Live and let live.

Now, however, she couldn't help but try to convince the boy he was making a mistake.

Despite her healing, he remained dangerously weak. He needed rest and plenty of good food to complete his recovery.

Gently smoothing the light brown hair from his forehead, she studied him with a worried gaze.

"Jacob, I don't think you're strong enough to leave," she said in soft tones.

He grimaced, one eye swollen and his bottom lip split.

"I have to," he muttered.

"If you're worried about the monks, I could contact them and explain—"

"No." Jacob grabbed her arm, his panic making him clutch her hard enough to bruise her pale skin. She winced, and Jacob instantly eased his grip, but his distress remained. "Please. I can't face them. Not yet."

Her lips flattened. Unlike those healers who worked for Valhalla, she wouldn't force him back to the monastery.

"Where will you go?" she instead demanded.

"I have a . . ." He paused, his gaze shifting away in a gesture that warned he was about to lie. "Friend I can stay with."

Her hand cupped his cheek, her healing power naturally flowing from her palm into his still-weak body.

"Jacob, if you're in trouble you can tell me."

He shuddered, his shoulders hunched. "I can't," he whispered so softly she barely caught the words.

"I swear that whatever you tell me won't go any further, and I might be able to help," she assured him.

"I—"

"Tell me," she urged when his words trailed away.

He slowly squared his shoulders. "I have something I must do first."

Bailey didn't like the grim edge in his voice.

Was he planning to exact revenge on whoever had attacked him?

Reaching into the pocket of her denim shorts, she pulled

out a crumpled business card that was printed with her cell number. She always kept them handy.

"Here's my number," she said, pressing the card into his hand. "You can call me day or night."

He studied the card, the tension that hummed around him a tangible force.

"You'll come for me?" he demanded, his voice low, intense.

A strange chill inched down Bailey's spine as she lowered her hand. There was something going on with this young man.

But what?

"Always," she promised.

Far from comforting the Sentinel, her words seemed to add to his distress.

"I have to go," he muttered, taking a quick step forward.

"Jacob." She halted his hurried retreat.

He grudgingly halted. "Yes?"

"Sometimes it's hard to know what's right or wrong," she told him in soft tones. "Listen to your heart."

He gave a sad sigh. "That's what I'm doing."

Without giving her the opportunity to respond, Jacob stepped through the magical barrier and swiftly disappeared in the thick foliage.

Bailey stood there for a long moment, her heart troubled.

She wished she could do more, but she wasn't going to force Jacob to stay.

He was old enough to make his own decisions.

Finally accepting Jacob wasn't going to have a change of heart and return, Bailey headed toward the nearby town to replenish the food she'd used during her patient's short visit.

Although calling Gilford a town was being extremely generous.

There was nothing beyond a dozen houses and handful of shops that were huddled near the vast monastery. The monks and their students were remarkably self-sufficient, but they did hire a few local workers.

And, of course, there were those hardy souls who called the swamps home. They depended on the stores in Gilford when they were in need of supplies.

Two hours later she was done with her shopping and had stopped by the home of a local witch who had become a friend since Bailey had arrived in the area several months before.

Walking back to her cottage along the narrow path, she was skirting the treacherous edge of a bog when the sound of a male voice filled the air.

"*Bonjour*, Bailey."

Pressing a hand to her racing heart, she whirled around to glare at the man who was standing only a few feet away.

For a brief second Bailey was staring at an exact replica of herself.

The same untidy halo of pale curls. The same heart-shaped face. The same slender figure that was casually dressed in white cotton shorts and a red halter-top.

Only the eyes were different.

While hers were a clear mint green, the creature standing in front of her had eyes of pure white that glowed with a frightening power.

"Boggs." She gave a shake of her head. "You startled me."

There was a shimmer before her image was replaced by a pale, hairless man who stood nearly six feet tall. His features looked as if they'd only been half-formed, giving him the creepy appearance of a larva while his thin body was covered by a heavy robe.

The eyes remained white even as the power faded, revealing he was completely blind.

Not that Boggs needed his eyes to see.

As a doppelgänger he was capable of sensing another

person's essence, allowing him to take their shape for a limited period of time.

He also had the ability to touch an object to have it "whisper" to him. She wasn't sure what that meant beyond the fact he would have a glimpse into the past or the future, or even the present. And that he couldn't control what he could hear.

Needless to say, his odd appearance and strange talents didn't make him particularly popular. Not even among the high-bloods who took weird to a new level.

Bailey, however, enjoyed his sporadic visits to the swamps.

Like her, Boggs had never found a place at Valhalla. They were both outsiders who enjoyed a life without rules and expectations.

Free spirits.

"Did you miss me?" the doppelgänger demanded.

She gave a toss of her silvery curls. "I missed beating the pants off you at chess."

Something that might have been humor twisted the half-formed features.

"You don't need to use chess to get my pants off, pet."

She shook her head. "Don't start," she warned. She knew Boggs was just teasing, but she didn't flirt.

Not with anyone.

Not since . . .

She slammed the door on the treacherous thought.

Nope. She was soooo not going there.

"A pity," he murmured.

She reached into one of her bags and pulled out an apple, tossing it in Boggs's direction.

Despite being blind, he easily grabbed the fruit out of the air and took a bite.

"Have you been out saving the world?" she asked. The doppelgänger claimed that he'd recently given information to end a threat by a crazed necromancer.

He shrugged. "Always."

"So what brings you here?"

Boggs took time to finish the apple before he tossed the core toward the thick line of cypress trees.

"I've missed your companionship," he said, his fingers smoothing down the front of his robe as he seemed to search for the appropriate words. "And—"

"No," Bailey sharply interrupted, abruptly sensing he was about to share a vision. It wasn't that she was morally opposed to psychics and clairvoyants. They often prevented tragedies for high-bloods. But she preferred to live her life without a safety net. "I've told you. No sneak peeks into the future. I like to be surprised."

Boggs made a sound of annoyance, clearly desperate to warn her. "You must take great care, Bailey."

"Boggs—"

"One that you trust will betray you," he said in a rush.

Bailey slapped her hands over her ears. "Stop."

Boggs held up his slender hands in a gesture of defeat. "So stubborn," he muttered.

"Yeah, I've been told that," she admitted wryly. More times than she wanted to acknowledge. "Do you want to join me for dinner?"

"Not tonight," Boggs said, his hand reaching out to lightly touch a curl that rested against her cheek. "Take care, pet. Danger stalks you."

With his unwelcome warning delivered, Boggs stepped back, and with his usual love for drama, he spread his arms and simply disappeared.

Bailey gave a shake of her head.

As far as she knew, Boggs was the only high-blood who could actually perform that little trick.

Even the guardian Sentinels who could use their magic to travel in a blink of an eye had to use copper posts that transported them from one monastery to another.

None of them could just . . . poof.

Shifting the bags of groceries in her arms, she continued around the bog, her feet sinking into the mossy ground as she at last caught sight of her small cottage, which was nearly lost in the gathering shadows.

She'd stayed in town longer than she'd intended, she abruptly realized.

Being a high-blood meant that she was harder to kill than a normal human, but she didn't possess the same strength as a Sentinel. There were plenty of things that crept through the swamp at night that could hurt her.

She picked up her pace, frowning as a strange prickle of alarm raced through her.

What was wrong with her?

It was one thing to be sensible enough to avoid unnecessary danger, and another to suddenly feel as if she were being stalked.

"Get a grip, Bailey," she muttered, beneath her breath. "It's only because of Boggs and his creepy warnings. . . ."

Her words trailed away as she heard a distinct rustle in the underbrush.

The wind?

An animal?

A ghost?

She shivered, judging the distance between herself and the cottage.

Too far to make it beyond the barrier if she was actually being hunted.

Turning, she continued to back toward the protective shield while scanning for any hidden intruders.

"Who's there?" she called out, her voice not entirely steady. "Show yourself."

Nothing moved beyond a startled squirrel that darted into a patch of milkweed, and the stirring of the thick Spanish moss as a sluggish breeze wound its way through the trees.

Okay. She was being ridiculous.

There was nothing but bugs and gators and . . .

An arm abruptly wrapped around her from behind, jerking her against a rock-hard body.

Bailey dropped the grocery bags to the ground, her lips parting to scream. Before she could make a sound, however, a hand was pressed over her mouth, stifling her cry of fear.

"Gotcha," a male voice whispered in her ear.

She sucked in a shocked breath, her heart coming to a perfect, painful halt.

Shit. She recognized that voice.

"Mika."

Chapter Two

Mika's lips twisted in a wry smile. He hadn't missed the dismay in Bailey's muffled voice.

Of course, to be fair, he hadn't been overjoyed when he followed the trail into the swamp and caught the sweet scent of jasmine.

The delicate fragrance might have been native to this particular area of the swamp. And even if it wasn't, there could always be some random woman wearing perfume.

There were a dozen explanations. But he knew the truth.

The scent didn't come from a plant or a bottle.

It was a unique, intoxicating aroma that could only belong to Bailey Morrell.

Damn.

He'd nearly turned on his heel and walked away.

Ten years ago, this female had ripped out his heart and stomped on it. Did he really want to endure some awkward reunion that was bound to end with yet another night of pacing the floor?

Hell no.

But then the realization of where they were had penetrated his shock.

Barely aware he was moving, he'd tracked the scent through the thick bogs until he reached a small clearing.

There.

His heart slammed with painful recognition.

Nothing had changed.

The curls that were so pale they looked silver in the gathering shadows remained a riotous, untamed halo around her head. Her pretty heart-shaped face with the wide, mint green eyes and slightly uptilted nose still gave her the image of a charming urchin. And her body remained as slender and perfectly curved as the last time he'd seen her.

A dangerous brew of regret and lust and yearning churned through him, but it was the overriding anger at the knowledge she was waltzing through the swamp as if nothing could hurt her that won top billing on his emotional meter.

Now, with his arm wrapped around her and his hand pressed against her mouth, he continued to whisper directly in her ear.

"Hello, Bailey." He smiled as he felt her shiver. It wasn't fear. It was the same combustible awareness that was searing through him. "It's been a long time."

For a gut-wrenching second Mika sensed the beautiful healer soften in his arms, her back pressed intimately against his chest as his hand rested on the flat plane of her stomach, which was left bare by the indecently skimpy halter-top.

A moan lodged in his throat, a brutal need that he hadn't felt for ten long years clenching his body.

He desperately wanted to bury his face in the satin halo of jasmine-scented curls while his hand slid beneath the teeny-tiny top to cup the soft swell of her breast.

But before he could give in to the madness, Bailey was suddenly squirming against him, grabbing his wrist to tug his fingers from her mouth.

"Let me go," she commanded.

Instantly Mika released his arm, stepping back to watch as Bailey spun around to study him with a wary frown.

She should be worried, he acknowledged, folding his arms over his chest.

The realization that she was so lacking in concern for her own safety was enough to make him nuts.

"What are you doing here?" he abruptly demanded.

Her lips thinned. "I live here."

His narrowed glare shifted toward the cottage. "Alone?"

"None of your business," she snapped.

It really, really wasn't, but that didn't stop the urgent need to know.

"It's a simple question." His voice was carefully stripped of emotion and his expression unreadable.

"Yes, I live alone." She impatiently brushed a silvery curl from her cheek. "Satisfied?"

He ignored the flare of vicious pleasure at the confession. The days when he had the right to consider this female as his were in the past.

Instead, he concentrated on the confirmation she was indeed living in this isolated space without protection.

"Not nearly," he growled. "You've always been impetuous and bullheaded."

Her brows snapped together. "Hey—"

"But to choose to live alone in the middle of the swamp is stupidly reckless even for you," he continued in grim tones.

"Great." With a glare that could strip paint off a wall, she turned to head toward the cottage. "A real pleasure to see you again, Mika."

Shit. He was going about this all wrong.

As usual.

Being a Sentinel meant that he was a natural leader who made snap decisions and expected others to follow his orders.

This female, on the other hand, had a perpetual allergy to any hint of authority.

Oil and water.

"Bailey."

She halted to glance over her shoulder. "We've had this conversation. I'm not interested in going through it again."

He moved until he was standing directly in front of her. "It bothers you that I'm worried about you?"

She met his steady gaze, her hands on her hips. She was half his size and quarter of his weight, but she never backed down from anyone.

Not ever.

"It bothers me that you think I can't be trusted to make my own decisions for my life," she said.

He grimaced, shoving his hand through his dark hair, which he'd left loose to fall past his shoulders. She had a point, but dammit . . . he better than anyone knew that this woman too often allowed her heart to lead her head.

Her unwavering belief in the goodness of others might be a large part of her charm, but it left her far too vulnerable.

"All I've ever wanted was for you to be happy," he said gruffly.

"As long as I followed your rules."

He heaved a deep sigh. Yep. She was right. They'd been over this waaay too many times.

He should walk away and leave her in peace.

Already the icy composure he used to protect himself was forming hairline fractures. Enough time with Bailey and it would shatter into a thousand pieces.

But his size twelve boots refused to obey.

In fact, they took a renegade step forward, bringing him close enough to reach out and brush his fingers through her satin curls.

"I assume you choose to live here so you can keep your strays hidden from Valhalla?" he murmured.

She stiffened, but made no effort to pull from his light touch.

"It's peaceful."

His lips twisted. This volatile female spread chaos wherever she went.

"You've never sought peace."

"We all change as we get older."

"I wish that was true," he husked, his fingers compulsively moving to brush over her flushed cheek.

She sucked in a startled breath, something that might have been yearning darkening her eyes.

"Mika," she breathed.

Desire jolted through him.

God. It'd been so long.

He'd almost forgotten the scorching thrill of satisfaction when she trembled beneath his light touch.

"Your skin is still as soft as silk," he murmured.

She licked her lips. "Mika."

He stepped closer, breathing deep of her sweet jasmine scent.

"I've missed you, little one."

She jerked, as if his soft words had caught her off guard.

"No, you haven't."

He cupped her cheek in his palm, studying her with a frown. "You're a psychic now?"

She held his gaze. "If you missed me, you would have contacted me."

He blinked. Was she kidding? He'd been busy preparing their wedding when she'd packed her bags and left Valhalla without so much as a good-bye.

"You disappeared."

A blush stained her pale cheeks. "You're the best tracker in the world. If you wanted to find me, you could have."

He didn't bother to admit that he'd tracked her movements from the moment she'd left the protected high-blood community. And that he hadn't halted his stalker routine until he was sure she was safely home with her parents.

"I was waiting for you to return," he said with simple honesty.

"And that says it all, doesn't it?" She heaved a soft sigh. "We're always on opposite sides."

"Perhaps," he muttered, wondering why he wasn't nearly as certain as he'd been just an hour ago.

He grimly shoved aside the treacherous thought, jerking his hand from her face as if he'd been burned.

Dammit, this woman had screwed with his head enough for one lifetime, thank you very fucking much.

As if agreeing with his inner dialogue, Bailey stepped back, her arms wrapping around her waist in an unconsciously protective gesture.

"Is there a reason you're creeping through the swamp?" she demanded.

He shrugged. "I'm working."

"Of course you are." She rolled her eyes. The constant demands of his job had been just one of many battles between them. "Always the dutiful Sentinel."

"I won't apologize for being good at my job."

She grimaced, almost as if she regretted having stirred up unwelcome memories.

"I'm sorry, I know it's important to you."

"Just as healing is important to you."

She gave a jerky nod, leaning down to gather the groceries that had tumbled out of the linen bags.

"Who are you hunting?"

He instinctively bent down to help her, gathering the apples and fresh vegetables that were spread across the mossy ground. His lips twitched at the familiar sight. God. How many dinners had they shared where Bailey had tried to convince him that tofu was an adequate replacement to his twelve-ounce T-bone steak?

"A young acolyte ran away from the monastery three days ago." He absently answered her question.

Bailey made a choked sound as she abruptly straightened, reaching to take the bag from his hand as he rose to his feet.

"Ran away?" She forced a stiff smile. "Do the monks keep them prisoners?"

He narrowed his gaze. He recognized that wary tone.

She knew something about the boy.

Something she didn't want to share.

God. Damn.

He'd been an idiot. No new thing when he was in the company of this female.

He should have suspected from the second he'd caught her scent that Bailey was involved. She would have sensed a wounded high-blood the second he'd stumbled into the swamp, and rushed to his rescue.

But he'd allowed himself to be distracted by the tangle of emotions that Bailey always managed to create when they were together.

Now he could only curse himself for his stupidity.

"No more than parents keep their children prisoners," he said, resisting the urge to grab her and demand that she tell him where the acolyte was. Yeah. That worked about as well as ramming his head into a brick wall. "They have rules and regulations to keep their students safe, and they expect them to be obeyed," he instead pointed out, hoping he could reason with her.

She grimaced. "Yes, I'm sure they're big on obedience."

"That's not fair," he chided. Bailey might be impetuous, but she wasn't a fool. She knew as well as he did the danger of rogue high-bloods. "Without proper training, many Sentinels would risk killing themselves or others."

She hunched a shoulder. "They should have the freedom to come and go as they please."

His lips flattened.

It was her standard line.

The one she threw out when she was losing the argument.

"Not until it's certain that they understand the danger of their superior strength and are fully capable of controlling their magic," he countered. "You wouldn't give a child a loaded gun and send him out in the world, would you?"

She bit her bottom lip, knowing that he was right.

"What happens when you find the student?" she asked.

He folded his arms over his chest, his expression hard. He wasn't going to pretend there weren't going to be consequences.

"First I intend to discover why Jacob was so anxious to leave that he was willing to run down a monk with his car."

Her lips parted in genuine shock. Clearly Jacob didn't feel the need to share that little tidbit of info.

"A monk was injured?"

"Yes."

She was instantly concerned. "Do you need me—"

"He's been healed," he interrupted. She would be headed to the monastery if he didn't assure her that the monk was well. For all her refusal to play by the rules, she was utterly committed to her role as healer. "He should recover within a few days."

She heaved a sigh of relief, but her expression remained concerned.

"Will the boy be punished?"

"Right now all I want to do is find him," he hedged. Until he knew what was going on, he wasn't taking anything off the table. Including punishment. "And I suspect you can help me."

Chapter Three

Bailey knew she was busted.

She had several talents, but lying wasn't one of them.

Especially not when she was with Mika.

Not only did he know her better than anyone on this earth, but he'd been trained to see through any attempt at deception.

Still, her first instinct was to try to protect the young man who she'd treated.

Not because she feared Mika would hurt him.

Sentinels were harsh in their training, but they never abused their acolytes.

"Me?" She awkwardly cleared her throat. "I don't have any contact with the monastery."

He gave a short, humorless laugh. "No, but you're notorious for taking in waifs and lost souls," he said. "If the boy came to you injured, you would never turn him away."

He knew her too well to deny his words.

"Why do you think he's injured?" she hedged.

"I found his car smashed into a tree."

"Ah." Bailey did her best to disguise her surprise. Odd. Although Jacob refused to tell her how he'd gotten his injuries, she'd assumed he'd been beaten. A car crash seemed . . . wrong. "Maybe you should have checked the local hospitals."

"We both know there's no need." He leaned forward, his gaze searing over her face. "I tracked him here."

She frowned. She'd been drawn to Jacob because he was injured, but he was far enough into his training to have learned to mask his trail.

"He's a potential guardian," she said. "How could you track him?"

"I could smell his blood."

Well, duh.

She wrinkled her nose. It'd been a while since she'd spent any time with a Sentinel. It was easy to forget just how dangerously acute their senses could be.

"Of course."

He studied her with a knowing gaze. "If you haven't seen Jacob, how did you know he was a guardian Sentinel?"

Well . . . hell.

She gave a shake of her head, suddenly wishing that Mika had never intruded into the swamp.

Okay, there might be an unexpected joy that bubbled deep inside her at the sight of his starkly beautiful face. And a treacherous voice might be whispering that she'd been an idiot to ever walk away.

But there was also a familiar pain that was threatening to rip her heart in two.

It was a pattern that she'd shared with Mika for as long as she could remember.

"I don't have anything to say to you," she muttered, covertly backing toward the cottage.

He frowned. "This isn't a game, little one."

"I never said it was." She sent him a glare, ridiculously disturbed by the sound of the pet name he'd called her for as long as she could remember. "And my name is Bailey."

His expression hardened, a hint of temper in his hauntingly beautiful eyes.

"Where's the acolyte?"

She took another step back. "I don't know."

He scowled, looking every inch the lethal Sentinel. "Bailey."

"Don't try to bully me," she warned, refusing to be intimidated.

"As if I could," he said with a roll of his eyes. "Why would you try to hide the boy?"

She made a sound of impatience. "I'm not hiding anyone, but even if I was, you know that my policy is never to ask questions of those I heal."

His jaw tightened, a silent disapproval of her long-held belief that her gift was meant to be shared without unnecessary complications.

"Even if they might be in danger?" he demanded.

She hesitated. Was he screwing with her?

That seemed very un-Mika-like.

"What do you mean?"

"Give me the boy," he repeated.

"Tell me why you think he might be in danger."

He shrugged, his emotions cranked down so tight they were impossible to read.

Dammit. She hated when he did that.

It meant he was hiding something from her.

"The monks are convinced he would never run off unless there was something troubling him," he at last said.

It wasn't a lie.

Sentinels never lied.

But that wasn't the whole story.

"He's barely out of his teens," she pointed out. "He's overdosing on testosterone, of course he's troubled."

"True. That was my first thought as well," he said. "Males tend to be highly erratic when they're at the mercy of their hormones." His lips twisted into a wry smile. "Especially if there's a female involved."

A ridiculous blush touched her cheeks at the memory of Mika's own battle with hormones.

They'd been childhood friends before they'd both gone their separate ways, Mika to the monastery and her to Valhalla.

It'd been years before he'd finally been allowed to come and visit her. High-bloods tended to age far more slowly than norms, which meant their training could take decades to complete.

But the moment they'd been reunited they'd instantly realized that their relationship had turned into something far more intense.

Over the next few years they'd become passionate lovers. Hell, they couldn't be in the same room without tearing off each other's clothing.

But eventually the fact that Mika was too often returning to the monastery for training or on the hunt as a Sentinel had started to undermine her confidence in his love. She'd started to feel as if they were strangers who hooked up for great sex, quickly followed by Mika's annoyance with her refusal to follow Valhalla's rigid rules and regulations.

She felt stifled. As if the life was slowly being smothered out of her.

So she bolted.

She told herself she had to escape. But deep inside, she'd always thought this man would come for her. . . .

Bailey gave a sharp shake of her head.

Dammit. She'd put the past behind her.

It was too late to go back now.

She forced a stiff smile to her lips. "They certainly don't think with their brains."

He studied her with a brooding gaze, his own thoughts clearly traveling the same sad path as hers.

"Some things never change," he rasped.

She flinched. Damn, this hurt.

Gut-deep, to-the-bone hurt.

She took another step backward, feeling the magical barrier press against her back.

"If he's chasing some girl, why don't you leave him alone?" she asked.

"Because the monks are worried. Brother Noland has asked for my help and I'm happy to offer my skill."

She grimaced. As usual, his simple explanation made her feel in the wrong.

"Fine. Go search for him."

The dark eyes flashed with a growing exasperation. It was the only hint that he was anything but his usual stoic self.

"You can't keep him hidden."

"For the last time, I don't know where he is."

He moved forward. "Bailey—"

"Good-bye, Mika."

With one last step she was through the barrier, watching with a childish satisfaction as he tried to follow.

"Not so . . ." Running into the invisible shield, Mika came to a sharp halt, his brows snapping together. "Damn."

She sent him a tight smile. "You see, I'm not so stupidly reckless as you assumed."

His hand lifted to press against the magical barrier. "How did you get a shield?"

"I healed a witch who was very grateful for my services."

He stepped back, his expression unreadable. "This isn't finished, little one."

"Is that a threat?"

He held her gaze for a long, heart-stopping minute.

"A promise."

The soft words were still floating on the air when Mika turned and melted into the thick undergrowth.

Bailey grimaced, any sense of smug pleasure disappearing as tiny tremors of shock racked her body.

Mika.

"Damn," she whispered.

* * *

The monastery was truly an astonishing sight in the middle of the bayou.

Built long before norms had made their way to the remote section of Louisiana, it was constructed of pure gray granite that had been mystically transported by guardian Sentinels from Scotland.

In the center was the great cloister that included an unexpectedly whimsical fountain, surrounded by a chapter room, the monks' and students' dormitory, a library, refectory and kitchens. There was also a large yard that was used by the Sentinels for their weapon training.

More recently the stables had been converted into a firing range, while a new garage that could hold up to twenty cars had been built near the gatehouse.

And surrounding it all was a ten-foot stone wall that effectively turned the place into a fortress.

Not that the walls were really necessary.

Who would be stupid enough to try to sneak into a place that held at least six monks and two dozen Sentinels-in-training?

That was the definition of a death wish.

Entering through the kitchens, Mika ignored the speculative glances from the various students who were stuck on dishwashing duty.

Acolytes were expected to do the majority of work around the monastery in between their training sessions, as well as learning some sort of craft that would teach them that there was more to their duties than just destruction. They could also create beauty.

Mika had personally chosen to work with the scribes, learning the delicate task of calligraphy as he translated ancient texts into modern languages.

Entering the central cloister, he headed directly to the back of the monastery where a small office was tucked next to the library.

At his entrance a slender man with a lean face and long, narrow nose straightened from behind a large desk to smooth his hands down his robe, made from a rough brown fabric.

At a glance Brother Noland looked like he was in his early forties. His short blond hair was untouched by gray and there were only a few lines that radiated around the pale blue eyes. But his position as the leader of the monastery meant that he'd been around at least a couple of centuries.

"You didn't find him?" the monk demanded.

Mika stayed near the doorway, his gaze instinctively skimming the tidy room lined with leather-bound books before returning to the monk.

He didn't expect to walk into a trap, but then again, he was always prepared for trouble.

Well, that wasn't entirely true, was it?

If he was always prepared he wouldn't have been blindsided by Bailey Morrell.

He grimaced, grimly shoving aside the thought of the beautiful healer.

During his return to the monastery he'd come to a few conclusions.

Number one, he wasn't done with his former lover. Not even close.

Number two, his decision number one would have to wait until Jacob was safely returned to the monks.

"I found the car, which had been run into the ditch," he said.

Brother Noland flinched. "He wasn't—"

"No. The crash wasn't enough to hurt him," he reassured the monk, revealing what he'd hidden from Bailey.

Not that it was a big secret. He suspected she'd been well

aware the boy's injuries had come from something besides a car ride into a tree.

"Thank God."

"There was, however, blood at the scene."

"Jacob?"

"Yes." He glanced over his shoulder, ensuring there was no one lurking in the long corridor outside the office. "I would guess that he was deliberately run off the road and beaten."

Brother Noland's breath hissed between his teeth, anger flashing through the blue eyes.

Monks were just as lethal as any trained Sentinel. "Who would do such a thing?"

"I intend to find out."

"I agree," the monk said. "But the most important thing is finding Jacob. Was there any sign of him?"

Mika's lips twisted. "I traced his blood to the middle of the swamp."

"Really?" The blue eyes widened, a sudden comprehension softening the tension etched onto his lean face. "Ah. Bailey must have found him."

"You know her?"

Mika didn't know why he was surprised. High-bloods usually sought out one another's company, unless they were trying to pass as a norm.

Of course, most high-bloods chose to live in Valhalla or one of the numerous satellite compounds spread around the world.

Not alone in the middle of the damned bayou.

"Our paths have crossed," the monk admitted. "Although she prefers to keep her distance from the monastery."

Mika gave a humorless laugh. "Don't take it personally. Bailey has a prejudice against anyone she thinks is a part of the vast conspiracy to enslave the high-bloods."

Brother Noland lifted a brow. "Enslave?"

"Her word, not mine."

"Ah." He shrugged. "She's a free spirit."

Mika clenched his hands. God. He really, really hated those words.

It implied that Bailey merely breezed through life without touching the world.

Not that she was a bullheaded wrecking ball who managed to create utter chaos.

"She's—" He bit off his words, giving a shake of his head. "Never mind."

The monk studied him with an oddly knowing gaze. "You have a past with the healer?"

A past. And a future. Even if she didn't know it yet.

"Yes."

"She's a kind woman who is always eager to help those in need."

No shit.

"Even those who don't deserve her help," he said, his expression stoic despite the frustration that simmered just below the surface.

"Yes, well, it's a rare person who doesn't judge others," Brother Noland murmured.

Mika narrowed his eyes. He didn't give a damn about others. Not when they put Bailey at risk.

"If she helped Jacob, then she could be in danger."

The monk gave a slow nod. "True."

"Unfortunately she's too stubborn to accept that she might need my protection."

"Then it's even more imperative that we find Jacob."

That much they could agree on.

"Can you show me his room?"

"Certainly." The monk was instantly moving to pass by Mika and step out of the room. "This way."

In silence they traveled to the acolyte dormitory, climbing

the narrow stone steps to reach the upper attic where the newest students were lodged.

Mika grimaced as he studied the four narrow beds that were shoved into the center of the dark loft.

In one corner was a washstand and in another a small shelf for the few belongings a student was allowed to have. Clean robes, an extra blanket, and one book from the monastery library.

That was it.

"I had forgotten how barren the cells are," he muttered.

"The fewer distractions, the less cluttered the mind." Brother Noland spoke the words that every monk clearly had memorized.

Mika crossed the loft, forced to bend over to avoid knocking himself out on the low, open-beamed ceiling.

"Maybe, but we all have a few secrets that are tucked away," he said, making a quick sweep of the seemingly empty room.

In less than ten minutes he'd uncovered a stash of hidden nudie magazines, a homemade bottle of gin, and stack of letters from a lovesick girlfriend. Then, pulling up a warped floorboard beneath one of the beds, he at last found something of interest.

Straightening, he unfolded the paper.

Brother Noland moved to his side. "What is it?"

"A map." He pointed toward the X that had been marked along a narrow road leading into the nearby swamp. "This is where I found the car."

"Odd." The monk gave a shake of his head. "Why there?"

"It's isolated. Other than that . . ." Mika shrugged, unable to think of any pressing reason someone would choose that particular spot.

Taking the map, Brother Noland turned it over to read the short note that had been written on the back.

Tuesday, eleven a.m.

"This isn't Jacob's handwriting."

Mika took back the map, studying it with a frown. Although acolytes weren't prisoners, as Bailey was so fond of claiming, they were cut off from much of the world.

No cell phones, no TV, and no unofficial visitors.

"Could someone smuggle in a message?" he demanded.

"It wouldn't have to be smuggled," the monk said. "We don't monitor the students' mail."

"Damn." About to toss the map aside, he instead lifted it to his nose as he caught an odd smell that clung to the paper. "Strange."

The monk watched him with a steady gaze. "What is it?"

"Antiseptic." Mika narrowed his gaze. "The sort of thing that a healer would use."

Without giving himself time to consider the late hour or the fact that Bailey was hardly likely to allow him into her cottage, he was headed toward the door.

He had questions and he intended to get answers.

Now.

Chapter Four

Bailey had been determined to scrub Mika from her mind.

What was the point in brooding on what-might-have-beens?

It wasn't like she could change the past. Even if a renegade part of her was whispering that she'd been a fool to ever walk away from the only man she'd ever loved.

But while she determinedly cleaned the small cottage from top to bottom and concentrated on preparing her favorite eggplant parmesan for dinner, she couldn't stop her thoughts from replaying her brief encounter with Mika.

Over and over.

Worse, she found her body unable to shake the restless desire that had been stirred to life by his arrival.

Damn.

She'd known plenty of handsome men over the years. Many of them far more charming than her stoic Sentinel.

But no man had ever made her feel as if she'd been struck by lightning just by walking into a room. And certainly none of them had made her *ache* with the need to be wrapped in their arms.

In the process of dishing up her dinner, Bailey abruptly stiffened.

It was one thing to be plagued with constant thoughts of the man she'd loved since she was a teenager, and another to actually feel his presence.

Which meant she was losing her mind—a very real possibility—or Mika was near.

Smoothing her hands down the casual yellow sundress she'd slipped on after her shower, Bailey sucked in a deep breath and forced her heartbeat to slow from hypersonic to a speed just below turbo.

Then, pulling open the back door, she stepped onto the porch and allowed the fragrant darkness to wrap around her.

Nearby she could hear frogs croaking and the cry of an owl as it hunted the small critters that scurried through the thick foliage. Farther away was the distinctive sound of a boat heading out of the swamp as the fishermen finished up for the day.

But there was no indication of an intruder.

Predictable.

Sentinels were not only trained to move in silence, but they had the ability to "will" others not to see them. Not that they were invisible. Not entirely. But a person had to make a deliberate effort to search for their presence.

It was only because Bailey was hypersensitive to anything related to Mika that she'd known he was nearby.

Searching the shadows, she at last caught sight of his lean form leaning nonchalantly against a tree at the edge of her shield.

Her breath was squeezed from her lungs as she took in the sight of his finely chiseled features that were perfectly outlined in the moonlight. His glossy hair had been pulled back and held at his nape with a leather string, and his dark eyes were locked on her with that unwavering focus that used to make her melt in pleasure.

Now it . . . oh hell, it still made her melt in pleasure, she acknowledged with a stab of annoyance.

She planted her fists on her hips, trying to match his detached composure when inside she was trembling from head to toe at the sight of him.

"What are you doing here?"

"I need to speak with you."

His expression was impossible to read.

"It's late."

"And?"

She bit back a curse. "And I want to eat my dinner and go to bed in peace."

There was unexpected silence, Mika's expression suddenly softening with some inner thought.

"Tell me, Bailey, do you still kick the covers off in the middle of the night?" he asked in a low voice.

She flinched. How the hell did he remember such a small detail of their all-too-brief time as lovers?

Somehow she'd assumed that he'd simply forgotten about her after she'd left. And why wouldn't he?

It wasn't like he'd tried to follow or even contact her.

"Is that why you're here?" she asked. "To ask if I still kick off the covers?"

"Not entirely, but I'll admit that it's a question that's bothered me over the years."

Bothered him? She frowned. "Why?"

"When we were together I could pull you into my arms and keep you warm." The dark gaze slowly skimmed down her body. "I didn't like the thought you might be cold and alone."

A soft sound of distress was ripped from her throat.

Damn him.

It'd taken her years to repair the damage done to her heart by this man.

Was he trying to rip open wounds that were barely healed?

"I . . ." She halted, forced to clear the lump from her throat. "Why are you really here?"

Something that might have been regret tightened his features before he was reaching into the back pocket of his jeans to pull out a folded piece of paper.

"This."

"What is it?"

"A map I found beneath Jacob's bed."

Okay. That was strange. Why would anyone hide a map beneath their bed?

"A map to where?"

"To the spot he was nearly beaten to death."

It took her a second to realize just what he'd revealed.

"Beaten?" She tried to look innocent. "But you said—"

"Bailey, the boy might be in trouble." Mika abruptly straightened from the tree, his expression somber. "Let me in."

She hesitated before heaving a resigned sigh.

Mika was right.

It was one thing to fear that Jacob had been caught by a bunch of locals and beaten because he was high-blood. It was another to fear he'd been actually lured there.

"Fine." Walking forward, she reached through the barrier.

Once she had a hold of his hand, he easily stepped through the shield, a wry smile twisting his lips.

"Was that truly so hard?"

"Yes."

Turning, she led him through the back door of the cottage and straight into the kitchen.

There was no point in standing outside. Not when the heat was still smothering.

Besides, she wanted her dinner.

Entering on her heels, Mika closed the door and bypassed her to take a slow inventory of the small space.

He quickly skimmed over the white painted cabinets and appliances that had seen better days, instead lingering on the framed pictures of her parents that she'd placed on a wooden shelf.

"Where are they now?" he asked.

She shrugged as she reached into the fridge to pull out a bottle of wine.

"I think they're still in the Congo," she said. "But the last letter I had from Mother said that they thought they would be traveling to visit me before they went to New Zealand for their next mission."

He turned to watch her pour two glasses of wine.

"Does it bother you that they spend so much time away from you?"

"Of course not." She automatically denied any regret that her parents always put their careers as teachers before their only child. They loved her. Of course they did. It was just . . . "Do you want some dinner?"

"Very much." He crossed the floor to watch as she spooned out two plates of the eggplant parmesan. "Smells good."

She snorted, even as she took a deep breath of his potently male scent.

Oh . . . hell. She'd missed that intoxicating combination of warm skin and sandalwood soap.

When he'd had to leave Valhalla, she'd slept with one of his shirts on just so she could be surrounded by the feel of his presence.

Now she struggled not to press her face to the curve of his neck and suck in a deep breath.

"You hate when I cook," she muttered.

He brushed a finger down her cheek, as if sensing her traitorous thoughts.

"Only when you try to make me eat tofu," he teased, flashing his rare, extraordinarily beautiful smile. Her heart came to a painful halt. For a breathless second their eyes locked, a dangerous awareness fluttering in the pit of her stomach. Then Mika dropped his hand and grabbed the two plates to head to the tiny wooden table that was pushed against one wall. "Besides, it's been hours since lunch. I'm starving."

She followed behind him with the wine, settling in her seat as she watched Mika sit across from her.

It felt disturbingly right.

She shoved aside the unwanted thought as Mika took a cautious taste of the eggplant.

"Well?" she prompted.

He swallowed, his expression genuinely startled. "It's good. I mean, really good."

She couldn't halt her burst of laughter. "You don't have to sound so surprised."

He went hunter still, the air heating. A Sentinel always ran hotter than norms, and when their passions were aroused they could actually affect the temperature.

A blast of lust raced through Bailey.

God, the memory of having that hot, hard-as-steel body pressing her into a mattress was something she'd battled against on a nightly basis.

"Your eyes shimmer like the finest emeralds in the candlelight," he murmured, his voice a soft caress.

Her fork dropped onto the plate, her body instinctively swaying forward.

Mika had been her one and only lover.

And even after all these years, he still could make her shiver with need.

Dangerous . . .

The voice whispered through her mind, and with a tiny gasp she forced herself to sit back in her chair.

God. What was wrong with her?

She'd built a new life for herself. It would be the worst sort of stupidity to open herself up to more pain.

"Tell me about the map," she abruptly demanded.

Just for a second his beautiful face hardened, as if he were considering the pleasure of knocking the table out of the way and hauling her into his arms.

Then, with an obvious effort, he leashed his raw desire, pulling the map out of his back pocket to toss it on the table.

"Here."

She reached for the folded paper, recognizing the glossy picture on the front as one she'd seen at a dozen gas stations between the bayou and Lafayette.

"You can buy this anywhere." She spread open the map to see the large X that had been marked at a location not far from her cottage. "It's not going to be much help."

"Smell it."

She arched her brows. "Are you serious?"

He sent her a wry glance. "Always."

Well, that was true enough.

Even when they were young, Mika had been a somber, oddly aloof young man. In part because it was his natural demeanor. But she suspected that the death of his mother when he was just five had added to his air of reserve.

Only when he was with her had he ever revealed his warm, unexpectedly tender side. The knowledge had always made her feel special.

She grimaced. A pain slicing through her heart.

Okay. Not going down that road.

Instead she lifted the map to her nose and sniffed.

"It smells like ethanol," she murmured, sending Mika a startled glance. "Antiseptic?"

"That's my guess."

"Why would . . ." Her baffled words came to an abrupt halt as she shoved herself to her feet, glaring at Mika in pained disbelief. Suddenly she understood why he was at her cabin. And it had nothing to do with old times, or the crushing desire that still held her in its grip. "Oh, my God. You think I gave Jacob this map?"

"Not anymore." He grimaced, pushing himself upright. "You're a terrible liar."

"Screw you."

Tossing the map at his face, she whirled to head into the narrow living room that barely had enough space for her battered sofa and one easy chair that was shoved next to the bookcase that was overflowing with her precious collection.

Places came and went, even people. But her books always traveled with her.

As a child she'd learned they were the one thing she could depend on in her crazy, unpredictable life.

She'd reached the middle of the room when Mika grabbed her arm and turned her to face him.

"Bailey, listen."

"Why should I?"

"Because I know you," he said, his grip softening so he could run his fingers down her arm in an unconscious caress. "You're as worried as I am about Jacob."

"That doesn't mean I'm going to let you insult me in my own home."

"That was never my intention, little one." He wrinkled his nose, regret shimmering in the depths of his dark eyes. "Where else would I find antiseptic in this area?"

She was still mad at him. The aggravating brute. But he was right.

She was desperately worried about Jacob.

"There's a small clinic in town and a healer at the monastery."

He nodded. "I've spoken to the healer."

She knocked aside his hand. She couldn't think when he was touching her.

"Did you accuse him of leading Jacob into a trap?"

He eyes narrowed. "Why do you suspect it was a trap?"

She made a sound of disbelief, taking a step backward. What the hell was he implying now?

"Are you serious?"

"Please, Bailey." He held up a slender hand. "I'm just asking for your opinion."

Oh . . . hell.

Bailey shoved her fingers through her short tangle of curls.

"Jacob wouldn't tell me what happened, but it was obvious from his injuries that he'd been beaten, and by more than one person." She pointed toward the paper he clenched in his hand. "If that map was sent to him to lure him to a precise spot, then obviously it was some sort of ambush."

"Or someone sent the map because they wanted to meet with Jacob and he was attacked by the unknown assailants before the person could arrive," he pointed out. "Which was the only reason I thought you might have sent it to him."

"Oh." She grimaced. "It wasn't me. I never met Jacob until I discovered him injured."

"Did the boy mention any friends or family in the area?"

"He wasn't much of a talker. He admitted that he was from the monastery and that . . ." She frowned, suddenly recalling the boy's parting words. "Wait."

"What?"

"When he left, he said he had a friend he could stay with."

The air prickled with a tangible tension. Mika was preparing for the hunt.

"Someone local?"

She shrugged. "I don't know for sure, but he wasn't strong enough to make it far."

A sudden buzz interrupted his next question, and pulling his cell phone out of his pocket, Mika glanced at the screen.

"It's Wolfe, I have to take this."

She shrugged, returning to the kitchen before Mika could glimpse her expression of frustration.

It was a familiar sensation.

When she was with Mika, they rarely had more than a day or two that wasn't interrupted by his duty as a Sentinel.

It wasn't unusual. The warriors were always on call. And even when they weren't hunting, they were expected to devote hours to training.

If she hadn't been so young and so sensitized by her parents' habit of forgetting her existence when they were wrapped up in their work, Mika's devotion to his position as a Sentinel probably wouldn't have made her so crazy.

With a shake of her head, she cleared away the plates and put the rest of the dinner in the fridge. Neither of them had eaten much, but at the moment she wasn't hungry.

She did, however, keep her glass of wine.

She didn't mind wasting eggplant.

But tossing out a fine wine . . .

Never.

She was leaning against the counter when Mika returned to the room, his expression more stoic than usual.

Always a bad sign.

"What's wrong?" she instantly demanded.

"Wolfe has been trying to track down Jacob's family."

She set aside her wineglass. "Did he find them?"

Mika moved to stare out the window over the sink, his profile grim.

"He discovered that Jacob had been left at the edge of Valhalla around ten years ago by a man who'd run off before anyone could speak with him."

She licked her lips, not needing to be a psychic to know that this story wasn't going to have a happy ending.

"Not unusual," she murmured. "Many families are embarrassed to realize their child isn't normal."

He gave a slow nod. They both knew that they'd been fortunate to have families who hadn't turned their backs on them when their gifts began to develop.

"Wolfe managed to track him down."

She blinked in surprise. The Tagos had managed to find

a stranger who'd dropped off a boy and then disappeared ten years ago?

"How?"

"It's always better not to ask."

Yeah. Probably a wise choice.

"Has the man heard from Jacob?"

"Impossible to say." Mika swiveled his head to reveal his bleak expression. "He was found beaten to death last week."

She pressed a hand to her lips. "Dear Lord."

"And he wasn't alone," he continued, his voice oddly harsh. "A healer who had been missing for the past three years was found decapitated in the man's basement."

Chapter Five

Bailey gasped, the blood draining from her face. "Who was it?"

Mika cursed himself for being so blunt.

Of course she would instantly fear that the dead healer would be someone she knew.

But dammit, he'd been sucker punched by Wolfe's grim report.

"Benjamin Lyman, a healer who lived in Cleveland," he revealed, carefully watching as Bailey paced the cracked linoleum floor.

There didn't seem to be any recognition of the name, but her expression remained troubled.

"Why?"

"The human police wrote it off as a drug deal gone bad," he said in disgust.

She turned to study him with eyes darkened to jade. "And Wolfe?"

"He managed to smuggle someone from the Order into the morgue where they're still holding the bodies."

The Order was a group of high-bloods who worked for Calder, the Master of Gifts. They were specifically tasked with finding high-bloods throughout the world. Some because they were a danger to themselves or others, and some because they simply didn't realize they'd been born with mutant powers.

"Did they find anything?"

"The man was a soul-gazer. Not strong enough to attract the attention of Valhalla, but he was definitely a high-blood."

She nodded. A soul-gazer could see the auras of others, giving them a glimpse of the person's inner nature, good or evil. Or more likely, a combination of both. It was a passive talent that often went unreported.

"What else?" she prompted.

His jaw tightened until it felt as if his teeth would shatter.

"The autopsy file revealed he'd been routinely beaten over the past three years and then healed."

Her eyes widened. "Why?"

"It could be a sick way to torture him, or some sort of scam. It's impossible to say." He shrugged. Right now he didn't give a shit about the *why*. All that mattered was the *who*. And how quickly he could dispose of them. "But the fact that Jacob was recently attacked and then healed is too much a coincidence not to assume it's related."

She shook her head. "It just doesn't make any sense."

He squared his shoulders, preparing himself for battle.

Bailey wasn't going to like what he had to say.

"I have to track down Jacob, but first I want you to return to the monastery with me."

"No," she said before he'd even finished speaking.

"Dammit, Bailey," he growled.

She met him glare for glare. "I'm safer here than I would be anywhere else."

Well hell.

He couldn't argue with her logic.

The shield meant that only a powerful witch could enter the cottage without Bailey's assistance. Besides, they still didn't know how or by whom Jacob had been contacted. It was quite possible that there was a traitor at the monastery.

That didn't, however, ease his gut-deep fear.

This was Bailey.

The Queen of Impulsive Behavior.

"As long as you stay behind the barrier," he pointed out.

"I don't have any intention of taking unnecessary risks."

He grimaced. Oh, if only that were true.

"Until someone needs to be healed, or Jacob asks for your help," he muttered.

"If he contacts me, I'll call you."

"You swear?"

Her lips flattened with annoyance. "I'm not an idiot."

He moved forward, gently cupping her face in his hands.

This female was, and always would be, the most precious thing in his entire world.

If he lost her . . .

A savage pain ripped through him.

"No, but you lead with your heart, and that makes you vulnerable."

She met his concerned gaze with a stubborn frown. "It's not a bad thing."

"No," he breathed, ruefully accepting he wouldn't change anything about her. Even if she scared the hell out of him. "Will you let me come back tonight?"

She frowned, a hint of wariness rippling over her face.

"Mika—"

"I know," he muttered, recognizing that expression. He'd seen it far too often when he they'd been together. "I'm smothering you. I just need to know you're safe."

Her lips parted, as if she was going to deny his assumption that she was feeling oppressed by his concern. Then she gave a small shake of her head.

"Okay."

He held his breath. "Okay?"

"You can come back here," she said softly.

Thank God.

Relief reverberated through him.

Leaning down, he pressed a swiftly, wholly unsatisfactory kiss against her lush lips.

Later, a voice whispered in the back of his mind.

Once he was certain she was safe he intended to devour her.

"Don't leave this cottage," he said, an edge of command in his voice. "Not for any reason."

"You're pushing your luck," she warned, narrowing her gaze. "Besides, you're the one who needs to be careful. If you get hurt—"

"I won't." Another kiss before he reluctantly pulled back. "Until later."

Without waiting for her reply, he was headed out of the cottage and through the magical barrier. The shield was created to keep people out, not in.

Then, pulling a gun from the holster beneath his shirt, he moved through the dense undergrowth with a slow caution.

He wasn't afraid of the local wildlife. He was a Sentinel, which meant that he was faster, stronger, and more lethal than any other predator. Plus, he had a natural immunity to most poisons.

But he didn't want to miss any clues that might lead him to Jacob.

Returning to where the monk's car had run off the road, he circled the area, hoping for anything that might reveal who might be interested in the boy.

Finding nothing, he headed toward the clinic at the edge of town.

Again there was no hint of Jacob, or anything that looked remotely out of place.

Dammit.

Slipping out of the back of the clinic, he came to a sudden halt, his senses on full alert.

Someone was near.

"Show yourself," he commanded, keeping the gun hidden behind his leg as he stepped away from the building.

He wanted plenty of room to maneuver.

There was the sound of shuffling footsteps before a man appeared from the shadows, his head bald and his thin body bent with age.

"Sentinel." The stranger's voice held the singsong rhythm of a local. "You on the hunt?"

Mika sucked in a deep breath, sifting through the various odors that clung to the man.

Tobacco. Home-brewed moonshine. And stale French fries.

No metal. Which meant he wasn't armed.

Not that Mika lowered his guard.

Right now he had to assume that everyone was the enemy.

"I'm searching for a young man from the monastery," he said, his gaze searching the darkness for any hidden assailants. The old man might be a distraction. "He was wounded."

"Don't know nothing about a boy. Most folk in this town know not to stick their noses in high-blood business." The man turned his head to spit out a stream of chewing tobacco. "You won't find what you be searching for here."

Mika nodded. He believed the stranger. Most norms preferred to avoid high-bloods.

"Do you have a suggestion of where I should look?" he demanded.

"Heard a rumor that strangers were seen out near Badger Island straight north of here." The human shrugged. "A smart man might start there."

Mika held the man's gaze. "I'm in your debt."

"Watch your back." The man stepped back into the shadows. "People who come to the swamps don't like trespassers."

"I'll keep that in mind."

Keeping the gun in his hand, Mika headed north, cutting through the swamp rather than following the narrow road.

He assumed that any guards would be focused on the main pathways.

An assumption that nearly got him killed.

Silently halting near the edge of a lily-clogged channel, Mika surveyed the narrow island. It was difficult to see through the thick cypress trees, but he thought he could make out the outline of a small structure and catch a glimpse of a lantern reflecting in a window.

He was busy trying to decide whether to try to get closer or to wait for backup before he continued to scout the area, when he heard a distinctive pop.

It was only his quick reflexes that allowed him to avoid the killing shot. Leaping to one side, he felt a searing pain as the bullet clipped his shoulder.

Shit. His gaze searched the darkness across the channel, belatedly locating the human male who was hidden in the upper branches of a tree.

His fingers tightened on his gun, the urge to shoot the bastard nearly overwhelming.

His wound wasn't fatal, but it hurt like a bitch.

Only the knowledge that whoever was on that island had not only military-grade weapons, but the skill of a trained sniper, had him melting back into the tangled coverage of the bayou.

This wasn't some local yokel who was taking potshots at stray intruders.

He needed backup.

Ripping off his shirt, he pressed it against the wound to prevent any blood from giving away his trail as he made a zigzag path through the deepest part of the swamp. If some one wanted to try to follow him, he wasn't going to make it easy.

It took nearly an hour before he finally finished his attempts to throw off any pursuers and circled back to Bailey's cottage.

Not surprisingly, he'd barely reached the edge of the

barrier when the door was thrown open and Bailey rushed toward him.

Her talents as a healer would have warned her that there was an injured high-blood in the area.

"Mika." Wrapping her arm around his waist, she led him through the magical shield and across the spongy ground into the welcoming comfort of her kitchen. "Damn you. I told you to be careful."

Bailey was furious.

She'd been pacing the floor since the moment that Mika had left, a ball of dread lodged in the pit of her stomach.

He could call her impulsive and headstrong, but she wasn't the one who was always charging into danger. And she certainly never thought of herself as invincible.

No, that was Mika.

And now he was hurt.

Dragging him across the linoleum floor, she pressed him into a chair and hurried to gather her supplies.

"It's nothing, little one," he assured her, pulling away the wadded-up shirt to reveal the wound that continued to leak blood. "Just a scratch."

She placed the leather bag on the table, opening it to pull out an antiseptic and some gauze.

"It's not a scratch, it's a bullet wound," she growled, carefully cleansing the narrow gouge in his flesh with a practiced expertise.

Inside she was battling against the pure terror that was threatening to overwhelm her.

God. He'd been shot.

She could have lost him.

She abruptly dropped the gauze, her legs threatening to collapse.

Mika reached up to grasp her hand, bringing it to his lips so he could press a kiss to the center of her palm.

"I was grazed, nothing more."

"You were shot at," she said between clenched teeth.

"Yes." He casually glanced toward the wound, which was already healing. "Hazard of the job."

She sucked in a pained breath. "Don't."

He frowned, slowly rising to his feet as he sensed her distress.

"Bailey?"

"Don't you dare tease about putting yourself in danger."

He grimaced, reaching to cup her pale cheek in his hand. "I'm sorry, little one, it wasn't deliberate," he assured her, his starkly beautiful face softening with a genuine concern. "I've called Wolfe to send more Sentinels. I won't go back alone."

She bit her bottom lip, reaching up to place her hand over the injury.

"Let me heal you."

Focusing her powers, Bailey sent small pulses of healing energy from her hand into his damaged flesh, acutely aware of his dark gaze that was examining her face with a fierce intensity.

"Is this why?"

"Why what?"

"Why you left?" he asked, his voice husky with emotion. "Because my job puts me in danger?"

She stiffened at the unexpected question, feeling the instinctive urge to scurry behind her façade of the free-spirited hippie who refused to settle down.

That was her comfort zone, after all.

But standing so close to Mika, she could see the bone-deep pain that shimmered in his dark eyes and feel the slight tremor in the hand that was pressed to her face.

Dammit. She'd wasted too many years.

It was past time for a little honesty.

"It bothers me. The thought you could be hurt or even . . ." She shivered, her hand no longer healing as it smoothed over the chiseled muscles of his shoulder. She needed to reassure herself he was alive and relatively well. Besides, she loved to stroke his skin. Heated silk. "Hell, I can't even say the word," she rasped. "But I understood that was the cost of being with a Sentinel."

His thumb stoked her lower lip. "But?"

"I—" She swallowed the lump in her throat.

"Bailey?"

"I told myself it was because I felt trapped."

His dark, beautiful face tightened with regret. "By me?"

"By our relationship. By the rules at Valhalla," she said, only now realizing that Mika had somehow blamed himself for her insecurities. Her fingers traveled up the back of his neck, tugging the leather band free so his hair could spill over his shoulders. "But it was just an excuse."

A sudden heat glowed in his ebony eyes, a fine tremor racing through him as her fingers threaded through his hair.

"What was the real reason?"

She wrinkled her nose. "It seems so stupid now."

His free hand grasped her hip, urging her closer to his hard body.

"Tell me."

Disturbed by the unnerving perception in his gaze, Bailey dropped her gaze to the smooth, sculpted muscles of his bare chest.

She already felt like a fool.

She didn't need to see it reflected in his eyes.

"I spent my entire childhood trying to compete with my parents' career. No matter what I did, how hard I tried, I could never claim more than a small portion of their attention. Their true love was saved for the children they taught." She sucked in a slow, deep breath, savoring the male heat that brushed over her skin like a caress. "I think I was threatened by your devotion to the Sentinels and your brothers. It felt like I was coming in second place. Again." She gave a slow shake of her head, wishing she could go back in time. "So I deliberately sabotaged our happiness. How shallow is that?"

His thumb slid beneath her chin, tilting back her face so he could capture her wary gaze.

"I'm sorry," he murmured, his expression somber.

She gave his hair a tug. Trust Mika to try to take the blame. Just another way of protecting her.

"It wasn't your fault."

"It was," he insisted, the heat of his skin branding her as his hand slid down the side of her neck. "I was battling my own fears, so instead of forcing you to talk to me, I kept letting you pull further and further away."

She blinked. This man afraid? It seemed impossible.

Even as a young man he'd always been so composed. So utterly in command of his emotions. Unlike her flakey, impulsive self.

"What fears?"

"That I didn't deserve you."

She made a sound of disbelief. What the hell was he talking about?

"That's ridiculous."

"No, it truly isn't."

"Why would you say that?"

Her breath came out as a soft gasp as Mika reached out to wrap his arms around her, pressing her tight against his bare chest.

"You were so unbearably young and innocent when we met," he breathed.

She circled his neck with her arms, her nipples hardening as the heat of his skin seared through the thin cotton of her sundress.

She swallowed a groan.

God. It'd been so long.

Years. And years.

To at last be back in Mika's arms made her ache with need.

Unfortunately, they needed to talk. Didn't they?

Her gaze drifted down to the sensuously carved lips, a flutter of anticipation making her heart skip a beat as she felt the hard thrust of his cock pressed against her lower stomach.

"I was only a few years younger than you," she reminded him, her voice breathless.

He studied her flushed face with a brooding gaze. "You were a mere babe in experience, but from the moment we met I knew you were destined to be mine." His hands rested possessively on her lower back, his gesture of blatant male ownership emphasizing his words. "Common sense warned me to give you the time and space you deserved to explore the world."

"I'd already visited half a dozen countries before we arrived at the reservation," she said dryly. "Trust me, the last thing I wanted was any more exploring of the world."

"It wasn't about distance," he said, covertly beginning to urge her backward, herding her out of the kitchen. "It was about having friends and going to parties . . . dating boys." His eyes flashed with barely leashed emotions as he continued to steer her across the floor. "But no matter what I told myself was best for you, I couldn't force myself to set you free."

"I never wanted to date other men," she muttered, her stomach clenching with excitement as they entered the shadowed darkness of her bedroom.

"But how could you know?"

She met his dark, searching gaze, understanding that this was important.

Mika had truly feared that he'd somehow driven her away.

"Because I've had years of meeting other guys, and not one has made my heart beat faster or my knees weak."

She could feel his body heating as his passions amped up.

"And me?" he demanded, his voice thick.

"Feel," she murmured, reaching to grab his hand and place it over her heart, which was racing with an eager desire he couldn't miss.

Mika pressed her against the wall of her bedroom.

His hands skimmed up her back, his hips easing forward so she could feel the heavy thrust of his arousal. Sweet passion sang through her blood, the intoxicating sensation making her head spin like she was drunk.

"Tell me that you missed me."

She leaned forward to press a kiss to the pulse that beat at the base of his neck.

"Every minute of every day."

"Yes." He trembled, his silky hair brushing her shoulder as he leaned down to whisper directly into her ear. "Damn, but I need you, little one."

Dear God, his skin was so hot it felt as if it was branding her, she acknowledged, allowing her hands to stroke over his bare chest.

Tilting back her head, she studied his lean face.

The wide brow. The proud nose. The high cheekbones. And the lush lips that begged for her kisses.

He was so beautiful.

Was it any wonder she wanted to rip off her clothes and demand that he take her?

Thankfully she wasn't completely lost to reason.

Leaning back, she studied his shoulder.

"How is your wound?"

A wicked smile curved his lips as he dipped his head down to trace the line of her throat with his tongue.

"What wound?" he teased, grasping the sides of her dress and slowly inching it upward.

Chapter Six

Mika swallowed a groan.

But the pain that was plaguing him had nothing to do with the bullet wound. Hell, that'd been forgotten the minute Bailey's healing touch had stirred to life his ever-ready need for her.

No.

His agony stemmed directly from the rock-hard erection that was pressed hard enough against his zipper to threaten injury.

And the hunger that raged through him like a tsunami.

His hands impatiently tugged up the skirt of her dress so his fingers could appreciate the satin skin of her thighs, his head lowering so he could nibble a path down the length of her jaw.

He wanted to devour her.

To toss her on the nearby bed and take her in a fury of heat and raw need.

Instead, he forced himself to savor each slow kiss, the taste of her beneath his tongue, and the jasmine scent that was filling his senses.

He'd waited years and years to have her back in his arms.

And after tonight, who knew if he would ever have the opportunity again?

He had to memorize every delectable moment.

Reluctantly pulling back, he tugged her dress over her head and tossed it onto the floor.

He hissed, feeling as if he'd been punched in the gut as his gaze slid down the beauty of her slender curves.

Oh . . . hell. He hadn't forgotten. The memory of her was seared into his brain. But the sight of her rounded breasts tipped with rose-tinted nipples and the gentle swell of her hips always managed to shock him.

She was so perfect.

And his.

All his.

Unable to wait another minute, Mika scooped Bailey into his arms and headed toward the bed in the center of the room.

He heard her breath catch as he lowered her onto the mattress and followed her down, pressing his hardness against her. Mika stilled, preparing himself for her rejection. Her body was soft and eager, but he hadn't forgotten the past.

She might now claim that it'd been her insecurity that made her flee Valhalla, but he'd spent longer than he wanted to remember fearing that it had been his bottomless need for her that had driven her away.

There was a nerve-racking pause that felt like an eternity to Mika before she smoothed her hands up his back and buried her fingers in his hair.

At the same time, she moved her hips in an unmistakable invitation.

"Bailey." He muttered a curse, shoving himself to his feet so he could hastily strip off his remaining clothing before he was once again covering her with his naked body.

They groaned in unison, the heat combusting between them with nuclear force.

Mika spread impatient kisses over her face, wondering

how the hell he'd survived so long without having this female in his arms.

Reaching her mouth, he slid his tongue between her lips. He moaned. She tasted of honey and gentle, glorious power.

His sweet, beautiful healer.

She stirred a hunger that went beyond lust. Beyond companionship.

This was a need that came from a place deep inside him that only she could touch.

Enjoying the feel of her fingers smoothing through his hair, Mika allowed his hands to trail over the curve of her ass to the softness of her inner thighs.

His cock twitched, begging for release.

Her skin was so warm. So smooth. So fucking perfect.

A blast of pleasure exploded through him as his fingertips explored down the back of her thighs and then up to the juncture between her legs.

"Mika," she hissed as he allowed a finger to dip into her moistness.

His teeth nipped a path down her neck and over her shoulder.

Mmm. Jasmine temptation.

"Little one, I want to be inside you," he whispered against her damp skin. "I want to feel you wrapped about me."

"Yes." Her face pressed into his neck, her hot breath sending a bolt of bliss down his spine. "Now, Mika."

He meant to say something profound. Something that would let her know how much this moment meant to him.

But he'd never had a talent for making pretty speeches.

Hell, he was usually lucky to give a grunt when the occasion demanded a response.

This time he managed no more than a low growl as she reached to grab his cock, sliding her fingers down the aching length.

Sweat beaded his forehead as he struggled against the looming climax. Shit. He hadn't even gotten inside her yet.

Using his thumb to circle her clitoris, he tilted his hips, the breath wrenched from his lungs at the sensation of her fingers giving his sack a gentle squeeze before her fingers explored back to the broad head of his arousal.

Oh . . . hell.

It'd been too long.

"Little one, I can't make this last," he rasped, kissing a path down her collarbone and over the swell of her breast.

Her fingers tightened on his cock, the small pain only increasing his fevered passions.

"Then don't," she commanded in hoarse tones.

He didn't. Seizing her nipple in his mouth, he allowed his teeth to gently press into her skin even as he settled between her spread legs and slid deep into her heat.

Bailey gave a startled gasp. Her head arched back as hands lifted to grasp his shoulders.

Mika paused, giving her the chance to adjust to his intimate invasion.

And more importantly, a second to gather his own control.

Had anything ever felt so good?

The answer was simple.

No. Nothing—nothing at all—could compare to this moment.

Waiting until she began to move her hips beneath him, Mika caught her slow rhythm and rocked himself ever deeper. His eyes closed as the pleasure cascaded through his body. The heat, the scent, the feel of her tight wetness was nothing short of pure bliss.

"Mika . . ." she whispered, her breath coming in small pants.

He claimed her lips in a kiss of sheer demand, sliding his hands beneath her hips as he stroked into her over and over. There was no sound but the meeting of their flesh and their mutual moans of pleasure.

Outside the cottage, Jacob was still missing, and some bastard still had to be punished for taking a shot at him.

In this room, however, the world had disappeared and there was nothing but this woman who had always been a necessary part of his life.

Opening his eyes to watch Bailey moving beneath him, Mika quickened his pace. He could sense she was rapidly nearing her climax.

Just for a moment he was distracted by her sheer beauty.

The delicate features flushed with pleasure. The eyes darkened to emerald. The lips parted in passion. It was a sight he never, ever wanted to forget.

She gave a choked cry as the orgasm overwhelmed her, and the soft clenching around his erection tumbled him over the edge.

The release slammed into him with shocking force.

With a rasping groan he straightened his arms and sank as deep within her as he could go.

"Mine," he gasped.

Bailey struggled through her morass of emotions, trying to decide how she felt.

Gloriously sated? Definitely.

With Mika sprawled on top of her and her heart slowly settling back to a steady rhythm, she wanted nothing more than to melt against his warm body and stay there for the rest of eternity.

God. It'd been so long since she'd felt . . . anything.

It was ironic, really.

She'd run from Valhalla, saying she couldn't be caged, and where was her freedom? She'd created a prison of loneliness.

But beyond the bone-deep joy was a growing sense of unease.

A rising fear that this happiness might be suddenly snatched away from her.

With a sudden, irrational surge of panic, Bailey fought her way out of his arms and scooted off the bed.

Mika called out her name, but ignoring his legitimate confusion, she rushed out of the bedroom and through the living room.

It was only when she hit the kitchen that she realized she couldn't keep running.

Not even her stupid cowardice would allow her to run naked through the swamp in the middle of the night.

Instead she reached for the bottle of wine she'd left on the counter and poured herself a glass.

She'd taken her first sip when Mika was suddenly standing directly in front of her, his lean face tight with frustration as he studied her with a brooding gaze.

"What's going on, Bailey?" he demanded.

She held up her glass, doing her best not to allow her gaze to take a slow, thorough survey of his bronzed body.

Okay, maybe she took a peek.

Just enough to appreciate the hard, chiseled muscles and the fact that he was once again fully aroused despite the fact they'd just shared a cataclysmic orgasm.

"I needed wine," she muttered, forcing herself to take in a deep, calming breath.

The dark eyes narrowed. "You have regrets?"

"No," she instantly said, only to wrinkle her nose as she realized she wasn't being entirely honest. "Well, not about what just happened."

His expression remained grim, the gentle lover from just moments ago replaced by the focused hunter.

"Then why did you run?"

She took another large gulp. "I'm not running. I'm drinking."

Without warning he reached to pluck the glass from her hand, setting it aside as he tilted her face up to meet his ruthless gaze.

"You couldn't get out of my arms fast enough."

She grimaced before allowing the truth to spill out. "You scare me."

"I see." A shocking pain darkened his eyes, as if she'd wounded him on a deep, cellular level. "I should go."

"No." She grabbed for his arm, instinctively knowing that if she allowed Mika to walk out of the cottage, she would never see him again. "Wait."

His body was rigid with a brittle tension, his head turned away to hide his expression.

"I think you've said it all."

"No, as usual I've put my foot in my mouth," she admitted with a deep sigh. This man was right when he said she was too impulsive. "What I mean was that my feelings scare me."

He slowly turned back to meet her wary gaze. "Why?"

Her hand skimmed over the bulging muscle of his arm, confessing her deepest, darkest fear.

"Because if I need you, then you can hurt me."

Sucking in a sharp breath, he moved to grasp her face in his hands, his eyes blazing with an emotion that melted the ice that had surrounded her heart since she'd walked away from Valhalla.

"Never." He said the word as a pledge of honor. "I swear, little one."

She gave a slow nod, her heart lodged in her throat as his fingers lightly traced her face before following the line of her throat.

The tips of his fingers struck sparks of pleasure against her skin, reigniting her raw, unquenchable need for his touch.

"I believe you," she husked.

"But?" he prompted, his head lowering as he pressed his lips to the curve of her neck.

A groan was wrenched from her throat, her head tilting to the side to give him greater access.

"I've spent a long time convincing myself it was better to be alone."

"Then it's my duty . . ." He kissed a scorching path down the line of her collarbone. "And my very great pleasure . . ." He caught the tip of her nipple between his lips, ravishing her until she was forced to grasp the countertop behind her to keep herself from melting into a willing puddle at his feet. "To prove that being together is much . . ." His mouth headed downward, exploring between her breasts and then the soft skin of her stomach as he lowered himself to his knees. "Much better than being alone."

Her lips parted to agree with his plan of action only to come out as a gasp when his hands tugged her legs apart so he could find the center of her pleasure, his tongue penetrating her with a skill that made her forget how to speak.

Which was just fine by her.

There was nothing wrong with a little nonverbal communication. . . .

Chapter Seven

The sun was painting a glorious canvas of pale rose, violet, and amber across the morning sky when Mika at last received the text from Wolfe that he was waiting at the edge of the road.

Not that he was eager to leave Bailey, he acknowledged, reluctantly untangling himself from her warm body so he could pull on his clothes.

It'd been a night that would be seared into his mind forever.

Not just because of the sex.

Although that would have a starring role in his memories.

Hell, his body was still quivering from the raw, earth-shattering pleasure they'd shared.

But more important had been the sheer intimacy of their lovemaking.

Ten years ago they'd had plenty of passion, but both of them had been too young and caught up in their own insecurities and selfish needs to be able to truly share their hearts.

It'd taken the opportunity to understand how barren life was without each other to appreciate what they'd nearly lost.

Not that they'd discussed their future. He grimaced as he

dropped a gentle kiss on her forehead, careful not to wake her, before he silently left the cottage.

No. There was no way in hell he was going to press Bailey to commit to returning to Valhalla with him.

Did that make him a coward?

Maybe. But he didn't give a shit.

Nothing mattered beyond rebuilding the relationship that he'd once feared shattered beyond repair.

They had plenty of time to decide what happened next.

First he had to finish his current job.

Traveling through the barrier, he forced his way through the thick undergrowth that surrounded Bailey's cottage.

Two steps from the narrow road, Wolfe abruptly stepped from the shadows, his black hair tied at his nape and his lean body covered by a pair of black jeans, black T-shirt, and black shit-kickers.

Nothing complicated about the Tagos.

He looked like a badass because he was a badass.

End of story.

"About time you got here," Mika muttered.

"Hmm. You're looking . . ." A smile curved Wolfe's lips as his dark gaze studied Mika's face. "Well satisfied. It wouldn't have anything to do with a pretty young healer, would it?"

Mika stiffened, struck by a sudden suspicion. "Did you know Bailey was here?"

Wolfe shrugged, the cresting sunlight shimmering against the white streak at the front of his hair.

"There are few things I don't know."

Well, shit.

It was rare for Mika to be played.

No. Not rare.

Never.

But there was no mistaking the smug expression that settled on Wolfe's lean face.

The bastard had known exactly what was waiting for Mika when he came to Louisiana.

"And that's why you chose to send me to track Jacob," he growled.

"I was tired of watching you mope around because your pride wouldn't allow you to go after your woman."

Mika scowled. "I don't mope."

"You're right. You brood." Wolfe gave a dramatic shudder. "Even worse."

Mika rolled his eyes. "Nice."

"Aren't you going to thank me?"

Mika was honest enough to admit that he owed his friend more than a thank-you. Being able to have a second chance with Bailey was priceless.

Not that he was about to admit it to Wolfe.

The leader of the Sentinels was arrogant enough, thank you very much.

"You make an ugly-ass Cupid," he instead muttered.

Wolfe slapped him on the shoulder, nearly sending him stumbling into the nearby bog.

"Yeah, you're welcome."

"Did you discover anything about the healer who was found dead?" Mika abruptly changed the subject.

He wasn't ready to discuss Bailey or their reunion.

It was all too new. Too fragile.

Taking the hint, Wolfe folded his arms over his chest, revealing the gun that was holstered at his side.

There was no doubt another gun was tucked in the back of his waistband and one strapped to his ankle, as well as a knife or two stashed in easy-to-reach locations.

"We think he'd been kept captive."

"By who?"

"Impossible to say."

Mika frowned. In the past he'd heard of psychics and clairvoyants being kidnapped. People always believed that knowing the future could somehow bring them wealth or happiness. And even witches could be forced to perform spells.

But a healer?

"It would have to be high-bloods," he said. "A healer would be worthless to a human."

Frustration tightened Wolfe's expression. The Tagos liked mysteries about as much as Mika.

"None of this makes sense."

Mika gave a shake of his head. They weren't going to figure anything out by standing there.

"This way."

In silence he led Wolfe through the swamp. Twice they had to halt, once for a hunter who was on the trail of a rabbit, and once for two fishermen who were headed for a nearby dock. None of them were aware of the two lethal warriors who were standing a few feet away.

At last they reached the banks of the channel, careful to remain hidden in the thick line of cypresses as they studied the small island.

Minutes passed. There was no sound. No movement. And still they waited.

It wasn't until nearly an hour later that Wolfe stepped out of the trees, making himself a deliberate target for any sniper.

"I think it's empty," he said when he wasn't shot.

"I must have spooked them," Mika said, disgust in his voice.

Dammit. If they'd fled the area, the Sentinels might not ever discover who they were or if they'd been responsible for Jacob's disappearance.

"You stay here," Wolfe commanded. "I'll circle to the other side and we'll approach at the same time."

Not giving Mika time to argue, the Sentinel disappeared into the swamp, his movements so graceful he barely disturbed the choking vegetation.

Less than ten minutes had passed when a whistle too high for human ears alerted him that Wolfe was in place.

Pulling a gun out of the holster he'd hidden beneath his T-shirt, Mika eased his way down the steep bank and entered the tepid water of the channel.

He grimaced as his boots sank into muck at the bottom, well aware that he was vulnerable to attack until he was on the other side.

Not the most pleasant thought.

Battling through the lilies, water moccasins, and one gator, Mika was at last on the island and threading his way toward the small cabin in the center.

Glancing through a broken window, he glimpsed Wolfe coming in through the back, his gun raised to shoot anything that moved.

Wisely waiting until Wolfe gestured for him to enter, Mika did a slow sweep of the barren front room that held a low couch, two armchairs, and a stained coffee table. He did a similar search of the two bedrooms and kitchen before returning to the front of the cabin where Wolfe was standing next to the heavy shackles that were bolted to the wall.

His jaw tightened as he caught a familiar smell.

"Jacob was here," he said, watching as Wolfe bent down to lightly touch the pool of blood on the warped wooden floor.

"And recently injured," Wolfe muttered.

Mika grimaced. "Yes." The blood was the only reason he'd been able to recognize the scent as Jacob's.

Muttering a curse, Wolfe breathed in deeply, his senses far more acute than any other Sentinel's.

"Humans," he at last said. "At least six."

Mika glanced around the cramped, rapidly rotting room. As far as he could see there was nothing of value.

The house couldn't be fully secured. The view was obstructed. He could smell gas that would indicate a generator, but there were few of the usual comforts that most humans desired.

The only thing it had to offer was privacy.

"What the hell were they doing here?"

Wolfe straightened, heading toward a narrow flight of stairs that led to an attic. Mika followed behind, his nose wrinkling at the unmistakable scent of antiseptic.

"What the hell?" Wolfe muttered, bending low to keep from cracking his skull on the low, open beams.

Mika joined his leader, his brows pulling together as he took in the metal-framed bed that looked like something that would be found in a hospital and the IV stand that still had an empty plastic bag and a long tube attached to it.

"Someone was receiving medical attention."

Wolfe gave a slow shake of his head. "Jacob?"

Mika shrugged. "I have no idea."

With a growl, the Tagos headed toward a metal cabinet in the corner of the room, pulling out a scrap of wadded-up paper that had been left behind.

Smoothing it open, the Tagos made a sound of disgust.

"The Brotherhood."

Mika arched a brow. The Brotherhood was a secret society of fanatic humans that had first been formed in ancient Samaria. They believed it was their sole duty to try and rid the world of high-bloods.

Thankfully, they were usually as cowardly as they were incompetent, and so far they'd proven more an annoyance than a true threat.

"How do you know?" he demanded.

Wolfe pointed toward the letterhead that had a stylized arrow running beneath the words:

ONLY THE PURE.

"This is their symbol."

"Symbol?" Mika arched a brow. "They sell merchandise?"

Wolfe gave a sharp laugh, shoving the paper into the front pocket of his jeans.

"I would find them funny as hell if they didn't occasionally grow some balls and do something stupid."

Mika glanced back at the hospital bed, a bad feeling settling in the pit of his stomach.

"What interest would the Brotherhood have in Jacob?"

"Hell, who knows?" Wolfe returned his attention to the cabinet, tossing out the gauze and needles and vials of human medicine as he searched for some clue. "He might have seen something he shouldn't have. Or he possesses a certain skill they need."

"Maybe."

The Tagos easily picked up on Mika's lack of conviction.

Turning, he moved toward Mika. "What are you thinking?"

Mika didn't like guessing. He wanted facts. They didn't lead a warrior down wrong paths.

Unfortunately, he knew that expression on Wolfe's hard face.

He wasn't going to stop digging until Mika revealed what was troubling him.

"If they intended to capture Jacob after they lured him to the swamp, then why did they beat him and allow him to walk away?"

Wolfe stilled, silently considering Mika's question.

"Could he have escaped?" he asked. "The idiots call themselves the Brotherhood and have fancy letterhead, but in the end they're only humans."

"No, his injuries were too severe," Mika said, trying to visualize what had happened after Jacob had been pulled from his car and then beaten nearly senseless. "And besides, if he was trying to flee his attackers, why wouldn't he remain with Bailey until he could contact the monks and be returned to the safety of the monastery?"

Wolfe paced the narrow floor, his brow furrowed as he considered the various possibilities.

"It's almost as if—" His words came to an abrupt halt as he sent Mika a worried glance.

Mika's heart missed a beat as the vague sense of unease became downright terror.

"As if?" he prompted.

"As if Jacob was the bait, not the target."

"Shit." Mika was charging down the stairs and out the door before Wolfe even finished speaking. "Bailey."

Bailey wasn't surprised that she woke alone.

Mika had warned her before she'd tumbled into an exhausted slumber that he would have to leave as soon as Wolfe arrived.

And astonishingly, her first reaction hadn't been to assume he was running out on her because he didn't find her important enough to stay.

Instead, she'd been able to simply enjoy the small aches and pangs that came from a night of thorough, delectably vigorous lovemaking as she stood beneath the shower.

No regrets. No clawing fear that she'd made herself too vulnerable.

It was . . . blissful.

Pulling on another loose sundress, this one in a pretty shade of peach, she combed her curls with her fingers and headed for the kitchen to make coffee.

She intended to keep busy while Mika was gone.

Not because of her old habits. But because she knew that if she sat around worrying that he might be in danger, it would drive her crazy.

Taking her coffee and cell phone, she sat at the kitchen table and began returning messages that had come in overnight.

The first was from her parents. She grimaced as she

opened the message, already preparing herself for their usual spiel: *So sorry we won't be returning home as planned, but the school in New Zealand has asked us to come early and we're sure you'll understand . . .*

She sent back a quick text saying of course she understood, blah, blah, blah.

There was no point in being disappointed.

It wasn't as if she could change her parents, or their obsession with their careers.

All she could do was build a stable, loving home for her own children so they would never feel second best.

She abruptly gasped, realizing where her thoughts had taken her.

Children.

Mika's children . . .

Excitement raced through her.

The mere idea should have been shocking.

Just a day ago she was certain that her life as the free-spirited healer was precisely what she wanted.

No rules. No restrictions. No disappointments.

Now she was once again Mika's lover, and a strange, wholly unexpected urge to start nesting was settling deep inside her.

Craziness.

Still trying to accept the cataclysmic shift in her world, Bailey caught the unmistakable smell of blood.

A high-blood was injured.

Keeping a hold of her phone, she headed out of the kitchen, already suspecting who she would see as she stepped into the early-morning sunshine.

The young man standing at the edge of the barrier had light brown hair that fell onto his forehead and a bluntly carved face that was bloody and bruised from a recent beating.

His gangly body was equally wounded, the loose shirt and cargo pants covered in filth.

Christ. He looked like he'd been tortured.

Sliding her cell phone into her pocket, she took a step forward.

"Jacob?" she breathed. "Who did this to you?"

He held up his hand, pressing it against the shield. "I need your help."

She took another step forward. "What happened?"

He licked his busted lips, one eye nearly swollen shut. "Can I come in?"

Bailey twisted her hands together, her every instinct urging to her rush to Jacob and bring him into her home so she could heal him.

It was what she did. What she'd been born to do.

Only her promise to Mika kept her standing in place.

"Tell me how you were injured," she instead urged.

"I was attacked."

"By who?"

"I . . ." His gaze shifted to the side, almost as if he was looking for someone hidden among the nearby trees. Shit. Was he afraid he was being followed? "The Brotherhood."

She blinked in shock.

She'd heard of the secret society that supposedly hated high-bloods, but she'd never realized there were any in this area.

"Why would they attack you?"

"Please, I really need to be healed."

Bailey shook her head, the hair standing up on her nape at the edge of desperation in Jacob's voice.

"I'm sorry, I can't."

Jacob sucked in a sharp breath. "What do you mean?"

"I can't let you into my home until my friend returns," she said. "He wants to speak with you."

"I can't wait." Jacob smacked his hand against the barrier, his panic a tangible force in the air. "I'll die."

Bailey stepped back, her brows drawing together at the boy's strange behavior.

It was true he was wounded. And no doubt in pain.

But he wasn't near death.

"No, you won't."

There was a rustle in the undergrowth before a man stepped out of the trees and pressed a gun to Jacob's temple.

"Yes, he will."

Bailey's heart thundered in her chest, her wide-eyed gaze taking in the stranger.

He was medium height and medium weight with mud-brown eyes and black hair that was neatly combed from his square face. Dressed in a pair of khaki slacks and a pressed cotton shirt, he looked more like a politician than a cult fanatic.

Well, as long as you didn't bother to notice he was holding a gun to the head of a poor, innocent boy.

"Who are you?" she rasped.

"I don't give my name to freaks," he said with patent disdain. Creep. Then he lifted his free hand, gesturing toward her. "Come here."

Her mind raced.

She didn't know why they were there, or what they wanted from her, but she knew it couldn't be good.

Her only hope was that she could keep the bastard distracted long enough for Mika to return.

"Screw you," she muttered.

Soul-deep hatred glowed in the man's eyes. The sort of hatred that allowed him to view her as an object in need of destruction, not a real person.

"Do it, or the boy dies."

"No." She forced herself to breathe even as her stomach twisted with dread. God almighty, could she truly stand there and watch the man kill Jacob just to protect herself? "Why are you doing this?"

"You have something we need," he said.

She frowned. What the hell would the Brotherhood need from her?

And how was Jacob involved?

"I can't heal humans."

A strangely mocking smile twisted the stranger's lips. "You would be surprised." He grabbed Jacob's hair and tilted the boy's head back, placing the gun directly beneath his chin. As if he felt the need to make the threat more dramatic. "Now, make your choice. Do you come with us nicely or does the boy die?"

As if there was a choice?

It didn't matter what she'd promised to Mika. Or even that she knew she was being manipulated.

She was a healer.

It was profoundly, utterly impossible for her to stand and watch someone being harmed.

"I'm coming," she said, resentfully moving forward.

Stepping through the barrier, Bailey wasn't surprised when two more men appeared from the trees. Dressed in matching jeans and muscle shirts, they had identical arrow tattoos on the side of their thick necks.

Bailey grimaced. She assumed the Bobbsey Twins were the muscle of the nasty trio.

They hurried forward to grab her arms in a painful grip.

"Check her for a phone," the leader commanded. "We don't want to be followed."

Bailey swallowed a groan. Dammit. She'd been depending on that phone to help Mika locate her position.

She didn't bother to struggle as one of the men ran his hand over her dress, swiftly locating her phone and tossing it into a clump of weeds.

What was the point?

It wasn't as if she could fight off the three grown men, even if they were human.

Besides, as long as they held a gun to Jacob's head, they had her between a rock and a hard place.

"Take her to Limburg."

Bailey parted her lips to demand to know who Limburg was, but before she could speak she saw the flash of a hand, then the world went black as the fist connected directly with her chin.

Chapter Eight

When Bailey woke, she knew two things.

One: She was in a dark, cramped room that reeked of rotting fish.

And two: She had the headache from hell.

Lying flat on her back, it took a painful minute to remember exactly why she was waking in a strange place with a throbbing brain.

The Brotherhood goon had knocked her out.

The bastard.

Rubbing her chin, she slowly forced herself to a sitting position.

"Damn," she muttered, forced to lean back against the moldy cement wall as her head began to spin.

"Are you okay?" a voice whispered from the darkness.

She frowned, waiting for her eyes to adjust.

She couldn't see in the dark like a Sentinel, but there was enough sunlight creeping beneath the heavy steel door to allow her to make out the wooden pallets shoved in one corner and the stacks of empty crates that threatened to topple over.

"Jacob?" she called softly.

"I'm here."

The young man stepped from behind the crates, moving to squat beside her.

Bailey took a close inventory of his face. His eye was only slightly swollen and most of the bruises had begun to fade.

Which meant that she'd been out around three hours.

"Where are we?" she demanded.

Jacob grimaced, glancing around the small space. "It's a warehouse near the Gulf."

Bailey didn't know what she was expecting, but it wasn't that.

"Why would they bring us here?"

"I think they're waiting for a boat to arrive."

"You mean the Brotherhood?"

"Yes."

Bailey lowered her hand from her aching jaw, stabbing her companion with a suspicious glare.

From the beginning she'd assumed that Jacob was a victim. Now she wasn't nearly so certain.

"You know them," she accused.

"No." He halted, grimacing as he heaved a sigh. Sentinels could technically tell a falsehood, but they were trained from the second that they entered the monastery that lying held dire consequences. Of course, that didn't mean that they always shared all the info. Or that they couldn't twist the truth until it was nearly unrecognizable. "I mean, I don't know all of them," he at last muttered.

"Which one do you know?"

"The leader. He goes by the name Limburg." Even in the darkness Bailey could make out the young Sentinel's sick expression. "He's my father."

She made a sound of shock before her brows abruptly drew together in confusion.

"I thought your father was dead?"

"Why would you think that?"

She struggled to think through the fog of pain that still clouded her mind.

"The Sentinels tracked down the man who left you at Valhalla."

"Oh." He gave a shake of his head. "That wasn't my father; it was my uncle." He paused, glancing toward the steel door as he leaned toward her. "You're sure he's dead?" he asked in a low voice.

Was Jacob indicating that there were guards outside the door?

Bailey grimaced, not for the first time wishing she possessed the enhanced senses of a Sentinel.

"Yes."

"Damn." Genuine regret touched Jacob's face. "They told me he was. But I'd hoped—"

"I'm sorry," she murmured as his words trailed away.

He gave a slow shake of his head. "It's okay. We weren't that close," he said. "My uncle wasn't exactly accepted into the Benson clan once he confessed he was a high-blood." Holding out his arm, he unfastened the wide leather band. Then, turning over his arm, he revealed the small black arrow that was tattooed onto his inner wrist. "See?"

Bailey had a vague memory of similar tattoos on the goons who'd grabbed her.

"I don't understand," she said.

"It's the mark of the Brotherhood," Jacob explained. "My family has been loyal members since the society first started." He gave a short, humorless laugh. "We're like royalty."

Oh . . . hell.

Bailey grimaced. "It must have been a shock when your uncle and then you turned out to be high-bloods."

Jacob abruptly wrapped his arms around his upper body, as if trying to protect himself from the pain of his memories.

"No one knew I was different," he said, his voice suddenly hoarse. "Not until—"

Her hand instinctively reached out to lightly touch his arm, allowing the power of her healing to ease his distress.

She might not yet be entirely convinced he wasn't playing some game with her, but she wouldn't withhold her skill. Not if she could help.

"What happened, Jacob?"

Jacob shuddered beneath her touch, breathing out a small sigh of relief.

"I was in training." His gaze was fixed on the far wall, his expression distant as he allowed his memories to return. "Despite my size I was always stronger and faster than the other kids. My father was so proud, telling everyone that it was our pure breeding that made me win every competition." A sudden heat filled the air as Jacob's pain shifted to anger. "Then one day I accidentally tossed one of my opponents through a door. I nearly killed him. My father had to admit that it wasn't superior genes that made me better than the other students."

It wasn't an unusual story.

Many boys might realize they were stronger or faster than other kids, but it wasn't until they'd accidentally injured or even killed someone that they understood how truly different they were from others.

"So he had you taken to Valhalla?" she asked softly.

"Not hardly." Without warning, Jacob surged upright, his face grim. "He intended to kill me."

Bailey wasn't naïve.

As a healer she'd seen the damage that people could do to one another.

But the thought of a father willingly destroying his own son just because he was a high-blood . . .

"Good God," she breathed.

Jacob suddenly looked far older in the darkness, his lips twisting with a humorless smile.

Sometimes age had nothing to do with how many years a person had been on the earth.

"Thankfully my father was so shamed by the thought he could have created a monster, he was determined to execute me in a grand ceremony," he explained, his voice harsh. "It was supposed to cleanse the stain from our family honor."

Bailey gave a sad shake of her head. "The bastard."

Jacob shrugged. "At least it gave my uncle the opportunity to hear what was happening. He managed to sneak me out of the cellar where I'd been locked away and take me to Valhalla. It was the one place not even my father could get his hands on me."

And now the uncle who had saved him was dead.

Poor Jacob.

"What about your mother?" she asked, unable to bear the thought that he was all alone. Although she rarely saw her parents, she knew deep in her heart if she truly needed them, they would come. "Surely she must have tried to stop your father?"

"I never knew her. My father refused to even tell me her name." Jacob once again glanced toward the door before he turned his attention back to her. "Until now."

Bailey drew in a slow, deep breath. Her jaw still ached and the stench from the fish was making her stomach queasy, but her attention was locked on Jacob.

"What changed?" she forced herself to ask even as she suspected she didn't want to know the answer.

"A few days ago my father contacted me, demanding that we meet."

The crazy-ass father had contacted him after he'd planned to murder him in a grand ceremony?

Ballsy.

"How did he know how to find you?"

Jacob shrugged. "I'm not sure, but I suspect they have spies in Valhalla."

Bailey gave a low snort at the thought of anyone being able to infiltrate Valhalla.

Not only was it protected behind layers of magic, but nothing got past the Sentinels. Hell, you couldn't sneeze without it being captured on camera.

Still, she needed to let Wolfe know that the Brotherhood had some means of tracking Jacob.

The suspicion he might have a potential security leak was going to make the Tagos . . .

She grimaced at the mere thought.

It wasn't going to be pretty.

"You didn't go, did you?" she instead demanded.

"I'm not an idiot. As far as I was concerned, Limburg stopped being my father when he condemned me to death."

"No one would blame you, Jacob," she said, understanding it had to be confusing.

The parent/child relationship was difficult enough without adding in a planned homicide.

Jacob hunched a shoulder. "I hoped he would leave me alone, but he sent me a message that said he was holding my mother hostage."

"Hostage?"

"It was the only way he could force me to meet with him." Jacob clenched his hands at his side. "He said he'd kill her if I didn't do as he said."

"Dear Lord." Bailey shook her head. The man was pure evil. "And he calls you a monster?"

"What else would you call a freak of nature?" a male voice demanded as the steel door was thrust open.

Bailey tensed as a middle-aged man stepped into the room, his frail body covered by a loose robe.

Her immediate thought was that the man was ill.

The knowledge didn't come from her healer skills.

It was obvious by the thinness that had nothing to do with the latest diet and the way the jowls sagged from the once round face. His skin was pasty and his head bald from his past radiation treatments.

The dark, sunken eyes, however, remained bright with a cunning intelligence as he studied her with a disdainful curl of his lips.

Right behind him was the jackass who'd punched her in the face.

Her gaze returned to the older man. Despite his age and fragile health, he was by far the more dangerous of the two.

"Who are you?" she rasped.

"Limburg." His smile was mocking. "Jacob's father and your new master."

Mika slammed into the invisible barrier with enough force to rattle his teeth, his heart beating at a frantic pace.

"Bailey, let us through," he called, raising his hand to bang it against the shield. "Bailey."

Wolfe halted at his side, his dark face grim. "She isn't in the cottage."

"Damn." Fear blasted through him. The sort of fear that could cripple a man. "I told her to stay behind the barrier," he growled. "She promised."

Wolfe made a swift sweep of the area, pausing to crouch down at the edge of the trees.

"There were humans here," he murmured; then with a hiss, he reached into a clump of trees and pulled out a cell phone. "Is this Bailey's?"

Mika's blood ran cold as he recognized the distinctive pink case.

"They have her," he rasped.

"We'll find her," Wolfe said, his words a rough pledge. Rising to his feet, he moved to lay a hand on Mika's shoulder, offering his comfort before he was turning to jog back toward the narrow road. "This way."

Mika took a moment to suck in a deep breath.

His every instinct screamed for blood. He wanted the bastards who took Bailey in his hands so he could squeeze the life from them. Then he would rip their carcasses into small pieces and toss them into the bayou as gator food.

It was a dangerous, explosive anger that could too easily cloud his mind.

Bailey needed him.

Until he found her, he would have to shove his terrified fury to the back of his mind.

He was a hunter.

Cold. Ruthless. Unstoppable.

Focusing on his finely honed skills, Mika jogged over the spongy ground to join Wolfe as the Tagos studied the tire tracks that were visible in the mud.

"Two cars," he said. "They headed south."

"Can you follow their trail?"

Wolfe grimaced. "No. Trying to pick out one particular scent in this area is like finding a needle in a haystack." He pulled his phone from his pocket. "I'll call for backup."

Mika's heart twisted with an agony that was so profound it was a wonder it didn't strike him dead.

"I can't lose her, Wolfe," he said, his voice not entirely steady. "It'll break me."

There was a faint pop, as if the air pressure had just shifted, then a strange, larva-like man abruptly appeared in the middle of the road.

"If you care so much, Sentinel, then why didn't you protect her?"

Mika had his gun aimed and his finger on the trigger when Wolfe lightly touched his arm.

The Tagos's gaze never wavered from the peculiar creature. "Boggs," he muttered, his voice carefully stripped of emotion.

Mika grudgingly lowered his weapon. He'd heard of Boggs, of course.

The mysterious doppelgänger was renowned for his ability to see glimpses of the past and the future.

He was also rumored to travel around the world collecting folk stories that related to the high-bloods.

"The Keeper of Tales?" he demanded, puzzled what would bring the elusive man to the middle of the swamp.

And what his connection was to Bailey.

"I warned her," Boggs muttered. "I told her she would be betrayed."

Mika's brows snapped together. "Betrayed by who?"

Boggs's weirdly unformed features twisted with anger. "Jacob."

Damn. If Bailey weren't in danger, Mika might have felt a stab of regret.

Sentinels were rare. To lose one to treachery truly hurt.

Wolfe was clearly thinking the same thing.

"He's a traitor?" the Tagos demanded.

The creature shrugged, his robe thankfully hiding the thin body beneath.

"Not by choice, but that doesn't help Bailey."

Mika shook his head. They could deal with Jacob later.

"Where did they take her?"

The pure white eyes turned in his direction despite the fact he was supposed to be blind.

"If I knew that, I would rescue her myself. We've done quite well without you."

Was he implying that he had some sort of relationship with Bailey?

"You son of a bitch."

Charging forward, Mika ran into a brick wall named Wolfe.

"No, Mika," his leader muttered, glaring at the doppelgänger. "Do you have any information that will help us track her?"

"I had a vision that related to Bailey."

"Well, what was it?" Mika snapped.

Boggs shrugged. "I saw an arrow."

Mika made a sound of disgust. "That's it?"

The white eyes glowed with an eerie light. "I saw the mother of the sun god at the edge of the water," he said, his voice distant, as if he was lost in the memory of his vision. "There was a boat approaching."

It was Wolfe's turn to growl with impatience. "What the hell does that mean?"

Mika frowned, pulling out his phone. Two bars, thank God.

Surfing the web, he quickly had the information he needed.

"There," he said, turning the phone to show his companion what he'd discovered.

"Leto Warehouse," Wolfe read out loud. "Is that supposed to mean something?"

"Leto is the mother of Apollo, the sun god." Mika arched his brows at Wolfe's astonished expression. "What? Some of us actually read."

"Hey, I'm not judging." Wolfe pointed toward the phone. "But as a clue, the mother of the sun god is kind of vague. Why do you think this warehouse is the place in the vision?"

"This is the only place with Leto in the name that's close enough to water that a boat could be approaching."

Wolfe blinked at the simple explanation.

"Good enough for me," he at last said. "Let's go."

Chapter Nine

Bailey struggled to breathe.

Dammit. She hated being afraid.

From the time she was a little girl she'd always thought of herself as a brave adventurer. More Xena than Cinderella.

But she couldn't deny a bone-deep terror as she watched the man named Limburg motion for his bodyguard to cross the small room and stand beside her.

She didn't know what they wanted from her, but she knew it wasn't going to be good.

Not that she was going to let them see her fear, she bleakly told herself.

She might not be a warrior princess, but she did have a little pride.

Besides, she knew one thing beyond a shadow of a doubt.

Mika was coming for her.

It didn't matter where they'd taken her, or how hard they tried to cover their tracks, he would find her.

The knowledge gave her the courage to stiffen her spine and meet Limburg's sneering glare with a tilt of her chin.

"Master?" She shook her head. "I don't think so."

The dark eyes narrowed. "I see you are in need of training," he murmured, pointing toward the door. "Jacob, leave us."

"Why?" the young Sentinel asked, his expression troubled. "What are you going to do to her?"

Limburg sent his son a warning glare. "I told you what would happen if you disobeyed me."

Jacob grimaced as he turned toward Bailey. "I'm sorry. I . . ." His voice cracked as he backed toward the door. "I truly am."

Bailey waited until Jacob was gone and the door closed before she made a sound of disgust.

"Does it make you feel like a big man to bully your son?"

Limburg folded his arms over his sunken chest. "Robert," he murmured to his companion.

Without warning the thug backhanded Bailey with enough force to slam the back of her head against the cement wall.

Holy shit.

Bailey's teeth snapped together and a groan was wrenched from her throat as blackness threatened to suck her under.

Only grim determination kept her from passing out.

"You will show me respect or I will kill you," Limburg purred, his smug tone making Bailey wish she had the strength to kick his ass.

"I don't think so." She lifted her fingers to wipe the blood from her lips. "You brought me here because you need me."

"Correction." The too-thin face hardened with seething hatred. "I need a healer. If I decide you aren't worthy to serve me, then I'll kill you and get another."

Bailey swallowed her angry words.

It wouldn't matter if Mika was on the way if she couldn't stay alive long enough for him to find her.

She grimaced, meeting Limburg's feverish gaze.

Easier said than done.

The creep clearly got off on watching her being hurt.

"Fine," she forced herself to say. "What do you need from me?"

"I should think it's obvious," he rasped. "I'm dying."

God almighty. How many times did she have to explain her powers only worked on high-bloods?

"I can't cure human diseases."

The man moved forward, the strong scent of antiseptic not entirely disguising the slow rot beneath.

"You can't cure me, but your powers of healing can keep me alive," he said.

She shook her head. Not to antagonize the idiot, but to warn him that any hopes he was harboring that she could prevent his looming death were futile.

"It's not possible," she insisted. "My skill can't affect a human."

"You think not?" He regarded her with a superior expression, stroking a finger down his loose jowl. "Let me tell you a little story."

She clenched her aching teeth. God, he was a ridiculous blowhard.

Unfortunately, for the moment she had to grin and bear it. *Please hurry, Mika.*

"Okay," she muttered.

"There once was a Brotherhood leader who was held in awe by his people," he grandly announced, his voice gaining strength as he became lost in the thought of his own glory. "He was destined for greatness, despite the disappointment of his son."

Bailey shifted on the hard ground. She didn't know which was more painful, sitting on the hard pavement or having to listen to the douchebag's yammering.

"Fascinating," she muttered.

He seemed impervious to her blatant lack of admiration. "Then the gods grew jealous of his splendor and they punished him with a foul illness."

She gave a lift of one shoulder. "Cancer isn't a punishment. It's a common disease among humans."

The dark eyes flared with fury at what he considered a curse by resentful deities.

"Death has invaded my body. I tried all the usual treatments." His lips twisted with bitter anger. "I even went to a Nostrum clinic."

Bailey blinked in surprise. Nostrum clinics were unsanctioned, backroom hospitals run by high-bloods who claimed they could heal everything from infertility to death.

Valhalla did their best to keep them from popping up, of course. Not the least of which was tossing a healer caught providing treatment to a human into prison for life. But as long as there was money to be made, there would always be unethical people willing to take advantage of the desperate.

"Then you must realize there's nothing more to be done," she said.

"I haven't finished my story."

She made a sound of impatience. God. This wasn't *War and Peace*.

"Then finish."

He stiffened, that unnerving fervor flaring through his eyes at her sharp tone.

"Apologize," he snapped.

Bailey didn't hesitate as Robert lifted his hand, clearly eager to dole out more punishment.

"I'm sorry."

A taunting smile twisted his lips. "It's nice to know you can be trained." He waved off the goon. "Shall I continue?"

"Yes."

Smoothing his hands down his robe, he began to pace the cramped space, seeming to enjoy the sound of his own voice.

"A doctor suggested that I have regular blood transfusions to stave off the inevitable," he said. Bailey nodded. She wasn't fully familiar with human treatments, but it seemed she'd heard there were some drugs that suppressed the formation of blood platelets. "Luckily I had a brother who could provide what I needed."

She couldn't hide her shock. "The brother you shunned because he was a high-blood?"

Limburg shrugged. The bastard was clearly undisturbed by the thought he'd treated his brother like he was trash, then demanded his help when he needed him.

"I'll admit that I briefly considered my previous belief that I would rather be dead than to contaminate my body with anything that came from a freak. Thankfully, my lust for life was greater than my hatred of your people."

Bailey blinked.

Wow. Just . . . wow.

"And your brother agreed?" she demanded.

"Not at first. He had to be convinced to do his family duty."

"You forced him."

Limburg waved a hand toward the goon. "Robert provided incentive for him to agree to my demands."

Bailey grimaced. Of course he did.

"Nice."

"It offered some relief, but I was still dying. And then one day Robert became . . ." He paused, as if searching for the proper word. "Overly enthusiastic."

Robert gave a short, humorless laugh. "It happens."

Bailey pressed against the wall, desperately wanting to put some distance between herself and the looming brute.

"What does that mean?" she breathed.

"While he was convincing my brother to help, he accidentally broke his neck." He spoke as if he was discussing a shattered teacup. "We had to find a healer to keep him alive."

Limburg's stark lack of emotion was . . . stunning.

She shuddered. "Good God."

Limburg smiled. "Yes, it was indeed an answer from the gods."

"Because you nearly killed your brother?"

"He was still in the process of being healed when my private doctor performed the blood transfusion," the man explained. "Instantly I began to feel better."

"The transfusion—"

"It was more than that," he interrupted, suddenly annoyed. "My vitals improved, my constant pain eased, and I was able to keep down a meal for the first time in weeks. Then, as the days passed, we realized my cancer had slowed."

She frowned. "It must have been a coincidence," she said, although inside she was assuming that it had to be the placebo effect.

"No." His hand slashed through the air. "I don't understand the medical mumbo jumbo, but so long as the blood being transfused still contains the power from the healer, it gives me a residual burst of magic." He grimaced, glaring down at the robe that covered his frail body. "It doesn't cure me, but it does keep me alive."

Bailey hesitated.

Good God. Was it possible? Had the brother proved to be a conduit, allowing the healer's magic to be transferred to a human?

She'd never heard of such a thing.

But then, had it ever been tested?

They'd recently found a healer who was able to alter actual DNA, so clearly there were still things to be discovered when it came to high-blood powers.

Giving a shake of her head, she shoved the startling possibility to the back of her mind.

Right now it didn't matter if it truly worked or if it was a figment of Limburg's imagination.

Her only concern was keeping the man preoccupied until Mika could get her the hell out of there.

"So if your brother was helping you, then why did you kill him?" she asked.

Limburg halted his pacing to turn and meet Bailey's wary gaze.

"The more aggressive my cancer becomes, the more powerful magic I need. Which means the more healing my brother had to receive." Again there was that appalling lack of concern. Did he care at all that his brother had been brutally beaten just to keep him alive? Seemingly not. "Eventually his body gave out."

She was forced to clear her throat.

Just being in the same room with the jackass made her want to gag.

"And the healer?"

"He knew too much."

The words were matter-of-fact.

A man was dead. An expendable casualty.

"You truly are evil." The words burst out before she could halt them.

Robert took a step toward her, but Limburg held up a restraining hand.

"As I said, your opinion has no meaning to me," he drawled.

She wrapped her arms around herself, feeling a chill that had nothing to do with the temperature.

"Tell me why I'm here."

"My doctor is convinced that the transfusions worked because my blood was so similar to my brother's," he explained. "Which means I need a new source of blood."

A smile curved Limburg's lips as he watched the horrified comprehension spread over her face.

"Jacob," she breathed.

* * *

Mika and Wolfe crouched behind the hedge that framed the small parking lot.

Ignoring the baking heat and the nearby fishermen who were unloading a shrimp boat, they studied the square, red-brick structure that was built at the edge of the water.

At a glance it looked deserted.

The windows were barred and the front door locked with a heavy chain. And if that wasn't enough, there was a large No Trespassing sign planted in the small patch of grass next to the stairs.

"This is the place," Mika muttered.

They were the first words he'd spoken since they'd commandeered a vehicle from the monks and taken off.

It'd taken everything he possessed to focus his Sentinel skills on locating Bailey. Any lapse in his concentration and the barely leashed panic would overwhelm him.

Now, however, the tightness that had made it nearly impossible for him to breathe was beginning to ease.

Bailey . . .

She was near.

Wolfe nodded. "I'll scout—"

"She's there." Mika nodded.

"You're certain?" Wolfe pressed.

"I can sense her," he admitted.

It was rare, but a few Sentinels formed a bond so deep they could actually feel the presence of one another when they were near.

Wolfe lifted a surprised brow. "Where?"

He nodded toward the warehouse. "Lower floor, south side."

"Wait," Wolfe commanded as Mika prepared to rush forward. He pointed toward the top of the warehouse. "There's a sniper on the roof and at least one guard on the front door."

Mika shrugged off his leader's hand.

He didn't care if there was a fucking army guarding the place. He was going to get Bailey.

Now.

"Keep them occupied," he muttered, keeping low as he headed toward the end of the hedge.

"Where are you going?" Wolfe rasped. "Mika . . . dammit."

Ignoring Wolfe's anger, Mika silently jogged along the edge of the parking lot, headed toward the path that led toward the boat.

Then, ignoring the startled fishermen, he plunged into the water, using the wooden docks to shield his approach as he swam toward the warehouse.

Reaching the stairs, he pounded beneath the wooden planks, his lips twisting as the guard predictably moved to peer over the edge of the dock.

He was still bending down when Mika's fist met with his face, busting his nose and sending him tumbling into the water with a loud splash.

Mika didn't hesitate.

Grabbing the top step, he pulled himself out of the water and vaulted onto the dock. He crouched low for a second, waiting for a second guard. When none appeared, he jogged toward the back of the building.

Predictably, the only entrance was a vertical steel door that was locked and chained, but Mika was a Sentinel.

With one massive jerk, he busted the padlock and shoved the door up to reveal a large loading dock. He peered inside, assuring himself that it was empty before he slid inside and headed toward the closest door.

He wasn't afraid of human guards, but the farther he could get without having to fight, the better.

The last thing he wanted was to alert his enemies that he was there.

They might take off with Bailey. Or worse . . .

No. He clamped down on that no-go thought.

The only possible outcome he was willing to consider was him finding Bailey and killing the bastards who took her.

End of story.

He entered a narrow hallway, pausing as his acute hearing picked up the faint sound of gunshots.

Shit.

Wolfe must have been spotted.

He hurried past a row of offices, sensing he was closing the distance to Bailey.

Just a few more seconds . . .

Focused on his bond with Bailey, Mika nearly missed the scent of a nearby male.

Coming to a halt at the end of the hall, he pressed his back against the wall as he peered around the corner, watching a young man who couldn't be more than twenty years old come down a set of stairs.

Mika stiffened. He recognized that scent.

Jacob.

With a smooth motion, Mika stepped around the corner, his gun pointed at the center of the young man's chest.

"Don't. Twitch."

Jacob went perfectly still, his eyes wide as he watched Mika prowl forward.

"Sentinel," he breathed. "Are you here for the healer? I can take you to her."

Mika held the gun steady as he patted Jacob down, quite prepared to put a bullet in the traitor's heart.

Once he was satisfied, he took a step back, his expression hard with warning.

"You've done enough," he said in cold tones.

Jacob flinched as if he'd been slapped. "I know. Forgive me, brother."

"Don't call me that," he growled. Bailey had taken this acolyte into her home. She'd healed him. Given him food and shelter. And how had he repaid her? "Traitors aren't tolerated by the Tagos. You're no longer my brother."

Jacob blanched, his hand reaching out to rest against the wall as if his knees were threatening to give out.

"They told me they were holding my mother hostage. I was terrified she was going to die before I could even get to know her." He gave a slow, pained shake of his head. "But now . . . I think it was nothing more than a trick."

Mika flattened his lips. Dammit. Either the young Sentinel was the best actor ever, or he truly had been blackmailed into helping the humans.

Not that Mika actually gave a shit.

Not now.

"You should have gone to the monks," he said without sympathy.

"I know." Jacob covered his face with his hands, his body, which that had yet to fully fill out with muscle, visibly trembling beneath the force of Mika's disapproval. "God. What a mess."

Mika lowered his gun, although he remained on full alert. He was well aware this could be a trick to distract him.

"Why did you kidnap Bailey?"

"It wasn't me." Jacob lowered his hands to reveal his ashen face. "It was my father."

Mika sucked in a sharp breath. "Father?"

Hunching his shoulders, the young man gave a brief, sometimes confusing explanation of his family history and the twisted reason that both he and Bailey had been targeted by the Brotherhood.

By the time he finished, Mika was holding on to his composure by a thin thread.

Goddamn, the bastards.

They were going to pay.

Not only for what they did to Bailey, but what they'd done to Jacob's uncle and the innocent healer.

"If they wanted her as a healer, then why not take her the first time they beat you?" he demanded, his voice thick with fury.

"They had to make sure I would be compatible." Jacob rubbed his inner arm, where there were still faint bruises. "I was taken to a cabin and forced to share my blood with my father." Well, that explained the hospital bed they'd found in the attic, Mika acknowledged. As well as the smell of antiseptic. "Once they were sure I was a suitable replacement for my uncle, they demanded that I lure the healer—"

"Bailey," Mika rasped. "Her name is Bailey."

Jacob gave a slow nod. "They wanted me to lure Bailey from behind her shield."

Mika took a deliberate step backward. "You dishonored your brothers and the monks who have trained you."

"I . . ." Jacob abruptly fell to his knees, his head bent. "Forgive me."

"Don't ask for my forgiveness. You're not getting it," Mika said, knowing he was being harsh, but unwilling to lie. Being a Sentinel wasn't just learning how to shoot a gun or kill with your hands. It was a life that was devoted to duty and loyalty and utter commitment to your brothers. It couldn't be any other way. Not when they were blessed with such dangerous gifts. Without rules, a Sentinel could easily become the monster that all humans feared. "As for Wolfe . . . good luck with that."

Jacob lifted his head, his expression resigned. "I understand."

Anxious to find Bailey, Mika gestured for Jacob to rise to his feet.

He didn't fully trust the Sentinel. He wasn't going to leave him behind.

"Stay beside me," he commanded, heading down the hallway. "You so much as blink wrong and I'll shoot you. Got it?"

Jacob swallowed, falling into step.

"Got it."

Chapter Ten

Bailey knew that Limburg was speaking.

His lips continued to move despite the fact that she'd blocked him out.

Instead she concentrated on the unmistakable sense of Mika.

He was close. And growing ever closer.

Desperately she lowered her head, terrified that her expression might give away her heart's sudden leap of joy. The last thing she wanted was to expose the fact that Mika had managed to track her.

Her effort, however, was wasted as the goon at her side abruptly yanked his phone from his pocket and gave a low hiss.

"Something's going on," he growled.

Limburg reached beneath his robe to pull out a gun.

"What?"

"An intruder."

"Shit. I'll go check it out." He pointed the gun at Bailey. "Don't take your eyes off her."

Robert stepped forward. "You should wait here until—"

"I may be sick, but I still give the orders," Limburg snapped, his face blotchy with a sudden anger.

"Yes, sir," Robert muttered, grudgingly conceding the older man's authority.

Limburg turned, taking a step toward the door when it was abruptly thrust open.

Bailey froze, her heart forgetting how to beat as Limburg lifted his gun, preparing to shoot.

Then, unexpectedly, Jacob stepped into the room. "Father."

"Jacob." As baffled as Bailey, Limburg lowered his gun, a scowl marring his brow. "What the hell are you doing?"

"I'm here to do what I should have done from the beginning," Jacob muttered, launching himself at his father with enough force to send both of them into the empty crates.

Bailey gasped, rising to her feet as the two crashed to the floor.

The young Sentinel was stronger, but Limburg had a gun.

Intent on the awkward struggle, Bailey nearly missed the dark form that slid into the room directly behind Jacob.

Unfortunately, Robert wasn't so easily distracted.

Even as Mika was rushing toward her, the goon was swiveling toward the door, squeezing off two shots.

"No!" she cried, instantly catching the scent of blood.

Mika didn't even slow as he rammed straight into the shooter, slamming him into the wall with enough force to smash a few ribs.

Robert, however, had obviously been trained. Dropping the gun, he yanked out a knife he'd hidden beneath his shirt, attempting to stab it into Mika's heart.

Forced backward, Mika looked remarkably relaxed as he pulled out a gun and pointed it between Robert's eyes.

"On your knees," Mika ordered.

"Fuck you." With a remarkably swift motion, Robert threw the knife directly toward Mika's face.

Mika easily ducked, but the human used the distraction to launch his own attack, knocking the gun from Mika's hand.

Bailey gasped, but a Sentinel didn't need a weapon. He *was* a weapon.

Using the attacker's momentum, Mika easily flipped him over his shoulder. Then, turning so Bailey couldn't witness the killing blow, he gave a sharp twist with his arms.

Not that he could disguise the sound of a neck snapping, or the heavy body hitting the floor with a lifeless thud.

Bailey grimaced, but she wasn't sorry the man was dead.

He'd killed Jacob's uncle and the healer in cold blood. And God knew, he would have eventually killed her as well.

He didn't deserve sympathy.

Assuring himself the man was dead, Mika turned his attention to where Jacob was seated on his father's chest, his hands wrapped around the older man's throat.

At last satisfied that the most pressing danger had been taken care of, he moved to squat next to her.

Her heart twisted.

Damn. His hair was tangled around his dark, lean face. His shirt was covered in blood from the bullet wound in his upper arm. And the dark eyes smoldered with a barely leashed need for violence.

And he'd never, ever looked more beautiful.

"Are you okay?" he asked softly.

She gave a choked laugh. He'd been shot and nearly knifed, but his only thought was for her.

How had she ever doubted his love?

Her hand lifted to touch his wound, a pang of fear racing through her at the knowledge he would put himself at such risk.

"You've been shot." She allowed her powers to flow from her palm into his damaged flesh. "Again."

He smiled, his fingers running through her curls, as if he had a compulsive need to touch her.

"It's a good thing I have a healer as my lover."

Once she was certain the bleeding had stopped and the

wound had started to close, she pulled her hand away and leaned against his chest.

Maybe she wasn't Xena, but she did have her own special superpowers.

"Better?" she asked softly.

"Christ, yes," Mika breathed, clearly not referring to his injury. His arms wrapped around her, holding her tight. "I thought I'd lost you."

She pressed her lips to his throat, offering him a silent comfort.

"I knew you would come," she murmured.

"Always." The word was a solemn pledge. "I will always come for you."

She didn't doubt that for a second.

"You won't ever have to," she assured him. "From now on I intend to stick to your side like glue."

His went rigid, his arms compulsively tightening around her.

"Is that a promise?"

She pulled back, meeting his wary gaze with a smile.

"Yes."

Lost in the sheer beauty of simply being together, Bailey ignored the dark-haired Sentinel who strolled into the room.

For the moment she just wanted to savor being alive and in the arms of the man she loved.

Of course, it couldn't last.

They were in a warehouse that reeked of fish, surrounded by the Brotherhood, who wanted all high-bloods dead.

Not really the time or place for a romantic reunion.

With a low growl, Wolfe strode across the room to pull Jacob off the unconscious Limburg.

"Don't kill him, you fool," he snapped.

Reluctantly, Mika helped Bailey to her feet, keeping his arm wrapped around her shoulder.

"That bastard is responsible for Bailey being kidnapped," he informed his leader.

"Yeah, well, if he's in the Brotherhood, then I want to give the psychics a chance to rummage through his brain," Wolfe said, leaning down to grab Limburg and toss him over his shoulder. "He could have information we need."

Mika made a sound of disgust. "Then do I get to kill him?"

Wolfe flashed an evil grin. "He's all yours."

"Good." Mika pretended he didn't see Bailey roll her eyes. "What about the guards?"

Wolfe headed for the door. "Tied up and left for the cleanup crew. Let's get the hell out of here."

Mika slid a finger beneath Bailey's chin, his expression somber.

"Will you come with me?"

A slow smile that came from her very soul spread across her face.

"Just try to keep me away."

Two weeks later

Mika walked backward down the narrow pathway that cut through the thick patch of trees, leading a blindfolded Bailey. Overhead the sun blazed from a cloudless blue sky, and a soft breeze carried the scent of wildflowers.

They were less than thirty miles from Valhalla, but they might have been a thousand.

There were no sounds beyond the scurry of small animals, no nosy neighbors, no constant threat they were about to be interrupted by their demanding jobs.

A perfect day to unveil his grand surprise.

His lips twisted in a wry smile.

Perfect day or not, he was as nervous as a schoolboy.

The past fourteen days had been nothing less than heaven.

Having Bailey sharing his rooms—his bed—had filled the aching emptiness that had haunted him for the past ten years.

And more importantly, they'd learned from their past mistakes.

Instead of retreating behind their mutual barriers when problems popped up, they actually discussed their feelings.

Wow. An amazing concept.

Still, he couldn't deny that he'd been holding his breath, unable to shake the terror that Bailey might suddenly decide that she was being suffocated by their relationship.

That was why he'd made the decision that morning to put his fears behind him.

Bailey had pledged to her love.

It was time to look to the future.

Holding tight on to his hands, Bailey heaved a soft sigh.

"Can I look yet?" she demanded.

He steered her out of the trees and toward the small home that was built of gray stone and overlooked the natural lake.

"Not yet."

"Mika."

He chuckled at her exasperated tone. "Patience, little one."

She wrinkled her nose, but she willingly allowed him to grab her shoulders and situate her so she would have the perfect view of the wraparound porch that framed the house and the small garden at the side.

There was even a white picket fence.

"Did you find out what happened to Jacob?" she asked.

"Yes." He'd spoken with Wolfe before they'd taken off for the day. "He's been allowed to return to the monastery, but he will have to return to the very beginning of his training. It's more than he deserves."

"What about his mother?"

"She died in childbirth."

She shook her head. "That Limburg really was a piece of work."

"No more discussion of the Brotherhood," he scolded, moving to stand behind her. "Today is all about us."

"You'll get no argument from me," she murmured, her voice lowering in a husky invitation.

Mika's blood heated, his head lowering to plant a kiss to the side of her neck.

"Temptress," he murmured, his hands lifting so he could untie the blindfold.

With a smile, he tucked the strip of satin into the pocket of his jeans.

He had plans to use that handy piece of material later.

A groan was wrenched from his throat of the thought of having Bailey spread across the four-poster bed that waited in the house, her hands tied above her head.

Then his X-rated thoughts were interrupted when Bailey gave a small gasp.

"Oh, it's lovely, Mika," she murmured. "Who owns it?"

His fingers brushed through her soft curls. "You do."

She made a sound of shock. "What do you mean?"

"I had this house built before you left," he admitted. "I hoped . . ." He halted to clear his throat. "I thought you might be happier if we had a place to call our own."

She slowly turned, her hand lifting to touch his face. "You kept it all these years."

He gave a slow nod, his arms circling her waist.

"I never came here, but I couldn't let it go," he admitted. "I think I unconsciously feared that if I sold it, I would have to give up all hope of having you back in my life."

"Oh, Mika," she breathed, going onto her tiptoes to press a soft kiss to his lips. "I love it."

He studied her upturned face, his heart filled with a happiness he'd feared he'd never feel again.

"Will you stay here with me, little one?" he asked, his heart in his hands. "Will you help make this a home?"

"Our home," she whispered, pressing her head to his chest.

"Yes." Scooping her into his arms, he headed for the front door. "Our home."

Scorpius Rising

Rebecca Zanetti

*After all,
it really is all of humanity that is
under threat during a pandemic.*

—MARGARET CHAN FUNG FU-CHUN,
Director-General of the
World Health Organization

Chapter One

Week 1
Eight people dead
Likelihood of Scorpius Containment: Definite

> *Extinction is the rule. Survival is the exception.*
> —CARL SAGAN

Wind whistled a mournful tune around aluminum buildings and across the jagged tarmac. Dr. Nora Medina shivered in the damp night air and ignored the water splashing over her flip-flops. The soldiers around her, armed to the nth degree, merely added to the pressure building in her chest.

Her nearly bare chest.

She fought to keep her balance while hustling up the metal steps to the third private plane of her day.

Enough.

She might be the only unarmed person on the quiet tarmac, and the only woman, but enough was fucking enough, because she was also the only person wearing a borrowed white blouse over a pink bikini top, barely-there wrap around her bikini-clad butt, and sandals.

Temper roared through her, and she planted her feet at the top of the stairs, only to slide across the wet surface.

"Ma'am," said the nearest faceless soldier, reaching for her arm.

She jerked free and rounded on him. "I swear, if one more person calls me 'ma'am' or apologizes for the inconvenience of dragging me off a very nice beach in Maui several hours ago, I will take his gun and shoot him."

The man's expression didn't change. "Yes, ma'am."

She bit down a scream. "All right. Listen up. We are in Seattle, and I know we're in Seattle." She pressed her hands against chilled hips and tried to stand taller. "Do you know *how* I know?"

"No, ma'am." Well trained, definitely at ease, the soldier kept his gaze above her right shoulder.

"I *know*," she said slowly and through gritted teeth, "because I looked out the bloody window when we were landing. The next time you kidnap somebody, you might want to blacken out the windows."

"Yes, ma'am." He nodded, ever so slightly, toward the doorway to the plane.

"This is kidnapping, and I've had it. We're in Seattle, and yep, guess what? I live here. So I'm going to head home, take an incredibly hot shower, change my clothes, and then call—well, somebody. *Anybody* who will tell me what the hell is going on." Her rant would end perfectly if she could just get past him on the steps, but he easily blocked her way.

"All apologies, ma'am, but our orders are to escort you. Please embark." He kept his voice level and polite.

She swallowed. There were six of them, one of her, and no way would she win a physical altercation. "Not until you tell me where we're going."

"Nora?" a voice called from inside the plane. "Get your ass in here."

Every nerve she owned short-circuited. Her gut clenched

as if a fist had plowed into her solar plexus. Slowly, spraying
water, she pivoted toward the opening. It couldn't be. It *really*
couldn't be.

The voice she knew well. Male, low, slight Scottish brogue
a decade in the States hadn't quite banished. Her heart thundered, and fire skidded across her abdomen to flare deep.
How was this even possible? She steeled her shoulders and
approached the plane opening as if a bomb waited inside. So
many thoughts rioted through her brain, she couldn't grasp
just one.

Warmth hit her first when she stepped inside, followed
by another shock wave. "Deacan Devlin McDougall," she
murmured.

He stretched to his feet from one of the luxurious leather
chairs, standing in the aisle—the only place high enough to
accommodate his six-foot-four frame.

All the thoughts zinging around her head stopped cold.

Nothing. Her brain fuzzed. The years had been good to
him, experience adding an intriguing look of danger to his
masculine beauty.

His green gaze, dark and piercing, scored her see-through
shirt, light wrap, and bare legs. "I'm sorry I wasn't there for
the extraction."

Her chin lifted. Heat seared through her lungs, lifting her
chest, and she slowly tried to control her body. No way would
she let him see how difficult he made it for her to breathe—
even after all this time.

He wore faded jeans over long legs and a dark T-shirt
across a broad chest—no uniform. But the gun strapped to his
leg was military issue, now wasn't it? The weapon, so silent
and deadly, appeared at home on his muscled thigh.

His dark brown hair, glinting with red highlights, now
almost reached his shoulders. Very different from the buzz cut
he'd had years before. His eyes, the green of a Scotland moor,
held secrets, unplumbed depths, and promise. Chiseled face,

hard jaw, and definite warrior features proudly proclaimed his ancestry, and even now, she could see the Highlander in him.

The door banged shut behind her, and she jumped.

He gestured toward the seat across from the one he'd occupied. The engines roared to life.

She faltered. "Where are we going?"

He reached into an overhead compartment and drew out a plush blanket. "D.C."

The plane lurched forward, and she stumbled. He grasped her arm, shooting an electrical jolt up her bicep.

His eyes darkened. "I'd wondered."

"Me too." As kids, they'd been combustible. So she hadn't imagined the spark from years ago. She blinked confusion from her vision and allowed him to settle her into the seat. The second he covered her legs with the warm blanket, she finally took a deep breath.

He sat down, gaze somber. "You haven't responded to my proposition."

Her head jerked back. "This isn't, I mean, you—" She gestured around the luxurious plane.

His lips twitched. "No. I did not execute a military extraction and secure three private jets to force you into making up your mind to meet me in person now that I'm settled in the States. Finally."

She plucked at a string on the blanket. "I didn't think so." They'd kept in touch through the years, and when he'd sent her an email two months ago, saying he wanted to meet up with her, she'd needed time to think about it. "I was hoping to use my vacation time in Hawaii to consider, well, us."

Thoughtfulness, sexy and focused, crossed his rugged cheekbones. "I appreciate that. I've been wondering lately if I should've fought the divorce."

Fought it eight years ago? Surprise and a silly feminine hope flushed through her. They'd been married at eighteen and divorced at twenty-five. They'd spent more time apart than together during the marriage with him in the military and her pursuing various degrees. "We were just kids." The plane lifted in the air, and she tried to relax against the leather. "You said you work for the government now, Deacan."

"I do." He tugged a table from the wall and secured the legs.

"Which branch?" she asked softly. What in the hell was going on?

He reached into a duffel bag to retrieve a laptop. "Doesn't have a name."

Yeah, she'd figured. Supersecret, code-name, hidden organization. "In your email, you said you had your head on straight and had finished your time as a soldier."

He placed the laptop on the table to their right, facing them. "I do. I work in the States and for the most part invent strategy and the like. No more violence, and I've dealt with the anger."

She nodded, her body rioting at his nearness. The gun strapped to his leg hinted at another agenda, and she needed time away from him to really figure out if she wanted him in her life again—even as a friend. Leaving him before had nearly destroyed her, and she'd built a good life in Seattle. A safe life. Okay, a boring life. "Why am I here?"

His very presence affected the oxygen, because her lungs quit working properly. He smiled, as if knowing, and waited until the laptop came on. "You're here because of this."

She leaned toward him and turned to the side to see a picture of a round blue shape covered by long spikes. Definitely a bacterium. "Coccus shape, mobile, looks a little like *Staphylococcus*." She frowned and squinted. "I don't recognize it, though."

Deke exhaled, and impressive muscles shifted beneath his shirt. "No. It's new."

She blinked. "New?" Fascinating, but not unusual. Her heart started to thrum harder. "What's the rate of growth?"

"It duplicates in an hour."

Fast, but not unheard of. She leaned back. "What's going on, Deacan?"

He scrubbed both hands down his face. "You're the best microbiologist in the country."

She bit back a snort. "Lynne Harmony would disagree with you."

He nodded. "Perhaps. It's probably a tie between you."

Now wasn't the time to discuss Nora's best friend from graduate school. "Why am I here, and why are you here? It's no coincidence." If the bacteria had been weaponized, then the CDC would be on it. "I work for a private company, not the government, and this isn't one of our samples or, ah, mutations."

"I know you work for a private company. Of course."

Yeah, she made her own schedule and only worked on projects she believed in. The government wouldn't allow her such freedom. Plus, the money was much better. "You know I don't trust the government."

"I do know." Deke punched a couple of keys, obviously unwilling to debate the issue. A picture of a rock came up on the screen.

"Looks like a meteorite," Nora said slowly.

"Aye."

Her brain clicked into gear as her mind connected a pathway from the bacteria to the meteorite. "No way. Really?"

"Yes. A group of twelve Stanford students took a field trip to the southern Nevada desert to go meteorite hunting, which is actually quite an industry out there. They found a good ten pounder and cut into it, each taking a piece. Apparently bacteria spores were let loose." He shook his head. "Can you believe it? Bacteria from outer space."

She glanced at the innocent-looking rock. "Well, yeah. I mean, NASA has been worried for years that we're sending bacteria into space with each shuttle mission, and we've actually tested bacteria that survives in the outer atmosphere."

He cut a hard look at the screen as if facing an enemy. "But from space."

She grinned. "Our entire planet was formed by materials from outer space. The bacteria on earth came from galaxies away when our planet formed. This isn't a surprise." She sobered. "That little blob might be the find of the century, but I wouldn't be here unless something else is going on."

He shut the laptop and faced her. "The students each took a piece of the rock, and all came down with fevers. Initially *E. coli* was suspected because they ate a box of doughnuts that morning, but the locality of the infection was in the brain, so anything abdominal was quickly ruled out."

"You want my research." For five years, she'd worked for BioGlax Pharmaceuticals, trying to create an antibiotic for drug-resistant bacteria. "Why isn't the CDC on this?" If her phone wasn't still in Maui, she'd call Lynne and ask that very question.

"They are. The head of the CDC National Center for Emerging and Zoonotic Infectious Diseases, your good buddy, Lynne Harmony, requested your help," Deacan said "I offered to meet your plane and get you up to speed."

"What?" Nora shook her head. Not only would Lynne never ask for help, she'd call herself and not have the military hijack Nora's vacation. "Lynne would've called me. We usually talk at least once a month." But they'd both been busy, and they hadn't talked in maybe, what? Two months?

"I have the CDC team locked down. No communications out or in."

Nora blinked. "You can't do that."

"I can and have." Deke cocked his head to the side, all patience.

Awareness cascaded through her, and the hair on the back of her neck lifted. "Exactly who do you answer to, Deacan?"

He lifted a shoulder.

"Deke?" she snapped.

He sighed. "The president. But that's just between us, darlin'."

Anxiety filled her abdomen. "The president. The actual president?"

Deke sighed. "Yes. Two years ago, after he'd been elected, I was on detail for a foreign trip. It went south, I saved his ass, and we had one of those foxhole situations that's top secret. Became buddies of a sort, and I've been working with him since—trying to move into more of a strategy and planning position instead of shooting and killing."

Emotion colored his words, although his expression remained stoic. For years, she'd wondered if his humanity would succumb to his need for action and adventure. She'd be crazy to get caught up in his world again. But she'd worry about Deke and his employment later, once she figured out why her vacation had been cut short. "All right. What happened to the students?" Something told her she didn't really want to know the answer.

Deacan kept her gaze captive. "All twelve were hospitalized, infected with the Scorpius bacteria."

She frowned. "Scorpius?"

"Yes. The meteorite was probably one of many that fell last year after the Scorpius Comet passed by the earth, hence the name. We had to call it something. Damn bug."

"Not a bug. Bacteria is different." Her brain spun. "The bacteria is airborne?"

"No. The kids all took a taste of the rock. A five senses type of thing." He shook his head. "Tasted salty, apparently."

Breath whooshed from her lungs. "That's unfortunate, but I'm glad the infectious agent isn't airborne." Of course, neither was Ebola, *E. coli*, or meningitis. "Give me the rest of the facts."

He sobered. "One student seems to have recovered fully. Nine died. Two are experiencing what can only be termed a psychotic break."

Holy shit. "Nine died? Scorpius killed that high of a percentage of infected?" Unbelievable. She calculated the statistics. "I'm assuming you have medical and historical profiles for each of the students?"

"Yes."

Sand, salt, and oil covered her arms, making them itch. She rubbed her elbows, hunching into herself. "The two survivors with mental issues. Any other symptoms?"

"Odd brain scans and low activity in the frontal lobe," Deke answered.

Nora frowned. "All right. How far has the infection spread?"

He lifted dark eyebrows. "Why do you think it has spread?"

She leaned her head back against the headrest. "You wouldn't call in a second team unless we were facing a pandemic. How many?"

"Not many."

She studied him. He'd always been tough, but as he'd shed the look of youth, he'd gained a masculine hardness with an edge. Sexy and dangerous. Intriguing enough that her instincts yelled for her to stay away from him while her heart dared her to jump right into his fire. "What's the urgency?"

Deacan leaned toward her, bringing the scent of wild forest and man. "The survivors continue to carry the bacteria."

Nora blinked. "You mean they're still contagious after surviving? That's unheard of."

"Yes. Trace amounts of the bacteria have been found in their saliva. If they bite and break the skin, well . . ."

"Are you sure?" Finding a cure was crucial, although many people were carriers of deadly bacteria, like MRSA, and they rarely infected people.

"Yes." Deacan leaned even closer. "One of the infected students is the president's daughter."

Nora stilled. "One of the survivors?"

"One of the two experiencing what seems to be schizophrenia. Maybe."

She breathed out. "Oh."

Deacan gripped her knees through the blanket. "It gets worse."

She shook her head. "No."

"Aye. She bit the president. He's fighting the fever right now."

Chapter Two

Deke finished showing Nora around her new digs in D.C. just as dawn broke. For now, the government had taken over a nice condominium high-rise a block from the Washington, D.C. office of the CDC, which normally dealt with policy issues. "We've created an emergency command post in the D.C. office of the CDC, and we've commandeered a new building with secured lab space for your research, as well as this condominium building," Deke said.

Nora shook her head. "This is serious, Deke. We should be at CDC headquarters in Atlanta."

"No. We need the experts here, close to the president, so we transferred Lynne Harmony's entire team from Atlanta for now. Her apartment is one floor up."

Nora whirled on him. Brown eyes, brown hair, fiery temper. A woman born in Argentina with the mind of a statistician and the body of a goddess. "I do not work for the government, Deacan."

God, he'd missed her.

For now, he had her exactly where he wanted her, and he intended to make good use of his time.

She somehow glared harder.

His lips tickled, and he bit back a smile. "You're going to

get a migraine if you don't relax your shoulders." Did she still get migraines? He hoped not. One time she'd been in so much pain, he'd wanted to knock her out until it passed.

"Fuck you," she said quietly but with impressive authority.

He let the grin loose. "When did you start swearing?"

She lifted an eyebrow. "Graduate school. I'd ask when you turned into such an asshole, but I already know the answer."

He lost the smile. Yeah, she knew exactly when he'd turned into a dick. "I'm sorry," he said.

Her eyes widened. "Huh?"

He'd never apologized, now had he? "I said that I'm sorry. Sorry I left you for war when you were only eighteen and returned so fuckin' damaged. Sorry I was a jerk to live with." He leaned back against her closed door, his gaze remaining steady. "More sorry I let you go when I did." Although she'd done well without him.

She blinked. "You're forgiven. Now you should leave."

Quick, wasn't she? Yet she didn't hide her emotions any better now than she had in the past. "I'm not forgiven."

"You are," she whispered, crossing her arms. "We were young, and it was a long time ago."

Yeah. Eight years seemed like an eternity. "I have somebody in Seattle packing you several bags of clothes, and I have extraction teams rounding up your team from BioGlax Pharmaceuticals."

Her shoulders straightened in pure defiance. "I would like clothes, but for now, I need to call my team and provide an explanation. The guys with guns will scare them." She dropped her chin, and her fingers played with a string from the small white top.

He shoved down a groan, remembering full well how those fingers had felt wrapped around him. "Sorry—no calls about Scorpius. We have the building blanketed and are monitoring every call."

Anger heightened her high cheekbones. "You can't do that. The government can't do that."

"Yet we have." He'd been entranced by her naiveté from day one. That and her serious side. The woman couldn't relax unless seriously wrestled to the ground. One of the highlights of their marriage had been his taking her down and exploring how to play and just have fun. Who lightened her load now? "You seeing anybody?"

Her mouth dropped open and then shut just as quickly. "You're joking."

"No." He wasn't. Not even close.

Her chin lifted. "None of your business."

"You're my wife. It is my business." The words escaped in a full-on Scottish brogue before he could think twice.

"We've been divorced for years." Bright red spiraled through her high cheekbones, and educated precision clipped her diction. Her brains, her sheer intelligence, had intimidated him once.

Now they impressed the hell out of him. "The second I saw you, I forgot about the divorce."

Her eyes flashed. "That's why we haven't been in the same state for eight years."

Actually, he'd been across seas, then dealing with the aftermath in his brain. Now, after years of working through the hell, he was calm. Settled. Alone. And alone, without her, was the last thing he wanted to be. "I've changed."

"I haven't."

"Good," he whispered.

She blinked, and a cute frown wrinkled between her brows. "We're not doing this right now. Leave, Deacan."

She was the only person in the world who'd ever used his full name, and the second she slipped back into using it, his world righted itself. Until that very moment, he hadn't realized he'd been off. "You want me to leave?" he asked.

Her stubborn chin lifted again. "Yes." Then she waited, daring him. Definitely daring him.

This was the most fun he'd had in years. "Fine. I'll make you a deal."

Her lip curled. "No deal."

He shrugged. "I could stay all night or put you under guard. Work with me."

She hissed and pressed both hands to her curvy hips. "You're going to blackmail me?"

He wouldn't, but besides anger, he could see something else in the eyes that still haunted him late at night. Interest. Definite interest. "Yeah. One dinner. You and me."

While he'd deny it to his grave, he held his breath as he waited for her answer.

Curiosity. Deep and glimmering, her eyes were full of questions. "Why?"

Why indeed. "I want to know you again."

Her head jerked.

Yep. She'd never expected the direct approach—not with her crappy childhood. Her mom had died when she was a toddler, and her father, a genius statistician with a definite antigovernmental agenda, had moved her to the States to be raised by a nanny. Not horrible, but not with much warmth.

She'd never been able to turn away from warmth.

His heart beat faster. So close. Finally. So close to her. He smiled and tried to appear harmless. "One dinner, and you're free." They'd always been too different, but he'd thought that his new job, new life, would be soothing to her. Well, before Scorpius had risen.

She rubbed her nose, her body visibly relaxing. "One dinner tonight—just to catch up."

"One dinner and one kiss."

She breathed out. "No kiss."

"Just one." He opened the door. "Unless you're afraid."

She scoffed.

His lungs compressed. Years ago, the woman could never resist a challenge. Hopefully she hadn't changed.

She hovered, for the slightest of moments, obviously fighting the impish side of herself. Her head went back. The devil lit her smile, she glided toward him, stood up on her toes, and brushed her lips across his.

Heat flashed into his belly so fast his vision narrowed in focus. To one woman and one moment. "That wasn't a kiss." His voice lowered to a huskiness he couldn't hide.

Her head tilted in a flirty move he remembered well. "Oh?"

Yeah. He'd forgotten. Actually forgotten how easily she could tempt him and how much the woman liked to play with fire. Even as the thought spun through his head, he moved.

His hands clamped her upper arms, and he dragged her into him. Her gasp breathed heat against his lips. The second her body slid against him, his cock tried to punch through his zipper. Yet he fought his natural inclination and slowly, so damn slowly it hurt, lowered his face to hers.

Then he forgot *slow*.

His lips covered hers, and he drove his tongue inside, swallowing her instant moan. Fire. Lava heated his blood, burning his nerves, lighting everything he was on fire.

He'd forgotten. How, he'd never know. But he'd forgotten the burn.

The incredible, unreal, so fucking deep shot of raw electricity only she could create. Even as he kissed her, bending her back, taking so hard, anger tried to claim hold. Fury at her for taking away *this*. This feeling nobody else on earth could actually experience. The feeling of *them*.

He tangled his fingers in her hair and twisted, tugging her head back so he could go deeper. His other arm banded around her waist and lifted. Her legs wrapped around his hips, her body gyrated against him, and her mouth filled his with soft little gasps. The male inside him, the one full of instinct with no intellect, roared for him to take. To yank off her clothes and spread her out on the floor. To feast for hours.

Her fingers curled into his chest, digging through his shirt, nearly unleashing everything inside him he'd tried so fucking hard to tame.

He jerked his head back, his chest panting.

Stunning. Her eyes had darkened further, glowing with hunger. Her lips shone red and tempting. She sucked in air. "No," she whispered.

"Why not?" he asked, already knowing the answer. When they'd been together, they'd been raw. Real. When they had ended, he'd been nothing. Had she lost herself, too?

She shook her head and released his shirt. "I can't do it again."

Yeah. He got that. Relying on training, sucking deep to remember who he'd become, he let her slide to the floor. Then he took a step back. He didn't know how to be coy, and he didn't have time for games. Plus, the woman deserved the truth and always had. "I want another chance, Nora." If for no other reason than to get her out of his fucking blood for good. Out of his dreams.

She blinked, her eyes widened, and she tried to step back, but the wall held her in place. "Absolutely not."

He respected her, and he'd walk away if she insisted. But too many emotions glimmered in her eyes. Anger. Fear. Denial. Beyond those, beyond the gates keeping him out, he saw something else. Desire. Yeah. It was there. So he smiled and stepped away. "We'll discuss it over dinner tonight, after what'll probably be a long day at work for us both. My place— right next to yours down the hallway. You bring the wine."

An hour after meeting with her bewildered team and being ferreted to the CDC, Nora strode into Lynne's temporary office in the D.C. location. "Your jeans are too tight on me," Nora groused.

"Nora." Lynne dropped a stack of papers onto her disaster of a desk, hustling around to give Nora a hug. "I'm sorry about the secrecy—I tried to call you." She leaned back, light green eyes warm but marred by dark circles beneath them. "They took our phones. I had to leave Dean Winchester with a neighbor."

"You are way too attached to that cat." Nora forced a smile and studied her best friend. Lynne had piled her curly dark hair up on her head, revealing a graceful neck and very pale skin. At five-six, they were about the same height, but Lynne was definitely more slender. "You look exhausted."

Lynne laughed. "I am." She tucked her arm through Nora's and pulled her from the room. "The jeans and shirt fit you fine. I've heard your ex is running the military side of this for the president, but I haven't met the Scottish bastard yet. Have you seen him?"

"Aye," Nora said in an imitation of his brogue. "Bossy as ever."

Lynne tugged her closer. "Sexy as ever?"

"Yes." Nora sighed. "Definitely bad boy to the bone."

Lynne sniffed. "Very bad. Doesn't care about the Constitution at all."

"I know, right?" Nora stiffened her shoulders. "My team just arrived, and they are not happy."

"None of us are happy." Lynne halted as Zach Barter loped around the corner, blond hair ruffled, tie askew.

He stopped, and his eyes bugged out. "Dr. Harmony. *The* Dr. Harmony."

Nora rolled her eyes. "Lynne, this is my assistant, Dr. Zach Barter. He's, ah, heard of you."

Zach shoved wire-rimmed glasses back up his nose. "I've read the paper you published last month about sequencing bacterial DNA. Twice."

"Twice." Lynne lifted an eyebrow. "That's nice."

Amusement bubbled up through Nora. "Actually, considering Zach has an eidetic memory, *twice* is quite the compliment."

Lynne smiled. "It's nice to meet you in person, Dr. Barter, although you refused my job offer a year ago."

Zach flushed a deep red across his clean-shaven face. "I went where the money was, Doctor. I'm a whore."

Lynne threw back her head and laughed, tightening her hold on Nora. "So is my best friend. Thank goodness she lets me borrow her fancy shoes when necessary." She launched into movement again. "We're heading to the main lab to look at the bacterium up close. Want to join us?"

"Well, sure. I'm not much of a lab guy and usually deal with the methodology. Not a big fan of the icky stuff." Zach pivoted and fell into step. "I've been studying the medical histories of the two students fighting what your doctors misdiagnosed as schizophrenia."

"Stop saying *icky*." Nora bit back a smile. "Zach. Gentle talk here about other doctors."

He squinted blue eyes through the glasses. "That was gentle."

Lynne sighed. "Geniuses."

"Yep." Nora glanced at her best friend as they wound through long hallways. Soon red and yellow biohazard signs became visible and then lined the way. "Aren't we geniuses?"

"Not like I am," Zach said without a hint of ego.

True. Nora nodded. "What's the correct diagnosis for the two surviving students who have changed behaviorally, oh brilliant one?"

He scratched his head and tripped over something on the smooth white tile. "Damage to the frontal cortex, I suspect. Scans show a decrease in activity but no physical abnormalities. Emotional changes and lack of empathy are the biggest indicators."

Nora lifted her head. "Did either of the students exhibit sociopathic tendencies before being infected?"

"Not that we've found," Lynne answered tersely. "We're just starting to get a handle on this, and I've even been studying up on the oxytocin receptor gene, even though it deals with aggressive behavior more so than empathy."

"Huh." Nora glanced into a pristine lab with advanced security measures. A red Biohazard Level 4 designation was displayed above one window. "I can't believe I'm being allowed to play in Lynne Harmony's lab."

"Just don't break anything," Lynne retorted.

A tech wearing a pristine white lab coat dodged around the opposite corner, blond hair swinging. "Dr. Harmony, here are the newest results." She handed over a stack of papers.

"Hi," Zach said.

"Bobbi, Zach," Lynne said absently.

Zach gave what could only be described as a half bow to the blue-eyed blonde smiling at him.

Nora bit back a grin. He was a dork, but a handsome one.

Bobbi batted long eyelashes. "Zach Barter? I read your dissertation for one of my advanced classes last year."

Zach's chest puffed out. "Just once?"

"No," the young woman scoffed, "about ten times."

Zach grinned.

Lynne cleared her throat. "Back to work, everybody." She turned and swiped a key card.

"See you later, Zach," Bobbi called out as they entered the first secured area.

"Romeo," Nora muttered, throwing him an elbow.

"Let's suit up." He grinned. "I don't usually get to say that."

Nora turned to make sure she had his attention. "You're not accustomed to lab work, but you're excellent, so we need you. Be careful, and if you have any qualms, don't do it."

He nodded.

Thirty minutes later, after suiting up in protective gear and checking each other's suits for rips or tears, they finally entered the lab. Machinery lined the outside counters, and the far wall held cages full of mice. Pipes hissed, and electrical machinery hummed. Nora settled into the familiar sounds.

Lynne maneuvered to a small fridge and pulled out a series of vials. "I've tried treating Scorpius with all known antibiotics."

"It's resistant," Nora murmured.

"Yep. The outer protein shell is incredibly strong and re-silient. So far, we haven't been able to completely breach it." Lynne set the vials on the counter and pointed to one with a clear, blue liquid. "I've tried everything from adding genetic material to adding chemicals to just yelling at the damn stuff."

Nora smiled. "That's a pretty blue color."

"Yes. I bombarded a sample with radiation and damaged its DNA. Well, I altered its DNA, and then I treated it with a combination of zinc and B12 by incorporating a catalyst of titanium oxide," Lynne said.

Nora hummed. "Interesting. A mineral and vitamin known to deal with brain function. Lynne, that's brilliant."

"Only if it works. So far, this just looks pretty. I'm hopeful we'll figure out something useful in it, and I'm very hopeful with the vitamin B." Lynne pointed to a dark green vial. "Now this one, this one is scary as hell. Another radiated sample combined with *Staph*, injected with a cocktail of catalysts, and it could be lethal within minutes." She stepped closer to a keyboard and brought up a computer simulation. "This is how the green interacts with human tissue."

She showed the bacterium at a minute level, increasing ex-ponentially and shooting green across healthy cells, creating deadly toxins.

"What the heck?" Zach breathed, stepping closer.

Lynne nodded. "The green multiplies so quickly it could conceivably cause death within minutes."

Nora stepped back and fogged up her mask. "That rate is crazy. Wow. Bad bacterial alteration. Horrible."

"Yes. The alteration made the bacteria even deadlier."

Lynne drew in air and turned around, her eyes oddly glowing in the mask. "Who knows what it could do inside the human body."

A chill skittered down Nora's back. "Does the military know?"

"Yes." Lynne leaned closer to whisper. "Once we find a cure, we'll destroy these altered strains as soon as possible. For now, we need to keep everything we have just in case there's a clue here to stopping the contagion."

Nora nodded and gulped. "Good." She and Deacan had always disagreed about the military role in scientific discovery, and now, more than ever, she could see the chasm between them. "What happens if you combine the green and the blue?"

Lynne's eyes lit up. "The blue slows the rate but not enough. I think a possible solution lies within some mixture of the two. I knew you'd figure that out right away."

Nora smiled. "I was the top student at grad school."

"Second top," Lynne retorted.

"Whatever. Well, we should probably get to work." Nora had developed several new possible antibiotics in the last few years and couldn't wait to give them a shot against Scorpius. "I assume I'm here to incorporate our new studies with nanoparticles and their ability to evade the immune system?"

"Yes." Lynne pointed to a laptop on a counter. "We've had your entire database transferred here." Beneath the mask, she blushed. "Darn government."

Nora sighed. "Fair enough. Let's see if we can get nanoparticles to zero in on Scorpius and its outer shell."

Lynne tapped her face mask. "Are you still working on wrapping nanoparticles in red blood cell membranes to remove toxins from the body?"

"Yes. If we can neutralize toxins produced by certain bacteria, we have a chance." Nora rolled her shoulders, accustoming herself to the biohazard suit. "The nanosponges kill the cells by poking holes in them, but each bacteria has a different structure, so I have no clue how it'll work with Scorpius."

"There's only one way to find out." Zach headed for the far counter. "Let's kill this sucker."

They worked through lunch and well into the afternoon, country music playing throughout the lab. In test after test after test, Scorpius won, although Nora's main experiments with the nanoparticles would take twelve to thirty hours to complete.

There had to be a way to curb the bacteria.

A knock on the glass door made Nora jump. She turned to see Bobbi holding a cardboard box of sandwiches. As if on cue, her stomach growled.

Zach leaned back against the counter and gave Bobbi a half salute. "My hero," he mouthed.

Nora tried to keep from rolling her eyes. He really was a goofball.

Bobbi twittered and winked at him. "Come and get it," she mouthed back.

Geez. Enough with the sexual innuendo.

Zach turned to finish up, and a quick clatter startled Nora out of her thoughts. She instantly focused on him.

"Damn it," Zach muttered, hustling across the lab and ripping off his glove.

Panic heated up Nora's throat, and she ran toward him. "What happened? Did you puncture?" The idiot had been flirting and not paying attention. God, had he infected himself?

He finished tearing off the glove and shoved his hand under a faucet.

Red welled beneath the knuckle of his left thumb.

Nora scrambled for disinfecting liquid to pour over the wound and glanced toward his station. "What was it?" she breathed.

"Original Scorpius strain. No mutations," he bit out, rubbing vigorously.

Shit. He'd punctured his own skin. Nora's gaze met Lynne's somber one.

Lynne nodded. "Zach? We need to get you to the infirmary. If you infected yourself, the fever will start within an hour."

Chapter Three

After a full day of monitoring the spread of outbreaks, Deke leaned back in his chair and eyed the president's chief of staff over the man's sprawling mahogany desk. They'd shut the doors, and quiet reigned for the briefest of moments inside the West Wing. "What happens now?"

George Ellis rubbed a bruised hand over his bald head. "Nothing for now. We're covering for the president, and as soon as his fever breaks, everything will be fine." Almost sixty years old, the stately politician filled out his expertly cut suit like he ran five miles a day, which he did. His eyes were a deep brown, his skin a shade darker, and intelligence all but emanated from him. "The fever has lasted longer with him than with the students, but he's only fifty-five and in great shape."

Deke exhaled. "Even so, fifty-five is different from twenty years old, like it or not. He's older and it's not unrealistic to believe it'll take him a little longer to fight off the infection."

"Don't tell him that when he's better."

"What happened to your hand, sir?" Deke asked quietly.

George winced. "I ducked when I should've dodged, practicing with Secret Service agents earlier."

Deke smiled. "I'm glad you took my advice about additional training."

George glanced at his hand. "I'm not." He flexed his fingers and winced. "The president's fever is at one hundred and four, so I'm thinking it'll break soon."

Deke swirled the brandy snifter. "We're going to scan his brain, right?"

"Yes." George took a deep swallow of his drink. "If he protests, we have a problem."

"He won't." Deke knew his friend, and he'd want to make sure his brain still functioned normally before continuing to lead the country. Of course, if his brain wasn't functioning, he might not agree. "How's Sally?" The president would want to know his daughter was doing better when he awoke.

George shook his head. "Not good. We're keeping her contained in the residence, and she's quieted. Is claiming she's better, but . . ."

Deke lifted an eyebrow. "But?"

"She doesn't seem right." George rubbed his chest. "I've known that girl since she was two years old, and now there's a different light in her eye. One I don't recognize—or like."

Bloody hell. So much for Sally's brain kicking back into normal. "We'll find a cure, I'm sure of it." Yet nothing was coming close. He'd checked in with Nora through the day, and so far, Scorpius was invincible.

George nodded. "I know." His gaze sharpened. "Just in case, I have the vice president under tight security."

Deke grimaced. "How's he feeling after the heart attack last month?"

"Not good." George rubbed his chin. "I'm glad we kept it quiet."

The government kept a lot quiet, but Deke was okay with that. For now. He lifted an eyebrow. "I hate to sound cold, but who's third in line? Just in case? Is it you?"

George's eyes widened. "Hell, no. How can you not know the order of succession?"

Deke shrugged. "Don't really give a damn until it matters to my job."

George shook his head. "Third in line is the Speaker of the House."

"A politician?" Deke winced.

"We're all politicians, jackass."

Deke snorted a laugh. "Oh yeah. I forgot."

George studied him like a hawk searching for dinner. "You've seemed more at ease since the crisis started than you've been all last year."

"How so?" Deke took another sip and allowed the aged liquor to heat down his throat.

George shrugged. "You're a man of action, McDougall. Always have been and always will be. Strategizing, being on the sidelines, hasn't been good for you."

Deke shifted in his chair. "I've done my time, and I've done my action. I've earned peace."

"Speaking of motivation and peace, how's the ex?" George's upper lip twitched.

"Spirited," Deke said. "Not happy to be taken off a beach in Hawaii."

George full-on grinned. "Has she figured out you waited until her first day of vacation before sending in the team?"

"No, but she will." There hadn't been a choice, considering BioGlax Pharmaceuticals would've noticed its number-one team missing. "We have nearly two weeks until her people need to report back to work, and we'll have the bacteria contained by then."

"I hope so. We've had reports of illnesses in Key West that match the Scorpius symptoms."

Deke rubbed the scruff on his chin. After the initial students had been released, they'd scattered for spring break until he'd had soldiers hunt them down and bring them back. "We knew there was a chance of some spread of the infection."

"I know." George stood. "I have a meeting on the Hill.

When this is all over, I'd like to meet your ex, at some point. I'm quite curious."

Deke followed suit and placed his glass on the desk. "How so?"

George tilted his head. "You're military, and she's well, antimilitary. Her people are from Argentina, yours from the Highlands of Scotland. Talk about opposites."

Deke grinned. "She's not an anarchist, George. She just thinks the government breaks too many rules." He cocked a shoulder. "She isn't wrong."

"No, she isn't." George crossed around the desk. "However, I learned a long time ago that there are two types of people in this world."

Deke turned for the door. "Do tell."

"The kind who believes the ends justify the means, and the other kind."

"Who are they?" Deke paused before opening the door and glancing at the older man.

"People who live the life they want because there are people out there, like us, making sure the ends justify the means." Wisdom, right or wrong, lit George's eyes. "For now, we claim the luxury of having two kinds of people." He opened the door and clapped Deke on the back. "If we don't get a handle on this infection, only one type of person will remain."

A chill sliced into Deke's temple. "Which one?"

"Survivors."

Deke nodded and turned down the hallway, his mind spinning. George had pegged him right. He did feel more like himself now that there was something to fight, and wasn't that all sorts of fucked-up?

He made his way through the building and out to his car, stopping then to check his phone. A text message from his contact at the CDC read: *One of the new team was infected. Fever started two hours ago. Call in.*

His legs stopped moving, and he slapped a hand onto the roof of his car. His gut clenched. What had he done? He quickly dialed Nora.

"Hello?" she answered.

"Nora? You infected?" He wrenched open the car door and slid inside, igniting the engine in one smooth motion.

"No. My assistant, Zach, was infected." Concern rode her voice.

Deke pulled out of the lot, driving one-handed. Thank all the gods. "I'm on my way." He clicked off to maneuver through traffic. What the hell had he been thinking? Not for one second had he thought about the danger to the research team. There were so many protocols in place. Nora ruled her lab, and he figured she'd be fine.

Yet her own team member now fought the fever.

Every instinct he had pushed him to yank her from the CDC, and he knew the urge came from the hardheaded warrior persona he'd tried so hard to shed. Was George correct? Did Deke belong in the fight and not behind the scenes? No, he'd tried too hard to banish the anger and deal with not only a crappy childhood but the things he'd seen in the service. Hell. The things he'd *done* in the service. Now he could be a normal guy just living his life.

He could be that guy. He really could. Right?

Traffic hampered him, but he finally arrived at the CDC. His card would get him through any secured door, but he had to go to reception in order to find Nora. As soon as possible, he needed to memorize the layout of the building. An escort arrived, a young intern by the name of Judy, who led him through the building to a heavy metal green door manned by two armed guards. An imposing red biohazard warning spanned the door.

"You go the rest of the way on your own," Judy said with a happy hop.

Deke nodded. He swiped his card, and the door buzzed.

Keeping his expression stoic, he yanked open the door and crossed inside, waiting until it closed before wiping his hand down his jeans. Give him ten armed assassins over a nearly invisible bacteria, any day. He could only kill if he could see the target.

A petite brunette with weary green eyes lounged against the stark white wall, measuring him carefully. He strode toward her and stopped far enough away that she wouldn't have to tilt her head to look at him. "Can I help you?" he asked.

She lifted one eyebrow. "Yes." Her tennis shoe tapped a rapid staccato against the tiles.

Interesting. It seemed Nora's buddy didn't care for him. Well, that was fine. At the moment, he didn't like her overmuch, either. "Would you please take me to Nora?"

The brunette lifted an eyebrow. "I'm Lynne Harmony."

No shit. He'd read her file and knew everything about her from her favorite color to her weakness for chocolate-covered raisins. "Deacan McDougall."

She chewed on that for a bit before speaking again. "So you're the bastard who broke my friend's heart."

Yep. That's what he'd figured she'd say. "Yes, ma'am," he said slowly.

"Do you want to tell me why?"

"Nope."

"Why not?" Lynne continued to tap her foot.

He glanced down the hallway. There was only one way to go, but he didn't want to tick off Nora's friend too much. "I don't figure it's any of your business."

By the woman's huff, she apparently didn't agree. "I'm the only family she has left in the world, which does make it my business."

When she sounded all outraged on Nora's behalf like that, Deke couldn't help but like her a little. "Now that's where you're wrong, Lynne Harmony."

She strode toward him, hand on hip. "Excuse me?"

Deke met her gaze, keeping his hands at his sides and trying to appear harmless. He had a point to get across, but there was no need to frighten the woman. "You're a friend, and from what I can tell, you're her best friend. That's good. But I'm her family. Period."

Lynne kept his gaze without blinking for several tension-filled moments, although a slight blush filled her face. Admiration welled through Deke at her stubbornness. Not many hardened men could hold his gaze for that long. Finally, Lynne nodded. "I guess we understand each other."

He grinned. His Nora chose her friends well. "I guess we do." He waited a beat. "She left me, ya know," he said softly.

"I know. But you let her go," Lynne said, stretching her neck. "You don't seem like the type of guy to give up something good."

Deke gave a short nod. "I'm not, but at the time, I didn't think I was something good. I figured she'd be safer on her own than with me."

"Was she?"

Now that was the big question. "I donna know."

"Fair enough." Then Lynne Harmony, brilliant scientist and good friend, threw back her head and laughed. "Man, I like you."

He smiled, feeling as if he'd overcome a deadly hurdle. "The feeling is mutual."

Lynne tucked her arm through his. "I'll take you to Nora. She's not doing well."

That quickly, Deke's gut roiled again. He shortened his stride so Lynne wouldn't have to run and allowed her to lead him through a labyrinth of hallways to a room outside a hospital bubble. Nora sat on a makeshift sofa, her gaze on the young man inside.

Lynne patted him on the arm. "I'm heading back to the lab. If there's any change, let me know."

Deke nodded and strode forward to touch Nora on the shoulder. For the slightest of seconds, she leaned against his leg.

Then she straightened. "His name is Zach Barter, he's twenty-two, and his fever is at a hundred and five."

Deke sat and slid an arm around her shoulders. "He's young and strong. The fever should break within the night." Pulling her into his side, he couldn't help but press a quick kiss to her curly hair. "You haven't slept in over twenty-four hours, baby." They hadn't been together in eight years, but Deke knew without a doubt she wouldn't leave her friend to fight the fever by himself. So he took care of her the best he could. "Close your eyes. I'll watch Zach."

Nora shuddered and leaned into him.

The situation sucked, but the rightness of the moment dug deep into Deke's gut and took hold. If they were such opposites, why did it feel so damn good just to sit and hold her?

Chapter Four

After a useless day of trying to penetrate Scorpius's protein shell, Nora had left her nanoparticle experiments to do their thing. Hopefully there would be results within sixteen hours.

For now, she stood outside Deacan's apartment door, not moving. Her knees wobbled. Agreeing to dinner had been a mistake. A huge-ass, what was she thinking, larger-than-life . . . mistake. She knew better. God, did she know better.

Yet when he'd asked, her heart had leaped. A hard thud against her rib cage—one she hadn't felt in eight years. The previous night, as Zach had battled the fever, she'd actually slept curled up into Deacan's side, feeling safe. Deke had awoken her around dawn with the good news that Zach's fever had passed. She'd waited for a while to talk to Zach, and the second he made a lame joke, she'd known. He would be all right, and more than willing to donate blood and get his brain scanned for a closer look at Scorpius.

So she'd returned to the lab to double her efforts to beat the crap out of Scorpius. The nanostructured materials so far hadn't worked, but she'd only tried silver and titania. She'd try ceria next.

Now, after a full day in the lab and a quick shower in her

temporary apartment, she hovered like a weenie outside Deke's place.

If she went inside, she knew exactly where the night would end. Where she wanted it to end—satisfying her curiosity about their past. Had it been as good as she remembered?

She lifted her hand to knock, but the door opened before she made contact.

"I gave you long enough to change your mind." Deacan grasped her arm to lead her into cool air.

She'd forgotten. The way he had of taking charge, of touching, of instantly enfolding her into his space. Even in his early twenties, he'd ruled the atmosphere around him. Now, in his thirties, seasoned and somehow calm, he still made air adjust to him.

Some things never changed.

She stumbled by him and shoved a bottle of wine into his stomach. "I bought red."

He lifted one eyebrow and shut the door, accepting the bottle and releasing her arm. "Thank you."

She swallowed and nodded, her gaze darting around a sprawling room decorated with masculine leather furniture. The room even smelled like him. Spicy and male.

He grasped her chin and lifted her face. "Nora, take a breath."

She tried to appear calm and meet his gaze, but her heart thundered in her ears. "I'm fine."

He blinked, his thumb brushing across her chin. "I won't hurt you, baby."

She frowned and tilted her head to the side, allowing his fingers to remain on her skin. "I'm not afraid of you."

He sighed and released her to run a hand through his thick hair. "Sure you are, and I don't blame you." He turned toward a spacious kitchen decorated with dark granite and stainless steel appliances.

Heat rushed into her lungs, and she grabbed his arm. Hard and sculpted, his muscles moved beneath her palm.

But he didn't turn back, and his shoulders remained stiff.

What was he thinking? She kept hold and walked around to face him. "Deacan?"

His gaze met hers, green and dark. "I remember how it was, and so do you. I've changed, but I don't expect you to believe just my words."

She shook her head, her mind fuzzing. "You're confusing me. I was never afraid of you." Afraid *for* him, sure. Definitely. But not one minute of their time together had she spent thinking he'd hurt her. Ever.

His brows drew together. "I punched the walls. A lot. I was so fucking angry. All the time."

She nodded, her heart hurting in a way it hadn't in so long. "I know. But you never hit me, and I never thought you would." There were times she thought he'd break his hand, but not once, *not once*, had she feared for herself. He'd been so young and angry. "You've never been a man who'd harm a woman, Deacan."

Even at their worst, when she'd yelled at him, he'd never yelled back. Had never even raised his voice to her. He'd needed her, and she'd run like the scared kid she'd been. Although they'd both changed during the ensuing years, he was still a soldier, whether he knew it or not, and she was still a scientist with a healthy suspicion of the government.

Were they on opposite sides? Especially since Scorpius could be eventually weaponized? She wouldn't allow any government, even her own, to have that kind of power.

"You were right that I needed to get my head on straight before I re-upped. I should've listened to you." His gaze softened, and he brushed a strand of hair off her face. "We were too young. Way too young."

She smiled, her body relaxing. "I know." Clearing her throat, she stepped back. "Where do you really live now?"

He chuckled and turned toward the kitchen. "I had a place in Georgetown, but the lease is up, so I just moved everything here for now. Maybe once you cure Scorpius, I'll actually buy a place. Settle in." He shrugged broad shoulders and reached for a plate of steaks.

Deacan McDougall in a permanent home? Hard to imagine. She followed him through the kitchen to a dining nook set against floor-to-ceiling windows looking out at the lights of D.C. He'd set the table with matching place mats, plates, and linens.

"Sit, Nora," he said, setting a pan in the center and pulling out her chair.

She sat, and amusement bubbled up upon seeing a tag sticking out from her place mat. "This is lovely," she murmured, discreetly tucking the tag under the blue woven material. She'd bet her last dollar he'd purchased matching tableware that day, and his cupboards were full of mismatched plates and chipped cups. "Everything looks so put together."

He leaned over a breakfast bar for salad and rolls before opening the wine and pouring them each a glass. Then he sat, overwhelming the oak chair. "I remembered you liked things to match."

She chuckled, absurdly touched that he'd made such an effort. They hadn't succeeded as a couple, but there had been some great times together. "Remember that teeny apartment we had by the base?" One bedroom, living room, tiny kitchen, and minuscule bathroom. Just painting the place had depleted their savings, but she'd wanted it bright and cheery for when he took leave, so she'd worked for a week to make a home.

"Yes," he said, taking a drink of the wine.

She followed suit, allowing the dark taste to warm her belly. It was time for some truth. "I'm thinking it's not much of a coincidence you had me extracted on day one of my vacation."

He reached for the salad to dish it on their plates before

adding the steak. "No. We needed to keep the relocation of your team under the radar, even from your employer."

Tingles flared alive in her abdomen. "Don't you think the public should be made aware there's a dangerous bacteria being transmitted?"

His green gaze met hers. "We don't need to cause a panic at this stage."

She lifted her head. "People have a right to know. You must understand your obligation to the public." Her gaze narrowed, and her breath slowed.

"It's too early for panic, Nora. Trust the government a little."

She set down her fork, her temper simmering. "You're kidding me."

"Nope." Deacan cut into his steak.

How could she trust an entity so comfortable keeping secrets? She wiggled on her seat. "Do other governments know about Scorpius?"

"Yes, and that's a problem. China accused us of creating Scorpius and is insisting we send along samples."

Nora coughed. "You said no."

He glanced up, his gaze direct. "Of course, but that just means we need to tighten security."

Her mind blanked. "Please tell me that once we solve this thing, Scorpius gets destroyed."

He leaned toward her, his gaze soft, his voice strong. "Probably not. We need to study it and prepare for any mutations, which I've heard has already happened. If Scorpius was in one meteorite, it'll be in another."

She shook her head. "I won't let you use any of my research as a weapon."

He lifted an eyebrow and gave a short grin. "Fair enough. Let's talk about something that won't get us into a fight. How about movies and current events?"

She laughed and started to argue about dramas versus

comedies versus sports. Dinner passed, and she finally set down her fork. "That was wonderful. Thank you."

He nodded, his gaze warming. "I know you've dated, Nora, but have you found anything close to what we had?"

Panic skittered down her spine, and she shoved back into her chair. "We were kids, Deacan." What she remembered, what haunted her at night, had to be a dream. A young girl's romantic rememberings of a time that couldn't have existed. She took a big gulp of wine. "What we had wasn't real."

"It was real, and you know it." He refilled both their glasses and then captured her gaze. His voice rumbled low and intimate, while his gaze heated. Seated and eating, he was every bit the slumbering lion, satisfied for the moment. Yet there was no doubt he'd be hungry again . . . and not for steak.

A shiver of warmth licked across her nerves. "I'm not sure."

"I am. I missed you."

The statement, so direct and honest, flared her nerves alive. Intrigue and want tempted her with a heated hunger, and she fought to keep control. To remain sane and unharmed. She pushed away from the table and grabbed her wineglass to head into the living room. "Thanks for dinner."

He reached her with a wisp of sound, tugging her down to the sofa. "Stay the night."

"Probably not a good idea." She gingerly placed her glass on the coffee table before she doused them both with Cabernet. The man radiated heat in the air-conditioned room, and she had to fight the urge to nuzzle into his side like she would've years ago. To feel that sense of belonging and home. "We tried, we failed, it's over."

He remained silent and placed his glass next to hers. "Are you sure?"

No. Hell to the nth of no. She'd been apart from him for eight years, and she'd dated several men, even going so far as to move in with one. Yet not once had her heart been broken when the relationship had ended. Was it possible that there was only one match for each person? She was a scientist and believed in soul mates as much as faeries or mermaids. But she couldn't help but wonder. Were they meant to be? "What are you asking me, Deacan?"

"Just for one night." He reached for her, so casually, so easily, and settled her on his lap, facing him, her thighs straddling his. "To find out if it was real. Any of it."

She could've fought him and kept her seat. He wouldn't have forced her onto his lap. Yet she allowed him to move her, to reposition her, to put her where she'd once belonged. Out of curiosity to find out if she'd still fit easily, and out of a bodily craving she couldn't deny. Yet she kept her voice level. "Are you joking?" The man wanted to get her into bed? She perched very still, trying not to appreciate the rigid muscles of his thighs between hers. In their years apart, he'd filled out, becoming even harder. "That's the worse come-on I've ever heard."

His upper lip curved. "Baby, if I just wanted ta get laid, I have plenty of options. I want more. A chance to see if what we had was real, or if I'm making up memories." He brushed her hair back from her shoulder. "Are you seeing anybody?"

"No," she breathed.

"When was the last time you had sex?"

Her shoulders went back. "None of your business."

"Oh?" He ran his hands over her arms and around her waist, pulling her along his legs until his erection nearly burned through her jeans. She almost managed to swallow her gasp. His eyes darkened to a color beyond green. "When was the last time you made that sound?"

Eight years ago. "Deacan—"

At his name, something in him snapped. His arm banded tighter around her waist, and his other hand tangled in her hair, gripping her with the promise of power leashed with determination.

The combination rippled through her, and she shuddered.

"Yeah." He held her in place. "*That*."

She tried to breathe, but the desire clawing through her gave no quarter. "You planned this."

"No. I wished for this." He met her mouth, enveloping her in desperate heat. No calculation, no seduction—just all male taking her under.

Her eyes closed, and her hands clamped onto his shoulders. For years, she'd felt so cold. Now, finally, here was warmth. She kissed him back, lost in the feeling, drugged by the familiarity.

He stood easily, holding her, continuing to demolish her mouth. The moment stilled, and she didn't care. When she dug her hands into his hair, he began to move.

She just didn't want the ecstasy to end.

Somehow he managed to maneuver through the condo, kissing her the entire time. They reached a bed, and he laid her down. He drew off his shirt, revealing rugged muscles adorned with battle scars. "I've waited a long time for this. Are you sure?"

She'd known he'd ask. Somehow, deep down, she'd known. Now they both needed to know if their memories were even close to true. "I'm sure," she whispered. One night wouldn't hurt her—she'd make sure of it. But she had to know.

His eyes glittered a startling green through the semi-darkness. "I've missed you, Nora." Quick movements had his belt wisping through loops.

She shivered at the sound and partially sat up.

"Let me," he rumbled, reaching for her shirt. "I remember what you like."

Did he? She held up her arms so he could remove her shirt. "Prove it."

Chapter Five

The second she acquiesced, something in Deke's chest unfolded. Something hard and foreign . . . and now gone. He'd missed her. If she'd decided to show up for dinner, he'd known she'd want to explore their past—to see if what they'd had was real. Hell, he'd been counting on it.

Now, with her daring him from his bed, he finally allowed himself to relax. When he reached down to remove her jeans and panties, his hands trembled enough to make him grin. "Did you know?" he asked softly, wondering if she'd be honest.

She unhooked her bra and tossed the lacy material across the room. Her breasts had filled out, but the hard pink nipples were familiar and so damn sexy. "Know what?"

He breathed out, the air burning his throat. "That we'd end up here tonight." Lying on his bed, naked, skin glowing in the muted light, the woman was a goddess. The years had been kind to her, sculpting her curves into delicate femininity. Red highlights in the hair spread out against his pillow caught and glimmered, and his cock hardened even more.

She smiled, the sight both enticing and a little sad. "I knew."

He crawled up her, careful to brush his skin against hers,

enjoying the hitch in her chest. Her nipples scraped his pecs, and he groaned. Reaching her face, he kissed her, trying to be gentle. Finally, he had a chance to show her who he'd become. He'd worked so hard to get rid of the anger, to find some sense of peace after so much blood and death. He'd never be that guy again.

She gripped his head, kissing him back, little moans trembling through her chest.

The man inside him, the primitive male, revolted against control. So he rolled them over. "God, Nora. I'd forgotten."

Her knees dropped to his sides, and her hot sex rubbed against his dick, coating him with wetness. "Forgotten what?" she murmured, her lips pressing hot, openmouthed kisses against his jaw.

"How damn small you are." He caressed down her flanks to her tight ass, and his cock jumped against her. The woman had taken such a prominent place in his heart, in his mind, in his dreams . . . she seemed so much larger in the abstract. Here, with her writhing on top of him, he remembered her fragility. He probably outweighed her by a hundred plus pounds. Nearly overcome, he gripped her head to hold her still, his fingers tangling in her curls.

She gasped, and more wetness coated his balls at the dominance.

Fire rushed through him, and he grinned. Some things didn't change. Thank the gods. "I'll keep you safe this time," he murmured, claiming eye contact, needing her to understand. To believe him.

She blinked and slid her hand down to grasp him with an incredibly soft hand.

Electricity sparked through his balls, and he shoved against her palm. "Nora—"

She levered herself up, all grace and strength, and positioned him at her entrance. Slowly, almost as if she enjoyed torturing him, she lowered herself, pausing several times and taking deep breaths.

Jesus. How long had it been for her?

Her butt hit his groin, and impossible heat captured his shaft. His eyes rolled back, and thunder rippled down his abdomen. "You're so damn tight," he gritted out, his muscles undulating with the need to move.

She chuckled, the sound throaty and breathless. "Now we talk." Her fingernails scraped across his chest.

His eyes opened. "What?"

"Your statement that you'd keep me safe *this time*. I'm assuming you're not talking about birth control, and lucky for you, I'm on the pill. Deke, I was safe last time." She lifted up and slid back down along his length.

Hunger roared through him, neck to dick. His hand tightened in her hair, and he clutched the bedspread to keep from grabbing her with the other hand. "I meant from me."

"So did I." Her eyes darkened to nearly black, and using his abs for balance, she lifted her butt again and then slammed home.

Agonizing need clawed his balls, and he had to bite his lip to keep from moaning. "I was angry. During and after tours."

Her internal muscles gripped around him, and he arched up into her. She smiled. "You were a scared, angry kid who'd seen hell, and I was a scared, lonely kid who didn't know how to help you. We're not those people now. You're not a soldier."

He paused. Something wasn't quite right in the statement, but at the moment, his body was sweating as he held himself back. "I'm not in the service." But he still wore a gun and dealt with violence. He was just better at it now. Did she understand that?

"Exactly." She wiggled her butt across his groin, igniting every nerve he had.

He snapped.

Both hands seized her arms, and he rolled them, already

pounding into her. She gasped and dug her hands into his flanks, clasping her ankles at the back of his waist. "Nora," he groaned, burying his face in her neck.

She met him with each thrust, her nails scoring him, her wet heat destroying him. "Harder," she breathed.

That quickly, with her plea, he forgot any concern. Securing her hip, he lifted her to meet him, fucking her hard. He hit a spot inside her that made her cry out, the sound echoing through his body. He drove harder, holding her in place, fighting to reach bliss.

Her body went taut, and her head pushed back against his hold, her neck elongating. Spasms rippled around him, gripping with a fierce hold. He changed his angle, brushing her clit, and she went off again, crying his name.

Lava poured down his back to collect in his balls. He stopped moving, held her tighter, and ground against her. Sparks of white flashed behind his eyes, and his own release nearly shattered him. Gasping, his lungs heaving, he slowly came down. Sex with Nora had always been all encompassing and wild. But this? After eight years, after knowing what he'd lost, this was more. Everything and absolute.

Finally. He'd returned home.

A quick swipe of his tongue against the pulsing vein in her neck made her sigh. He rose up on his elbows and released his hold. "Are you all right?"

She blinked and then slowly smiled, her eyes remaining at half-mast. "I'm perfect."

Yes. She damn well was. He rolled to the side, taking her with him to hold, wrapping the bedspread over them. "It's as good as I remember."

"Better." Her voice thickened and sounded drowsy. Mere minutes later, she slipped into sleep, her body relaxing against him.

The feel of her, so soft and trusting, awoke emotions he'd thought he'd buried. A primal need to protect gripped him, surprising in its rawness. He'd been an orphan, a kid who survived losing crappy parents and relocating across the ocean, and then he'd moved on to the service. In the marines, he'd found a purpose. In the vulnerable woman sleeping with abandon in his arms, he'd found a home.

One he'd lost.

Now he'd found her again, and maybe it was possible to show her peace. The instinctive animal deep inside that had made him such a good soldier, a good survivor, could be quelled.

No matter how he tried to convince himself, his instincts hummed. Even if he could find peace, Scorpius wouldn't let him.

For years, as a soldier, his instincts had told him when danger stalked near. Now more than ever, he was sure.

The war had just begun, and the peaceful guy inside him, the one Nora would love, had to disappear. Only the soldier could remain. He pressed a kiss to Nora's head, wanting to hold tight for the night.

Then he'd let her go.

Chapter Six

Nora studied Deke over a mound of piled scrambled eggs and tried to sit comfortably in the diner booth. The previous night had been explosive, and she'd used some very out-of-practice muscles. "I appreciate you absolutely insisting on taking me to an early breakfast before we get back to work, but I need to return to the lab for results expected in about an hour."

He finished chewing and swallowed. "We burned a lot of calories last night, and you need protein. If I'd allowed you to go right to the lab, you would've stressed out all day. Here we can analyze the situation together, calmly, and then reach a mutual decision so you don't have to fret."

Fret. Had he just said *fret*? She set down her fork. "I'm not some frail girl from last century, Deke." For some reason, with his only slightly mellowed accent, he came across as more arrogant and self-assured than he would've with a modern drawl. "I can handle my own thoughts."

He smiled, transforming his face into a powerful masculine beauty no man should be able to wield. "You're the smartest person I've ever met."

She sat back, slightly appeased, desire warming at just being near him.

"But you're one to fret, sweetheart." He dug back into his ridiculous stack of pancakes. "I thought to cut that off at the pass."

She blinked. "Excuse me?"

Male suffering filled his sigh as he set down his utensils. Green eyes, Scottish and true, lasered right into her. "Ar-right. Let's do this now so we can eat. Have you wondered about us through the years?"

She crossed her arms. "I don't think—"

"Nora." He didn't snap, he didn't raise his voice, but a new tone, a bite of command, filled it. "Just answer the question. Have you wondered?"

"Yes," she huffed.

"I donna want to know about other men, but has it been like that with anybody else?"

Heat climbed into her face. "Deke—"

"Nora." Another command.

Fine, and that voice should not be wetting her panties. "No. But sex is just sex." Even as the words tumbled out of her, she didn't believe them.

"Uh-huh." His gaze dropped with longing to his pancakes before returning to pin hers. "So we have two choices. I spent a lot of time thinking last night—"

"Thinking?" She squinted and narrowed her focus. "There was no time for thinking. Hell, we barely had time for sleep." They'd had sex four times during the night. *Four times.*

He grinned. "Between rounds one and two, you slept a little. I thought."

She pressed her fingers to her closed eyelids as a headache roared in. "We don't have time for this right now. Too much is going on."

He reached over and gently pried her fingers away. She opened her eyes. He released her. "There's always too much going on, and for right now, we're working together. Last night, after round one, I figured this was a one-night deal, and that we would just get some closure," he rumbled.

Hurt, surprising in its sharpness, sliced into her chest. "Okay."

"But then, between rounds three and four, I decided *fuck that*." He took a bite of pancake.

"Uh." She couldn't find words. What words were there?

He grinned. "I figure it'll take more than one night to get closure."

She couldn't hold back a chuckle. "Your plan, the one you came up with while I slept, was to keep having sex with me while I'm in town."

He nodded, amusement lightening his too-knowing eyes. "Exactly."

"You're terrible." She took a bite of eggs.

"That's not what you said last night."

She shook her head. There was no way she could continue sleeping with Deacan McDougall and not lose her heart again. They'd nearly destroyed each other once. "Not a good idea."

A corner of his mouth twitched. "Ah, to have lived centuries ago."

She couldn't help but return the smile. "When you could've just kidnapped me instead of cajoled?"

He grinned. "Aye. We'd still be married, and you'd be thoroughly tamed by now."

She rolled her eyes at the teasing, but even so, studying him, she could see his proud heritage. Rugged features and battle-hardened green eyes. He would've made a hell of a Highlander, an incredible warrior. She had no doubt he would've tamed her way back when. But now she had rights, and a brain—and the desire spiraling through her abdomen could just stop it. "Pity for you to be born in this time."

"Aye," he breathed. "However, I am now as modern as a

man can be. I've mellowed and learned to control not only my temper but the actual anger."

She tilted her head to the side. "You make it sound as if the anger was already in you before you went to war."

"'Twas." He shook his head. "The anger has been with me since I was a kid. My da was a prick, my ma not much better. When they died and I moved to the States, I was already screwed up." His long fingers played idly with his unused knife.

"I know," she said softly. She knew well his childhood hadn't been safe, with a father who hit and a mother who drank. "You moved past the pain." At least, she had thought he'd found peace with his childhood. Of course, then he'd entered the military and had seen things that had only brought back the anger. "Right?"

"Mayhaps. Hell, Nora. Maybe the anger lives in my blood anyway." He rubbed the whiskers on his hard jawline. "Maybe my people all have it."

The descendants of the Highlanders seemed to hear a distant call nobody else did. She wasn't prone to fancy, but every once in a while, she'd seen a faraway look in his eyes, as if he sensed something. As if a whisper, across the times, demanded his attention. She shivered. "I appreciate the offer but think I'll opt for self-preservation. Any truce between us is temporary."

"What about my new mellow life and attitude?" he asked evenly.

She bit back a smile. "It's temporary. I know you, Deacan. There's an edge to you, always will be, and you need the action. The fight."

His eyebrows lifted. "I don't agree, but even if I did, so what? Right now, we're fighting together. Common goal and common enemy."

Right now. She sighed. "The second we cure the Scorpius

infection, our goals diverge. Science is about saving lives, and we both know the military will want to weaponize and further mutate the bacteria."

He sighed and set down his utensils. "Having weapons is necessary to saving lives, and you know it."

"Science shouldn't be used that way," she said softly.

He leaned back and rubbed his chin. "Remember when I first got to the States? A couple of kids at school, the ones on the boxing team, tried to mess with me?"

She sipped her tea. "I do."

"Do you remember what happened?" His voice rumbled low. Intimate.

She inhaled the scent of peppermint herbs, remembering him well as a handsome, lost, pissed-off kid from Scotland. "You beat the ever-livin' shit out of them, Deacan."

He nodded. "Aye. What happened then?"

She frowned, studying him. "Well, nothing happened."

"Exactly."

She set down the cup. "It's different."

"No—it's the same. We have a weapon; the world knows we'll use it if pushed, so they don't push, and we don't use. Simple as that."

Yeah, and that was why they'd never see eye to eye. "We're going to end up on opposing sides." She'd destroy the bacteria when it was no longer needed, and that might even be illegal, according to current law. Who knew?

He lifted an eyebrow. "Your best friend works for the government. Have you thought about that?"

"Yes." But Nora knew Lynne, and she was a healer, not a killer. "I trust her."

"Hmm. You may not know her as well as you thought."

Nora frowned. "What do you mean?"

"Ask her." He paused while the waitress refilled his coffee. "How did you two become friends, anyway?"

Nora smiled. "Oh, we weren't friends the first semester of grad school. Didn't like each other, actually."

A grin split Deke's face, masculine and way too handsome. "Don't tell me. You two competed. Big-time."

"Yes." Nora blew on her tea. "In every class, on every quiz or test, one of us earned the top grade. We saw each other constantly at the library or in class, and we pushed each other."

Deke settled back. "And then?"

"Lynne's a klutz. A serious, should be bound in bubblewrap klutz." Nora chuckled, memories assailing her. "One night, we were the last two in the library, and she needed a book on the top shelf. She climbed it, no big deal, but then . . ."

Deke winced. "She fell?"

"Yes. The entire shelf started to come down, and I just reacted." Nora shrugged. "Moved without thinking, tackled her, and got her out of the way."

Approval mingled with amusement in his green eyes. "So you saved her?"

"I broke my right wrist." Nora sighed. "Which wasn't a huge deal, because in most of our classes, we could use recorders during the lectures. But in Dr. Mobsey's advanced biology class, the complete dickhead, no computers or recorders were allowed. Taking notes was tough."

"And?"

"After class one day, I was trying to decipher my lefthanded notes, and Lynne sat down with a typed set of hers." Nora shook her head and heat tingled into her face. "I told her to stuff it, that I didn't need her help, and thanks anyway."

Deke chuckled. "And?"

"She said I probably couldn't understand her notes because she'd used big words." Nora chortled. "We laughed, and she shared her notes. Then we started to study together, and before second semester was over, we were best friends. Still are." They'd seen each other through breakups, job problems, and good times. Yet now Deke hinted that Lynne was keeping secrets. He had to be wrong.

His phone buzzed, and he read the face. Tension gathered along the sides of his mouth.

Nora leaned toward him. "What is it?"

He slipped the device back into his pocket. "We'll have to finish talking about us later." He slipped a series of bills on the table. "The president just slipped into a coma."

Chapter Seven

After breakfast, Nora headed back to the new temporary CDC labs. Upon going through security, she swung by the lab to find the experiments about another hour from spitting out results, so she went searching for Lynne. She stepped into Lynne's office to see her reading charts, scuffed boots up on the desk. With a sigh, Nora inched inside and dropped into a chair.

"That was an 'I had crazy monkey sex last night and am sore' sigh," Lynne mused, her gaze not leaving the papers.

Nora coughed, and heat climbed from her chest to her face. "Shut up."

Lynne looked over the top of the file, emerald eyes widening. "Oh my. I was just kidding." Her boots dropped to the floor. "You've only been here a day. What were you thinking?"

"Meow? Take me harder? Oh thank you, God?"

Lynne snorted. "How was it?"

"Amazing. Four times over—amazing."

Lynne's mouth dropped open. "Four times? Really? Does he have a brother?"

"No." Nora studied her friend. Tired. Definitely exhausted. "What are you reading?"

"Your boy's brain scans."

Nora lost her grin. "And?"

"Zach seems fine." Lynne closed the file and slid the mass over the desk. "Activity in the central cortex lights up as normal."

Nora flipped open the top sheet to see a nice blue and green blend around Zack's frontal cortex. "Why do you sound worried?"

"He's a boy genius, and we don't know what his cortex looked like *before* the infection." Lynne clasped her hands on her desk. "Also, I don't like that he's now a carrier and was infected in my lab. He's twenty-two, for goodness' sake. We need to find a cure and fast."

Nora tapped the printout. "We sure do. Then we can destroy the mutated samples, right?"

Lynne arched one angled eyebrow. "I thought that was our plan."

"Me too." Nora planted the file back on the desk. The current experiments wouldn't be finished for at least an hour, so it was time to get to the truth. "What aren't you telling me?"

Lynne frowned. "Huh?"

"Deacan said you had a secret."

"Oh, did he?" Lynne rubbed her elbow and blushed a very pretty shade of pink. "It's not a secret. You and I haven't had time to talk, and it's not something you exactly Skype about. Geez."

Curiosity roared through Nora, but a shadow by the doorway caught her eye. She turned to focus. "Zach."

He stood in full protective gear, face behind a mask. Even so, something about him looked like a clean-cut movie star from the 1950s. Thick blond hair, blue eyes, trembling smile in a pale face. "I wanted to thank you for staying outside my bubble the first night." His voice emerged tinny through the faceplate.

She glanced at Lynne. "The full suit isn't necessary, is it?"

Lynne shook her head. "From a safety protocol, no. From a workplace and emotional standpoint, hell yes. Everyone is nervous as wet cats around here."

Pressure built behind Nora's eyeballs. "We're all scientists—screw emotion. If he's no more infectious than a carrier for regular *Staph,* typhoid fever, or even MRSA, then we shouldn't treat him like he's carrying the plague."

Zach snorted behind the helmet. "I don't mind, to be honest. It was my fault I got infected, and I deserve to be a little uncomfortable. Apparently walking is good for my joints, because the doctors suited me up to head down for yet another MRI."

Nora studied him. "You look so much better."

"I'm glad, because I feel like somebody punched me in the head with a Buick," he said.

Lynne nodded. "Aptly put. Other than that, feeling crazy?"

"No." Zach shrugged. "I'm not sure I would know, however." His eyes clouded behind the rimmed glasses. "How contagious am I now?"

Lynne exhaled. "The bacteria is still alive in your saliva, blood, and probably semen. For now, you can't kiss, give blood, or have sex until we find a counteragent or a cure for Scorpius."

Red flushed across Zach's cheekbones. "How long do I need to stay in the protective room at the CDC?"

Lynne swallowed. "For a while yet, Zach. I'm sorry."

His Adam's apple wobbled. "Okay. Let me know my results when you get them." Turning awkwardly in the suit, he disappeared down the hallway.

Nora shook her head. "Semen? Man. You didn't have to embarrass him."

Lynne's lips twitched. "I wanted to make him laugh." She rubbed her nose. "Sorry we have to keep him contained. But at least here he can continue working with that huge brain of his."

Nora grimaced. "I don't agree with the containment."

"Neither do I. The fever has passed, and he's out of the woods. Basically, he's a carrier, and there are tons of people who are carriers of dangerous diseases—especially *Staph*. But we have public relations concerns, and for the time being, he stays put."

Nora nodded. "I know."

Bobbi poked her head in the doorway. Today she'd worn a bright pink top with tight jeans and looked like a cheerleader from any California college team. "The samples of the president's blood have arrived, and they're in the lab. The White House is expecting a cure today."

Nora snorted. "Then we'll get right on that."

Bobbi nodded. "Have you seen Zach?"

"He's getting an MRI down in Imaging." Lynne rested her elbows on the desk. "If you end up in his contained room with him, there's no kissing, no sex with Zach. You wear gloves and don't touch anything."

Bobbi rolled her eyes. "I know, but talking is okay, right?"

Lynne lifted a shoulder. "Talking is fine."

"Good." Bobbi stretched her neck. "I've been receiving the stats from across the country, and the contagion is spreading, but doctors don't know what it is. At some point . . ."

"I know. We're waiting for approval to announce." Lynne swallowed. "Would you make sure Zach found Imaging?"

"Yep." Bobbi hopped away.

Lynne's phone buzzed, and she answered it. "Hi. No. Lunch? Probably not, but I can meet tonight after setting up our next batch of tests. They should take at least twelve hours to come to fruition. Okay. You too." She slid the phone back onto the desk.

Nora lowered her chin but kept quiet. No way. She knew that look. "Oh, my God. You totally are seeing somebody."

Lynne's eyes widened. "Shhh. My door is open."

Nora shoved hair out of her eyes. "So? This is a secret? Why is it a secret?" She stood. "He's not married, is he?"

Lynne rolled her eyes. "For the love of Pete, of course he isn't married. Geez. I just try to keep my personal life private, you know?"

Nora planted both hands on her hips. "Why didn't you tell me?"

Lynne swept both hands out. "It's pretty new, just a few months, and I figured I'd dish all when we met next month for our Vegas weekend."

"Oh." Nora's mind spun. She leaned against the chair. "Well? Dish now."

Lynne smiled, her eyes glimmering. "His name is Bret Atherton, he's smart and sexy, and he's from Atlanta. We met at a fund-raiser for a local kid's ranch. Our first date, he took me for a picnic."

Nora squinted. "Bret Atherton? As in Congressman Bret Atherton?"

Lynne wrinkled her nose. "Yes."

Nora snorted. "You're dating a politician. A congressman from Georgia." She laughed. Her wild, free, brilliant friend was dating a politician. A blond, sexy, sharp politician. Her mind clicked through what she knew. "Wait a minute. After the last elections . . . didn't he become the Speaker of the House?"

"Yes." Lynne sighed. "I like him, politics and all, but we're taking it slow."

"You slut. You've done him."

Lynne rolled her eyes. "Look who's talking. You're back in the same air as your ex for one day, and you can barely walk."

"Shut up," Nora said without heat. "I've seen your guy on television. Definitely charismatic."

Lynne shrugged. "I know—he's pretty amazing. May make a bid for the presidency next time. The guy has quite an ego, you know? For some reason, I keep finding that incredibly sexy." Her phone buzzed, and she glanced down. "My newest results are spitting out in the lab, and shouldn't yours be available sometime today? The new ones on the nanostructured oxide? For now, you can help me. We can talk men later."

Nora sighed and rose. "Between the two of us, we really know how to complicate our lives."

"Amen, sister."

Deke sat on a flowery chair across an antique coffee table from Sally Phillips, who relaxed on a matching sofa in the residence of the White House. "I'll ask you again, do you understand me?" he asked quietly.

She rolled her eyes, looking like any other put-upon nineteen-year-old co-ed. "Yes. I get you. If I move, if I try to lunge and bite you, you'll have no choice but to protect yourself." Her pretty pink lips pouted. "When did you become such a wimp?"

"When you infected your father, the President of the United States and my boss, with a deadly bacteria." He kept his expression bland but watched closely.

Nothing. No emotion, no regret, no anger. "That was an accident, Deke. I promise." She fluttered her eyelashes.

He rubbed his whiskered chin. Damn it. He'd forgotten to shave again. Wincing, he set his hands on his knees, careful not to touch anything else in the room. "Listen, Sally. I want to help you."

She rubbed her hands down jean-clad thighs and sighed. With her blond hair in a ponytail and wearing a Stanford T-shirt, she looked like any pretty teenager. "I appreciate your offer, but the doctors are wrong. Sure, I might've been kinda crazy right after the fever when I bit my dad, but I feel fine now. And awful about Dad." She smiled, flashing twin dimples. "He's strong and will be fine."

"I know."

She huffed again. "I feel okay and don't want to bite anybody else. When can I get out of house arrest?"

Deke sighed. "Your last brain scans still show lack of activity in your frontal cortex."

She snorted. "My brain is working just fine. Give me a break. They can't tell from a bunch of colors what's going on in my head."

Good point. "I'm inclined to agree with you there." He leaned forward, his hands dangling between his knees. "For now, we have to make sure you're all right before letting you loose. You understand that."

She leaned back her head. "I do, but I'm so sick of being cooped up. What if my brain scans never get colorful? I mean, if they were colorful before. Maybe they weren't. Maybe I'm somebody who doesn't have a lot of colors flashing from machinery in a freakin' lab." She lowered her chin, and tears glinted in her eyes. "It's like they *want* me to go crazy."

Being held inside without any freedom would drive him up the wall, too. "I'm sorry, Sally. I'll talk to the scientists at the CDC and determine if there's any other way to test your brain than what they're doing." More importantly, the girl had a point. What if her brain scans didn't ever really light up? Was that a true sign that she was dangerous? Somehow, he wasn't buying it. "I'll do my best."

She rolled her eyes again. "Why are you in charge here? I mean, you're not Secret Service or in the military. What exactly are you?" Her focus narrowed.

"Special Strategic Advisor to the President of the United States," Deke murmured.

She chuckled. "Sounds like a complete bullshit title, now doesn't it?"

"Aye."

"I've been around politics my whole life, you know?" She glanced toward the heavily curtained window and then back.

He breathed out, his shoulders tightening. "That kind of sucks."

"It really does," she said softly. "But you know what? I can recognize a soldier, and I can recognize a killer. You're both, aren't you?"

He couldn't really blame her for being pissed. "I've been a soldier, and I've killed."

"How many?" Her eyes glittered.

He shook his head.

She clucked her tongue. "I'm in trouble because I bit my dad while under a fever, and you're an advisor to the president because you've killed tons of people." She leaned toward him, gaze intense. "You believe in hell?"

"Yes." He had to concentrate to keep his brogue at bay. Tension lifted the hair on the back of his neck, and he paid heed.

"Me too." Her shoulders slumped, and her gaze dropped to her knees. "At the worst of the fever, I almost died." She lifted her gaze, her lips twisting. "I didn't see a light, Deke. I heard a darkness."

Chilled nails ticked down his spine. "And now?"

She rested her chin on her hand and let out a low sigh. "I don't hear anything and just want to go shopping."

Now that sounded like a normal kid. His body relaxed. "I'll see what I can do." He rose and edged around the coffee table. "Give me a little time."

"Okay." She scratched her elbow.

"Call me if you need anything." He passed the sofa and headed toward the door, his heart heavy. Poor kid. They had to be able to figure out the brain scans and whether the colors really meant anything.

A wisp of sound.

He partially turned, only to be attacked by a hurtling female body. Pain thumped into his shoulder. All instinct, he pivoted and shoved. Hard.

Sally flew across the room and smashed into the couch, bunching instantly to leap toward him again, nails out, teeth bared. Saliva slid down her chin.

He settled on his feet, waited, and took the hit by grabbing her arms. A quick turn, and he planted her on her face.

She struggled, spitting, an inhuman snarling jerking her body.

Holy fuck. The kid probably weighed a hundred pounds, but her strength was beyond what it should be. "Restraints," he yelled toward the closed door.

Sally kept trying to turn her head toward him, teeth snapping. He clasped the back of her neck and held her still. "Take it easy, Sally," he tried to soothe like he would a wild animal.

She kicked and howled.

A Secret Service agent ran inside with zip ties.

"Stay away from her mouth," Deke ordered. Shit. He was tying up and might have to gag the president's daughter.

The agent's eyes widened, and she handed over the ties. "Did she bite you?"

"No." But she'd hit him hard enough to bruise his shoulder.

"I thought Sally was better," the agent said.

Deke nodded. "So did I." Fuck, was he wrong.

The agent lifted both eyebrows. "I just received word."

The atmosphere thickened around Deke. "And?"

She leaned over to whisper in his ear. "The president is dead."

Chapter Eight

Week 2
50 people dead
Likelihood of Scorpius Containment: Probable

Nae man can tether time or tide.

—ROBERT BURNS, SCOTTISH POET

After days without positive results, Nora had left experiments running and headed to her apartment for a very late dinner with Lynne and Bobbi. They devoured her homemade chicken-surprise dish, and she clicked off the phone after giving directions for Amanda Bison to play first base and July Newcomb to cover for shortstop.

As she slipped her phone back into her pocket, both women stared at her with various expressions of *what the hell?*

She sighed. "Last year, one of my bunko friends needed an assistant coach for a girls' softball team. The Tigers. I played softball as a kid and somehow ended up volunteering." She had a blast with the girls and the team. "We won the division last year."

Bobbi raised both eyebrows. "You play bunko?"

Nora nodded. "Yes. I do have a life outside of my job, you know." She played bunko with a fun and tipsy group of friends, jogged regularly, and coached softball. "I miss my life." The calmness and order of it.

"You'll get back to it soon," Lynne said, patting her hand.

Would she? Although she'd only been gone a week, she wondered if life would ever get back to normal. Scorpius was spreading. "I hope so." When the president had died, they'd had to announce his passing to the world, but the government had lied by saying it was a stroke. "We need to cure this thing and now. When will the neurologists from Johns Hopkins head this way?" Nora asked.

Lynne set down her beer bottle and rubbed her bloodshot eyes. "Tomorrow morning."

Bobbi scratched her head. "Why aren't they here already?"

"Their medical facility in Baltimore is the best. Now they want a firsthand look," Lynne murmured, reaching for another scan. "Zach's brain scan is bright and colorful."

"He is a genius." Bobbi snorted, her gaze remaining sober. "But he's still contagious."

Lynne nodded. "I know. Any thoughts on that one?" She lifted an eyebrow at Nora.

Nora shrugged. While she'd been watching Zach carefully, he really did seem to be all right. Cheerful, smart, and nerdy as usual. "Being contagious sucks, but it isn't the end of the world. I mean, there are many carriers of MRSA, and they live normal lives. They can only infect people who have wounds, and it's rare. But possible."

"We don't know enough about Scorpius yet, so I can't release him from the CDC's secure facility," Lynne said on a strong exhale. "I think I'd almost prefer if Scorpius were a virus."

"No." Nora flipped open another manila file folder. "With a bacteria, we can create an antibiotic or at least a nanosponge to take it out. Hopefully."

Lynne yawned until her jaw popped and then glanced at her watch. "Crap. It's midnight. Let's all get a few hours' shut-eye and meet in the main lab at four. The enzyme experiments should be concluded by then. Hopefully they've done their job and discovered a way to break up the DNA of Scorpius."

Bobbi groaned and pushed away from the table. "Four a.m.?"

Lynne stood and rolled her eyes. "All right. Five a.m., but everyone be ready to go." She glanced at the cluttered table. "You need help cleaning up?"

"No." Nora wanted a few more minutes of work. "You'll just make it more disorganized."

"I'd object to that statement if I wasn't so tired." Lynne stood and inched toward the door.

Bobbi hovered. "Thanks for dinner, and thanks for letting me work with you two. I really like Zach and want to help him."

"You bet." Nora smiled. Ah, young love. She remembered how quickly it could happen.

Lynne and Bobbi took off.

Less than a minute later, a knock echoed on the door. Nora glanced around the table. What had Lynne forgotten now?

Humming and shrugging stiff shoulders, Nora crossed the living room and opened the door. Her mouth gaped open. "Zach."

He stood in pressed pants and a crisp shirt, looking like a clean-cut superhero. A bouquet of roses filled one slender hand. "I wanted to thank you for staying at the hospital all night, and I figured we should get some things straight."

Her body stiffened in pure instinct. "Uh, what are you doing here?" She blinked. He hadn't been released from the CDC.

He wiped a hand across his brow and shrugged. "My key card still works, and I just changed into doctor attire. Nobody expected me to leave, so nobody was watching."

Well, hell. Good point. "You dropped by your place for fresh clothing?"

He glanced down at the ironed clothes. "Yes. I wanted to look good for you."

Oh, shit. She shook her head. "You're not thinking clearly."

He lowered his chin. "I almost died last week."

She swallowed. Was his brain going wonky? Had they missed something in the scans? "I know."

"I think wasting time is a bad idea. Hell. This thing could still kill me." He sighed.

She shook her head. Fear made her hands tremble. Could she get to her phone? "We won't let that happen. We'll figure out Scorpius. In the meantime, you just need to take care of yourself and be vigilant until we find the right antibiotic and vaccine."

"Life is short, Nora," he whispered.

Now that she knew. How could she get through to him? Blood roared through her head, making her dizzy. "I think maybe something is going on with you. How about we head into the lab and take a look at your scans?"

Zach stood close—too close—his gaze on her lips. "I know you are hesitant about us because you're kind of my supervisor right now, but I've faced death, so we need to stop playing around. Enough is enough." A young firmness entered his voice and gave her pause.

"Zach, let me help you."

"I don't need help." In a surprisingly fast move, his hip hit hers, shoving her back into the apartment. He shut the door.

Panic roared through her.

He grasped her arm. "Let's discuss this rationally."

Okay. This shouldn't be happening, but it was, so she needed to deal, and now. "You're having issues. Use your big brain and slow down." She planted a hand against his chest. "Trust me."

"It's time you shut up and trusted me," Zach hissed, his face contorting.

Holy shit. Who was this guy? His brain scans had been normal. What had they missed? Nora angled to the side. "Listen, Zach, something's up with the way your brain is working. Let's call Lynne and go take additional scans."

He grabbed her arm and pushed her toward the hall closet. The flowers dropped.

The image of the red petals gliding down and scattering against the white tile skittered a chill down Nora's back. Her breath caught. She hadn't realized how tall Zach stood. Now as he looked down, his handsome features held a hardness she'd never seen on him.

"Pack a bag. We need to go discuss this somewhere we won't be interrupted," he said.

Possibilities flashed through her brain. She could fight, or she could flee. But maybe she could reason with him. An idea struck her. "Don't you want to see what's happening in your brain right now? You're the most curious I person I've ever met."

"No." He cocked his head toward the living room. "Get packed."

Her gaze slid to the side to where her cell phone sat on the kitchen counter.

"Don't even think of calling the soldier. He's not right for you." Zach remained motionless.

Terror trickled through Nora's gut. "Please let me help you."

"No." Zach's calm expression didn't twitch. "I thought I had time to court you right, but with Deke in the picture, we need to get a move on now."

"I'm not leaving with you," she snapped.

He smiled, and the once charming expression now held menace. "Oh, you are."

She couldn't get to the phone, and she didn't want to get anywhere near the bedroom and bed. So she went on instinct.

And nailed him in the balls.

He doubled over with a shocked *oof* and fell to the side. Her breath panted out, and fear heated the air. She had to avoid his teeth and mouth. She pivoted and kicked him in the hip, throwing him against the coat closet. Then she yanked open the front door, grabbed his hair, and propelled him outside.

Her heart thundered in her chest, and she fumbled locking the door. The second the bolt engaged, she jumped for the phone.

It rang just as she grasped for it. "Hello," she nearly screamed.

"Nora? What's wrong?" Deke asked, the sound of movement echoing through the line.

Zach pounded on the front door.

Nora turned her head to yell at Zach. "I'm on the phone with Deke. Just stay there until we can get you some help." She really didn't want to go hand-to-hand with a pissed-off Zach now that he was prepared for a physical fight.

"Damn it," Deke bellowed. "I'm on my way. What's going on?"

The pounding stopped. Nora eyed the room wildly. "I think Zach is having mental problems. Please send somebody to take him in for tests. Somebody trained and armed. He's dangerous. But don't hurt him."

"Get in the bathroom and lock the door. I'll be right there." Deke's voice lowered to calm and direct.

She breathed out, her head swimming. Pounding footsteps echoed down the hallway. "He's gone. Damn it. We have to find him."

"I'll send out a BOLO and call in my men. Stay there."

Nora nodded, her gaze taking in the scattered rose petals. What now?

Nora opened the door on Deke's knock and let him into her apartment, her hands gesturing, even though she was sucking in air to calm down. Thank God Deke was there. "Lynne and I have called everyone Zach knows, and nobody has seen or heard from him. Bobbi is really upset and is trying Twitter and Facebook to find him."

Deke shrugged out of his jacket. "I have men scouring the city for him. He's only been gone two hours, so he can't have gotten far."

The guy was a genius and would know how to hide. "This is so bad," she murmured. "I should go and try to find him."

Deke lifted an eyebrow. "Where exactly would you look?"

She bit her lip. "No clue."

"Exactly. Stay here, stay safe, and we'll get him. Where's Lynne?" Deke tossed his coat toward the sofa.

"She left about five minutes ago, for the second time, after giving everybody orders to get a couple hours' sleep—especially me. The poor woman could barely stand, yet she's worried about me." Too much energy, probably adrenaline, roared through Nora's veins. "I think I may head into the lab and get to work early." None of her results would be ready, but she just couldn't sleep.

"Absolutely not. You're staying here and getting some rest, and you're under guard until Zach is caught. I'm protecting you tonight while my men find him. Period." Deke's jaw clenched. "There's nothing either one of us can do right now, so we're catching rest."

Nora's mouth gaped open and then closed on a snap. There was the bossy asshat she'd once married. Yet instead of ticking her off, she was almost giggly. It must be because she was so tired. "Your time of ordering me around has long past, Deacan McDougall."

He rubbed whiskers that had grown rougher in the few hours they'd been apart. A black gun nestled in the harness strapped around his right leg, and a polished knife handle gleamed at his belt. In a dark shirt with faded jeans, he looked like a mixture of badass soldier and dangerous warrior from years gone by. "I've never ordered you around," he said.

"Sure you did. Remember when there were those robberies in my neighborhood before we even got married?" She flushed hot.

He blinked, his green eyes narrowing. "That was different."

Her head lifted. "Oh yeah? How?"

"Jesus, Nora. When it comes to safety, to danger, I fuckin' know a lot more than you do about survival." At the outburst, his brogue came on strong. "Right now, you have a guy stalking yer every move. He was alone with you in your own apartment."

She blanched, and bile rose in her throat. The realization of how easily Zach could've bitten her rolled her stomach over. "You don't need to sleep over."

Deke grinned, and seeing the tension leave his face was like viewing the sun after a monstrous storm. "I'll just stay until we catch Zach, and that might even be tonight. All right?"

She paused, studying him. Well, at least he'd asked. Truth be told, she wasn't a dumbass who wouldn't accept protection when necessary, especially since she didn't quite know what she was dealing with concerning Zach. Deke was trained, and he was dangerous. He could handle any threat. So she nodded and gave him what he wanted. "I would very much appreciate your protection while Zach is on the loose."

At her acquiescence, Deke's eyes darkened. "Ah, I do so like you sweet and agreeable, Nora McDougall."

Heat flared down her torso, and she didn't correct his use of the wrong name. "I wouldn't know the feeling, Deacan. I've never seen you agreeable or sweet."

His chin lowered, and intent mingled with the amusement in his amazing eyes. "Sassy now, are you?"

Her very blood sparked with the need to challenge him. Life had turned dangerous, and she wanted an escape. Just a moment to be a woman and have some fun. With Deacan. She was way too keyed up to sleep and needed to burn off some energy, and there wasn't much she could do in the lab until the current experiments were concluded in the morning. Hopefully the charged nanoparticle experiment would work. "Sassy, I am. Think you can handle me?"

His eyebrows rose, and the amusement disappeared. "Yeah. I know I can." That deep voice lowered even more, rumbling with a masculine truth he made no effort to mask.

Anticipation stiffened her limbs. "Prove it."

His head lifted while his eyelids dropped to half-mast, giving him a primal look only a true predator could wear. "Run," he said softly.

A nervous chuckle tickled up her windpipe. Trembles vibrated her legs, and her mind kicked into gear with a sense of warning. "I don't think you can catch me." Yeah, she was enjoying being a woman all of a sudden, completely ignoring reality.

His head cocked, ever so slightly. "Last chance. *Run*."

As if her body were his to command, she turned and leaped into a mad dash. Around the sofa and over a stack of books. He caught her before she'd cleared her doorway, propelling them both hard and fast toward the bed to hit with a thud. She flipped onto her back and kicked, laughing, striking out with her hands to hit solid muscle.

He pressed a knee between her thighs and grabbed her wrists to stretch above her head against the pillows. Hard as she writhed, she couldn't gain purchase to counter him. Masculine smugness angled his jaw as he stared down at her. "Appears you've been caught."

Her struggles were useless, and she sobered at how quickly, how easily, he'd subdued her. Instead of providing caution, the reality speared fiery awareness through her. The power of the thigh between hers caught her breath in her throat.

He leaned up to gain better hold of her wrists, and that hard leg muscle pressed against her sex.

She gasped, and her body involuntarily shoved up into him.

He glanced down, eyes darkening, just as her nipples hardened to points inside her bra, causing small spikes of pleasure through her breasts. Holding her in place with merely one hand around her wrists and one thigh between hers, he quickly unfastened his harness and dropped the gun by the side of the bed. "Are you going to fight me?" he asked, the tone merely curious.

The game of run and chase had been fun, and playing with Deke was a lot more enjoyable than fighting with him. "And if I do?" she teased.

"You'll lose." One swipe down her front scattered buttons. "I may even tickle."

She gasped. "Hey."

He lifted a broad shoulder and tugged her bra up, revealing her needy breasts. "Spoils of war and all that." His voice thickened.

Cool air caressed her flesh, providing an erotic contrast to the heat boiling inside her. Her skin ached, and a hollowness echoed throughout her. Even though they were playing, enough truth hinted in the air to flutter hunger through her abdomen. "Deacan."

His head lifted, as did her skirt. He wasted no time removing her panties and instead snapped the sides away. His jeans were shed, the movement so quick she didn't have time to move. Then he was above her.

Gaze to gaze, groin to groin. "Nora?"

"Yes," she breathed. "Definitely, yes."

He didn't ask twice. A hard lunge of his hips, and he sheathed himself completely.

Pain zipped through her, followed by an unreal pleasure. The combination overwhelmed her, and she closed her eyes.

His hold tightened on her wrists. "Open yer eyes."

She blinked several times, a strangled plea buried in her breath. He possessed her, so strong, so male. No way could she have moved, even if she'd wanted to. Not for the first time, she wondered if she'd even come close to plumbing the depths of Deacan McDougall during their marriage.

Keeping her gaze, his expression inscrutable and his eyes filled with a light she couldn't quite decipher, he pulled out and then shoved back in, setting up a pounding that rocked the headboard against the wall.

She gasped, her eyes widening at the powerful treatment. Even so, her hips lifted to take more, whether her mind could or not. The second she rubbed against him, he thrust harder, controlling her body, not allowing her to move. More of his weight descended on her, preventing even the small lifting of her hips.

All she could do was take it.

An orgasm rushed through her so quickly she could only gasp. He kept pounding, sweat drifting off his chin and onto her chest. It was raw and way too real. At the thought, electricity uncoiled inside her. Deep inside, way deeper than she'd known existed, the unfurling swept her up. She stiffened, trying to fight, needing to clutch at any semblance of control.

The hard pounding was slipping from the warmth of pleasure into the heat of pain, and she couldn't stop the fire. She detonated, her body arching, his name spilling from her lips. With a smile akin to a snarl, he shoved hard inside her, his body jerking with his release.

Moments later, her heart thundering and her breath panting out, she tried to back away from the intimacy and return to playfulness, even as her eyelids began to droop. "I guess you won, right?" she murmured sleepily.

The glimmer in his eyes somehow darkened even further. "Not yet, no. But I fully intend to."

Chapter Nine

Early morning, after dropping Nora off at her temporary CDC office, Deke finished searching Zach Barter's makeshift hospital room. The plastic gloves covering Deke's hands pulled at his skin, and he fought the urge to rip them off.

Instead, he gingerly grabbed a leather-bound book from the night table to open it. Genius boy kept a diary, and he'd obviously left the journal to be found.

Deke sighed. He had an ex-wife who hadn't quite realized her importance in his life, a possible bacteria from outer space that was killing people, a dead president, a weak vice president, and a stalker he needed to stop but not kill. To think that just the week before he'd been trying to mellow out his life.

Taking a deep breath, he flipped through the beginning pages of Zach's writing, noting equations, theories, and quotations about Einstein. Every once in a while, personal notes about Zach having a crush or wanting to ask a girl out but lacking the courage filled the pages.

Deke turned to the last couple of days. Pencil drawing after pencil drawing of Nora. At her desk, staring dreamily into space, nude on a bed.

Zach had gotten her tits wrong. They were rounder at the base.

The fire of his ancestors blazed through Deke's chest. He continued to read as Zach detailed how much he hated his formal self for being such a wimp. The last entry stole Deke's breath.

I'm finally free. No worries, no concerns. How could I have been so fucking weak? So unwilling to take what I want? This fever created a god. I'll take what I crave, and tonight I start with Nora. That bitch has ignored me long enough.

HEY SCOTTISH DICKHEAD: I put this in big letters so you'd see it, you fucking idiot. You might be a soldier, and you might have fucked her, but I'm smarter than you. I'll get her, and she'll be mine. You lost her.

Deke shut the journal. Fury made his hands shake. Scorpius had taken a nice guy and turned him sociopathic. Did the bacteria work harder, stronger, on already nice people? Impossible.

Zach had even left him a note, so focused was he on Nora.

Slowly, deliberately, Deke withdrew his phone and called his men. "I want Barter found and right now." The fact that Zach had tried to kidnap Nora was just the beginning.

Obviously Zach's brain scans hadn't told the whole truth. Or any truth, really. Deke left the room and endured the many decontamination steps before emerging into clean air. He jogged for the stairwell, his mind focused, his hands calm. Training dictated he drop into a mode of thought ready for action, and he allowed himself to do just that. The last thing he wanted to do was scare Nora off now, but every instinct he possessed bellowed she was in danger.

The real kind.

He'd stand between her and any threat, whether she liked it or not. This danger to Nora had forced the soldier, the warrior, deep down inside him to the surface again. To face the light of day.

He couldn't help but wonder if the return had always been inevitable.

Hours after Deke had rocked her world in a way that left her both satisfied and incredibly uneasy, and hours after not enough sleep, Nora worked with her best friend handling test tubes, meteorites, and a piece of brain matter from a dead student. Finally all of the supplies had arrived. For now, as she worked, special lights illuminated the space, and Lynne looked more like a Martian in the white protective suit than an expert in biological contaminants.

"Any news on Zach?" Lynne asked, dropping blue liquid on a slide.

"No." Nora stretched her back and slipped a slide under her microscope. "Everyone is looking, but so far, nothing."

Lynne nodded. "We'll find him, and we'll cure him."

Hopefully. "I know." Nora wrinkled her nose in the helmet. "How's Bobbi doing?"

Lynne snorted. "Not great. I hadn't realized the depth of her quick crush. She's a maniac on social media right now trying to find Zach. It'll probably work, too."

Good. "Whatever works. So long as we get him back." Nora adjusted the device. "We've had twenty more cases reported throughout the country since last night."

"I know." Lynne shook her head. "We'll figure it out."

"Yes," Nora said.

"Speaking of crushes, with all the danger, we haven't had a time to talk, just the two of us. The Scot is every bit as sexy as I expected," Lynne said through the headset in her suit.

Nora rolled her eyes and leaned closer to peer through the

microscope lens. "You're looking for a biological killer. Worry about my love life later."

"Aha," Lynne said, peering to look into a different microscope. "You said *love*. You luuuuv him."

"Shut up," Nora said without heat. "You're one of the most respected scientists in your field, and you sound like you're in junior high."

Lynne snorted, the sound emerging tinny from the helmet. "Talk about protesting too much." She paused and reached for another slide. "I have to tell you, when he dipped into that brogue of his, I almost orgasmed."

Nora chuckled. "Knock it off, Lynnie. Last I checked, you were dating one of the most powerful men on the planet." The guy now second in line to the presidency. How weird was that?

Lynne shook her head. "Ehh. He's kind of intense, and right now I have my hands full."

Nora blew out air. "I know."

"Hmm." One of the many whirling machines beeped, and Lynne moved to read the computer printout. Turning, she read a large computer monitor. "Interesting. My mutation, the green vial, is resistant to everything and kills instantly." She turned and frowned, the expression oddly garish through her faceplate. "This may be the most dangerous biological weapon I've ever touched."

Holy shit. Nora shook her head, her heart kicking into gear. "We have to destroy it."

"I know." Lynne turned back toward the computer. "Not until we cure Scorpius, just in case there's something in the concoction, in how quickly it divides, that might help. If we could duplicate the speed of division with a containing agent, we might be able to isolate the bacteria and starve it to death."

A bacteria from outer space. "This whole thing is crazy," Nora said.

"I know, and it's the find of a century. We need to get a handle on it before we announce to the world, however."

"I really don't like the public being told the president died from a stroke."

"Me either," Lynne murmured.

Nora swallowed, her mind spinning. They'd found bacteria in the middle of a meteorite from somewhere else, and now she was part of a governmental cover-up. It was too fantastic to think about.

Nora's gaze caught on a series of vials with different colored liquids. "That's quite an array."

Lynne glanced over her shoulder. "Yes. So far the green shade is the most dangerous, and the blue the most interesting. We have hope."

Nora nodded. She stretched her back and winced when something popped. "It'll be an hour before my newest test results are ready. How about I head down to the cafeteria and grab us sodas and something healthy? Maybe pizza?"

Lynne chuckled. "Make mine macaroni and cheese."

"Fair enough." Nora waddled into the first decontamination area and followed all protocols. Nearly twenty minutes later, she finally emerged into cool, air-conditioned air. Fighting a shiver, she strode to her locker and drew out a sweatshirt and her key card.

The door opened behind her, and she turned with a greeting. The words stalled in her throat. "Zach," she whispered.

He nodded and stepped inside. The door swished shut and locked automatically. He'd dyed his blond hair a deep brown, and a new dark suit covered his body. A wild glint lit his eyes. "Nora."

She gulped and tried to look normal. The FBI disguise was a good one since so many new agents were suddenly milling around the temporary CDC labs. "How did you get in here?"

He smiled, the expression a parody of the sweet look he'd given her the previous month. "I borrowed a card. No big deal. Why do you keep forgetting I'm smarter than, well, everybody else around here?"

Nora tried to reach for the phone in her pocket. "What happened to the guard outside?"

Zach drew a gun from behind his back and pointed it at her. "He's in a supply closet right now, hopefully bleeding out. Now toss your phone over here." He flicked the gun toward where Lynne stood beyond the glass doors, her eyes wide. "Move, and I'll shoot you," he mouthed clearly. He waited for her nod before turning back to Nora. "Now."

Lynne was across the entire lab from a phone. Nora took out her phone and tossed it at him.

He dodged to the side, and the phone spun by to smash against the wall. "Good enough." He gestured toward a chair. "Sit down."

She took a seat, her gaze meeting Lynne's frantic one. "Zach, I don't really think you want to hurt me," Nora said.

"I don't." Zach walked toward her and yanked a pair of handcuffs from his jacket. "From the guard. Moron."

Panic bubbled up in Nora, and she tried to push off the chair. Zach clicked her hands into place, securing her to the leg of the heavy oak desk. She could remain seated, but her arm dangled at a painful level. "Please let me go."

"We'll leave in a minute." He turned and approached the lab, yanking open the two protective doors and kicking stoppers into place to keep them open.

"Zachary, don't go in there," Nora hissed.

He continued on. "Why not? I've already had the infection, and since it's Scorpius, you can't catch it in the air. Now just sit there and shut up."

She shook her head, tugging uselessly on the cuff. "What the hell are you doing?"

"I'm curious about this bugger," Zach said, crossing toward Lynne.

Shit. The woman was hampered by the big suit and

wouldn't be able to fight well. She backed away, her hands up. "Nora, how tight you bound?" Lynne yelled.

"Can't move. Cuffed," Nora screamed back. "If you can get by him, run."

Lynne winced. "The suit is probably contaminated."

Zach laughed, the sound high and slightly off. "What exactly is this bacteria, doc? I've felt better in the last week than I have in years. Years and years. Talk to me."

Lynne's gaze sharpened. "You feel different since recuperating?"

Zach walked toward her, smiling as she backed away and hit the counter. "I do. No more doubt, no more silly thoughts. I'm meant to be here and get what I want."

Nora's chest compressed. "Zach, leave her alone. Please. I'll go with you right now."

He turned and smiled, his expression the closest to evil Nora had ever seen. "You'll go with me when I'm ready."

Taking advantage of his momentary change in focus, Lynne dodged forward and hit him in the gut. He turned, faster than Nora would've thought, and tackled Lynne to the floor.

Nora screamed as loud as she could.

Zach released the zipper and yanked the helmet off Lynne before straddling her. She yelled, trying to fight him off, her gloved hands useless. Laughing, Zach reached up for one of the test tubes.

"No!" Nora jerked against the cuffs. He'd grabbed the deadly green strain, and they had no idea what it'd do to a person. "Let her go. Please."

For answer, he flicked off the cover and shoved the end in Lynne's mouth. She coughed, shoving at him, her body jerking. Green spat over her face. The vial clinked on the floor. Then, almost in slow motion, Zach slapped his hand over Lynne's mouth, forcing her to swallow several times. She flapped against him, her legs kicking the tiles.

Finally, Zach stood, turned, and shot a back kick into one

of the monitors. Sparks crackled, and the screen tumbled over the desk to the floor. In an almost manic series of hits and kicks, he destroyed every piece of equipment in the lab.

Lynne turned over, coughing, and tried to crawl away. Her chest heaved and a mournful groan rumbled up from her chest.

Nora struggled against the cuffs, tears blurring her vision. "Inject the blue. It's your only chance."

Zach watched Lynne, his face passive. Then he smiled as she pulled herself up the side cabinet to stand, weaving back and forth.

"Fuck, it hurts. Hurts so bad," Lynne mumbled, both hands clapping against her temples. "God, please help me."

Zach tipped back his head and cackled. "I am God, and I'm not likely to help you. Bitch." Venom filled his words.

Nora shook her head, trying to clear her eyes. "Leave her alone."

Lynne dropped to her knees, her hands clutching her chest, fumbling up for the blue vial.

"Zach, please help her," Nora yelled, fear ripping into her. "Drink the blue, Lynne. Now. We can make more."

Lynne's eyes widened, a continuous keening coming from her until her voice cracked. She grasped a syringe and filled it with blue liquid, her hands shaking. The vial dropped to the floor.

Sucking in air, she stuck the needle into her arm and depressed the plunger. She dropped all the way down, face-first, her body going into convulsions. The scream that erupted from her sounded like it came from the depths of hell.

Aqua blue filled the visible veins at the back of her neck, brightening and then winking out.

Nora gasped, her gaze on her friend.

Zach frowned and stepped over debris to reach the downed woman. Humming to himself, he reached down and flipped her over. Quick motions had the suit removed. Frowning, he ripped open her shirt and unclasped her bra.

Blue glowed up from Lynne's skin. How was that possible? Nora shook her head, trying to clear her vision. Lynne's heart was a bright greenish blue, cascading out in arteries and veins. Blue morphing into a bright aqua. She lay limp, unconscious.

Zach palmed a breast, and she didn't move.

Nora gagged. "Let her go. Zach, this isn't you. Please."

He looked up and squinted as if he'd forgotten her. Then he smiled. With another almost absent pinch to Lynne's cheek, he stood.

He stalked toward Nora, a bizarre smile lifting his lips.

Fear ricocheted through her. She hissed out air, her feet kicking to somehow move the chair. "Leave me alone."

He reached her and bent down, his face an inch from hers. She stopped breathing and pressed back into the cushions.

Zach licked his lips.

Nora shoved down a whimper of terror.

The door opened, and one of Lynne's techs strode in. His name was John or Joe, or something like that. "Where's the guard?" he asked, munching on a bagel.

Zach shot forward and tackled him into the metal door. His head impacted with the sound of a melon on concrete, and he slid to the tile unconscious.

"There's no way to get you out of here unwillingly. Not through all the hallways and security." Zach sighed. "Any chance you'll come with me?"

Nora slowly shook her head. The man had completely lost it, but he had to have known she wouldn't cooperate. "Why did you come?"

He shrugged. "I wanted to see the green vial and what it would do. My normal curiosity seems to have moved into obsession. Like it has for you. I have a couple of things to take care of, and then I'll be back for you." He paused at the door and blew her a kiss. "You and me, Nora. It's gonna be great."

Chapter Ten

Deke set his gun on the night table, his senses on full alert. Behind him, Nora perched on his bed, way too quiet.

He sighed, his gaze remaining on the darkness outside his window. His gut roiled, and his fingers curled with the need to extract vengeance. With great pain. "Are you sure you're not infected?"

"I'm sure," she said softly. "The infection is spread by bodily fluids."

He shut the blinds and turned to face her, masking his expression. "So only kissing, sex, blood, urine, semen?"

She shook her head. "Those for sure, but it's like any bacteria. If it's on a surface, and you touch the surface and then your eyes, nose, or mouth, you can catch it."

He nodded, his chest heavy. The memory of having to wait while they'd performed so many tests on her would haunt him forever. "It's contained for now?"

She winced. "Lynne's team got her into isolation, and she's being treated with the highest protocols. Then they disinfected the entire room and everything in it. I stayed with her for a couple of hours while you looked for Zach, but she hasn't regained consciousness."

Deke scrubbed both hands down his face. "Our biggest problem now is Zach Barter."

"I don't know what's going to happen next. He wanted to infect Lynne, so maybe he wants to infect other people. Perhaps part of the bacteria's strength, when it strips the brain, is to push for more infections. There are contagions with similar symptoms." Nora clasped both arms around her knees, looking unbelievably fragile.

Deke remained still. "Great."

Nora leaned her chin on her knees. "You should've seen Lynne's chest. It turned blue. I mean, her heart glowed almost aqua. I've never seen anything like it. Ever."

"You're sure you're not infected," Deke said.

Nora huffed. "No, I'm not infected, they did plenty of tests and they know how the bacteria works."

His temper pricked his shoulders as if the old fury really wanted out. Yet his woman had been through an ordeal, and now wasn't the time for him to lose it. "If there's a chance you're infected, then I want you in the hospital with doctors all around."

She dropped her gaze. "He didn't touch me after being in the containment area. There's no way, Deke. I'm going to head back into the lab and find something new to work on while I wait for more results."

"No." Deke kicked off his boots and set a knee on the bed, the pressure in his chest easing. He believed her, and thank the gods. All of them. "We have a couple of hours to sleep, and then I need to go out hunting again." He'd spent hours trying to find Barter, with no luck; he had to contain the bastard, and soon. "Now we sleep."

Dark smudges marred the pale skin beneath Nora's eyes, and weariness hunched her shoulders, yet her eyes shot sparks. "Just because we're in a crisis right now doesn't give you the right to tell me what to do."

He lifted his chin. "You're right."

She blinked. "I am."

"Aye. I'm telling you what to do because we're together, and it's my job to keep you safe. If you're passing out from exhaustion, it makes my part more difficult." He kept his voice level and tried to add some humor, but he spoke the truth, and damn it, she could tell.

"We're barely together, and that doesn't give you rights," she muttered.

He needed sleep, as did she. So he skipped the argument and instead grabbed her up and shoved her under the covers. Her halfhearted struggle did nothing but make him more determined. Then he reached over his head to turn off the lamp before lying down.

"You're not getting in?" she asked, her voice small in the darkness.

"No." Deke could get enough sleep lying on top of his covers. Getting through the security system he'd installed that morning would be nearly impossible for a guy not trained in systems. Even so, Deke would be prepared. "Go to sleep, Nora."

"Fine." She rolled over, and even the rustle sounded huffy.

He shut his eyes and relaxed his body from the bottom to the top as he'd been trained. The slightest of movements in the bed caught his attention. Then another. A soft, muffled sob came from next to him. *Well, shit.* He stood and kicked off his pants and shirt before sliding under the covers and turning her to face him. Her fight this time was a little more impressive, but he was patient, and before long, he'd tucked her wet face into his neck. "Let it out."

She smacked his ribs. "I thought you had to be vigilant."

He sighed against her hair. "No way can Barter get inside this place without my knowing it." Truth be told, Deke had wanted to sleep on top of the bed to keep from reaching for her. Even now, with her so warm and soft against him, his groin stirred.

She hiccupped, and the slight knock of her knee against his balls seemed deliberate. "You're not the boss here, and I'm going back to work, jackass. Now let me go, and get out of my way."

So she wanted to fight, did she? A good brawl would make her forget her troubles for a while, but she'd have to cry it out and face them sooner or later. "No."

She pushed against his chest. "I'm not going to sleep, so I might as well head back into the lab and work."

"You're exhausted, and that's where mistakes are made. Rest a little, and you can go back to work."

She shoved against him, her nails digging in. "Let me go."

"No." His quick smack to her ass reverberated up his arm. "Knock it off."

Her gasp heated his collarbone. "Oh, you did not," she hissed.

The roar of his blood through his veins filled his head, and he struggled to contain himself. "Go to sleep, or I'll do it again. I'm in no mood, Nora." Wrong thing to say, and he knew it the second the words left his mouth. But enough was enough, and his hold on his temper was rapidly failing. A sociopath wanted his woman enough to taunt Deke in a fucking journal. "Go. To. Sleep."

She kicked against him and landed a punch near his mouth.

Damn it. He rolled them over, flattening her to the bed.

She got off another good punch, this time nailing his bottom lip.

"Fuck." He grabbed her hands and manacled her wrists.

Her tight nipples scraped across his chest, and she groaned. Then she widened her legs, making room for him. "Deacan," she breathed.

"No." He could barely make out her face in the darkness, so he lowered his closer. His emotions were raw, and he needed time to gather himself. "I'm garna release you, and you're going to roll over and go to sleep. You feel me?"

She wiggled her butt in the bed and rubbed her wet cunt against his dick. "I definitely feel you."

Hunger clawed through him. He shut his eyes, struggling for control. While he understood her need to escape reality, and sex was a good way to do that, he wasn't ready. Gentleness lay nowhere within him at the moment. Shit. From the second he'd busted his ass to get to the hospital and seen her, so pale and frightened, huddled under a blanket as the medical teams tested her, he'd wanted to beat somebody bloody. So he took a deep breath and slowly released her wrists. "Nora, heed me."

"I'm trying to *heed* you," she hissed, rubbing herself against him.

He swallowed, his biceps quivering with the fight to keep from implanting himself so deep danger never found her again. "I'm not in control." Damn, he hated admitting that. "If I take you, baby, it's gonna be my way, and that ain't gentle." Nowhere near, actually.

She laughed, the sound deep and throaty. "No kidding. Geez. What do you call the other day?"

He paused and blinked. The other day? What other day? Realization dawned. "That was play. We were playing." The woman really didn't know him if she thought that was him out of control.

She leaned up and licked along his jawline. "Let's play again."

His cock hardened to the point of pain. His chest burned, and his vision hazed. "Let go. Time to sleep." His voice sounded as if he'd eaten glass.

She shifted against him, her nails scraping his palm. "Stop being such a pussy. You want me? Take me."

His body actually jerked as if held by invisible chains. Her use of the word was deliberate, and he bit down a retort. He drew in air through his nose, trying with every ounce of strength he had not to take her up on the offer. Or dare. "Trust me, Nora."

"I do." She freed her hands and reached for his hair to yank, and the pain shot straight from his scalp to his throbbing dick. "You've always held back, haven't you." Wonder filled her voice as she made the statement that didn't remotely sound like a question.

"Aye." The breath caught in his chest, and he forced it to remain there. Held. Waiting. Like a jaguar about to strike, everything in him coiled.

She went still beneath him as if instinctively knowing how close he was to the precipice. Then slowly, with pure deliberation, she released his hair and caressed down his neck, back, and buttocks, her nails lightly scraping. She reached his hip bone, and he stopped breathing.

Tension filled the room, smothering any oxygen still left.

Then she slid over his hip and wrapped her hand around the base of his shaft. Tight.

He growled, the sound more animalistic than human.

Her shoulders came off the bed, and her lips brushed against his. "You want me, Deacan McDougall? Then fucking take me."

Nora knew the second his control snapped. She not only heard it, she could *feel* it. After the fear of the day, after the sadness, she just wanted to get lost. Pushing Deacan McDougall to lose control was by no means a smart move. But it was all she had, and once she'd started, she couldn't stop.

He reared back and flipped her around.

"Hey—" she protested, trying to lift her face from the pillow.

He grabbed her hair and pulled back—hard. She scrambled

up onto all fours to keep the ache at bay, her mind swirling. Her chest filled until her lungs protested, and she tried to breathe out. Deke had taken her from behind before, and this shouldn't feel like a big deal. But something . . . was different.

One broad hand was planted between her shoulder blades and shoved down. Her arms gave, and her face hit the pillow again, leaving her ass in the air and exposed. Desire, raw and hot, warmed her head to toe. He grasped one cheek and squeezed, shoving a knee between her legs to widen them. "Move from this position, Nora, and I swear to fucking God I'll make sure you don't sit again by giving you the spanking I should've years ago."

A protest rose in her, and she began to lift her head, when the bed shifted. He pulled up on her thighs, tilting her, and his mouth found her core.

She cried out, sparks of light flashing behind her eyes. Strong, determined, and with a mission, he ate at her. From behind, his head between her legs, somehow he found the right angle. No finesse, none of the teasing licks he usually used. The scruff on his jaw scraped her thighs, and he went at her for his pleasure. Damn hers.

The first orgasm hit her with a flash of light, and yet she fought it, fighting him. But the waves took her over, pounding through her, and she came down with a soft moan. He moved again, and his fingers replaced his mouth. His chest arched over her back, and his heated breath brushed her ear.

She shook her head. "I can't."

"You will," he said, his free hand squeezing one nipple, his cock hard against the back of her thigh. "Your mind may not be clear, or your heart. But your body knows who owns it." His brogue thickened to the point she could barely understand him. "Before this night is over, I'll hear it from you."

She opened her mouth to argue, but he pinched her clit, and she went off again. His talented fingers prolonged the ecstasy until she moaned into the pillow, pleading for relief. Finally, he relented.

Air whooshed from her lungs, and she turned her head on the pillow to breathe.

Both hands grabbed her hips, he levered himself up, and in one hard thrust impaled his cock so deep, he'd always be there. She gasped, and small tremors rippled inside her. That quickly, that easily, a renewed craving for him consumed her.

He tethered her hair again, this time drawing back. "Now you get up," he said. She planted her hands and knees and rose, forced to arch her back as he kept a tight hold. The sensation of being controlled, of being vulnerable, filled her with a hunger so hot it burned.

His thighs settled on the outside of hers, one hand tangled in her hair, and the other clamped on her hip strong enough to bruise. Then he thrust. Harder and faster than she would've thought possible, he hammered into her, taking everything. Her arms trembled, and her vision hazed.

The devastating pleasure he pounded into her edged close to pain, all the sharper for the thin line. A set of mini-detonations exploded inside her, and she gasped, her body stiffening. The next thrust threw her into such an intense orgasm, she vibrated head to toe and screamed his name.

Her body stopped shaking, and her sex relaxed.

Still, he pounded.

"You're killing me," she moaned, trying to free her head.

His mouth nipped at her earlobe. "Definitely not my intention." He reached around her and slid two fingers along her clit.

She moaned. "God, Deke. So much."

He continued to hammer into her without even a hitch in his pace, his fingers sliding, plucking, and pinching. Sensation upon sensation whirled through her, taking over, stealing her will. She rose higher and higher, her breath catching, her heart maybe stopping. Time extended with no beginning, with no ending, and he showed no sign of slowing. Of weakening. As if he had a point to make, one he'd held back, he gave her everything he had without mercy.

She kept climbing, bombarded by sensation. When she reached the top, the world stopped. Then she fell.

She screamed his name, pummeled by waves, the explosion so powerful she'd never recover. He held her tight, his body jerking as he found his own release.

Then he stopped moving. Still inside her, with the aftermath of the pounding still echoing in the silence, he placed a searing kiss between her shoulder blades.

He released her hair, and her head dropped forward. Breath panted out from her lungs, and her mind blanked. Sleep half claimed her, right then and there. Deacan pulled out and turned her around.

She flopped onto her back, her body beyond exhaustion. Everything inside her quieted almost to the point of numbness. Yep. She was going to be sore the next morning.

He smoothed the hair off her forehead and traced a path between her breasts to her still-vibrating core, his broad hand hot. "Say it," he murmured, his green gaze intent.

She frowned, trying to follow his words. "Hmm."

His hand flattened over her already sore mound, and her eyelids flew wide open to study him as a threat. "I said to say it, or we'll go for round two." The set of his jaw didn't allow for any misunderstanding.

She blinked, her body too satiated to find any outrage. "You're such a throwback. Highlander."

His chin lifted. "Aye. Now, Nora."

Sleep tried once again to entice her, and she wanted to fall into it. "Fine." She yawned. "You win. I'm yours. Do with me what you will . . . after I sleep."

In the early dawn light, his face changed. Not in an obvious way, and not in a way she would've noticed had she not been watching. What she saw there was absolute and carved in stone as ancient as those around his homeland. "Again, Nora. Without the yawn, in this moment and in this place. Ye will say it."

Her mind cleared to razor-sharp focus, the feeling unpleasant after her dreamy state. Her body felt well taken and overcome, and her heart beat in tune with his. On some level, a purely feminine one that had nothing to do with logic or reason, she felt his call. His demand. She also knew, after she'd pushed him, after what they'd just shared, he wouldn't allow her to evade or diminish the moment. He wouldn't let her deny what had passed between them, whether she liked it or not. Whether she fully understood it or not. "Fine, but it goes both ways. If I'm yours, you're all mine." It was as close as she could come to finding some balance.

"True. One more time. No qualification." The look on his face, determined and dark, stole her breath.

Nerves tingled across her abdomen at the possessive tone, and she had to take a deep breath before speaking. Sometimes words held meaning that changed lives, and he was demanding acknowledgment of something easier left unsaid. Knowing full well what he was doing, to be sure.

Yet she had to answer. "I'm yours." She gave him the only words that would satisfy him.

His chin lifted and for several long, quiet moments, he studied her. "You are mine. And you won't be forgetting it again." He lay next to her and rolled her into his embrace, covering them with a blanket.

Warmth seduced her, but something, a flare of awareness, opened her eyes. His hard body all but enclosed her. "I never really knew you, did I?" she murmured.

His breath brushed her hair. "You knew half of me."

She sighed and closed her eyes. "Now I know all."

"Aye, you do. God help you, Nora." His hold tightened. "Now you *have* all of me."

Chapter Eleven

After only two hours of sleep with Nora in his arms, Deke jerked his truck to a stop in a small driveway just as a local squad car screeched to a halt behind him. "Stay here," he muttered to her, halting her reach for the door handle. When the call had come in, he hadn't had time to get her to safety, and he sure as shit wasn't leaving her at his apartment, alarm system or not.

She nodded, her face pale, her eyes wide. "The newest nanoparticle results will be available in about two hours, maybe three. I need to be there to see if the charges reversed when the particles found the bacteria. I've been working with zinc oxide nanoparticles, since Lynne thought zinc affected Scorpius somehow."

He had no clue what charges she was talking about. "I'll make sure you're back by then." He jumped from the truck and squinted in the sun before giving a short nod to a gnarled Metro Police deputy. "The FBI has secured the scene. Keep the neighbors back."

The cop rested his hand on his hip, his bushy eyebrows rising toward Nora.

"Keep an eye on her. She doesn't come near the house." Waiting for a grim nod, Deke stalked toward the front door and knocked, leather gloves covering his hands and making them sweat. An FBI agent in full black suit opened the door. "What?"

Deke flashed his badge, the serious one nobody fucked with.

The agent's eyes widened, and he stepped back. "All righty. Want to tell me why I was called down to secure an attempted rape scene?"

Deke sighed. "No. Go outside and wait for the CDC."

The guy pivoted and took off, mumbling something sounding suspiciously like *dickhead*.

A trilling ambulance siren blasted through the day, and Deke glanced back toward the cop, who waited far away. "Don't let them come in unless the CDC is with them and geared up." Deke had called the CDC workers at the hospital the second he'd gotten the report of the assault.

"Yep," the cop said, hand on his holster.

Deke walked around the vestibule to a quaint living room where a young woman sported a nasty black eye and split lip.

Anger and lingering fear darkened her pretty blue eyes. "Who are you?" she asked.

"Hi, Mandy. My name is Deke McDougall, and I'm with the police." He remained on the other side of the room to keep from spooking her, having no problem lying about his affiliation. "An ambulance is coming, and they're going to take you to the hospital."

She shook her head. "I'm fine. Fought the prick off."

Deke nodded. "I know, and good job, by the way. You sure it was Zach Barter?"

"Yes." She fingered the crack in her bottom lip and winced. "We went to undergrad together and have kept in touch. When he got into D.C. last week, he gave me a call, and I hoped we'd get a chance to meet up." She flushed. "He's cute, you know?" Red stained her cheeks.

Deke lowered his voice. "This wasn't your fault, and don't think for a second that it was. Tell me what happened."

She patted the couch next to her. "I'm not scared. You can come sit down."

He sighed. "Honey, I'm going to tell you something, and I don't want you to get too worried. Okay?"

She blinked and her movements halted. "That doesn't sound good."

"It's not. There's a possibility Zach is infected with some sort of bacterial pathogen." Deke tried for reassurance, but as the ambulance pulled into the driveway, panic crossed the girl's face. "Stay calm. Trust me."

She pressed a hand to her chest.

"You're probably just fine." Deke ignored the ruckus behind him. "But we need to make sure, you know?"

She gulped, and tears filled her eyes. "Okay."

Deke nodded. "Tell me what happened."

She glanced beyond him and then focused back. "Zach called, and I invited him to dinner. When he got here, he came in, and almost immediately, he grabbed me and kissed me."

Fuck it all. Deke nodded. "Then?"

"He tried to rip off my shirt, and I panicked. Starting fighting back. Hit him in the nose." A tear fell down her cheek.

"Good job." Deke glanced over his shoulder to see two workers from the CDC donning protective gear outside on the lawn. "Did he bleed?" Deke asked.

"Yes. We fought some more, and then he ran out." Mandy shrugged. "I don't understand."

Neither did Deke, but it seemed that Zach had tried to infect the girl. He moved to the side. "Thank you. I know this is difficult. I'm going to let the CDC take over, and they'll get you to the hospital just to run some routine tests. As soon as I can get in to see you, I will."

Fear all but cascaded from her, but she lifted her chin. "How bad is this?"

He shook his head. "I'm sure it's fine, but we need to double-check. Do you have any idea where Zach would've gone?"

She rubbed her eye. "No. Sorry."

He forced a smile, hoping it held some reassurance. His gut was brewing, and he didn't like it one bit. "Be strong, sweetheart. Don't worry. Everything will be fine." He moved out of the way and walked outside as the CDC workers, looking like something from a science fiction movie, approached the house.

The first one, a short black guy, stopped near him with a plastic bag. "Did you touch anything?"

"I just knocked on the door." Deke slid off the gloves to deposit in the bag. "She's hurt and she's scared. Be easy with her."

The guy nodded. "Not my first rodeo, pal."

Deke paused and then moved toward the cop. "Keep the onlookers away from the scene. More FBI should be arriving soon."

The officer returned to his squad car with an uneasy glance at the CDC guys before turning around. "We've been canvassing per FBI instructions with the picture of the suspect. Two restaurants blocks over said he'd been in earlier."

Deke frowned. Jesus. "Did they mention any weird behavior?"

"Not really. Just said the guy ate from the salad bar."

"Fuck. Call them back and shut them down. Then call the CDC and have them go test the restaurants, especially salad dressing or anything he could've contaminated." Deke paused at his door.

The deputy winced. "You think he spit in the salad dressing?"

"Hell if I know." Deke sighed and jumped into his truck. Apparently the cop had figured out there was a contagion on the loose. Of course, with the CDC stomping around in full suits, it wasn't a huge leap.

"Well?" Nora asked, her arms crossed.

He glanced at her, not liking the pallor of her usually tan skin. They had things to discuss, and now wasn't the time. "Zach attacked her, but she's okay. I mean, depending on whether he was able to infect her or not."

Nora shook her head. "It's like he wanted to infect her."

"Yes, and it's interesting he sought out somebody he already knew." For whatever reason, Zach was fixated on Nora. "He'll come for you again."

She nodded. "Let him come."

Now that was Deke's badass woman. "Right. For now, I have to go coordinate a manhunt. You want to stay with me or go back to the CDC labs?"

She swallowed. "CDC labs. I want to check on Lynne and see if I can do anything."

That's what Deke had figured. "We will have a serious chat, and soon."

She cut him a look. "Uh-huh."

He ignited the engine just as his radio beeped.

"McDougall," the FBI dispatcher called.

"Yes," he answered.

"We have a report of a rape over on Miller Street, three blocks from your current location. Student from the college was knocked out and just woke up to call nine-one-one," the dispatch said, her voice crisp.

A rock hit Deke's gut. "I'm on my way. Did she mention a suspect?"

"No. Just said it was a blond guy who looked like a movie star from the fifties."

Shit. Zach Barter.

After dropping by the lab to discover the experiments were still running, Nora was frisked by a Secret Service agent and then escorted through another hallway to find Lynne. A man stood outside a plastic bubble, his gaze on Lynne, lying inside the bubble and all alone. The last round of tests had been conducted, and the CDC health workers had gone to decontaminate and find some answers.

The extra security made sense, but Secret Service?

Lynne sat up in her hospital bed, pale and wan, her chest glowing a bright blue. "Nora, meet Bret Atherton."

Nora stood up straighter. Aha. The man now second in line to the presidency. "Mr. Speaker."

Bret Atherton half turned, deep blue eyes twinkling. "Bret."

"Okay." Tight and trim, he stood to about six-two with thick blond hair and worried eyes. Even with tension cutting lines into the sides of his mouth, charisma flowed from him. She had the oddest urge to study pheromones. "What's the news?" she asked.

"None of it good," he said, turning back to face Lynne. "The country is in unrest, and as soon as the truth gets out, the stock market will plummet. We have foreign enemies gearing up to make attacks because they think we're weak, and they don't even know the details about Scorpius yet, although their spies have been pretty effective." He sighed. "Although at the moment, I'm more worried about Sweetcakes."

Nora blinked. Once and then again. "Sweetcakes?"

He grinned. "She hates that."

Yes, Lynne would hate being called that. Nora eyed her friend. "If you two need a moment, I can come back."

"No," Bret said. "I have to get back to work and figure out if we should make an announcement to the American public yet or not. The White House is against it at this point." His gaze darkened as he studied Lynne. "If you need anything, you call me. I mean it."

Lynne nodded. "I'll talk to you later."

Bret turned and nodded at Nora. "It was nice to meet you, Dr. Medina."

"You too," Nora said. "For the record, I think it's time to announce."

He nodded. "Me too."

She waited until he and his guards had cleared the door and had time to walk down the hallway. "What the fuck is with the blue?" she asked through a speaker set into the wall, at a loss for any other words.

Lynne nodded and glanced down. "I know, right?" Her voice emerged weak, and the monitor to her left recorded a slowed heart rate. "The altered bacteria and experimental antibiotic did something freaky weird to me."

Nora tried to smile. "I don't think 'freaky weird' sounds very scientific."

Lynne sighed and leaned back against the pillows. Sweat dotted her brow from the high fever. "It's all we've got. So far, the tests show a ramped-up bacteria that's attacking my cells. If it keeps going like this, I'll be in a coma within a day or so."

Tears pricked the back of Nora's eyes, but she kept her voice calm. "You'll be fine. We'll figure this out." Guilt threatened to swamp her. "I'm so sorry, Lynne."

Lynne glanced her way and rolled her eyes. "Knock that shit off," she said. "Seriously. Your shy assistant, Zach? Who would've thought it?"

Nora half chuckled. "Not me." The idea was too crazy to believe. "Anyway, I'm sorry."

Lynne glanced down at her chest, glowing a bright blue under the hospital gown. "I should've destroyed the green strain the second I saw its power. I thought maybe we could use it to contain the illness somehow."

"I was there," Nora said softly.

Lynne shut her eyes. "I know. Any news on poor Zach?"

Nora bit her lip, her chest aching. "Four attacks that we know of right now." Two rapes and the other two assaults, both with an exchange of bodily fluids. The lunatic was trying to infect people. The idea that the man she'd known and trusted for months was capable of rape nauseated her. Deke, the Metro Police, and the FBI were dropping a net on D.C. in the hopes of catching him. If he got out, somehow made it to another city, things could get bad. Really bad.

Lynne opened her bloodshot eyes. "Let's hope they find him soon." She rubbed her lips with a pale hand.

Nora nodded. "They will. So Bret came to see you."

"Yes." Lynne coughed. "He's under a lot of pressure. Don't tell anybody, but the vice president is fighting heart problems."

Wow. So the guy could actually be named president. "Do you love him?" Nora asked. If she could keep Lynne thinking happy thoughts, that wouldn't hurt.

Lynne shrugged. "I don't know. Sometimes I think so, and then sometimes he turns into a narcissistic asshat."

"Isn't that the very definition of a politician?" Nora asked. Heck. "Doesn't a person have to be a narcissist to want to be the president?"

Lynne snorted and rubbed her eyes. "Probably."

The woman needed to rest. Nora forced a smile. "Why don't you get some sleep, and if I hear anything, I'll let you know?"

Lynne snuggled back against the pillows, and her eyelids lowered to half-mast. "First, talk to me about anything but Scorpius or my love life. Let's talk about *your* love life. Tell me about your Scot and if you're going to screw it up again."

The mention of Deke seared heat through Nora's abdomen. She needed to get back to the lab, but whether she wanted to admit it or not, her friend was running out of time, and this might be the last time they talked. The thought made her chest hurt. So she dropped into a chair. "I'm out of my depth."

"Good." Lynne grimaced and readjusted her blankets. "You love him?"

Nora frowned. "We just started dating again."

"So the hell what?" Lynne whispered, her voice cracking. "I'm beginning to see how short life is. You've loved that man since you were sixteen. Why the hell are you waffling?"

Because she hadn't really known him. After the previous night, she'd caught a glimpse of the dangerous being she'd always suspected of living inside Deacan McDougall. "He's too much, you know?" she said softly. "It's like he was born in the wrong time."

Lynne's eyes glazed. "Maybe he was born in exactly the right time." Her voice dropped to almost dreamy, almost trance-like. "If not this illness, then the next one. Or the one after that." Her eyes fluttered closed.

Nora stood and approached the plastic, a chill trickling down her spine. "What do you mean?"

Lynne sighed. "At some point, human beings are done. You know that. Just waiting for the right pandemic."

Nora gulped down fear. Sure, as a scientist, she knew the human race was due for a natural disaster, be it illness, comet strike, or nuclear bomb. But as a human with hope, she clung to faith that she'd survive it. "What's your point, Lynnie?"

Lynne's eyelids fluttered open. "We've forgotten that living and surviving are two different things. They require different skills." She shut her eyes again and curled onto her side. Her voice, slight and whispery, continued. "Your Scot, dark as he may be, is a survivor. Don't let go of him." She fell into sleep.

Nora's shoulders trembled, and she clasped her hands together. It was just the fever. Lynne had been talking nonsense from the fever. Yet no matter how hard she tried, how hard she rubbed her arms, Nora couldn't ban the chill of truth.

At some point, human beings are done.

Chapter Twelve

Week 3
2,017 people dead
Likelihood of Scorpius Containment: Poor

> *Only the dead have seen the end of war.*
> —PLATO

After four full days of hunting Zach Barter, Deke was ready to kill somebody. He strode inside his temporary office at the CDC and tossed his phone across the desk. Fuck it all to hell. He'd stalked Barter through three states, only to come up empty in Virginia. The bastard was smart . . . and raping his way across the East.

When he wasn't attacking women, he was spitting in restaurant salad dressings.

The determination to infect people might be part of the illness, but Deke didn't give a shit.

Barter needed to be taken out, and now.

Infections were springing up in hospitals throughout the East, and soon the CDC would have no choice but to make an announcement. Hell on earth was about to break out, and although the government currently had a blanket over all news, at some point the truth would get out. Hell, the bloggers were already announcing a new pandemic.

Sure, he might be overreacting. But his gut had never failed him, and he didn't figure it was off target right now, either.

A shadow at his door caught his attention, and he half turned. "Mr. Speaker."

Bret Atherton strode inside while two agents covered the door. "I was just saying good-bye to Lynne. They fly her out in an hour."

Deke nodded and gestured toward a chair before crossing to a file cabinet and fetching bourbon and two glasses to pour generously. "I spoke to Lynne an hour ago. She's strong and stubborn." He'd met the Speaker a few times throughout the last couple of years, and the guy seemed all right. "The hospital in Maryland is better equipped to care for her, and it's a short jaunt there for you."

"I know." Bret took a chair and accepted a drink. "I just like her closer to me so I can control everything."

Deke laughed. "That sounds so wrong."

Bret lifted his gaze and smirked. "Yet you know exactly what I mean."

"Aye." Deke grinned because the guy was right. Deke had no intention of allowing Nora out of town until he captured Zach Barter. Guards were now posted throughout the laboratory section of the temporary CDC building. "How's the president's daughter? I haven't had an update since I got back into town."

"Same." Bret took a deep drink of the potent liquid. "As the doctors have described it to me, the bacteria attacked her brain and stripped away her humanity."

"We'll find a cure," Deke said.

"Maybe. Lynne's brain scans are good, though." Bret sighed.

"Although the scientists couldn't see anything abnormal in Zach Barter's scans."

"Maybe the scans aren't a good way to determine anything," Deke said.

"They're not." Bret shook his head. "Apparently not all brains show a change. Or rather, we don't have pre-Scorpius scans to study in order to see if there's a change. Brains differ. Even the brains of psychopaths vary. Some have abnormalities. Some don't."

Deke swirled the amber-colored drink in his glass. "Well, I'm hopeful for Lynne. What's the latest on the infection?"

"At least two thousand are dead and ten times that have been infected. Maybe more. The infection is being spread by Zach and maybe others who've survived the fever." Bret coughed. "I've convinced the White House we need to go public."

"Good." Deke studied one of the smartest men on the Hill. "Do you think we can still contain the illness?" he asked.

"No."

Deke's stomach rioted. "Me either." The noises from outside grew louder. "Sounds like they're about to take Lynne."

Bret nodded and stood. "I already said good-bye, and I can't go through it again. Call with any updates." He set down the glass. "We need to secure a copy of the stronger Scorpius strain, the green one that infected Lynne, and send it to the lab up north. Just in case."

Deke nodded. "I know." Boy, would Nora be pissed. For now, he had to make good on a promise. He'd talked to Lynne earlier, and she'd asked him for a favor. One he'd grant without question.

If Nora agreed.

Exhaustion weighed down Nora's limbs and made it difficult to hold back tears. The last several nights, she'd slept alone, when she'd slept, as Deke tried to find Zach. She'd missed him far more than was healthy.

To think on a normal week it'd be her turn to host bunko, and she'd be worrying about what salad to make. But she steeled her shoulders and spoke softly into the speaker set in the wall, her gaze on her friend in the plastic room. "You'll be okay, Lynnie. The hospital in Maryland is prepared for you, and I'll be along as soon as I can."

Even pale and gasping for breath, Lynne Harmony rolled bloodshot eyes. She lay in the hospital bed, not moving, the pallor of her skin lighter than the white blanket covering her rapidly diminishing form. She now needed oxygen to breathe, and the strong antibiotics being pumped into her veins were doing more damage than good. "They're gonna move me in a minute, and I need a favor from you first."

"Anything." Nora slid closer to the plastic. "You're my best friend." *And you're dying.* Bret had fought tears when he'd left earlier. "I'll do anything for you."

Lynne's lips trembled in a parody of a smile. "Call it a deathbed wish, if you like."

"You're not going to die," Nora snapped out. "Fight this, damn it."

Lynne's eyelids fluttered. "I will. Promise. For now, you said anything."

Nora nodded. "Yes."

With an obvious struggle, Lynne forced her eyelids open, and her green eyes focused. "I always thought we'd be at each other's weddings. You know, ugly bridesmaid dresses and all."

Nora frowned, her instincts humming. "Me too."

"Well, this is fucking ugly." Lynne glanced down at the hospital gown. "Fugly, if you will."

Nora tilted her head. "Lynnie—"

"No." Color suffused Lynne's face. "No silliness, no protest, no self-protection. I want this, and you promised." Her voice slurred on the end.

Nora shook her head. "Want what?"

"You. Safe and protected." Lynne gasped for air. "It's all I want."

Oh, man. The fever was taking her brilliant friend away. Nora nodded. "I'm safe, Lynne. I can protect myself."

Lynne snorted, the sound tinny over the line. "Bullshit. With what's coming, with disaster, you can't protect yourself. He's stronger than you. Meaner. A survivor." Her eyelids fluttered. The monitors beeped.

"Lynne!" Nora clapped her hands.

"What?" Lynne groused, opening her eyes again. "Oh yeah. Marry him so I can die in peace. I need to know you're protected."

Nora's head jerked back. Her stomach dropped. "Marry him?" Where had her friend's head gone? She was perfectly capable of protecting herself. Wasn't she?

"Yes." Lynne sighed.

The door opened, and Deke stalked in, his gun at his hip and a frown on his face. Behind him loped a gray-haired pastor in full robes.

Her heart jumped hard, and her abdomen warmed. Harsh lines cut into the sides of his mouth, and his green eyes held anger. But damn, it was good to see him. Then Lynne's words hit her. "Oh, hell no," Nora swore.

Amusement lightened Deke's green eyes to the color of a spring river. She gaped, not having seen the expression on him for nearly a month.

He nodded at Lynne. "I take it you made your deathbed request?"

Nora turned and punched him in the arm. Hard. "She's not on her deathbed."

Deke shot her a warning glance and rubbed his bicep, leaning over to speak in the mic. "I'm not sure about marrying this wild woman, Lynne. She just hit me."

Lynne coughed out air, and a tremor shook her body. The blue heart shone bright from beneath the covers. "You promised, McDougall."

"Aye, I did." He turned and looked down at Nora before grabbing her hands in his big ones. "Start the vows, Pastor."

Nora shook her head and tried to jerk free. Without success. "You set this up," she accused Deke.

"No," Lynne said weakly. "I talked to him this morning. Asked him. Please, Nora. I want to hear the words before I go."

Nora gaped, looking from Lynne to Deke. This couldn't be happening; the fever was seriously screwing with Lynne's brain. "This is crazy, Deacan," Nora whispered.

He lifted a massive shoulder. "I always figured on marrying you again, and why not make your friend happy? Give her some peace."

"Please," Lynne groaned.

On all that was holy. Fine. Bloody Deacan McDougall had no problem taking advantage of the situation, now did he? Nora could grant a deathbed wish, if the vows would give Lynne peace. Then she'd march her ass down to the courthouse and annul the damn thing. Nobody was going to force her into marriage. She showed her teeth to Deke, and his chin lifted.

Nora pushed out air. "If I marry him, you have to promise to live, Lynne. Promise me."

Lynne nodded. "It's a deal."

Nora glanced back at Deke. "Fine."

The pastor was fast and kept the vows simple. Within five minutes, Nora found herself married to Deacan once again. When he slipped on her wedding band, the same one from before, she gasped.

"You threw it at my head when you left," he said calmly.

"You kept it?" she whispered.

He looked down through heavy-lidded eyes. "Aye. Figured I'd put it back in place at some point."

Lynne smiled at the end, her eyelids closing. "You all come visit me in Maryland for your honeymoon," she whispered before falling asleep.

"You can kiss your bride," the pastor said.

Nora stilled and opened her mouth. Deke leaned down and grasped her shoulder, pulling her into him. His mouth covered hers, so much power in the move that she rose to her tiptoes out of instinct. He kissed her hard enough her head fell back, and she had to grab his rigid biceps to keep her balance. His tongue swept inside her mouth with masculine insistence, staking his claim, and desire spiraled through her flesh to her blood. Maybe deeper.

Finally, he released her.

She blinked, her body rioting. With a gasp, she released his arms.

He took her hand and led her from the room and down the corridor. She tripped beside him, trying to control herself. Finally, he paused.

She freed her hand from his. "I can't believe you went along with that," she hissed.

He rubbed her arm, his expression unreadable. "Your friend is worried about the future and wants you safe. I want you to be mine again. The timing worked."

Nora drew away, facing him fully, needing to lift her head to keep his gaze. Man, he was tall—and big. Sometimes she forgot about his sheer size. "I'm not staying married to you."

His eyes darkened, and his face hardened in a way she hadn't seen before. "Aye, you are." He leaned in, bringing the scent of male with him. "You run this time, Nora, and I swear to all the Scottish gods watching over me, I'll come after you."

Chapter Thirteen

That evening, after a frustrating day in the lab, Nora waited in what was now her office, trying not to cry. The CDC had taken Lynne away, and her chances weren't good. But she'd sure made things interesting before leaving, now hadn't she? Leave it to Lynne, the world's most dignified romantic, to arrange Nora's love life before leaving.

Married. Lingering rays of moonlight slanted through the partially drawn shades, catching Nora's simple platinum band. She was once again married to Deacan McDougall. Before, she'd been able to somewhat handle the boy. Now he was all man. Could anybody handle him? Even though it had only been four hours, she felt different.

The way he'd looked at her, the way he'd touched her after the ceremony . . . had been different.

Purposeful. Protective. Possessive.

The part of him he'd always contained seemed present now. Out free and wild.

Judging from the kiss he'd given her, he didn't have any intention of subduing himself. The guy she'd glimpsed during her first week in D.C., the cheerful strategist whose biggest concern was creating battle plans for faraway places, was gone. Instinct told her the existence of that Deke had been fleeting, anyway. A man's true nature couldn't be contained, and she knew now, more than ever, that Deacan would never be restrained.

Even if the CDC contained the spreading infection, even if life continued on as it was, Deacan wouldn't remain a mere advisor.

That much she knew.

What he'd do, she wasn't sure. But he was a fighter, a warrior, and those characteristics lived in his very blood. She'd known it years ago, and she'd run.

Was she strong enough to stay this time?

A shadow crossed her vision, and Deacan filled the doorway. Solid, strong, and steady. "The FBI has a new lead on Zach Barter in Texas."

She swallowed. "I see."

He reached out a hand. "Let's go home. We need to talk."

They needed to talk? Seriously? Steam nearly boiled from her ears, and she shot to her feet. "That's the understatement of the year."

"I know." He waited, ever patient, until she'd crossed the room to take his hand. "While I've been finishing up with the FBI, have you been in here plotting my death, planning your escape, or accepting your current situation?"

"If I were plotting your death, McDougall, you'd be dead." Head held high, she began to sweep past him.

And forgot he had her hand.

She jerked to a stop and let out a low snarl.

He fell into step beside her. "I say this time around, any time we wanna fight, we do it naked."

She snorted. Though she'd never admit it out loud, if they fought naked, she'd lose. "Sounds like a good way for you to be seriously damaged, McDougall."

He paused. "Good point."

She laughed, catching herself off guard with the sound. When was the last time she'd laughed? She pondered the question as they climbed into his truck and drove the block to the apartment building. In the parking lot, she paused to look at him. "We both know you're done creating strategy. What's next for you?"

He blinked and stepped out of the truck, crossing to open her door. With a gentleness only a big man could show, he helped her from the vehicle. "You and I will make a decision as to our future. Afterward." His hand at the small of her back felt both familiar and new as he propelled her toward the door. At the entrance, he swept her up.

She yelped and grabbed his chest. "What are you doing?"

He grinned and carried her through the entryway and up the flights of stairs to his apartment door. "Figured we'd do it right."

Her heart hummed in her chest as he crossed his threshold and finally set her down inside. "You said we'd discuss your career *afterward*? After what?"

He kicked shut the door. "After we consummate the marriage. We wouldn't want an easy out, now would we?"

The breath caught in her throat, and she took a step back. "Ah—"

"Ah, what?" he asked, crossing his arms.

She blinked, desire weakening her knees. He wanted to *consummate*. Her nipples hardened instantly. Man. She had it bad. "We should talk now."

He stared down at her, not blinking, obviously contemplating. Heartbeats later, only a twitch of his jaw showed he'd reached a decision. "Nope." Faster than a man his size should be able to move, he ducked, and she found herself over his shoulder. Air blew through her hair when he stood, and the blood rushed to her head.

She smacked him as hard as she could on the ass.

His smack beat hers, hands down. Pain rippled through her butt, followed by instant heat. "Damn it, Deke," she muttered. She caught a glimpse of the sofa, a doorway, and then a bed before he flipped her back over in the bathroom. He used one hand to steady her shoulder and the other to reach in and turn the shower knob.

She tried to clear her mind. "You want to consummate in the shower?"

"Aye." He tugged her shirt over her head along with her bra. "We've been at the CDC all day, and I want warmth and woman. I can get both in the shower." He unbuckled her jeans and shoved her clothes down her legs.

Her mind spinning, she kicked out of the jeans and her sneakers, leaving her completely nude. She swallowed.

He lifted an eyebrow in a silent command.

Oh. Well, okay then. Her hands trembled as she unhooked his belt and jeans to push them down his legs, revealing a fully erect cock. Her body sizzled with hunger at the sight. He helped her by toeing off his boots and kicking everything across the room. "Shirt," he said.

She thought about defying him, but then she'd be without the sight of his impressive chest. He had to duck to help her, but soon he stood nude.

A soft sigh breathed out of her. He was strong and scarred, with hard ridges of muscle down his arms and across his chest. She flattened her hand over his heart. "You're beautiful," she whispered.

He grasped her and kissed her in a combined move of strength and gentleness. Lifting her, he walked into the shower, setting her shoulders against the dark tile, protecting her from the spray with his body. Holding her aloft, he leaned back. "I wanna be married to you again, Nora. Truth be told, I've never felt without you."

Such sweetness from such a dangerous man ambushed her every time. She ran her hands through his wet hair. Life had changed, and things were going to get worse. One or both of them could be gone in a week if the bacteria continued to spread. She couldn't hold back any longer. "I've missed you."

His eyes darkened, and he pressed between her legs, slowly pushing all the way inside. The second he filled her, it felt like coming home. Finally. She swallowed and leaned forward to drop a kiss above his heart, her entire body vibrating.

His chest hitched, and his fingers tangled through her hair, drawing her head to the side. "You're willing to give us another chance? A real one?" he asked.

She looked into his eyes, absorbing the different colors of green, noting the question in them. Had she ever felt separated from him? Really? Probably not, and life was too short to miss out on Deacan. He was difficult and deadly, but he was hers. "Yes," she breathed.

At her acquiescence, a lump of pain he'd become accustomed to having in his gut disappeared. Gone for good.

Her pretty brown eyes sparkled, and a light flush covered her high cheekbones.

Deke gripped her harder, sheathed to the root, feeling as close to heaven as he'd ever get. "I won't let you down," he said softly, leaning over to brush his mouth across hers. Soft as petals, her lips opened under his, taking him. This petite woman had owned his heart since he was sixteen years old and a newcomer to her country, and she'd never given it back.

He pulled out and gently worked his way back inside her. Where he belonged.

She gasped, and her thighs trembled around his hips. He grinned and leaned down to suck one pink nipple into his mouth. Her curves had filled out in the years they'd been apart, but during the last few weeks, she'd lost weight from stress. As her husband, he'd do a much better job of taking care of her this time.

Steam rose around them in a cocoon of intimacy.

He licked down her shoulder and over her breasts again. The second he scraped a nipple, she rippled around his dick.

His groan mingled with hers. She clasped him tighter with her legs, and he slid out and then back in. Harder this time.

Sharp nails scraped his chest, and sparks lit his balls.

There were so many things he needed to say to her, so many decisions to be made. But at the heart of it all was right now. He wanted the night, and he needed to make her his. For good this time, no matter what the future held. They'd been married, and while he'd aroused her by promising a consummation, the primal male deep inside him wanted that union. Proof that they were man and wife.

Her eyelids fluttered closed, and her head rested back on the tile. "Deacan," she moaned.

The sound torpedoed right to his heart, blowing it wide open. For her. He thrust harder, holding her up, tilting her pelvis to take more of him. He'd tried. God, he'd tried to be somebody else. To have a quiet life and be a quiet man.

That was over, and he figured they both knew it. Even so, the words would come later.

Now he fully intended to claim her and go deep enough she'd never be free of him.

Electricity burned down his spine. He released her hair to flatten a hand against the tile by her head, hammering inside her, his mind blanking. Only here and now mattered. Only this woman forever.

Little ripples cascaded inside her, milking him. He pounded faster, and her body arched against his. She opened her mouth and cried out his name, vibrations moving through her to grab his cock and hold on tight.

He shoved hard, holding her to him, and exploded.

Chapter Fourteen

Morning light filled the office at the CDC, and Nora readjusted her weight on the chair and bit back a wince. The previous night had been wild, and they'd certainly consummated their marriage.

Three times. Enough that the soreness extended to places inside her she hadn't realized could become sore.

Yet they hadn't talked. The night had overcome them, and they'd run with it, finally succumbing to sleep. Deke had been called to the office early in the morning to update the White House, and he'd dropped her off at the CDC labs, which were nearly in lockdown.

Experts milled around the building, ranging from CDC health workers to FBI agents to MPD. The CDC was about to hold a press conference and announce the truth, finally.

At the moment, as they tried to contain the infection, the world seemed to be holding its breath.

Whether it knew it or not.

She glanced at the newest printout on her desk. Several of Zach's local victims, including the first one, Mandy, had died from Scorpius. Her shoulders slumped.

Nora's phone buzzed, and she picked it up. "Yes?"

"Nora? It's Bobbi."

Nora sighed. She'd taken over for Lynne as the head of infectious diseases and had left Bobbi in the lab cataloging results. "Hi, Bobbi. Have you finished with the new samples?" The test results from the previous week were dismal, so she'd kept systematically trying different methods and different materials for the nanoparticles. They'd also tried using several different catalysts to get antibiotics through Scorpius's protein shell, and the results should be ready soon.

"Um, yeah, but well, we have a problem."

Nora lifted her head. "Define *problem*."

"Two vials of altered Scorpius, the new green strain, are gone. No record, no transfer . . . nothing."

Nora's breath caught. "I'll be right there." She hung up.

Deke poked his head in, his gaze roaming her head to toe as if taking inventory. A feminine part of her bristled, and she lifted her chin. He grinned with no small amount of masculine smugness. "You're looking a bit worse for wear, darlin'."

The endearment, normally used with a nice Southern drawl, came out as *dorilin* in his deep brogue. She lowered her chin as her mind spun. As she tried to deny reality. "No more so than you."

"True." Someone called his name from down the hall, and he turned and gave a jerk of his head before focusing back on her. "Just got word the FBI is tracking Zach Barter back this way. There are guards posted by the labs and at the end of this hallway. You don't move without me by your side. Got it?"

Fear sizzled along her skin, yet she kept her composure and lifted an eyebrow. "Did you take Scorpius samples from the lab?"

He stilled. Then his head lifted, and his green gaze lasered right in on her. The atmosphere in the small room was charged. "No."

She stood and planted both hands on the desk. "Do you know who did?"

"Aye." His eyelids dropped to half-mast in a curiously dangerous look.

"Damn it all to hell, Deacan," she exploded. "Scorpius is not a weapon."

He drew in air through his nose. "It could be if used against us."

She pinched the bridge of her nose between two fingers and fought the urge to punch him in the face. "I won't be part of creating a weapon we might use against other human beings. No matter what happens."

"We need a secondary location to keep Scorpius, just in case something happens to this one," Deke said levelly. "Nobody is asking you to be part of weaponizing anything. Your job is to find a cure, so I suggest you do it."

Her chin lifted. "What's your job?"

"To protect and defend by any means necessary." He lifted a shoulder. "It's who I am, and I'm not garna change. What we have, you and me, it's good. Maybe we don't agree on much, but we agree on each other. We shouldn't have given up so easily last time." He glanced down at his vibrating phone. "I have to go. We'll discuss us later. Don't leave the building, *wife*." Without another word, he turned and disappeared down the corridor.

Her temper exploded inside her head with enough force to rattle her teeth. How could he?

The phone on her desk buzzed, and she snatched it up. "What?"

A pause came across the line for a moment. "Um, Dr. Medina?"

Nora took a deep breath and tried to keep from throwing something. She and Deke were going head to head at the nearest opportunity. "I'm sorry, Bobbi. What's going on?"

"Well, I, I'm not sure what to do. I tried to call Lynne because I heard she still wanted to be informed of major developments, but she's out of range, and maybe not even conscious, and I, just—"

"It's okay." Nora lowered her voice to soothing. "I'm covering for Lynne, and I can help. What's going on?"

"I found the missing samples," Bobbi whispered, her voice muffled.

Nora's head jerked up. "Where?"

"By Loading Dock C. After I saw they were gone, I figured I should do something since Lynne wasn't here, so I went to talk to Geo Flanks in the security room? The cute one with the beard?"

"Bobbi—to the point, please." Nora skirted the desk and headed into the hallway. Where was Loading Dock C? Somewhere south, right?

"Well, he let me watch the security cameras and recordings, and I saw the vials being removed. The cooler containing them is in C right now. Just waiting." Bobbie cleared her throat. "What should I do?"

Nora sped up, smiling at people she passed. "Nothing. Do nothing right now—I'm on my way." She sucked in air. "Who took the vials?" *Please, don't let it be Deke.*

Bobbi sniffed. "Don't get mad, but it was the sexy-as-hell Scot. Your man."

Nora doubled over as if punched in the gut. If he thought she wasn't smart enough to stop him, to stop the government, he didn't know her at all. "Hold tight. I'll be right there." She tried to remember the map she'd been given earlier so she could maneuver around the CDC and find the vending machines. They probably hadn't figured she'd use it in order to avoid the guards.

While her memory wasn't as good as Zach's, it was darn close. Nora avoided the guard points, took several more hallways, found the stairs, went down, took several more hallways, and finally ended up at Loading Dock C. Quiet and boring. She shoved open the double doors to a quiet warehouse-like room.

Dust filled her nose and trickled like a warning across her skin.

Bobbi slowly came out from behind a box of masks. Her blue eyes sparkled and her color was heightened. "Dr. Medina. Or is it Dr. McDougall now?"

Nora swallowed and glanced around the deserted area. A chill swept through her. Something was definitely wrong. She casually reached for her phone. "McDougall." Awareness spiraled through her stomach, and she edged away from the girl. "What's going on?"

The assistant smoothed down a yellow T-shirt. "I needed to see you."

Nora peered closer. Something was definitely off. Had Bobbi been infected? "How are you feeling?"

"Better." Bobbi rubbed her pointed chin. "The Scorpius bacteria is a bitch to get over. I was so sick."

Heated air burst from Nora's lungs. "You were infected?"

"Yes. Zach came over the night before he left town, and we, ah—" She blushed and swayed.

Oh shit. "Did he rape you?"

"No. Well, not really. I mean, I fought him, but after the fever, I see that it was love." Bobbi tilted her head to the side. "I was sick for twenty-four hours—thought I was going to die." She frowned. "I kept in touch with Lynne, saying I was searching for Zach, but I didn't die, and now Zach and I can be together. I mean, once you're out of the picture." She drew a pointy gun from the back of her waist. "There are a couple of ways this can happen. I can shoot you, but Zach would be pissed. Or I could bite you, but Zach . . . would be pissed." She sighed. "He wants to bite you himself."

Nora glanced around for some sort of weapon. Going hand-to-hand with the girl was a bad idea, since the bacteria still lived in the saliva of a host, even one that had recovered from the infection. "Why does he want to infect me?"

Bobbi wrinkled a very pert nose. "He thinks those who survive the infection become immortal."

"And you don't?" Nora asked, peering closely.

"Nah. I feel stronger and maybe smarter, but I don't feel like a god." Bobbi jerked the gun toward the outside door. "There's a nice, quiet parking lot out there that nobody uses."

Nora eyed the weapon. If she rushed the girl, she'd get shot. "Why are you doing this?"

"I love him." Bobbi's aim wavered. "When you love somebody, you'll do anything to make them happy. Right?"

"No." Nora shook her head. There was an odd glint in Bobbi's eyes. Fever? Or possibly insanity. "So there weren't vials stolen?"

"Oh, we're missing two vials, that's for sure, but I have no idea who took them and don't really care." Bobbi shrugged and pointed the gun at Nora's chest. "I'd love to just shoot you."

Nora blinked and tried to remember the layout of the building. The exit let out at the side parking lot; there was a chance somebody would be out there. Not a great chance, considering the main parking area was on the other side of the building. If she let Bobbi take her outside, she'd be at a disadvantage. So she set her feet. "I don't think so. And if you try to bite me, I'll knock your ass out."

The girl's head jerked back. "Well, Zach figured you'd say that." She fired, and three red darts plugged Nora in the neck.

So, not bullets. Interesting. Nora's eyes fluttered shut, gravity took over, and the last thing she felt was the hard cement floor.

Deke finished meeting with the FBI profilers, and his temples pounded at the newest update. Zach Barter was probably back in town. Fair enough.

"We'll get him," FBI Director Siles said around a worn toothpick as they maneuvered down the hallway. "We knew he'd come back."

Deke nodded and headed toward Lynne's office. Well,

Nora's office now. She was probably still pissed at him, but they both had their ways of dealing with life, and they'd have to agree to disagree. He wasn't losing her again, damn it. "Aye." They'd known Zach would return for Nora, but Deke had thought he'd have a little more time to prepare. "Warn your men about Zach. There's no cure for the bite, and you can only hope to beat the fever."

So far, based on the newest data from Zach's reign of terror, most people lost the fight. The CDC had released information to the drug companies, and they were rushing to find a cure. Or vaccine. Or hopefully both. But with the foremost experts in the country still unsuccessful, their chances looked bleak.

Deke reached the office. Empty. He turned toward Siles. "Have you seen Nora?"

"Nope." Siles's phone rang, and he glanced at the face. "It's the vice president. No, I mean the newly appointed president. I bet your girl is either meeting with agents or is in the break room. Call me if you can't find her." He turned for the nearest exit.

Deke nodded, glancing down the bustling hallway. A month ago, he'd enjoyed the peacefulness of his job and slow days. Now he could barely find a spot to think. Where the hell had Nora gone? The back of his neck tickled, and he shoved down impatience. She was fine. Zach Barter couldn't have gotten into the building, considering his face was plastered everywhere, and Nora wouldn't have gone outside without protection, even if she was pissed about the missing vials.

Where the hell was she?

He scouted the building, going office to office, asking everybody if they'd seen her. All he got were shrugs and head shakes.

He sucked in a deep breath, everything inside him calming. Okay. She wouldn't have gone anywhere. So he needed to relax and just find her. Yet he couldn't help but hurry as he headed for the control room.

The men let him in and didn't question him as he ran through recordings of the last two hours. *Damn it.* He watched the meeting between Nora and Bobbi, and his gut clenched when Bobbi fired. Nora hit the ground, and then the aide had carried Nora outside with surprising ease. The camera outside captured them getting into a white SUV with a man driving. Probably Zach.

Bile rose from Deke's gut. If Zach had Nora, and if he'd bitten her, Deke was too late.

Chapter Fifteen

Nora's head rolled on her shoulders, and she caught herself in a snort. Her eyes opened.

Candlelight. Tons and tons of candles surrounded her.

She blinked and shook her head, trying to focus. Pain lanced along her wrists, and she glanced down. Rough rope bound her wrists to an old-fashioned wooden chair. A gasp escaped her at seeing the pale-pink, see-through teddy barely covering her. "What the hell?" she asked. The room was sparse with only a twin bed in the corner and her chair.

The door opened.

Her heart slammed into her gut. "Zach."

He smiled, the expression full of charm. "Nora. I've missed you." An odd glint filled his movie-star blue eyes, and somehow, his voice had deepened. "Did you miss me?"

Hell no. Her mouth tasted like sand. "Where am I?"

"Bobbi's aunt's house. She's quite the helpful girl," Zach said.

Bile tickled the base of Nora's throat. "Where's the aunt?"

"On a cruise."

"Why am I tied up?" She tried to keep her voice level.

He shrugged and shut the door behind him. "You've been playing hard to get, so I figured I'd just go ahead and catch you." His chuckle filled the room with a slightly manic sound. "Some women like these kind of games."

The blood rushed through her head. "Did you infect me?"

His eyebrows rose. "Not yet. I figured we'd do that the old-fashioned way." His perfectly coiffed blond head jerked to the bed.

"Why do you want to kill me?" she whispered.

He frowned. "You won't die. Sure, it's a rough few days, but you'll live through the fever. Then we'll be together forever."

She jerked against the restraints. "Most people catching the infection are dying, Zach. If you care about me at all, you won't want to kill me."

He licked his lips, his gaze dropping to her breasts. "You'll live."

A shudder wound through her. "Where's Bobbi?"

Zach shrugged. "She served her purpose."

Oh no. He hadn't killed the young scientist, had he? "You've gone mad."

He smiled again. "They do say that most genius is akin to madness, right? Trust me. You want this feeling." His tennis shoes made little sound as he crossed the room to kneel in front of her, his hands clasping her thighs. Calluses marred his palms and scratched her skin as he caressed up her legs.

Nausea kicked into her gut. She tried to push back, to kick him, but his hold was absolute.

He frowned. "Stop fighting me, or I'll bite you right now."

Her legs trembled. Fear bit like fire through her. What should she do? If she fought him, he would infect her. His fingers reached the edge of the pink panties. "Please, stop," she whispered.

He groaned and reached up to tug down the bodice. Cool air brushed across her nipples. Terror ricocheted through her arms, and she pulled harder against the ropes, shredding her skin.

"I've waited so long to taste you," he murmured.

She shook her head, trying to get away. "If that's so, why did you leave?" If she could get him to talk, maybe she could buy herself some time. Deke had to be looking for her by now.

Zach blew warm breath over her skin. "I had a job to do. Infecting all of those people took time, and it also kept the authorities busy."

"Zach, look at me." She had to get his focus off biting her, damn it. Her voice trembled as she asked, "Why did you infect all those people? I mean, why would you do that?"

He blinked, clearly perplexed. "To thin the herd. You really don't get it, do you?"

"No," she whispered.

He sat back. "This is new. I'm something new—in the chain of evolution." He glanced down at his arm. "Since I survived the infection, I'm stronger. Smarter even. It's time for the next species on earth—it's time for me. People who survive the illness are different. Surely you know that."

The tests were still coming in, but was it possible? Could it be that the infection actually allowed its host to use more of the brain than humans normally were able to access? "Then we should get you into a facility for testing, don't you think?" she asked, hoping to reach the scientist he used to be.

His gaze sharpened. "No. Why would I let lemmings study me? If the scientists survive, once we've gotten rid of lower beings, then I can be studied. No problem."

A tear rolled down her cheek while her brain fought to get through to him. "I'd like to study you. Please let me."

His lips spread in a pleased grin. "As soon as you prove you're worthy, we'll find a place to study each other. Now I've waited long enough to taste you. Stop trying to distract me." His gaze intent, he leaned toward her breasts.

"No!" She shoved back against the chair. His saliva was infected, but so long as she didn't have any cuts, she'd probably be all right. She kicked out again and nailed him in the ankle.

He growled and slapped her across the face. Hard. Agony bloomed along her cheekbone.

Her vision blurred, and her ears rang.

"Bitch. Now I bite." He bared his teeth and grabbed her neck, moving toward her breast.

She screamed.

The door burst open, and Deke barreled inside. He took one second to assess the situation and ran full bore for Zach, manacling him around the waist and lifting. Zach flew through the air to strike the wall and fall down. Hard.

Deke turned toward Nora just as Zach stood up and rushed him.

"Deacan!" she yelled.

Deke pivoted and kicked Zach in the chest, sending him sprawling again. Circling around, Deke kept his body between Nora and the threat. The image of her, pale and terrorized, half-naked in the chair, would haunt him forever.

Zach shoved to his feet and smiled, blood covering his teeth.

"Don't let him bite you," Nora said, her bare feet slapping uselessly against the floor.

Sirens trilled outside, while blue and red lights swirled through the partially closed blinds. "My backup is here," Deke said calmly. "Get onto your knees, and I won't have to shoot you." He drew his gun and pointed.

Zach smiled. "You won't shoot me. They need me alive."

"No. They *want* you alive. I'm okay with you dead." Deke kept his gun pointed levelly. If he shot, blood would spray. While he could probably block Nora's body with his own, he couldn't be absolutely sure no blood would get on her.

Zach spat blood toward him.

Nora cried out.

He turned his head to avoid the liquid touching his face.

The door opened, and the blonde ran inside, knife in her hand, heading for Nora.

Time slowed. Deke's focus narrowed. Drawing on training, drawing on history, he launched himself into action. Spinning, he kicked Bobbi full in the jaw, throwing her back into the door. Her head hit with a sickening thud, and she dropped hard, eyes closed. Without missing a beat, he turned just as Zach leaped for him.

Deke clasped the man in a bear hug, pivoted, and slammed him face-first onto the floor. Blood arced over Deke's hands and flew in every direction, along the floor, spattering Nora's feet. Zach slumped into limp unconsciousness.

His hands slipped, but Deke clicked handcuffs into place. He jumped to his feet. "Any cuts on your feet?"

She shook her head, tears washing down her face. "Have to get clean. Have to get you clean. Cuts on your hands?"

He glanced down at his shaking hands, covered with blood. "I don't think so."

FBI agents burst inside, guns out.

"Cut her free," Deke said, yanking off his shirt and kicking out of his clothes. He waited until the nearest agent had cut Nora free. "Get into the shower. Now."

She nodded, gulping air. With barely a glance at the agents, she shimmied out of the teddy and ran, buck-assed naked, for the hallway. Deke followed her, waiting until she'd stepped inside the shower. "Use soap. Wash it all off."

He kept his hands away from his body and dropped to one knee, peering at her feet. She scrubbed them with soap until they were pink. He breathed out. No cuts, not even a scrape. Good.

She stepped out. "Your turn."

He nodded and shoved by her, careful not to touch. Minutes later, he'd washed off the blood and reassured himself he didn't have any cuts or wounds.

The first agent poked his head into the bathroom. "You're

both to stay here until the CDC guys come for you. They're bringing decontamination chemicals."

Deke nodded and flipped off the water, not wanting to touch anything else in the room.

Nora shivered next to the shower but didn't reach for a towel. "Anything in here could be contaminated."

"I know." He wanted nothing more than to reach for her, but just in case he was contaminated, he kept his distance. "Are you all right?"

"Yes. He didn't bite me." Her lips began to turn blue. "How did you find me?"

His chest hitched. "Saw Bobbi take you on video, tracked her through town, did a search for anybody she might know. The aunt and her address popped up. The SUV is in the driveway." He shook his head. "I thought I'd be too late."

Her hand trembled as if she wanted to reach out and touch him. Reassure him. But they had to follow protocols. Instead, she gave him a smile. "We'll be okay, Deke. I promise."

"I can't live without you." Standing, dripping cool water, having just faced death, he gave her the truth. "I've loved you since I was sixteen years old, and I don't want this life, any life, without you."

Color bloomed in her face. "You pick the darnedest times."

He chuckled. "I know."

She smoothed water from her hands. "You live by different rules, but you're true to them, and you'll be true to me." Her smile brightened the entire room. "You'd go through hell for me. How could I not want you?" She faced him fully, shivering but with determination in her eyes. "I love you, too." As she gave him the words, as she gave him herself, she met his gaze. "It's always been you, Deacan."

Yeah. He smiled. "I'll make you happy, baby. I promise." More importantly, he'd keep her safe, because the woman had pegged him right. Hell was definitely coming, and he fully intended to storm the flames for her.

Chapter Sixteen

Week 4
29,071 people dead
Likelihood of Scorpius Containment: Impossible

> *The Romans fell, their last moment a quiet movement of time. The Athenians fell, their blood soaking the earth. The grand Highlanders fell, their mighty swords still clanging in history. Now it's our time to fall. The difference is, in this time and with you . . . we will rise again.*
>
> —DEACAN DEVLIN MCDOUGALL

Nora stretched her neck as she shoved open the door to Deke's apartment. The statistics of the infected, crazy, and dead were going to give her nightmares. The public finally knew the truth, and society was holding its breath.

The aromatic scent of spaghetti rumbled through her to warm her belly. How could she be hungry? But she was. Yep. That was Deke. It was toast, steak, or spaghetti if he was cooking.

She closed the door, kicked off her boots, and wandered to the kitchen, where he stirred the pot.

He turned, his gaze serious.

Her system instantly went into overdrive. "What?"

He handed her a glass of wine, took another, and grasped her hand to lead her to the living room. His hold was firm and warm. "The noodles need another three minutes, and you and I need to talk."

She slipped onto the sofa and took a sip of the Cabernet. Warm and robust, it exploded on her tongue. Protecting herself, she tucked her feet under her. "All right."

He set down his glass. "Our tests came back, the third round, and neither of us was infected by Zach."

"I know." The CDC had called her, too. "I actually spoke with Lynne earlier."

Deke's eyebrows rose. "How is she?"

"Not great, but hanging on." If anybody could survive the beginning of the pandemic, it'd be Lynne. "Said she's basically a pincushion in the name of research right now."

Deke nodded. "That makes sense, although I feel for her."

"Me too," Nora said, plucking at a loose thread on his shirt. "Also said that sleeping with the second in line to the presidency hasn't given her any more power, darn it. They won't let her leave."

Deke rubbed his eyes. "They're an odd couple, don't you think?"

Nora squinted and took a moment to digest the news. "No. They're both strong, stubborn, and smart. Probably a good match, really." She sighed. "Any news on Zach or Bobbi?"

"No. They're still in custody and being studied." Lines cut into the sides of Deke's generous mouth. "I'm still wondering if I should've put a bullet in each of their heads instead of letting them live."

"You did the right thing." She cleared her throat and steeled her shoulders. "I'm no closer to getting inside Scorpius, though." She focused on him, needing to look at something good. To feel something strong. "So you wanted to talk. Talk."

He rubbed the scruffy shadow covering his jawline. "The infection is spreading, and we're going to need national containment measures." Green and dark, his eyes sizzled with an impenetrable light.

She blinked. "You've been asked to be part of the, well, whatever it is."

He nodded. "Yes. I'm sure they'll come up with a grand acronym, but basically, it's a first line of defense against the threat, and right now we're calling it the Brigade."

Front line of danger, that was. Her hands shook. "You took the job?"

"Not yet." His head lifted, his look all male. "I figured I should talk to you first."

"What if I say no?" she asked quietly.

He didn't answer.

She lifted an eyebrow.

He cupped her jaw. "We're in a war, Nora. A new one. Most people who catch the infection die. A few live, and a few are different. Dangerous."

She swallowed. The truth of his statement carved fear through her, but they'd faced terror before and won. "You're going to hunt them down."

"Yes." He kept hold of her jaw, trapping her gaze. "I tried to be somebody else. To get you back, to make you love me again, I tried. God knows I did."

"Deacan—"

"No." He brushed a finger cross her lips. "I'm a fighter, and I'll always be a fighter if there's something needing to be fought. This disease? It needs to be fought. The people trying to spread it need to be stopped. I canna sit on the sidelines and watch."

She'd known. From the first day they'd met, she'd known he was different. Special. Dangerous. A deadly predator now created havoc amongst them, and there wasn't anybody she'd trust to stop it more than Deacan McDougall. They were going to argue about government and freedom, and she'd stick to her guns. But she would be there for him as he did his job. If he needed her support to do it, then she'd square her shoulders and help him.

If nothing else, she'd learned that life was short, and no way did she want to live it without him. "I love you as is. Always have and always will," she said softly. She couldn't ask him to be less than he was. Less than the man she loved.

His head lifted, and his eyes glittered. "I love you, too."

"I know." She reached up and took his hand. "It's you and me, Deacan. Together. No matter what happens next."

He took her mouth, kissing her deep. When he leaned back, the look in his eyes, true and absolute, was for her. Just her. "Aye," he said.

Phantom Embrace

Dianne Duvall

Chapter One

Yuri closed his eyes and let the night sounds serenade him. How he loved the quiet.

"I don't miss the city," Stanislav murmured beside him.

Yuri smiled. As usual, his friend had read him well. Stanislav might not have been able to peer into one's thoughts as telepathic immortals often did, but he *could*—like Bastien—discern one's emotions through touch. And his shoulder brushed Yuri's as they strode through the somnolent college campus.

"Nor do I," Yuri responded, opening his eyes.

Duke University's students appeared to have all retired for the night. No parties raged at the frat houses. No lights brightened the windows of the sorority houses. No music *thump thump thumped*, the bass pounding through the streets while students blew off steam and got drunk off their asses, providing easy targets for vampires.

Instead blissful silence embraced him, broken only by nocturnal creatures that scavenged about whilst the humans slept.

Or most of them, anyway. The occasional straggler or two staggered wearily through the campus. Up late cramming for exams, Yuri supposed, or returning home after a late-night tryst.

"Do you think Seth will transfer us back to New York?" Stanislav asked, his sharp eyes scouring every shadow.

"I don't think so. Not for quite some time, anyway. Whenever we quash one enemy, another rises. There seems to be no end to the troubles here in North Carolina."

"There is also a proliferation of new immortals in the area," Stanislav countered.

Almost half a dozen transformed in just the past few years. Quite an astonishing number. But Yuri wasn't concerned that it would render the two of them obsolete.

"Every one of us will be needed until no more threats arise."

Stanislav nodded.

Until a few years ago, all had been the same old same old: Immortal Guardians hunted vampires nightly to reduce their numbers and keep them from preying upon humans. Nothing more.

Then Bastien had raised his vampire army and pitted it against the Immortal Guardians, aided by a weasely scientist named Montrose Keegan. Unbeknownst to Bastien, Keegan had fostered ties to a budding mercenary group that possessed a very dangerous sedative. A sedative they had developed with the sole purpose of torturing Ami, the petite mortal female in the Immortal Guardians' midst who had come to them from another world. Ami had suffered six months of torture before Seth and David, the two eldest and most powerful immortals, had found and rescued her, welcoming her into the fold.

Then the mercenaries had tried to get their hands on her again and, in the process, had discovered that the sedative worked on immortals and vampires, too.

Thank you, Bastien, Yuri thought sarcastically.

No other drug had been capable of affecting an immortal

until then. None at all. The odd, symbiotic virus that infected immortals replaced their immune system when they transformed and was hyperproficient when it came to repairing any and all physical damage they suffered, including that spawned by drugs. Except for this one unique sedative.

Twice mercenaries had attempted to use the sedative to capture an immortal they could use to create an army of supersoldiers. And twice the Immortal Guardians had defeated them. The immortals had killed *everyone*—every single mercenary—in the last epic battle.

Things had been pretty quiet since then. But considering the troubles the Immortal Guardians had faced here since Bastien's initial uprising, Yuri doubted it would stay that way.

A pale flash of color caught Yuri's eye, drawing his attention to one side.

A woman strolled parallel to them, her feet making no sound that carried to his preternaturally sensitive ears. A long, cream-colored dress adorned her slender form. Casual, not formal. The skirts so long they hid her shoes. An oddity today when skirts so short they showed *everything* if the woman bent over were more en vogue.

Sleeves encased her slender arms to just beneath her elbows. The bodice hugged a narrow rib cage and even smaller waist. The only thing that wasn't demure about the dress was the neckline, which dipped low enough to provide a tantalizing glimpse of cleavage.

Were she wearing stays and panniers and petticoats, she would have fit right in with the mortal aristocrats he had rubbed elbows with . . . oh . . . about two and a half centuries ago. She certainly carried herself with the grace those women had practiced.

Stan mumbled something Yuri didn't catch.

Too entranced. Yuri couldn't seem to pry his eyes away from the woman.

She was a beauty, with raven hair that tumbled down her back to her waist in thick midnight waves. Her profile displayed a small nose and pert chin. Full lips that bore no smile.

A cat slipped around a corner of the building a few feet away and stopped short upon glimpsing her.

The woman stopped, too, and smiled at the ragged little creature. Bending forward, she appeared to speak to it.

Yuri strained to hear her words, but failed to catch any.

The cat dipped its head and crept forward, every movement cautious until it reached her.

She knelt down, her pretty face brightening with a soft smile.

The cat lay down and rolled over onto its back, begging for a belly rub.

"Cats are strange," Stanislav said.

The woman, reaching a hand toward the stray, looked around at the sound of his voice.

Yuri's heartbeat picked up. Moonlight spilled across her nose and chin, leaving her eyes in darkness. But he could feel her gaze upon him like a touch.

"Don't you think?" Stanislav asked.

"What?" Yuri murmured. "Oh. Right. Yes."

"What's wrong? Your heartbeat just picked up."

He *would* notice that, damn him.

Yuri surreptitiously put more distance between himself and his friend so Stanislav wouldn't brush his shoulder and feel the attraction and whatever the hell else it was that claimed him in that moment.

"Ah," Stanislav said. "I smell them now. How many are there?"

Frowning, Yuri tore his gaze away from the woman and drew in a deep breath.

Vampires. Six of them.

"Half a dozen," Yuri told him. A century older than

Stanislav, Yuri should have caught the vampires' scents first, but had allowed himself to become distracted.

The two stopped walking and let their ears and noses determine the vampires' location.

When Yuri glanced to the side once more, only the cat stared back. The woman was nowhere to be seen, though he had not heard her leave.

A faint whimper floated to him on the night's breeze.

Yuri caught Stanislav's gaze and pointed northeast as the wind ruffled his hair.

Nodding, Stanislav drew a pair of shoto swords.

Yuri drew his treasured katanas and shot forward without another word.

They found the vampires in the shadows behind a building Yuri didn't care enough about to identify. Six vampires. Two victims. All male.

Vampires were humans who had been infected with the same rare symbiotic virus that transformed immortals. As with immortals, the virus replaced their immune system and lent them many of the characteristics that had been found in vampire folklore over the centuries — greater speed, strength, and regenerative capabilities, coupled with heightened senses, photosensitivity, and a frequent need for blood. It also spawned progressive brain damage in every human infected with it that resulted in a rapid descent into madness. A madness Yuri and the other Immortal Guardians were spared thanks to the protection provided by the advanced DNA with which they had been born.

These vampires, Yuri swiftly discerned as he watched them do their damnedest to draw forth every drop of blood from the humans they had slain, were a mixed bag. Two had long since embraced the madness. Their ragged clothing and filthy bodies reeked. Their oily hair hung in limp straggles around faces stained with both new blood and old blood from the previous night's kills. Their eyes glowed blue and green with mirth as they cackled over the torturous deaths they had just inflicted.

Three others had not yet completed their descent into madness. They made at least a minimal effort at maintaining basic hygiene. And they seemed a bit leery of the insane vamps. But they clearly had taken pleasure in hurting their victims. Any sense of right and wrong that had been instilled in them by their parents had packed its bags and headed for the door. Little conscience remained. Only some basic sense of self-preservation that told them the older vampires might just be psychotic enough to turn on *them* one night.

Yuri met the sixth vampire's glowing blue gaze as that one noted their presence and rose in a slow, controlled movement.

Towering at least a head above the others, the sixth vampire nearly matched Yuri in height. Crisp, clean clothing adorned a form packed with muscle. Neatly cropped hair, almost military in its appearance, accompanied an air of I-can-and-*will*-kick-your-ass-at-my-discretion. The vamp's iridescent eyes bore no insanity, indicating he had only recently been turned. And when they latched on to Stanislav . . .

Yuri frowned.

He would've sworn those blue eyes lit with triumph. As though the vamp had merely been biding his time until Yuri and Stanislav had made an appearance.

The other vampires looked up at Vampire #6, followed his gaze, then rose, growling and hissing like B-movie vampires.

Instinct telling him the sixth vampire was trouble, Yuri spoke not a word. Issued no warning. He simply left the weaker five vampires to Stanislav and shot forward, his gaze never leaving the big vamp.

Vampire #6 reached behind him—so quickly his movements blurred—and drew a weapon.

Yuri barreled past the slovenly vampires and swung his katana . . . just in time.

Cold steel cut through the flesh of the arm the vamp raised to aim what appeared to be a handgun at Stan.

The gun tumbled to the ground with a clatter as crimson liquid poured forth from the vamp's brachial artery.

Yuri breathed a quick sigh of relief. Immortal Guardians rarely carried guns, the loud reports of which tended to draw unwanted attention to their battles. Vampires usually didn't carry them either, having heard rumors of this or that careless vamp experiencing an excruciating death in a sunlit cell after being taken into custody by law enforcement officials.

Rumors Immortal Guardians had spawned. Such had served them well thus far.

But vampires weren't always the brightest bulbs in the box.

Had this vampire fired his weapon, campus security would have swarmed toward them. Police would've joined them as residents nearby called 911 to report gunshots. And Yuri and Stan would've been up to their ears in chaos.

The large vampire roared with rage as he clutched his injured arm and struggled to stanch the flow of blood from the severed artery. It was a fatal wound. Both knew it. Unlike immortals, vampires died if they lost too much blood.

But this vampire wasn't ready to throw in the towel. Swirling around, he delivered a roundhouse kick that sent Yuri flying through the air.

Dust and mortar exploded around Yuri in a cloud as he struck the side of the building. Landing on his feet, Yuri raced forward, leapt over the two lesser vampires Stanislav had already slain, and swung hard at Vampire #6 before that one could retrieve the gun.

The vampire stumbled backward and drew two short swords.

The expertise with which the vamp wielded those swords astonished Yuri. He fought as though he had been trained by an Immortal Guardian.

Yuri pressed forward, keeping the vampire on the defensive. The vampire countered Yuri's every strike until blood loss slowed the vamp to near-mortal speeds.

Yuri struck a second killing blow, slicing the vamp's carotid artery.

Vampire #6 dropped to his knees. His weapons fell from lax fingers as he wavered, then pitched forward.

A blade parted the material of Yuri's coat and sliced through his hamstrings.

Hissing in pain, Yuri swore and spun around.

The two vampires Stan had taken out had begun to shrivel up like mummies as the virus they housed devoured them from the inside out in a desperate bid to continue living. Stan now battled two others and held his own very well. The last vampire had snuck up behind Yuri with two big-ass Bowie knives, thinking to slay Yuri while the sixth vampire had distracted him.

Yuri parried a blow that otherwise would have severed a limb, then countered it with a strike that broke the blade of the other's Bowie knife.

The vampire gaped at what remained of the jagged blade, then started swinging wildly as fury and fear battled for dominance in his glowing silver gaze.

Trained by a master swordsman, Yuri defeated this one easily.

The vampire's body dropped to the ground, then began to shrivel up like the others. Yuri started to step over him, then stopped when the two vampires Stanislav fought fell limply to the pavement.

Stanislav looked at Yuri. "You okay?"

Yuri nodded and pointed to the big vamp. "This one actually had some skills."

Vampires rarely had any real training with regard to fighting or swordplay. Most were college students who had spent much of their time prior to being transformed in sedentary pursuits like gaming or surfing the Internet. So they tended to take the easy route, aiming for the hamstrings to bring their opponent to his knees, then falling on him like jackals.

"Reminded me a bit of the fencing-instructor-turned-vampire we encountered back in 1843," Yuri continued.

Stanislav laughed. "I remember him." He nodded to Vampire #6. "Did I see him pull a gun?"

Yuri nodded and glanced around, but didn't see it. "He must have fallen on it."

"Dumbass," Stanislav muttered. "Good thing you kept him from firing it."

Yuri laughed. "I know. What about you? Are you injured?"

His friend glanced down at his left arm, then shrugged. "A few cuts. Nothing more."

Stanislav had an impressively high tolerance for pain, thanks to the sadistic vampire who had turned him. So *a few cuts* could refer to anything from shallow slices that didn't need stitches to deep gashes that left his arm barely attached.

Yuri studied his friend's movements as Stanislav sheathed his shoto swords and bent to retrieve the weapons the vampires had dropped. Satisfied that Stanislav's wounds indeed posed no threat, Yuri sheathed his own swords, drew his cell phone from a back pocket, and made a quick call.

"Reordon," Chris Reordon, who headed the East Coast division of the human network that aided immortals, answered.

"It's Yuri. Stanislav and I just took out six vampires at Duke."

Chris grunted. "Any human casualties?"

"Two. Both slain before we arrived."

"Where are you?"

Stanislav, whose preternaturally sharp hearing enabled him to hear both sides of the conversation, identified the building for Yuri.

Yuri passed it along to Reordon.

"I'll have a crew there in five minutes," Chris vowed.

Yuri pocketed his phone, then pursed his lips and looked at Stanislav. "I should've asked him what to do with the gun."

Stanislav shrugged. "Just toss it in a Dumpster with the rest of the weapons. I'm sure anything a vampire would carry would be far inferior to the arsenal of weapons the network keeps at its disposal."

True.

Yuri waited another minute for Vampire #6 to finish disintegrating, then gathered his clothing and weapons together with that of a couple of the other vampires in one fell swoop and deposited it all in the nearest Dumpster.

Stanislav did the same while they waited for Chris's crew to arrive and collect the human victims.

Cat entered the home of David, the second eldest and second most powerful immortal on the planet. Located in the North Carolinian countryside with no nearby neighbors who might panic upon seeing powerful warriors come and go with bloodstained clothing (hunting insane vampires was a violent, messy business), this sprawling one-story home appeared to be the hub of the Immortal Guardians' world here on the East Coast.

Cat had been drawn to this place—and to these people, these warriors—ever since her brother Bastien had raised a vampire army and done his damnedest to bring the immortals down.

What a terrifying time that had been. Terrifying and frustrating and heartbreaking. She had known Bastien was in the wrong, that he had focused his quest for revenge upon the wrong man, but had had no way to convey it to him.

And she had feared every day that it would be his downfall.

Had Seth, the Immortal Guardians' leader, not been so forgiving, she knew her brother would be dead now, killed in that final battle between his vampire army and the Immortal Guardians.

American and British immortals Ethan and Edward entered David's home behind her and strolled past, their long black coats glistening with the blood of the vampires they had slain.

Krysta and Étienne, still newly wed, called greetings and offered the duo smiles.

Étienne's twin, Richart, and Richart's wife Jenna added their own hellos.

Yes, Cat thought, as she watched the immortals smile and trade jests, it was the people who drew her here time and time again. They were different. And not just because they were infected with the same virus that afflicted vampires. No, these men and women, these immortals, had been born like Cat—with special gifts no humans or vampires possessed.

Krysta could see auras. Étienne and his sister Lisette were both telepathic. Richart could teleport. Jenna, as the descendant of a healer, had been born with far greater regenerative capabilities than ordinary humans enjoyed.

Roland, considered the antisocial one of the group, and his wife Sarah entered from the hallway on the opposite side of the room. Roland could heal with his hands and bore some telekinetic abilities. Sarah had prophetic dreams.

Bastien, Cat's brother, could discern one's emotions through touch and determine truth from falsehood. His wife, Dr. Melanie Lipton, had minor precognitive abilities.

And Cat? Cat had always been able to see an object's history, glimpse those who had held it and the like, by touching it. She just hadn't understood *why* she could until she had begun haunting David's home after David and Seth had captured her brother and pretty much forced him to join the Immortal Guardians' ranks.

Every immortal, or *gifted one*, as they had called themselves before being infected with the vampiric virus, had been born with advanced DNA, the origins of which Cat still didn't understand.

That advanced DNA lent immortals their gifts and, thankfully, offered some protection from the more corrosive aspects of the virus that infected them. Immortals didn't suffer brain damage the way humans did and, thus, weren't driven insane. This enabled them to live . . . well . . . forever, unless their heads were stricken from their bodies. The older the immortal, the more powerful and plentiful his or her gifts, because their bloodlines had been less diluted by ordinary human DNA.

David, who had lived thousands of years, was such a powerful healer that he could reattach severed limbs. He could also shapeshift, among other things, and could withstand several hours of exposure to daylight before he began to suffer the consequences younger immortals suffered immediately.

Seth . . .

Well, she'd yet to find anything the immensely powerful Immortal Guardians' leader *couldn't* do.

Bastien and Melanie entered, laughing and holding hands like teenagers.

Dawn must be approaching.

Many of the immortals in the area congregated here at David's after each night's hunt. Some spent the days there, too.

Frowning at the bay window, Cat wondered how the two Russian immortals she had followed earlier had fared in their battle.

For a moment, when she had knelt down to address the stray cat, the taller one—Yuri—had seemed to look right at her.

Excitement had skittered through her.

Then she had heard the vampires coming.

After spending two hundred years with Bastien and his psychotic vampire friends, Cat could no longer abide being near the fiends. And when the immortals inevitably defeated the vampires in battle, setting their spirits free . . .

Cat shuddered.

No. She'd had to leave.

The front door opened once more and, as though conjured by her thoughts, Yuri and Stanislav entered.

A little thrill darted through her as it always did in Yuri's presence. She wasn't sure why. There was just something about him that drew her to him and always compelled her to single him out with her gaze, even when a host of other warriors surrounded him.

She didn't think it was because he was handsome. They were *all* handsome.

Although Yuri did seem to be even *easier on the eye*, as she'd heard one of the female Seconds say, than the others.

He stood about six foot four, just under a foot taller than her own five foot five. He kept his black hair short in back and on the sides, but long enough on top to reveal a tendency to wave. Dark brows hovered over piercing brown eyes that seemed to miss nothing. She'd once heard him tell Bastien that his patrician nose used to be crooked from being broken in a brawl in his youth, but had straightened when he had transformed. His lips were a little fuller than most men's, but were by no means feminine. A perpetual five o'clock shadow hugged his strong jaw.

Broad shoulders. A slender, yet muscular build. A smooth stroll that did odd things to her insides.

Cat drifted into a corner and watched the other immortals call greetings and trade gibes with him before Yuri headed down the hallway toward the basement stairs. No doubt he intended to wash the night's hunt off him in the bedroom he'd claimed when Seth had transferred him to North Carolina a couple of years ago. Just before he turned into the basement stairwell, Yuri glanced over his shoulder and looked in her direction.

Perhaps, Cat thought, her attraction to him simply resulted from times like this when he *almost* seemed to acknowledge her presence.

The others never did. Except for Marcus, who had only done so once. He had bellowed at her to get out when he had been arguing with Ami and Cat had inadvertently intruded.

Speaking of whom . . .

Marcus and Ami passed Yuri in the hallway and joined the others in the living room. Ami was about a foot shorter than her husband, with slender arms and legs and a huge protruding belly that turned her walk into a waddle.

The couple sank onto a cushy sofa and began to chat with Roland and Sarah.

Cat eased forward, her eyes on the petite redhead.

Ami shifted, as though the babe in her belly wouldn't allow her to get comfortable.

Cat claimed the empty space beside Ami and lowered her eyes to Ami's round tummy.

A few minutes later, her careful scrutiny was rewarded when the babe shifted. What appeared to be the faint shape of a knee slid across the knit shirt that molded itself to Ami's torso.

Ami absently placed a hand over the knee and gave it a pat.

Pleasure and pain warred within Cat.

She remembered how that had felt. Her married friends had expounded upon the beauty of feeling a child move within them when they were breeding. But in the privacy of her bedchamber, when Cat had lowered the bedcovers and raised her nightgown to watch this limb or that shift and slide and press against her skin from inside her belly, she had thought it a strange combination of funny and creepy.

Her chest tightened.

How nervous she had been. Nervous and excited and

afraid all at once. She had barely been more than a child herself and had had no idea what caring for a babe would entail. Nor had she known what childbirth would bring. Women had spoken of it only in the most generic of terms back then. She'd known it would be painful. That it would be messy. And that she might not survive it.

But she had loved the baby within her so much that she had thought it well worth the risk.

Ami gave her big belly one last stroke, then dropped her hand to her lap.

Ami carried a baby girl.

All of Cat's friends—her mother, too—had thought Cat had carried a boy.

Her eyes burned. How many times had she wondered, with something akin to panic, what she would do with a boy? If raising a son would be harder than raising a girl in the male-dominated world in which she had resided? How great a role she would be able to play in his life? If he would love her as much as she already adored him?

Immortals continued to move about the room, but Cat paid them no heed.

Eyes burning, she reached a hand out and rested it on Ami's belly.

Ami didn't react, just kept chatting with Sarah.

On Ami's other side, Marcus frowned at Cat and looked— for a moment—as though he would shove her hand away from his wife and unborn babe.

But he didn't.

It only made Cat want to weep more.

She liked to think she would've been a good mother. That she would've raised a fine young man. As fine and honorable as the warriors in this room.

How she regretted having been denied the chance to do so.

How she hated her husband for murdering her before she could birth their child.

Cat squeezed her eyes shut as memories of violence and death attempted to intrude. A tear slipped down her cheek. She couldn't think of that tonight. Couldn't bear it.

Lifting her lashes, she withdrew her hand from Ami's tummy, glanced away, and looked directly into Yuri's warm brown eyes.

Her breath caught. When had he seated himself across from her?

Her heart did an odd trip-hammer thing in her chest as he continued to meet her gaze.

Or *appeared* to meet her gaze. Did he *see* her?

He couldn't possibly. Only Marcus could see her because the gift with which he had been born enabled him to see spirits and ghosts.

Frowning, she glanced over her shoulder.

Tracy and Nichole, two of the Seconds or human assistants who aided immortals, sat behind her, laughing and talking as they explored something on one of those electronic tablets.

Ah. He must be looking at one of them.

Cat turned back around, cursing herself for feeling so disappointed. For a moment . . .

Again Yuri seemed to meet her gaze.

No, it wasn't just his looks that drew her, she thought. It was the uncanny way he had of appearing to look right at her.

It happened with others from time to time. She would find herself standing between two people and one would seem to look her right in the eye. But it happened often enough with Yuri to make her wish it weren't coincidence.

She sighed.

And now even more sadness afflicted her.

Well, she didn't want to stay here and watch Yuri admire whichever woman behind her had caught his attention.

Rising, Cat strolled across the room and, passing through a few walls, looked in on the kittens snoozing in David's study.

Chapter Two

Yuri had never been much of a talker.

He wasn't antisocial, like Roland. He just would rather listen and observe and toss in a word here or there than do the constant back-and-forth thing.

Lounging on the sofa, he let the conversations of his brethren flow around him and tried to forget the tear that had slipped down the cheek of the beauty beside Ami.

Who *was* the mysterious woman who haunted both David's home and Yuri's thoughts? Why did she linger here? Why did she follow Yuri on his hunts on occasion?

Was she an Immortal Guardian who had been slain in the line of duty? Or a Second?

He'd lost so many Seconds of his own over the centuries. Mortal men he had loved like brothers.

"How did tonight's hunt go?"

Yuri looked around at the ___ current Second's inquiry.

Dmitry stood next to hir ___ apple.

"It went well."

Dmitry nodded. "Whe ___ apons?"

"In the armory."

"I'll clean and sharpen them for you. Anything else you need me to do?"

"I could use a new coat," Yuri said. "A vampire tried to hamstring me, so mine's looking a little ragged now."

Dmitry scowled. "I hate it when they do that. Why don't the bastards just learn how to fight?"

"One of the vampires we fought tonight *did*," Yuri admitted with a wry smile. "He actually proved to be quite a challenge."

"Really?" Surprise lightened Dmitry's blue eyes. He knew Yuri wasn't easy to defeat. "Do you need blood?"

"No, I'm good." His wounds had been superficial enough to heal without an infusion.

"Okay. I'll have a new coat for you before tomorrow night's hunt. Anything else? Something to eat, perhaps?" Dmitry held up a second apple.

Smiling, Yuri held out his hand. "I'll take it."

Dmitry tossed it to him. "Let me know if you need anything else."

Yuri shook his head and rose. "I think I'm going to turn in." Leaving the living room, Yuri resisted the urge to peer into every doorway he passed in search of the woman in the long, cream-colored dress.

David's home boasted a basement that, with a few recent additions, was twice the size of the ground floor. A large sparring or training room took up a lot of square feet on the left. The rest of the basement provided bedrooms that now had all been soundproofed for any immortals who chose to spend the day there.

And a lot did. Almost every immortal in the area, in fact. They had really been sticking close to offer their support and protection to Ami, the first mortal woman ever to conceive a child by an immortal.

Yuri strode down t███████ay. Entering the bedroom he had claimed for hi██████d the door behind him.

Blessed silence.

Tugging off his boots, he sank down in one of the two chairs in his reading nook. He and Stanislav had spent many a morning in those chairs, poring over books filched from David's extensive library.

Now Yuri retrieved his favorite dagger and applied it to the apple.

No sooner had he placed the first slice between his lips than the woman in the cream-colored dress walked through his door.

Yuri paused, then began to chew slowly as he watched her.

Sadness clung to her, weighing every movement, though no tears stained her cheeks, he noted with some relief.

He cut another slice, slipped the fruit—both tart and sweet—between his lips.

This wasn't the first time she had visited his quarters. She had been to his room more times than he could count since Seth had transferred him here.

Yuri hadn't known how long or how brief a time he would spend in North Carolina, so he had simply claimed this room at David's home rather than choosing a house and going to the trouble of moving all of this things down from New York.

She meandered around the room, studying his possessions.

There hadn't been very many personal effects at first. Yuri had thought his stay would be brief, so he hadn't brought much with him.

Then this lovely spirit had begun to visit and had seemed so curious about the few items he had brought with him.

Giving in to what he had considered an absurd urge to please her, Yuri had asked Richart to teleport him to his apartment in New York so he could retrieve more.

Sap. A smart-ass voice spoke in his head.

Yuri ignored it.

Every week or so, he put out something new. His first pocket watch—now an antique. His mother's brooch, also an antique. Hell, almost all of his favorite things were antiques. Even his favorite quill.

And each time the beauty in the cream-colored dress would find the new objects, she would pause and admire them, then appeared to touch them.

Could she touch them? he wondered idly. Some spirits were endowed with that ability. Some weren't. Or so he had observed over the centuries.

Could she touch *him*? he wondered next, then cursed the flutter of excitement and, yes, arousal, that struck at the notion. Of course she couldn't touch him, nor would she. The woman hadn't even spoken to him.

He continued to munch the apple.

He found he didn't mind her silent company. He was a quiet man himself, so the fact that she never spoke didn't bother him. Much. He wouldn't mind having his curiosity appeased, though curiosity had proven detrimental in the past.

She seemed curious about *him*. Or so he thought. Why else would she spend so many hours here, sitting with him while he read or watched television or continued to try to figure out the electronic gadgets Dmitry kept buying him?

And if Yuri were honest with himself, it had become harder and harder in recent decades to keep loneliness at bay. It was actually kind of nice, having her here with him.

Setting the dagger and the half-eaten apple on the night-stand, he rested his head against the chair's high back and closed his eyes.

So odd to know that someone was in the room with him, yet to hear no heartbeat, no clothing rustling, or the like. With his hypersensitive ears, he *never* enjoyed such silence in another's presence.

Her grief called out to him, though, niggling him until he did something he had vowed never to do again.

"I can feel your sadness," he murmured, not knowing why he spoke. "I wish I could alleviate it, little one."

No response came, of course.

Sighing, he opened his eyes, half expecting her to be gone, and found her staring at him from across the room.

"*Is* there anything I can do to alleviate it?" he asked her.

She glanced behind her, as she always did when she caught him watching her, then returned wide eyes to him. "Can you see me?" she asked in a whisper, her expression a mixture of hope and disbelief as she touched a hand to her chest.

"Yes."

If anything, her eyes widened more. "You can *hear* me?" Her words carried a British accent.

He smiled. "Yes." And he thought her voice lovely.

Her face lost all sadness and acquired such a look of astonishment that he had to laugh.

She took a hesitant step closer. "You . . . Are you like Marcus, then? You can see . . . ?"

"Ghosts? Spirits?"

She nodded, but didn't seem fond of either term.

"Yes. For as long as I can remember. Though I can probably count on one hand the number of spirits with whom I've conversed."

She stared at him.

He smiled. "I see I've surprised you."

"Yes, you have." She took another careful step closer, as though she feared he might bolt if she stood too near. "So, you were looking at *me* upstairs? I thought you were looking at Tracy or Nichole."

He shook his head. "I was looking at you. And I saw you at the university tonight as well."

"I thought you were looking at the cat!" she exclaimed, her features brightening with a beguiling grin.

Again he laughed. "Stanislav was looking at the cat. *I* was looking at *you*."

She motioned to the empty chair. "May I join you?"

He stood and motioned to the chair. "Of course." Once

she perched on the edge of the cushioned seat, he reclaimed his own.

"If you've seen spirits all of your life," she asked, "why have you conversed with so few?"

He picked up his apple and dagger and carved off another slice. "Some spirits never acknowledged my presence." It felt odd, unmannerly, not to offer her a piece. "They didn't seem to see me, or those around me. Rather they went about whatever chores they were performing as though they were alone."

She nodded. "I've seen such spirits. There is something different about them."

He eyed her curiously. "Have you ever spoken with them?"

She shook her head. "They ignore me as they do you."

Interesting.

"What about the other spirits?" she asked. "Spirits like me? Why did you not converse with *them*?"

He placed another apple slice in his mouth, buying time and considering his words. "Some spirits," he said at length, "are like the vampires I hunt. They delight in inspiring fear and sparking chaos. If one acknowledges them at all—one need not even say a word, just making eye contact will do— the spirits will do everything they can to make one's life a living hell."

Her pretty face grew somber. "Sometimes the vampires' spirits are like that. They terrify me."

"Is that why you left as soon as we encountered the vampires earlier?"

She nodded. "I didn't want to be around when you killed them and freed their spirits."

Another mystery solved.

"What about the others?" she asked.

Yuri hesitated. "May I be honest with you, at the risk of hurting your feelings?"

"Yes. I always prefer honesty to lies."

She might change her mind once he spoke. Yuri feared what he intended to say might come across as rather harsh.

He set the dagger and apple core aside. "When I was a boy, I was told more than once never to feed a stray dog. When I asked why, I was told that if I fed the stray, I would never be able to rid myself of it, that it would keep coming back. I learned, rather painfully, that the same held true for spirits."

She clasped her hands in her lap.

"I spent most of my childhood fearing the spirits only I could see, so I didn't attempt to speak to one until I had approached, oh, ten and eight summers or thereabouts and thought myself invincible as all young men do. He seemed a benign spirit. Not menacing at all. So I thought it safe to try." Yuri drew in a deep breath. "Well, once the spirit learned I could see and speak with him, he stuck to me like glue. I never had a moment's peace afterward. Never had a moment's privacy. And I could not rid myself of him no matter how hard I tried."

She bit her lip.

"Even had he been a more likable fellow, it would've aggravated me," Yuri continued, irritation rising at just the thought of that pain in his arse. "But this spirit felt he had to offer his opinion—usually a critical one—on *everything*. And he wouldn't even give me privacy when I, uh, sought the company of women."

Her cheeks acquired a rosy glow.

Perhaps he shouldn't have mentioned that part. "I'm a quiet sort," Yuri explained. "I appreciate my privacy. Yet he wouldn't *give* me any. The damned man, spirit, whatever, was still dogging my heels when I was attacked and transformed by a vampire and would no doubt *still* be plaguing me today had Seth not done something to rid me of him."

"What did he do?"

"I don't know. He wouldn't tell me."

Her brow furrowed. "I can see it angered you."

He grimaced. "Did I raise my voice?"

She nodded.

"Forgive me." He offered her a wry smile. "It wasn't the best period of my life."

"So you never spoke to a spirit again?" she posed tentatively.

"Actually, I did. Several decades later. I found myself living in a city with an alarmingly large spirit population. One in particular drew my sympathy, so I spoke to her."

"And?"

He laughed. "And she and all of the other spirits in the vicinity did their damnedest to make me their errand boy once they discovered I could see and hear them."

She frowned. "I don't understand."

"They wanted me to carry messages to the living for them." He could laugh about it now, but it had not been the least bit funny at the time. "In the movies, ghosts always have some meaningful message they wish whoever can see them to tender to their loved ones."

"I don't know if that would work," she said. "Who, other than your immortal brethren, would even *believe* you if you approached them and said you had a message for them from their dead husband or wife or father?"

"No one would, or did, as far as I could tell. But then I was never asked to carry any noble messages. One spirit wanted me to fetch some jewels he had stashed in his favorite gentlemen's club and take them to his mistress because he didn't want his wife to get her greedy little hands on them. His words. Not mine. And there were other, uglier errands. I ended up having to ask Seth for another transfer to get away from them all."

"How . . . unpleasant."

"Yes."

A long moment passed.

"With such a track record," she said softly, "I'm surprised you ventured to speak to me tonight."

"I fear it was inevitable. I've been wanting to speak to you for a long time now," he admitted.

Her lips curled up in a faint smile. "You have?"

"Yes. I almost *did* the night I moved here and saw you for the first time."

"What made you change your mind?"

"You walked through a wall. I didn't realize until you did that you were a spirit."

She stared at him, her brown eyes wide. "You see me that clearly?"

"Yes. Even knowing you were a spirit, I wished to speak to you, but past experience taught me that there is *always* a catch. I didn't want to find out what that catch might be with you."

"Yet you spoke to me tonight. Why?"

"I couldn't bear your sadness."

She lowered her head.

"Will you tell me the source of it?" he implored gently.

She shook her head, avoiding his gaze. "I don't wish to speak of it."

When sadness crept back into her visage, Yuri hastened to change the subject. "Then why don't we formally introduce ourselves?" Rising, he sketched her a gallant bow. "Yuri Sokolov, at your service."

Cat rose and smiled up at the handsome immortal warrior. "Catherine Seddon." She executed a curtsy. "My friends called me Cat."

"May I count myself among your friends?" he asked with a roguish grin.

She laughed. "Yes, you may."

"Then it's a pleasure to meet you, Cat."

"A pleasure to meet you, too, sir."

"Yuri," he corrected.

"It's a pleasure to meet you, Yuri." And how intimate it felt to address him so informally. When she had last been a living member of society, the rules had dictated that she address men such as Yuri by their titles.

Yuri offered her his hand.

Once more, excitement skittered through her. If he could see her and hear her so clearly, would he also be able to feel her?

It had been so long since she had experienced the touch of another.

Cat placed her hand in his. Disappointment pummeled her as her hand passed right through it. "Oh," she breathed. "I had hoped, since you can see me so clearly . . ."

"That I could feel you, too?" he asked, sympathy and disappointment suffusing his deep brown eyes.

"Yes."

"I hoped so, too." He continued to hold his hand out to her, palm up. "Let us try again, shall we? Slower this time."

Cat saw little purpose in it, but did as he requested and placed her hand over his, making sure, this time, that her hand didn't keep going and pass right through it. Again she felt no skin-on-skin contact. Did not feel the pressure of his fingers closing around hers when he attempted such.

But she did feel *something*.

Warmth. Her palm felt warm where it merged with his.

She raised her head and stared up at him in wonder.

"Can you feel me?" he asked, an amber glow entering his brown eyes.

She had to swallow before she could speak. "I feel warmth."

He cupped his free hand over hers, encapsulating it in more warmth.

It wasn't what she had hoped. But to feel anything at all

after two centuries of nothing . . . "Can you feel me?" she whispered.

"I can't curl my fingers around yours. Can't raise your hand to my lips for a kiss," he murmured, "but my skin tingles where we touch."

Was tingling a good thing or a bad thing? "Is it uncomfortable?" she asked.

A slow smile stretched his lips. "No. It's quite pleasant, actually."

Butterflies fluttered in her belly as Cat found herself utterly smitten with him.

Oh, who was she kidding? She had been smitten with Yuri ever since he had moved into David's home. Tonight hadn't been the first time she had followed him on his hunt. Nor was it the first she had joined him in his bedroom.

An unpleasant thought arose. If he could see her, then he must know she had been tagging after him on his hunts and sitting with him and Stanislav while they read and reminisced.

Dismay rose.

Yuri had said he loved his privacy. And like the spirit he had found so annoying as a young man, Cat had denied him that privacy time and time again.

A bell rang.

Cat jerked her hand back and looked toward the door.

Since all of the bedrooms down here had now been sound-proofed, they had been outfitted with doorbells in case knocks went unheard.

"Your friend is here to read with you," she announced. Risking a glance up, she found Yuri scowling at the door.

"I'll tell him I'm going to be late," he muttered.

"No," she protested and backed away. "I'll go. Thank you for speaking with me tonight." It had been a rare treat.

"Cat—"

Spinning on her heel, she hurried through the wall into the next room, then stopped short. "Oh!"

Roland Warbrook, the antisocial British immortal, and his American wife were making passionate love in their huge bed. *Intensely* passionate love.

Eyes wide, Cat sidled around the bed. It had *never* been like that when she had lain with her husband. Blaise had never done anything to her that would make her loose such sultry moans and cries or throw her head back and reach down to grab her husband's . . .

Face and body flushing, she raced through the wall and out into the hallway just in time to see Stanislav entering Yuri's room.

The door closed behind him with a quiet *snick*.

Cat leaned into the frame of a large window behind the massive desk in David's study. The sun's rays, almost blindingly bright and sparkling with dust motes, poured through the clean panes and passed right through her, imbuing her with warmth . . . much as Yuri's touch had.

The house around her was quiet. All the immortals slept. Many of their human Seconds slept as well, having worked until noon or thereabouts, running errands and conducting whatever business they did during the day for the immortals they served and protected.

Even David slept, exhausted by the long hours he had kept of late, aiding immortals in North Carolina and surrounding states whenever emergencies arose, then spending the moments in between poring over medical textbooks in search of any information that would help him and Seth carry Ami safely through her difficult pregnancy.

Outside, Roland's cat, Nietzsche—as cantankerous as his owner—crept toward a squirrel.

The squirrel continued to nibble on an acorn, watching the cat from the corner of its eye.

"There you are." A pleasant male voice spoke, startling her.

Her head snapping around, Cat stared at the tall figure in the doorway.

Yuri graced her with a charming smile as he entered and closed the door behind him.

"Why aren't you asleep?" she asked, telling her treacherous heart to stop slamming against her ribs. She had never understood why she had continued to feel that particular organ after she had breathed her last breath. She never felt hunger. Never felt thirst. But her heart seemed to thump away in her breast. One of many mysteries for which she had no explanation.

"I was looking for *you*," he said, tucking his hands in his pockets as he strolled toward her. He wore the usual garb of an immortal. Black pants. Black T-shirt stretched taut over the thick muscles of his chest, shoulders, and arms. Heavy black boots.

From what she understood, immortals and their Seconds dressed thusly so bloodstains would be less apparent to any looky-loos who saw them after a hunt.

She frowned. Was that the right phrase? Looky-loos? It sounded odd.

Regardless, the clothing suited Yuri, accenting his dark hair and chestnut eyes.

She straightened as he approached the desk.

"I've only caught the briefest glimpses of you these last few nights," he commented.

Because she had been careful to avoid him since their talk. As soon as he had entered a room, Cat had left it. She had even resisted the temptation to follow him on his hunts.

He arched a dark brow. "Are you avoiding me?"

For a moment, Cat considered denying it. But she had told him she valued honesty. So she nodded.

"Why?" He cocked his head to one side. "Did I offend you in some way?"

Shaking her head, she glanced down. "I fear it is I who

offended you." She forced herself to meet his gaze. "I owe you an apology."

His expression remained impassive. "For what?"

"Now that I know you can see me, that you've *always* been able to see me, I realize . . ." Mortified, she looked away and began to pleat her skirts with anxious fingers. "You said you value your privacy, and I denied you that on many an occasion, visiting your chamber and following you on hunts. I—"

"Cat."

She shook her head and met his gaze. "I don't want to be like that first spirit you mentioned, the one you spoke to. I don't want to irritate you or make you uncomfortable. I—"

"You don't," he interrupted with a kind smile. "You didn't." He sighed as he circled the desk. "I feared this might be the reason for your absence." Stopping a few feet away, he leaned against the wall on the opposite side of the window, careful to avoid the sun's rays. "I confess I enjoyed your presence each time you joined me in my room or on a hunt." His smile widened. "The former more than the latter. The latter proved dangerously distracting on more than one occasion."

"Oh. I'm sorry."

"I'm not," he said, and glanced out the window.

Cat followed his gaze.

Without warning, Nietzsche raced toward the squirrel.

The squirrel dropped its acorn and shot up the nearest tree, not stopping until it reached the highest limbs, well out of the crazy cat's reach. Spinning around, it barked a peculiar little bark at the disgruntled feline, its tail flicking wildly.

"It's been so long, Cat," Yuri murmured, his profile drawing her gaze. "It's been so very long since I've spent time with a woman around whom I can relax and be myself." He cast her a smile, both wry and sad at the same time. "Five hundred years or so, if you can believe it."

She couldn't.

"Even when I was mortal, I had to hide my strange ability to see spirits. If I didn't, I was believed to be quite mad." He shrugged. "Once I became immortal, I had a great deal more to hide."

Surely there had been women over the centuries. Even Bastien had not remained celibate since his transformation.

"This life is not conducive to forming lasting relationships with women," he went on, almost as though she had spoken the thought aloud. "Human/immortal relationships never end well. Most end bitterly when the human ages and the immortal does not. The human always seems incapable of believing that the immortal who loves her will continue to do so as she grows wrinkled and stooped with age. That disbelief sows distrust. The elderly human convinces herself the immortal must be seeing a younger woman on the side and launches accusations each night as he leaves to hunt. The immortal always grows bitter himself that the woman he loves has so little faith in him."

He grew quiet, his handsome face pensive.

"Does it never work?" she asked.

"Very rarely. When it does, it always ends in tragedy when the human inevitably dies. Until Roland met Sarah, the same held true for immortal/*gifted one* relationships. Sarah is the first *gifted one* in history who actually asked to be transformed so she could spend eternity with an immortal. In the past, *gifted ones* always refused, which spawned even more bitterness."

He faced her once more. "I suspect you were born in another era, so I hope this will not offend your sensibilities, but . . . casual, meaningless sex has held no appeal for me for the past . . . oh . . . four hundred years, give or take a decade. After a century or so it just grew . . . tiresome and interested me about as much as eating the same meal for dinner every night for hundreds of years would. Periodically one feels the need to sate the hunger, of course, but it's just the scratching of an itch. There's no real satisfaction in it. And certainly no affection."

She fought back a blush. No man had ever spoken so plainly to her.

"I miss the company of women," he said with something akin to apology in his voice. "And while I was a bit wary of you the first few times you joined me in my room, I soon found I enjoyed your presence there. Enjoyed the companionship you provided. Enjoyed watching your expression change as you listened to audiobooks with me when Stanislav didn't join us."

Revelation struck. "You started listening to them for *me*, didn't you?" she asked.

"Yes," he admitted. "I couldn't help but notice the looks of longing you cast the books on my shelves." He glanced at the floor-to-ceiling bookshelves around them. "Or these."

What a thoughtful gift he had given her. Cat had always been a bit of a bluestocking when she had lived, burying her nose in a book whenever she could. "Thank you."

He inclined his head. "I even enjoyed watching television with you." He smiled. "As though we were an old married couple."

That enigmatic heartbeat of hers quickened.

"You brought me a peace I haven't experienced in many long years, Cat. I've missed that these past few days."

She swallowed. "I didn't want to be like that other spirit. I didn't want to make a nuisance of myself."

He huffed a laugh. "If you knew how much I've missed your company since we spoke, you'd understand just how impossible that is."

Hope and disbelief battled within her. Could she be so lucky?

He straightened away from the window frame and took a step toward her.

Cat reached out instinctively to push him away from the sunlight. "Careful," she admonished. Warmth suffused her hands when they touched his chest and started to pass through him. She jerked them back. "Oh. I'm sorry. I—"

He raised a hand to stop her apology, then held it out to her, palm-up, as he had that night in his room.

Cat stared down at the large, masculine hand as sunlight bathed it.

"I'm old enough that I can sustain some exposure without suffering."

"Oh." Cat glanced up at him, then tentatively placed her own hand atop his, careful to ensure hers wouldn't pass through it.

That wonderful warmth filled her where they pretended to touch.

Smiling, Yuri leaned down and mimicked kissing the back of her hand.

More warmth suffused her where his lips contacted her intangible skin.

He straightened. "Dmitry downloaded a new audiobook for me today at my request."

Cat smiled. One of the many things she had learned about Yuri in the time she had been haunting him was that he was not at all comfortable with the electronic devices and advanced technology of this time.

"He teased me mercilessly about it," he continued with a wry smile.

"Why?" she asked.

"Because I asked him to download something called a paranormal romance."

Paranormal romance. The term sounded familiar. "I think Tracy likes those."

He nodded. "According to Marcus, female readers love

them. Some men do, too. Though some—like Dmitry—mock them for it."

"Why?"

"Romance is considered a woman's genre by many. Love and happily ever after and that sort of thing. I think most men equate romance novels with chick flicks."

"Men don't like love and happily ever after?"

He shrugged. "I don't have a problem with it, but don't know that I'll enjoy listening to it for twelve or thirteen hours. Marcus claims paranormal romances also have a lot of action and violence in them, though, so I thought it might be something we could both enjoy."

"That was thoughtful of you," she said, pleased by the overture.

"My reading, or—in this case—listening preferences can be a bit dull and dry," he said apologetically.

"No, not at all," Cat protested.

He arched a brow.

She bit her lip. "It's just . . . some crime stories . . ." She tried to think of a diplomatic phrase that wouldn't offend.

"Bore the petticoats off you?" he supplied, his brown eyes twinkling with amusement.

She laughed. "Yes. I've watched too many of those police shows on television with the Seconds. The stories all seem to blend together now."

"Well, let's see if this paranormal romance will spark your interest, shall we?"

"Shouldn't you be sleeping?" she asked, hoping he would say no. It had been hard to stay away from him this past week. She had missed his company.

"Yes, but let us at least listen to the first chapter or two and get a taste of it. I'll turn in after that."

She grinned. "I'd like that."

He circled the desk and headed for the door.

Cat followed, as excited as a girl being courted for the first time. As he reached for the door handle, she passed through the wall beside the door. In the hallway, she turned and found him holding the door open for her.

Both laughed.

"Forgive me," she apologized. "Habit."

He shook his head. "I claim the same. Opening doors for women is second nature." He stepped out into the hallway with her. "This will be fun, I think," he said with a smile. "Never a dull moment."

Cat agreed wholeheartedly and accompanied him down to his room.

Chapter Three

The days and nights that followed were . . . *surreal*, Yuri supposed would be the best word. He hunted by night and spent his days with Catherine.

Or Cat. *His* Cat, as he soon began to think of her.

She was such a delight. Although Yuri had never considered himself a chatty sort, he and Cat never ran out of things to talk about. He loved that she called herself a bluestocking. Such an old-world term. Loved that she was well versed in the classics and philosophy and many subjects that women of her time had not been encouraged to explore. Yuri caught her up on some of the wonderful literature that had been written since her death, even playing audiobooks for her while he slept.

It was nice to be with a woman who, though three hundred years younger than he, was nevertheless nearer his age. A woman around whom he could be himself. A woman who wouldn't wrinkle her nose and complain about him being old-fashioned.

She made him laugh. Often. Made him happy in a way he hadn't thought he could be again. A perpetual smile seemed to touch his lips now. Even Dmitry had remarked upon it.

For the first time in a very *long* time, Yuri didn't feel as though he only existed to hunt. His life, for centuries, could've been summed up as succinctly as the instructions on a shampoo bottle: Instead of *wash, rinse, repeat*, it had been *hunt, sleep, repeat*.

But now he actually found himself wanting to put off falling asleep and looked forward to waking. Hunting and slaying vampires was no longer the center of his world. Cat was.

At last, he felt like he was living, not just going through the motions. And it felt good.

He felt good. He felt young again.

And Yuri suspected—*hoped*—Cat felt the same way.

If the centuries had seemed to pass slowly for Yuri, what the hell had it been like for Cat? At least Yuri had had his Seconds, Stanislav, and fellow immortals to take the edge off his loneliness. Hobbies to occupy his hands. Books to occupy his mind. Cat had had nothing. No books . . . and she *so* loved to read. No one to talk to. No one to even acknowledge her presence.

It broke his heart to think of it. So he made her laugh whenever he could and delighted in every smile he coaxed forth.

Though she was as old-fashioned as he, she seemed at ease in his presence. Seemed to enjoy his company and to care for him as much as he cared for her. Seemed to long for his touch as much as he longed for hers.

Yuri found his gaze drawn to her lips more and more often. How he wished he could taste them. And he had seen her gaze fall to *his* lips, and imagined her thinking the same.

The damned paranormal romance audiobooks they listened to didn't help. Cat's face flushed crimson each time a love scene rolled around. Yuri had had no idea those scenes would be so explicit, describing in vivid detail all of the things he wanted to do to Cat's lithe body, making him shift in his chair and sparking an intriguing flare of desire coupled with curiosity in Cat's shy gaze. As though she had never experienced such passion herself and wondered what it would be like to find it with him.

"Are you in love with Lisette?" she blurted one morning while such a scene titillated them both.

His eyebrows flew up. "What?"

"Lisette. The pretty French immortal," Cat said, her eyes on the skirt she pleated and unpleated with nervous fingers. "Are you in love with her?"

"No."

"You spend time with her," she muttered, still avoiding his gaze.

Yuri nodded. "We both like sports." Although *like* didn't quite cover it with Lisette.

Lisette was a sports *fanatic*. Any sport would do. But her brothers weren't interested in baseball. So when she had discovered that Yuri liked baseball shortly after his transfer, she had declared him her new sports buddy.

"That's all?" Cat asked. "The two of you don't . . . haven't ever . . ." Her gaze slid to the speakers that currently broadcast a description of the hero taking the heroine passionately in the shower.

"Made love?" he suggested for her.

"Yes."

Ah. So that's where her mind had gone. "No. We don't have that kind of relationship," he assured her. "We're just friends."

He wanted to be so much more with Cat. And judging by the relief that filled her blushing features, she wanted the same.

They touched each other . . . in that peculiar way that made his skin tingle. First casually. Her hand on his arm. His hand curling around hers and passing right through if he didn't take care. Then with more affection. Her fingers stroking his face, his shoulder. His own hand brushing her arm or lower back or lovely hair, wishing he could feel the strands slide across his fingers.

It might be a mere shadow of a touch, but Cat seemed to crave it, to enjoy having even that hint of contact she had been denied for so long.

Even now, as Yuri sat at the long table in David's dining room alongside his fellow immortals and all of their Seconds, he felt Cat come up behind him. Felt his back tingle and imagined her leaning against him. The tingle spread to his right shoulder and chest. Glancing down, he saw she had wrapped an arm around him (at least as much as she could in her spirit form) and smiled inside, though he kept his face impassive.

The voices of his comrades flowed over him as he basked in her presence. It would seem someone in the area was raising a new vampire army, one that was highly trained like the skilled vampire Yuri had slain the night he and Cat had spoken for the first time.

Very unusual for vampires. Even Bastien's army had not known martial arts or been as adept with weapons as some of these new vampires were.

Yuri glanced around the table as speculation flowed and found Marcus staring at him.

Marcus's gaze rose and settled upon Cat, standing behind Yuri, then returned to Yuri.

Cat leaned down to whisper in Yuri's ear, "I'm sorry. I forgot for a moment that he can see me. I'll go."

Yuri wanted to protest. He liked having her near. But he couldn't.

"Be safe on your hunt tonight," she implored. Then her presence vanished.

Disappointment filled him.

When the meeting ended, Yuri headed to the armory, eager to get the night's hunt out of the way so he could return to Cat.

Dmitry handed Yuri his cleaned and sharpened katanas.

A number of daggers followed, and throwing stars Yuri tucked in the long coat that would hide his small arsenal from humans.

Ready to leave, he strode toward the doorway only to find it blocked by Marcus.

"Got a minute?" the British immortal asked.

"Yes."

Marcus nodded in the direction of the basement stairwell.

Yuri followed him downstairs to the quiet room Marcus shared with his wife, Ami.

Marcus entered, held the door open, then closed it behind Yuri.

Yuri glanced around. This room was larger than his own and included a crib for the baby they all hoped would soon safely be born, as well as a rocking chair. He looked at Marcus and found him scrutinizing him a little too carefully. "What?"

"Are you insane?"

"No. Why? What's the word on the street?"

Marcus failed to laugh at the jest. "Why didn't you tell me you can see ghosts?"

Yuri shrugged. "I saw no purpose in it."

"Why didn't you tell me you can see *that* ghost? *Her* ghost?"

"I didn't see any reason to. You seemed uncomfortable around her—"

"I'm uncomfortable around *all* of them. As should you be."

Yuri shook his head. "Normally, I am, but—"

"You're talking to her."

"Yes."

Marcus shook his head. "There is *always* a catch, Yuri. I know I'm three hundred years older than you, but you've lived long enough to have learned that lesson many times over, I'm sure. There is *always* a downside to talking to them."

Yuri couldn't deny it. "I know."

"Then why did you do it? Why *are* you doing it?"

No point mincing words. "I enjoy her company."

The reprimand left Marcus's expression. His brow furrowed. A long moment passed.

"Really?" he asked, his tone perplexed.

"Yes."

"So . . ." Marcus backed away and leaned against the crib, his expression no less concerned. "You . . . what . . . converse?"

"Converse. Watch television. Listen to audiobooks together. Sometimes I read to her. I'm even teaching her to play chess."

Marcus's frown deepened. "How long has this been going on?"

"Not long. A few weeks."

Another minute dragged by, encapsulating them in heavy silence.

"Did she tell you who she is?"

Yuri nodded. "Catherine Seddon."

"And?"

"And what? You asked me who she is. She's Catherine Seddon."

Marcus straightened. "Yuri, haven't you ever wondered why she is the *only* spirit Seth and David haven't banished from this house?"

Yuri frowned. He hadn't really thought about it, but now that Marcus had mentioned it, it did strike Yuri as odd. Seth and David maintained homes all over the world, inviting immortals and their Seconds to visit whenever they wished to as David did here, doing their damnedest to foster a family atmosphere amongst them. This was the first time Yuri had ever encountered a spirit in one of the elder immortals' homes.

Why had they allowed Cat to stay?

"Is she the spirit of a deceased Immortal Guardian?"

"No."

"A fallen Second?"

"No."

Unease suffused him. "Who is she?" he forced himself to ask, almost afraid to hear the answer.

"She's Bastien's sister."

Shock tore through him. "The one Bastien thought Roland murdered?"

"Yes."

Bastien had raised his vampire army and pitted them against the Immortal Guardians a few years earlier for the sole purpose of avenging his sister's death, unaware that his sister had actually been slain by the husband she hadn't known had turned vampire.

Marcus sighed. "She didn't tell you?"

"No." Yuri had avoided asking her how she had died. He'd thought it a rather morbid question. And he certainly hadn't wanted to bring up painful memories.

Painful. He cringed as details of her murder swam through his head. He had only heard little snippets here or there since his arrival, but it had been enough. "She was with child when he killed her," he whispered.

Marcus nodded. "That's why she's so interested in Ami's pregnancy." His brow furrowed. "I don't mind telling you . . . it makes me nervous as hell when I see her touch Ami's belly. But I feel so damned sorry for her that I can't bring myself to tell her to keep her distance."

"Thank you for that," Yuri murmured, understanding now the sadness that claimed her in such moments. "Why did her husband kill her?"

"We don't know. He managed to convince Bastien he was lucid for several years afterward, so the madness had not yet claimed him. Maybe he simply meant to feed from her and lost control."

Yuri's heart hurt for her. "Does Ami know?"

"That Catherine touches her belly?"

"Yes."

Marcus shook his head. "She's having a hard enough time with this pregnancy. I don't want to throw in phantom hands touching her without her knowledge on top of everything else."

"She doesn't feel anything at Cat's touch?"

"No. If *you* do, your gift must allow you to feel it."

"What about Bastien? Does *he* know?"

"That his sister's ghost is hanging around? No."

"Why didn't you tell him?" Yuri sure as hell would want to know if he were in Bastien's shoes.

"At first I didn't tell him because I *hated* his ass. Ewen was a friend of mine."

And Bastien had killed Ewen when the Scottish immortal had attacked him, believing Bastien a maddened vampire preying upon an innocent woman.

"Seth wouldn't punish the bastard," Marcus continued, "and—I don't know—not telling him about his sister seemed a sort of punishment to me in my anger." He sighed. "Then I found out how kind Bastien had been to Ami, helping her recuperate from the torture she had suffered and boosting her confidence when those bastards who hurt her left her with almost none. He tested the antidote on himself so none of us would be hurt if it went really wrong. He helped us hide Ami's pregnancy in the beginning and has proven helpful in taking her mind off her worries." He shook his head. "I doubt we'll ever be best buddies, but I don't hate the guy anymore."

"So why haven't you told him about Cat?"

"It just seems cruel to me now. I mean, Bastien has probably assumed all this time that, although she suffered a tragic death, his sister found peace in the afterlife. Isn't that what we're always told? *Yes, she suffered, but she's at peace now.*" Marcus frowned. "Don't you think it would pretty much kill him to find out that instead, she's been stuck here—existing, but not *really* existing—for two damned centuries? That she's likely had no one to talk to in all of that time? That she was there with him the seven or eight years he continued to pal around with her husband, not knowing he was giving his loyalty to her killer? Or that she was there with him throughout his entire crap-hole life with the vampires, witnessing every atrocity they committed? She was born in the eighteenth century. She lived an incredibly sheltered life, then spent what must have felt like an eternity with psychotic killers, seeing all of the sadistic shit they hid from Bastien. And she *still* hasn't found peace."

Yuri recalled again the way she always vanished when he encountered vampires.

What she must have seen during those two centuries.

"I just thought it kinder not to tell him," Marcus finished.

Yuri had to agree.

Cat must also, because she had not once asked Yuri to let Bastien know she was there or to convey a message to him.

"Seth and David see her?" Yuri asked after a time.

"I'm sure they do."

"Do they speak to her?"

"I don't know. I don't think so. At least, I've never seen them do it. Probably for the same reason *I* don't talk to spirits. Because there really *is* always a downside."

"Why do they let her stay?"

"I think they feel sorry for her. I mean, even though he can't see her or hear her, Bastien is all she has left. What would she do if they banished her and took her brother away from her?"

Yuri swallowed. And if they had removed her from this house, Yuri would never have met her.

"So," Marcus spoke after a pause, "have you found it yet?"

"Found what?" Yuri asked absently, his mind a maelstrom.

"The catch. The downside to speaking with her."

Yuri responded with a slow nod.

"What is it?" Marcus asked curiously.

Yuri tried and failed to force a smile. "I'm falling in love with her."

Marcus swore.

Yuri encountered no more of the unusually skilled vampires in the nights that followed, though slacker vamps continued to proliferate. Sometimes he hunted without Stanislav and asked Cat to accompany him so they could speak freely and enjoy the night—or most of it—together. Sometimes he hunted *with* Stanislav and counted the hours until he could end his hunt and return to David's to spend time with Cat.

Seth had suggested that younger immortals hunt in pairs until the Immortal Guardians discovered the source of the new vampire uprising. Yuri had seen five hundred years and Stanislav four hundred. Both had no difficulty holding their own in battles with multiple slacker vampires. And Yuri felt confident they would also have no problem defeating any of the more skilled vampires they might encounter.

But something about this uprising left Yuri uneasy. And he found himself worrying about Stanislav when they hunted separately. The two had lived near each other and hunted either together or in the same area pretty much since Stanislav had been transformed and Seth had dropped him on Yuri's doorstep, naming Yuri Stanislav's mentor and trainer. Yuri loved Stanislav like a brother. And even though he knew his friend could handle himself exceedingly well in battle, Yuri just felt better hunting with him while this unknown army thrived around them.

Yuri opted to hunt with Stanislav again tonight. Cat didn't mind and hied herself off to haunt network headquarters, where her brother and his wife, Melanie, spent most of their nights.

Damn, he couldn't wait to get back to her.

It ended up being a good night. Yuri and Stanislav slew two different sets of vampires before the psychotic bastards could attack the humans they stalked. All were swift, clean kills. Neither immortal suffered more than the most inconsequential of injuries. And they managed to return to David's earlier than usual only to discover that many of the other immortals in the area had also ended their hunts early, having had an easy night.

No immortals had suffered serious injuries.

No more skilled vampires had made an appearance.

Laughter and conversation flowed freely.

Yes, it was a good night.

The only thing that would make it better, Yuri thought as he followed Stanislav into the kitchen to raid the refrigerator, would be Cat's return.

Dmitry and Alexei joined Yuri and Stanislav and helped them heap two huge platters high with fruits and breads and cheeses.

When the two Russian immortals carried their bounty into the living room, immortals and mortals alike pounced.

Over their heads, Yuri saw Cat appear on the opposite side of the room.

A moment later Bastien and Melanie entered through the front door.

Yuri gave the couple only a fleeting glance, his interest drawn to Cat.

She wore a pale yellow dress tonight, as demure as the others he had seen her wear, and looked as innocent as a girl in the first flush of womanhood. Her gaze searched the many immortals, humans, and *gifted ones* present until it fell upon him. Her face brightening with a smile, she offered him a little wave.

Yuri's spirit lightened. Grinning, he winked and hurried to set his platter on the nearest coffee table so he could wade through the throng to sit with her. He might not be able to speak to her without raising eyebrows and prompting unwelcome questions, but he could enjoy her presence. He would have motioned for her to follow him down to his bedroom so they could be alone if he didn't know how much she enjoyed the camaraderie these men and women shared. And all and sundry appeared to be in high spirits tonight.

Yuri found a love seat on the fringes of the room and claimed it for his own, his heart thumping madly as it always did when Cat seated herself beside him.

"Did your hunt go well?" she asked.

He nodded. Those delightful little tingles shot up his arm where it brushed hers, and he wished for the millionth time that they could truly touch. That he could hold her in his arms and feel her slight weight against him.

Laughter erupted, but Yuri missed whatever joke Darnell had cracked.

Cat watched it all with an envious smile.

As far as Yuri could tell, every immortal in the area was present save Lisette, whom he hadn't seen very often of late. Even Seth and David had taken some time off, relaxing amongst the others and watching Ami with affectionate indulgence.

Yuri shook his head when Ami's baby began to hiccup in the womb. He had never heard of such before. But then, he hadn't spent any time around pregnant women since acquiring preternatural hearing.

He glanced at Cat, wondering if she could hear it, if seeing Marcus smooth his hand over his wife's round tummy would spark that familiar sadness.

But Cat wasn't looking at the couple. She was staring at the bay window that graced the front of the room. Unease swept her features as her throat moved in a swallow. She reached for his hand, forgetting she couldn't grasp it.

Yuri frowned.

When she met his gaze, she looked terrified.

Alarm bells rang. "What is it?" he asked softly, uncaring if the others heard.

"Something's coming." Rising, she shook her head and began to back away, placing more distance between herself and the window. "Something's coming, Yuri," she repeated.

What the hell?

Before Yuri could ask her *what* was coming and why it frightened her so, Seth spoke.

"Marcus, Ami has spent too many days and nights cooped up inside. Why don't the two of you go for a ride? Roll down the windows. Get some fresh air. Enjoy the night."

"Sounds good to me," Marcus replied. "Are you up to it, sweetling?"

Yuri kept his gaze on Cat, wishing like hell they were alone.

"Absolutely!" Ami said.

Cat glanced at the eldest immortals. "They know. They know something's coming. They want Marcus to take Ami to safety."

Yuri followed her gaze and saw David toss Marcus his keys.

"Take my car," David said. "More room for you both to stretch your legs."

Everyone called cheerful good-byes as the couple left through the back door.

Silence fell as the others in the room began to glean that all was not well.

Tension rose as all eyes went to Seth and David.

Outside, David's car started and tore off down the drive, accompanied by Ami's fading laughter.

The two elders rose as one. Their faces turned to stone.

"Everyone out," Seth ordered.

"What's going on?" Roland asked, rising.

Yuri rose, too.

Everyone rose.

But none left.

The air began to crackle with static electricity.

Cat wrapped her arms around her middle, her anxiety ratcheting up enough that Yuri could damn near feel it himself.

Yuri glanced down as the hair on his arms rose. The hair on the back of his neck did the same.

Thunder rumbled on the night.

Seth shook his head, his eyes beginning to glow. "No time. Just go."

"Use the escape tunnels in the basement," David instructed beside him, his eyes glowing a vibrant amber.

Yuri had known David, one of the most even-tempered immortals, for five centuries. It took a hell of a lot to spark the kind of fury he now saw in that one's eyes.

"Don't return until we summon you," David finished.

"Fuck that!" Bastien blurted. "I don't know what the hell is coming, but we aren't going to leave you to face it alone!"

Yuri silently agreed and curled his fingers around the hilts of the daggers he always carried, even after disarming at the end of a night's hunt.

"Just go!" Seth snapped. "Get the Seconds out while you can. They—"

The large bay window exploded inward. Shards of glass rocketed through the living room, finding purchase in mortal and immortal flesh, as something catapulted inside as though it had been shot from a cannon.

Instinct driving him, Yuri spun around, dove for Cat to protect her, and ended up passing right through her. As he hit the ground, he saw the married immortal men all do the same for their wives, trying to shield them from the threat.

The coffee table near Seth and David splintered as a bloody body struck it. The unconscious male who had been tossed through the window hit the floor and rolled twice before coming to a halt near Yuri, lips parted to reveal fangs. A second body flew bonelessly through the bay window, knocking more shards free as it went. It hit the floor just beyond the first. Another vampire. Unconscious. His face and form shredded and bloody.

"There!" a voice bellowed outside as wind whipped the curtains.

The word shook them all from their shocked paralysis. Everyone lunged for the weapons they had removed earlier, rose, and braced themselves for a fight.

Everyone except Seth and David, who glared into the night through the broken window.

Drawing his daggers, Yuri peered into the darkness outside and wished he had his katanas.

Cat stepped up beside him, her fear palpable.

Lightning streaked across the sky, momentarily illuminating a figure who strode toward the house, still yards away, a black silhouette with . . . wings? . . . carrying something or someone in his arms.

"There's your fucking proof!" The male, damned near seven feet tall by Yuri's estimate, leapt through the gaping hole in the window and faced them with furious defiance.

He did indeed bear wings. Huge, dark wings with partially translucent feathers that made him appear even larger when he spread them, and damned formidable.

An immortal, then. A shapeshifter? But one Yuri had never seen before.

Little bits of feather, sliced away by the fragments of glass that remained in the window frame, floated on the breeze and settled quietly on the floor.

The male's eyes glowed golden like Seth's, very unusual. Almost all immortals had brown eyes that glowed amber whenever they were in the grips of strong emotion.

The male's face twisted with pure, animalistic rage.

Yuri's astonished gaze fell upon the limp form cradled in the intruder's arms.

Lisette.

"What the hell?" her brother Étienne shouted and leapt forward, swords flashing.

The winged immortal looked at Étienne.

Étienne seemed to hit an invisible wall and flew backward. *Shit!*

Étienne's twin, Richart, vanished and reappeared behind the intruder, daggers raised.

Without even turning around, the winged male sent Richart flying, too. "She tried to warn you it wasn't me!" he snarled at Seth.

Yuri caught Stanislav's eye.

Stanislav nodded.

Yuri looked just beyond him to Roland, older than Yuri by a good four hundred years.

Roland met his gaze and nodded, his face grim.

"She tried to tell you I couldn't have raised the new vampire army," the intruder bellowed, "because I was too busy being fucking tortured!"

Confident the three of them could take him, Yuri jerked his head toward the male.

As one, he, Roland, and Stanislav leapt forward.

That furious golden gaze speared Yuri.

A wave of power rippled through the room, the winged male at its epicenter.

Yuri swore as it hit him like the blast wave of a fucking A-bomb, sweeping him—and every other immortal and mortal present, save Seth and David—off his feet.

Yuri hit the floor hard and heard Cat scream. Looking up, he saw her form flicker, then vanish. Not the way she usually did: there one second, gone the next, like a teleporter. But like a hologram that had short-circuited, or a mirror that had shattered.

Fear rose within him, clamping a fist around his heart and making it difficult to breathe.

"I didn't . . . fucking . . . do it!" the winged male roared. "And because you wouldn't believe us, because you couldn't believe one of your *precious* Immortal Guardians would betray you, the new vampire army *I didn't fucking raise* grew unchecked!"

Had Seth accused this man of raising the new vampire army?

"Well, there's your proof!" the intruder roared and nodded at the vampires. "Read their minds! Unbury their memories! You won't find me in any of them!"

Yuri tightened his clasp on his daggers and glanced around frantically, hoping Cat would reappear—if only for a moment—to let him know she was okay.

Seth held out a hand to the intruder, palm facing out in a *just stay calm* motion, and slowly backed toward the vampires. Kneeling, he placed a hand on the first vampire's blood-soaked head.

Yuri gained his feet, feeling as if he had been kicked in the chest by a mule. Minutes ticked past as he fought the urge to race through the house in search of Cat, his gut telling him something was wrong, that something had happened to her.

Seth touched the second vampire.

The other immortals rose to their feet, faces pained. Mortals rose more slowly, some requiring the aid of their immortals.

Finally, Seth stood.

"You see?" the winged male demanded, the two words filled with wrath.

Seth shared another look with David. "What have you done to Lisette, Zach?"

"Watched over her. Tried to protect her when you wouldn't."

Zach? Yuri couldn't recall ever having heard any mention of an immortal named Zach. And this was clearly an elder.

"What happened tonight?" Seth asked.

"Lisette and I went hunting together."

Lisette *knew* this male?

Seth opened his mouth.

"That's right! Together!" Zach bellowed before Seth could speak. "Did you think I was going to leave her unprotected while you pissed away your time and let the vampire army grow in strength and numbers? Let them get their shit together? Let them nearly capture her?"

Yuri stared. No one spoke to Seth like that. *No* one. Who the hell *was* this immortal?

"The two of you were hunting," David said, his voice calm. "What happened next?"

"We took on a dozen of the new breed of vampires. I thought with me at her back she would be safe. But . . ."

"You can defeat a dozen vampires without lifting a weapon," Seth pointed out.

"Killing one or two with a thought wouldn't draw any notice," Zach said. "But the kind of power it would take to kill a dozen would have alerted the Others to my location. If they found out about her, learned what she means to me—"

Others? Other *what*? Other vampires?

"You just exerted more power than that here," Seth pointed out.

"They'll assume it was you."

"Fuck this," Ethan, a young American immortal who had been trained by and had long been smitten with Lisette, blurted and clambered to his feet. "We don't have time for if-I-woulda-coulda-shouldas. What's wrong with Lisette?"

Yuri agreed.

Zach swallowed, nostrils flaring, moisture rising in his

iridescent eyes. "I can't wake her." He clutched Lisette closer, rubbed his chin across her hair. "Her presence in my mind vanished, and when I turned around . . . she was falling."

Seth took a step forward. "Give her to me."

"Fuck you! I'm not letting you anywhere near her! Not after that little conversation you had with her." His gaze circled the room. "Do your Immortal Guardians all know you accused *her* of collaborating with the vampires?"

Still searching the room for a glimpse of Cat, Yuri felt his mouth fall open. *What?*

"What?" Richart and Étienne demanded, echoing his thought, as their heads snapped toward Seth.

Seth's face remained impassive. "If you don't want me near her, why did you bring her to me?"

"I didn't." Zach looked at Melanie. "I came here for you." His gaze shifted to Bastien. "And for you."

Bastien sheathed his weapons and strode forward, broken glass crunching beneath his boots. Melanie glanced at Seth and David, waiting for their approval, then followed with caution.

Again, Yuri glanced around, hoping to spot Catherine.

Melanie felt Lisette's pulse, then peeled Lisette's eyelid back. "Any major arteries severed?" She began checking them herself even as she asked.

"No."

"So not a lot of blood loss?"

"No. Most of the blood that coats her is vampire."

Seth took a step forward. "You didn't give her your blood, did you?"

Zach glared daggers at him. "Of course not. I'm not an idiot."

What the hell did *that* mean? Yuri wondered.

More calmly, Zach told Melanie, "We were holding our

own against them very nicely before she collapsed. She suffered no major injuries as far as I could see, hear, or smell."

Melanie glanced around at the debris-covered room, then motioned down the hallway. "Could I get you to place her on a bed in the infirmary so I can examine her more thoroughly?"

Zach's arms tightened around Lisette as his eyes flashed brighter.

Melanie raised a hand. "Okay. It's okay. I'll just . . . see what I can learn here for now so you can have another minute to . . ." She floundered. "So you can have another minute."

Yuri wasn't sure another minute would be enough. The male—Zach—appeared pretty savage. And disinclined to relinquish his toy. Or treasure.

Zach looked as terrified for Lisette as Yuri felt for Cat.

What the hell had that wave of power done to her?

Melanie proceeded to run her fingers over Lisette's arms and legs, across her abdomen, applying pressure here and there along the way. When her fingers slipped between Lisette and Zach's chest, she gasped and jerked her hand back.

Bastien stiffened. "What?"

A bead of blood formed on the tip of one finger. Frowning, Melanie slowly felt along the same path, then drew her hand back.

Utter sickening disbelief lashed Yuri when she held up a tranquilizer dart.

It couldn't be.

Melanie listed to one side, eyelids drooping.

Bastien hastily wrapped his arms around her, his face darkening with concern. "Melanie? Sweetheart?"

She squeezed her eyes closed and shook her head. "I'm okay," she said, but slurred her words as though drunk. Unsteady on her feet, she clung to the arms Bastien wrapped around her. "I just . . . I just pripped . . . pricked my finger."

Yuri swore silently. A pinprick had done *that*?

"They must've . . . must've upped the dosage again," she continued.

Silence took the room. Men and women stiffened with shock.

They, meaning the mercenaries who were all supposed to be dead, had upped the dosage again?

Twice the Immortal Guardians had battled mercenaries in recent years. Mercenaries who had been intent on capturing an immortal and procuring the virus so they could build an army of supersoldiers they could then hire out to the highest bidder. Mercenaries who possessed the only sedative known to affect immortals and vampires, who—until then—had been unaffected by every drug in existence.

The first time immortals had defeated the mercenaries, the elders had buried the survivors' memories. The second time, the mercenaries had upped the dosage of the sedative so much that it had taken double the usual dose of the antidote Melanie had developed to enable immortals to rouse and function again. And they hadn't functioned normally. They had functioned, at least briefly, as if they were high on cocaine. Juiced up. Heart racing. Not thinking clearly before they acted.

Seth strode forward. "That isn't possible."

"Stay back!" Zach barked.

"Fuck off!" Seth barked back.

Yuri tensed, ready to spring forward in an instant should Zach move to harm the Immortal Guardians' leader.

Seth took the tranquilizer dart from Melanie's limp fingers and brought it to his nose. He drew in a deep breath. His eyes flashed gold again as thunder rumbled outside. "How the fuck can this be?" he growled. "We didn't even bother to bury memories this time. We killed fucking *everyone*!"

They had. Not one mercenary had been left alive. *No one* outside the Immortal Guardian family and the network of humans who aided them should possess that drug. How the hell had vampires gotten their hands on it?

"It doesn't matter how it happened," Bastien spoke. "Not right now. We need to get Melanie a small dose of the antidote and see what, if anything, we can do to revive Lisette."

If anything. The two words filled Yuri with dread.

Keeping one arm around his wife, Bastien shifted to stand at Zach's side. He reached around and touched Zach's back beneath his wings. "Come on. The infirmary is just down this hallway. Let's make Lisette comfortable and see if we can't help her."

Bastien had to give Zach a gentle push to get him moving.

Stiffly at first, as though his feet had cemented themselves to the floor in front of the bay window and didn't want to part with it, Zach allowed Bastien to lead him from the room.

Seth followed.

A raindrop hit the grass outside with a swish. Another followed. Then more, racing each other to their doom as the sky opened up and enveloped the house in a downpour.

David eyed them sternly. "Not one word."

Étienne glowered at him. "David—"

"Not. One. Word," the elder repeated. "Your grievances will be heard at a more appropriate time. For now . . ." He motioned to the vampires. "Richart, take these two to the network and place them in separate holding rooms. Bring Chris back with you when you return. He needs to know what's going on. And ask him to send someone out here to replace my window. The rest of you, see to your wounds, then clean up this mess."

He turned without another word and headed down the hallway, disappearing through the infirmary's doorway.

His and Lisette's Seconds, Darnell and Tracy, followed, closing the door behind them.

"You heard him," Roland, nearly a thousand years old, said. Turning to his wife, he began to brush small shards of glass from her clothing. "Now isn't the time for questions." He speared the d'Alençon brothers with a warning glare.

"*Or* for recriminations. Now is the time to circle our wagons. We don't know who or what might come through that window next."

Hell, Yuri still wasn't clear on who *Zach* was.

"We should post guards," Stanislav said, "in case another of his ilk should follow."

Roland nodded. "As the strongest present, Sarah and I will patrol the grounds. Stanislav, you and Yuri go below and keep your ears open. Ensure no one enters through the escape tunnels."

Every bedroom in the basement included a wardrobe with a false back that hid a subterranean tunnel that would provide safe passage into thick groves of evergreens for any immortal who might be forced to escape an attack during the day.

Yuri nodded and zipped down to the basement, Stanislav on his heels.

"You take this end," Yuri instructed.

Stanislav positioned himself at the base of the stairs.

Yuri peered into the large training room. Upon finding it empty, he strode down the hallway opposite it.

He opened every door he passed, giving each bedroom a quick once-over.

Stanislav didn't question him, so he must think Yuri searched for other intruders.

In truth, Yuri sought Cat.

He didn't like the way she had disappeared. As though she had had no control over it.

And her scream still echoed through his mind.

Yuri found neither Cat nor additional intruders in the bedrooms.

Concern rising, he positioned himself at the opposite end of the long corridor and struggled to remain calm as he waited.

Chapter Four

Twenty-four hours later, Cat still had made no appearance.

Not knowing what else to do, Yuri waited for Marcus to stride past his bedroom, then yanked him inside.

Marcus stumbled a bit as Yuri closed the door behind him. Straightening, he arched both brows. "You wanted to speak with me?"

"Have you seen Cat?" Yuri blurted.

"No. Not today."

Yuri swore.

"Why?" Marcus frowned. "What's wrong?"

"I think something has happened to her."

"She's a ghost, Yuri. Nothing can happen to her. Nothing tangible can harm her."

"That thing Zach did," Yuri protested, "that odd blast of power or whatever the hell it was that knocked us all on our asses . . ."

Marcus frowned. "Roland told me about that. He said it felt like the blast wave of a bomb hitting him. What about it?"

"I think it did something to her," Yuri told him, finally voicing his fear.

"Like what?"

"I don't know. But she disappeared when it hit her and I haven't seen her since."

"Maybe she's at the network."

Hope rose. "Did you see her there last night, when you took Ami to the network to keep her safe?"

"No," Marcus replied with reluctance. "But I've seen her there other times. Maybe she went there after we left. Maybe she hasn't been around because she's afraid of Zach."

And the mysterious elder immortal Zach remained in David's home, refusing to leave Lisette's side until she awoke from what Melanie had begun to call a coma.

"Cat wouldn't stay away without telling me," Yuri said with certainty. "She'd know how much I would worry."

Marcus studied him. "The two of you are really that close?"

"Yes." Yuri waited for Marcus to again question his sanity or to lambaste him for doing something so stupid as to fall in love with a ghost.

He didn't. "What exactly do you think has happened?" Marcus asked instead.

Yuri shook his head, helplessness rising within him. "I don't know. When that blast of power hit her, she seemed to . . . fragment . . . or shatter like the glass in a dropped picture frame, then vanished. I haven't seen her since."

Marcus swore.

"What? Do you know what it means?"

"No. I've never seen that happen before."

Yuri's anxiety rose. He didn't know what to do. "Would Seth and David know?"

"Possibly. But both are busy pouring all of their energy into healing Lisette and trying to wake her from the damned coma or whatever the hell it is that drug has done to her." He thought for a moment. "I tell you what. I'll have Richart teleport me over to the network after I get a few hours' sleep. I'll tell him I think I left something behind when I was there last night with Ami. And I'll have a quick look around to see if Cat's there."

"Thank you." Yuri would go himself, but didn't want to leave until he had to hunt in case Cat should return.

"I can't stay more than a few minutes," Marcus added. "I don't want to stray too far from Ami. But it shouldn't take me long."

Yuri nodded and thanked him again.

Marcus headed for the door and gripped the knob, but didn't turn it. A minute passed, during which he seemed to debate over whether he wanted to say something more. "I understand, you know," he murmured and looked at Yuri over his shoulder.

Yuri frowned. "Understand what?" His concern for Cat?

"The position you're in. I can empathize," the elder immortal said. "I loved a woman I couldn't have for eight hundred years before I met Ami."

Yuri had almost forgotten Marcus's peculiar history.

"At least the woman you love can love you back." Marcus turned the knob, then hesitated again and arched a brow. "She *does* love you back, right?"

"I believe so," Yuri said. "But . . ."

Marcus waited for him to finish.

"We can't . . ." Yuri wasn't sure what drove him to continue. "I can't touch her."

"When she leaned against you at the meeting, it looked as though you could feel her."

"I feel a tingling sensation," Yuri told him. "But I can't touch her skin. Can't feel the weight of her against me." And how he longed to.

Marcus sighed. "I'm sorry. I was going to say that sucks, but that just doesn't cover it, does it?"

"Not even close."

Marcus considered him, features thoughtful. "She was a *gifted one* when she lived, wasn't she?"

"Yes."

"Do you know what her gift was?"

"She had psychometric abilities, could see the history of an object when she touched it. Still can, actually."

"Oh." Marcus's brow furrowed. "That's too bad. I was hoping she might've been a telepath or a dream walker. Then perhaps she could've visited you in your dreams." He smiled wryly. "Sex can be very real in dreams."

Yuri hadn't even thought of that.

"I'll let you know what I learn at the network as soon as I return," Marcus promised, again preparing to leave. "And, Yuri?"

"Yes?"

"If I had to choose between a woman who shared my love, but whom I couldn't touch, and a woman I could touch, but who meant little to me . . . I'd choose the woman I loved every time." Opening the door, he stepped out into the hallway, then closed it behind him.

Two long days and nights passed without Yuri catching so much as a glimpse of Catherine. Had whatever Zach had done that night banished her forever?

Marcus had not seen her at network headquarters. Nor had he seen her here at David's.

Ami's pregnancy had progressed far enough and was becoming so difficult that Marcus had stopped hunting entirely to remain close to her. And, sympathetic to Yuri's plight, Marcus had been keeping an eye out for Cat while Yuri was out hunting.

Several times, Yuri had wanted to seek Seth and David's counsel. But both elders were exhausted from pouring healing energy into both Lisette, who had still not awakened from her coma, and Ami to help her carry her baby to term. And as much as Yuri loved Cat, he couldn't bring himself to ask either elder to cease tending the living so they could help him locate a spirit.

Yet.

In truth, Yuri wasn't sure *what* he would do if Cat remained absent much longer.

Growing ever more desperate, Yuri had gone to the infirmary that afternoon to ask Zach what he had done to Cat, to ask him if he could reverse it and bring her back. But Zach had rendered himself unconscious pouring too much healing energy into Lisette in an attempt to wake her, his hand clutching Lisette's to his chest, his head resting on the bed beside her.

Despair rising, Yuri let the conversation of the immortals gathered together in David's living room flow over and around him without paying it much heed. He slumped in his favorite wingback chair with his boots propped on a coffee table scarred from years of other boots doing the same. Yuri knew his somber silence worried Dmitry, but had no desire to explain himself.

Marcus and Ami sat on a sofa catercorner to him. The pair had had a difficult day. Ami had begun experiencing contractions again, and Seth had had to use his healing gift to stop the premature labor.

Everyone else present, like Yuri, had made it through another night's hunt without incident. None had encountered any of the new skilled vamps. None had been seriously injured or tranqed. All had resolved to sleep at David's place until Lisette awoke.

Yuri found himself wondering if the gun drawn by that big vampire he had fought the first night he'd spoken to Cat had been a tranquilizer gun. He hadn't paid any attention at the time and—

Marcus kicked Yuri's feet.

Scowling, Yuri glanced over at him.

Marcus met his eyes, then looked pointedly toward a far corner of the living room.

Yuri followed his gaze. His breath caught.

Cat stood there. In the same place she had been standing the night the blast had hit her. Garbed in the same yellow dress. Brow creased.

Relief rushed through him, so intense it damned near left him light-headed.

Heart pounding, he rose.

Cat stared at the bay window in confusion, finding no evidence that it had ever been broken. Clean panes revealed darkness outside overlaid by reflections of light and the figures inside the room. No lingering shards of glass littered the floor. No splinters from the broken windowpane frames stuck out of upholstery. No stray feathers from the winged male who had leapt through the window rested upon the floor.

Brow furrowing, she looked around the room. The coffee table that had been shattered by the first vampire's body had been removed and replaced. The chairs and sofas that had been overturned in the immortals' haste to get out of the paths of the shattering glass and the bodies hurled inside had been righted and now provided seating for Immortal Guardians and their Seconds as they engaged in casual conversation as though nothing had happened.

Her eyes fell upon Marcus, seated next to his wife. For once he neither avoided meeting her gaze nor looked uneasy. Instead he appeared to . . . *welcome* her presence?

A figure near Marcus rose.

Yuri.

Relief suffused her.

He was all right, then, his face and form as perfect as ever.

His eyes met hers and began to glow a faint amber. He cocked his head toward the hallway.

Nodding, she started toward it, weaving her way through the men and women present. She had never grown comfortable with passing through the living, so she ducked and dodged them as she would have had she still been alive herself.

She and Yuri reached the hallway at the same time.

As they passed the infirmary, she glanced inside and saw the winged man, *sans* wings, sitting beside a bed, clutching the hand of a slumbering Lisette. Seth sat at Lisette's head, his hand resting on her shoulder and glowing.

Cat followed Yuri downstairs to the basement. Though he was taller and walked with much longer strides, she had no difficulty keeping up with him. Another peculiarity about her existence. No matter how slow her steps, she could progress forward as quickly as she wished.

As soon as they were ensconced in the privacy of his room and could not be overheard, he swung around to face her.

"What happened?" they asked simultaneously.

She bit her lip.

"Me first," he insisted. Even that defied the norm. Yuri had not been born in this century and still bore the *ladies first* mind-set.

"All right."

"What happened?" he repeated. "Where were you?"

The questions only heightened her confusion. "What do you mean? I was upstairs."

"Not just now," he said, raking a hand through his hair. "Before. Where have you been since Zach arrived? I've been so worried about you."

"Who is Zach?"

"The winged immortal who tossed two vampires through David's bay window, then dove in after them with Lisette in his arms."

"I don't understand. That just happened while I was upstairs. While we *both* were."

Yuri frowned. "What?"

"That just happened," she repeated, bewildered. "Minutes ago. It just happened. But . . . I don't . . ." She glanced up at the ceiling, recalling how normal the room and its occupants had appeared, then met his gaze once more. "How did you get it all cleaned up so fast? I didn't see . . ." She trailed off. Immortals could move fast, but they couldn't move *that* fast. They couldn't have cleaned it up so quickly that she wouldn't have seen at least *some* of it unfold.

Yuri stilled, his iridescent amber gaze sharpening.

Didn't his eyes only glow when he was gripped by strong emotion?

"You think Zach just arrived?" he said.

"Well, yes. Didn't he?"

A quiet moment passed while he considered her. "Tell me what you remember."

Anxiety rose. "We were sitting in the living room. Together. On the love seat you'd claimed. The bay window shattered when two vampires were tossed through it. Then the winged man leapt in after them with Lisette cradled in his arms. Richart and Étienne tried to attack him and failed to get close enough to wound him. You, Stanislav, and Roland tried to attack him. And then . . ."

"Then?" he prompted.

She shook her head. It didn't make sense. "Then everything was back to normal."

He continued to stare at her, the amber glow fading from his brown eyes.

"Yuri?" The longer he went without speaking, the more worried she grew. "Yuri, I don't understand. Is that not what happened?"

"Cat," he said finally and took a step toward her, "Zach shattered David's window three nights ago."

"What?" Gaping up at him as he drew closer, she shook her head. "That's not possible."

"When Stanislav, Roland, and I attacked him," Yuri continued, "Zach hit everyone in the room with a blast of power so great it knocked all of us—every immortal and mortal present save Seth and David—off our feet. When the blast of power hit *you*, you screamed and disappeared. Your form appeared to short-circuit or shatter like glass."

Cat had no memory of that, but knew Yuri wouldn't lie to her.

"I haven't seen you since that blast wave hit you," he told her. "Not until now. I thought . . ." He shook his head. "I didn't know *what* to think. I feared Zach had . . . I don't know . . . exorcised you or banished you the way Seth and David can when they choose."

She watched him with wide eyes. "I've been gone for three nights?"

"Yes." His voice grew hoarse with emotion. "For three *very* long nights."

She took a step toward him. "I'm so sorry, Yuri. I didn't know." How she wished she could touch him then. Smooth the furrow from his brow. Burrow into his arms and remove that look of anguish from his handsome face. "I don't even know where I was. To me, it's as though only minutes have passed."

His shoulders slumped. His head bowed. Closing his eyes, he took the last step that separated them.

Warmth raced down the front of her where their bodies merged.

"I thought I'd lost you," he whispered.

Her eyes burned with tears. "I'm sorry."

He shook his head. "It wasn't your fault. I'm just so damned glad you're here."

She lowered her own head and wished she could rest it upon his chest, feel his heart beating beneath her ear.

"How I wish I could hold you in my arms," he murmured.

The words mirrored her thoughts so closely he might as well have read her mind. "As do I."

Sighing, he backed away and sank down on the foot of his bed. "Sit with me for a moment."

Cat sat next to him, so closely that heat from his hip seeped into hers.

"Are you okay?" he asked, voice gentle.

She nodded. "A little scared, perhaps. It's a bit frightening to know I vanished and to have no memory of where I went or know why I went there."

He nodded.

She thought of the men and women upstairs. "Marcus almost looked happy to see me."

"He knows how worried I've been."

"He knows I disappeared?"

"Yes."

"Do you think he would know where I went?"

He shook his head. "Marcus is even more strict about avoiding contact with spirits than I am. He *did* help me look for you, though."

"Really?"

"I didn't want to leave longer than it took to hunt vampires because I didn't want to miss you if you returned. So he searched network headquarters for me to see if you were there."

"That was kind of him."

"Yes."

"Would you thank him for me, please? I don't think he would want me to do it myself."

A faint smile touched his lips. "I don't know. I think he may be coming around." Something new sparkled in his eyes. "In fact, he said something to me while you were gone that made me think."

"About what?" she asked, uncertain what that new light in his eyes reflected.

"You were born with psychometric abilities."

"Yes."

"Have you acquired any others since you . . ."

"Died?"

His face tightened. "Yes."

"No."

"None at all?"

"Not that I'm aware of, aside from being able to walk through objects. Why?"

"Have you ever tried to visit someone in their dreams?"

She frowned. "No. I wasn't born with that gift."

"But you exist in a different realm now. Physically, you're as intangible as dreams. And I've heard that ghosts who delight in frightening people can sometimes infiltrate their victims' dreams and twist them into nightmares. At least, they do in movies. Maybe *you* could find your way into that other realm and visit me in my dreams."

"I already visit you here. Why would you—?"

"I could *hold* you in my dreams," he interrupted, voice deepening.

Her breath caught.

"I could touch you in my dreams."

Excitement sizzled through her.

And how she wanted him to touch her, wanted to discover if she could find the same passion with him that paranormal romance heroines found with their heroes.

She swallowed. "I don't know how to enter your dreams," she whispered.

The hope in his eyes began to fade.

"But," she hastened to add, "I think I may know someone who does."

"Who?"

"A spirit like those you mentioned. One who enjoys frightening the living. One who may very well haunt both people *and* dreams."

A troubled frown drew his brows down. "Cat, I don't want

you to place yourself in danger. If anything were to happen to you—"

"It won't," she assured him, but already dreaded the confrontation to come. "I can handle this particular spirit." She drew phantom fingers along his cheek and hoped she would soon be able to feel the rough rasp of his beard stubble. "If all goes well, I will see you in your dreams this morning."

His throat moved in a swallow as his eyes darkened with the same longing that had been her constant companion since she had first spoken to him.

Rising, she thought of the estate she wished to visit.

Yuri's bedroom disappeared, replaced by sunny English countryside.

Cat stared up at a sprawling three-story home and willed away the trepidation that threatened to crush her.

Thinking of Yuri helped, filling her with purpose and courage.

Striding forward, she scaled the wide steps that led up to a pair of imposing double doors and passed through into the home.

It had changed over the centuries, had been remodeled many times over.

Servants went about their daily chores and paid her no heed as she strode past them, searching one room after another until she found herself in what had formerly been the library.

It still boasted tall bookshelves, but had been transformed into a modern home office.

A man with short, auburn hair lightly peppered with gray sat at a large oak desk, typing away at a computer. The current homeowner, she assumed.

Another man—a spirit like herself—with tousled dark blond hair slumped in one of the two chairs that faced the desk, singing a bawdy tavern song under his breath as he watched the other man work. The spirit leaned forward and reached a finger toward a coffee mug that rested a foot or so away from the computer. A grin splitting his face, he jabbed his finger into the side of the mug.

The mug skidded a couple of inches across the wooden surface, sloshing coffee over its rim.

The man behind the desk jumped and gripped the arms of his chair. "Shit!" His wide eyes fastened on the mug, then swiftly searched the room. Had she been able to hear it, Cat was certain his heart would be pounding a rapid rhythm in his chest.

A long moment passed while the man eyed the mug warily.

When nothing more happened, he pulled a tissue from a box on the opposite side of his desk and reached toward the spilled coffee, every movement stiff with anxiety.

The spirit's grin widened. When he again stretched a finger toward the mug, Cat spoke.

"Hello, Blaise."

The spirit jumped even more violently than the homeowner had when the mug had seemingly moved without assistance. Leaping up, he spun around and regarded her with wide eyes, his gleeful smile vanishing. "Catherine." Her husband's face filled with unease and shame and she-couldn't-identify-what-else as she studied him.

Cat had been there the night Roland had slain him. Hers had been the first face her husband and murderer had seen as his spirit had left his body. And as the madness with which the vampiric virus had infected him had fallen away, a new sort of madness had taken its place as he faced the truth of the atrocities he had committed.

He had begged her forgiveness for all he had cost her. Had wept over killing their babe.

Cat had felt nothing but bitterness, and wondered if bitterness was what drove him to torment the living as he did now. Bitterness or boredom, she supposed, and thought he really couldn't disappoint her more.

"W-what are you doing here?" he asked.

"You owe me a great debt," she told him.

His gaze fell. "Yes."

"You have knowledge I require."

He looked up, curiosity erasing some of his unease. "What knowledge?"

Chapter Five

Stretched out in his king-sized bed, Yuri stared up at the dark ceiling.

Cat was going to try to visit him in his dreams. And damned if insomnia hadn't chosen to rear its head.

He swore.

When was the last time he had had difficulty sleeping? During his transformation? Certainly not since he had become immortal. Immortals possessed tremendous control over their bodies. They could control their temperature, their pulse, their metabolic rate.

And they could damned well fall asleep whenever the desire struck them.

Hell. Maybe he was just too excited to sleep. Just the idea of finally being able to hold Cat . . .

Or maybe he was *afraid* to fall asleep. Afraid she might not be able to find him in that realm. Afraid of losing the hope Marcus had given him.

He sighed.

"Just suck it up and do it," he grumbled.

Closing his eyes, he slowed his breathing, relaxed his body, and let sleep claim him.

* * *

A crush of people surrounded Yuri, buffeting him alongside a crisp winter breeze. Noses and cheeks glowed red in the cold. Warm breath formed puffs of white fog in front of smiling faces. Excitement filled the air, as did sparkling lights, the noise of hundreds of thousands of voices all talking at once, and the scent of alcohol.

Times Square on New Year's Eve. What a thrilling place to be. Masses of individuals all eager to ring in the new year, emitting so much positive energy one could practically get high on it. *If*, that was, one didn't have to weed out the vampires that slithered through the crowd, preying upon humans who remained trapped in place by the throng.

Yuri eyed one such vampire who had buried his face in a human woman's neck. Had he bitten her yet?

Her head fell back, her eyes closing as her lips parted in apparent pleasure.

Yeah, he had bitten her.

When vampires and immortals transformed, glands formed above the retractable fangs they grew. Under the pressure of a bite, those glands released a chemical that behaved much like GHB, leaving the victim sluggish and willing to accede to anything the vampires wanted to do to them. Tomorrow morning, the woman would have no memory of this.

Palming a dagger, Yuri shouldered his way through the throng, nodding and smiling at those he passed even as he dodged their big blue top hats. He glanced at the clock.

Perfect timing. They were about to begin the ten-second countdown to eleven o'clock.

Yuri bumped into the vampire.

As expected, the vamp removed his fangs from the woman's neck and spun around to snarl at Yuri.

Yuri buried his blade in the vampire's heart and twisted it to ensure the wound wouldn't heal before the vamp bled out.

Gripping Yuri's shoulder to help him remain on his feet, the vampire gaped up at him.

Yuri withdrew his dagger and drove it into the vampire's abdominal aorta just as the countdown began.

The vampire tried to draw a weapon.

Yuri snatched it from his hand and pocketed it.

The vampire staggered, then sagged against Yuri, any sound he made going unheard amidst the shouts of the revelers.

The woman the vampire had bitten teetered a step or two to one side.

"Dana?" the woman next to her shouted over the noise, frowning up at her and gripping her arm to steady her. She looked past Dana to Yuri and the vampire, whose face was pressed to Yuri's chest.

Yuri grinned and shook his head. "Too much to drink!" he shouted over the noise.

She laughed. "This one, too, it looks like!"

Rolling his eyes in feigned amusement, Yuri started to make his way through the crowd. Not an easy task in this crush of humanity, particularly while supporting the vampire's weight until the virus that infected him went to work. It didn't take long for the vampire to deteriorate completely and leave Yuri holding only a jumble of clothes.

Fortunately, everyone in the crowd was so busy cheering and admiring the pyrotechnic display while they shouted into their phones, took selfies, and blew whatever the hell those annoying noisemakers were called, that they didn't notice. The few who did notice Yuri just thought he was, at first, taking a drunk friend home and, moments later, carrying a spare coat.

As Yuri neared the edge of the crowd, he felt a tug on his coat sleeve.

Glancing back and down, he halted. Pleasure and surprise filled him. "Cat." Wadding up the vampire's coat, he tossed it at the nearest building so no one would trip on it, then turned to face her. "What are you doing in New York?"

She smiled up at him. "You invited me."

He shook his head. "What—?"

"This is a dream. You asked me to visit you in your dreams."

"Check it!" a guy beside Yuri yelled to his friend. "This chick is so wasted she thinks she's dreaming!"

Laughter erupted.

Someone bumped Cat from behind.

She stumbled into Yuri.

Yuri grasped her arms to steady her . . . and stilled. "I can feel you," he murmured.

"What?" she called over the noise.

"I can feel you!" he shouted, joy and amazement rising within him.

Nodding, she grinned up at him. "Marcus was right!"

Yuri drew her into a crushing embrace, hugging her as close as he could get her and resting his cheek on her hair.

She didn't wear a coat and felt small and delicate against his taller, broader form, her head only reaching his shoulder.

Loosening his hold, he eased away just a bit.

Tears glistened in her eyes when she tilted her head back to look up at him.

Yuri cupped her face in his hands, smoothed his thumbs over her soft, soft skin. Lowering his head, he did what he'd fantasized about doing ever since he had first glimpsed her in David's home. He brushed his lips against hers.

Fire flashed through him at the contact. His heart began to pound in his chest.

Cat surprised him yet again, sliding her arms around his waist and increasing the pressure.

Yuri deepened the kiss, tasting those pink lips with his tongue before delving within. He tightened his arms around her, locking her against his hardening form. Damn, she felt good. And he had wanted this for so long.

Somewhere a male laughed. "Dude! It's not midnight yet!"

"Yeah," another male added with a laugh. "Save it for the new year!"

Yuri broke the kiss and stared down at Cat. "I can't wait that long!"

Face flushed, she shook her head. "I can't either!"

Opening his coat, he looped an arm around her and tucked her up against his side. Curses and disgruntled shouts rose around them as he muscled his way through the crowd, but Yuri would let no one deter him from leaving.

When they finally reached the edge of the massive horde, Yuri took Cat's hand and began to jog past the men and women just arriving.

Cat's laughter reached his ears, lightening his spirit until a huge grin split his lips. He felt so happy. And young. And carefree.

It seemed to take forever to reach a street with no pedestrians.

Stopping, he released Cat's hand, bent, and lifted her into his arms. "Hold on tight," he told her.

She smiled. "I will."

Cat's breath caught as the tall buildings around them blurred and Yuri carried them through the streets of New York at preternatural speeds.

She couldn't believe she had done it. That she was here in his arms. That she could feel him against her. His shoulder beneath her cheek. His muscled chest against her breasts.

She laughed again at the pure joy of it and heard a responding rumble in his chest.

As the noise faded, she buried her face in his neck, drew in his scent, reveled in the feel of his warm skin.

Yuri.

Her Yuri.

Yuri stopped in an alleyway, tall structures on either side of them. The building he turned her to face was old and worn and boasted a single, nondescript door that rested at the top of three steps.

Yuri climbed the steps and, balancing her with one arm, dug some keys out of his pocket.

"Where are we?" she asked.

"My home. Sort of. The network owns this apartment building," he told her as he unlocked the door and opened it. Stepping inside a stairwell, he closed the door behind him and locked it.

He dropped the keys back in his pocket. "Humans live on the lower floors," he murmured, reclaiming his hold on her with both arms. "All of them are single, early-to-bed-early-to-rise professionals who are dead to the world during most of the nighttime hours. The top two floors have been sound-proofed and provide apartments for Immortal Guardians. Stanislav, me, and six others. Our Seconds have adjacent apartments. This is our private entrance," he said, nodding to the door through which they had just passed, "so none of the other residents in the building will see the damp patches on our clothes or blood smears on our skin and panic."

The stairwell blurred and cool wind whipped Cat's hair as he raced up she-didn't-know-how-many flights of stairs and stopped before another door. Opening it, he stepped into a hallway that reminded her a little of Sublevel 5 at network headquarters. Just beyond the door lay a desk, behind which half a dozen men sat. Instead of wearing black fatigues, however, they wore suits.

All still bore automatic weapons, though.

One of the men rose. "Evening, sir."

Yuri nodded at them and strode past.

Cat felt the curious gazes cast her way. But none questioned him.

Yuri jogged up another set of stairs and, at last, stopped

before what she assumed was his apartment. Lowering her to her feet, he opened the unlocked door. Then he took her hand and led her inside.

He flicked on a light.

Cat got a quick impression of a large open space with modern furnishings before he closed the door and turned a lock on it.

She stared up at him, pulse racing.

"I can't believe you're here," he whispered. Drawing her into his arms, he hugged her close and buried his face in her hair. "I can't believe you did it. That it worked."

Cat burrowed into him, so happy to finally feel his big, hard body against hers, to have his arms tighten around her instead of passing right through her.

"I know I said the tingling your touch inspires is pleasant," he murmured, pressing his lips to her ear, "but this is soooo much better."

Cat laughed, tears rising, and nodded against his chest.

"Let me get this coat off."

Stepping back, she surreptitiously wiped her eyes while he shrugged off his coat, then tugged the sweater beneath it over his head, revealing a plain black T-shirt bereft of bloodstains.

Once more, he cupped her face in his hands, smoothed his thumbs over her cheeks.

Cat reached up and curled her fingers around his wrists, needing to touch him again. "I don't know how much time we have," she whispered. "If you should awaken for any reason . . ."

A slow smile curled his lips. "I'm a sound sleeper. But just in case . . ."

He lowered his head and claimed her lips in a long, slow kiss that made her pulse race. Sliding a muscled arm around her waist, he drew her up against him. Without the coat as a buffer, she could feel how hard he already was for her.

Her heart began to pound with excitement . . . and with a hint of nerves.

"What's wrong?" Yuri murmured against her lips, resting his hands on her hips and slowly walking her backward, farther into the apartment.

How had he known?

"Is your heart pounding because you want me?" he asked, his glowing amber eyes peering into hers, "or because you're nervous?"

"Both?" she responded with some despair. She wanted to be bold and passionate like Sarah and Krysta and the other immortal women she'd accidentally caught making love with their husbands. But . . . "I've only ever been with Blaise," she admitted.

"Your husband?"

"Yes. And it wasn't . . . It didn't . . ." make her throw back her head and moan in ecstasy.

Yuri arched a brow. "It didn't knock your socks off?"

She laughed. "Yes. It wasn't like what we heard in the romance audiobooks." How those had made her flush!

"Don't worry," he said and pressed a light kiss to her lips, "I won't do anything you won't like." He kissed her again. "And will do *many* things you'll like," he purred.

Cat's nervousness dissipated as she smiled up at him.

"That's what I want to see," he said. "Now put your arms around me."

When he leaned down, she slid her arms around his neck.

He straightened, taking her with him and lifting her feet off the floor. Fisting his free hand in her long skirt, he drew it up to her knees. "Wrap your legs around me."

Cat did as bidden, heat climbing her cheeks.

The glow in his eyes brightened as he released her skirts and slid a hand over her bottom.

The heart of her rested against his erection, still separated by their clothing. His eyes never leaving hers, he strolled down a hallway and into a smaller, darker room illuminated only by the light that spilled into it from the living room. Every step created delicious friction. Sparks of what Cat came to understand was desire shot through her with every brush of him against her core.

When he halted, she didn't want the wonderful feeling to end and arched against him.

He hissed in a breath. "You aren't going to let me do this slowly, are you?"

She rubbed against him again. "Not if everything you're going to do will make me feel like this."

He shook his head and released his hold on her, moaning when she slid her legs down his body and leaned against him. "This is just the beginning."

Stepping back, he kicked off his big boots and tugged his shirt over his head.

Cat visually devoured the muscles he exposed.

A belt circled his hips, equipped with several sheaths that held blades of various sizes. He unbuckled the belt and set it on a dresser behind him. "In all of the times you came to my room," he said, his hands going to the button on his pants, "did you ever peek at me while I was in the shower?"

She shook her head, her gaze fastening on his hands.

"Did you want to?"

She nodded as he unbuttoned the button and drew down the zipper.

"Shall I turn the lights on then, or leave it dark?"

"Lights on," was all she could squeeze out.

Taking two steps backward, he reached over and flipped a switch.

Light flooded the room.

Then he tucked his thumbs in the waistband and drew his pants and boxers down.

Cat's heart began to thud even harder. She had never really seen a naked man before. Had only caught glimpses . . .

He kicked the pants aside and let her have a nice long look.

"You're beautiful," she murmured. All muscle and sinew and strength, his arousal jutting toward her.

He approached her with panther-like grace. "Now it's my turn."

His fingers went to the buttons that ran down the front of her blouse.

"I wanted to dress like the women of this time," she admitted as he eased the first button free and moved on to the next. Another mystery in this existence: All she had to do was imagine clothing and it would appear on her form. "A short skirt. A low-cut blouse." Something that would set him aflame. "But it felt like I was wearing a costume."

He shook his head and moved on to the third and fourth buttons, his long fingers surprisingly deft. "I wasn't born in this century, Cat. I was born long before *you* were, as you know. And *this*"—he gave the material a little tug—"is what I enjoy seeing you wear. I don't need your breasts shoved up to your chin in one of those push-up bra things and spilling out of your blouse. I don't need a skirt so short it leaves nothing—and I mean *nothing*—to the imagination when you sit down or bend over. I *like* using my imagination. I like getting just a hint of cleavage that makes me long to see what is hidden beneath all this material. I like guessing what your lovely curves look like unclothed." He drew the end of her blouse up and out of her skirt. "I like knowing," he continued as he reached the last button at her waist and parted the soft cloth, revealing the nearly transparent chemise beneath, "that I'm the only man who can see you like this. The only man you'll *allow* to see you like this."

She let him draw the shirt down her arms, heard it hit the floor with the faintest sound.

He reached behind her, unfastened her skirt, and let it fall to the floor at her feet.

Beneath she wore the bloomers that had been popular in her time, nearly transparent like the chemise.

He rested his hands on her hips, tightening his hold as he examined her. The amber glow in his eyes intensified. "I love old-fashioned underwear," he hissed.

She bit her lip. "You don't prefer the tiny panties and bras women today wear?"

He shook his head. "If you knew how many times, as a boy, I tried to catch a glimpse of underwear like this beneath frothy skirts, you'd know that *this* is what turns me on."

She smiled, imagining it.

Then he slid his hands up her sides and drew his thumbs over the hard peaks of her breasts.

Cat sucked in a breath as sensation shot through her. Surprised, she looked up at him.

A sensual smile curled his lips. "I told you you'd like it."

Cupping one breast in his palm, he leaned down and closed his lips over the other, his tongue rasping over the sensitive peak and dampening the thin material of her chemise.

Cat moaned and buried her fingers in his hair. His soft, thick hair that she could touch at last. Every pull of his mouth, every flick of his tongue, made liquid heat pool low in her belly. Made her want to writhe against him. She gave his hair a little pull. "Take it off."

He raised his head. "What?"

She reached for the hem of her chemise. "Take it off. Now that I can finally feel you, I don't want anything between us."

He smiled, a low growl rumbling in his throat. Releasing her breast, he gripped the delicate material. One tug and it tore down the back. He dipped his long fingers in the front of her bloomers and tugged again. Wispy material floated down to the floor, leaving her bare to his gaze.

"I love your strength," she declared.

Grinning, he picked her up and tossed her backward.

Cat shrieked as she flew through the air, then landed on the soft cushion of an enormous bed she hadn't even realized rested behind her.

* * *

Yuri dove after Cat and drew her beautiful body up against his, settling them on their sides. "You feel so good," he groaned. "I still can't believe I'm touching you." He slid a hand down over her hip, hooked his fingers behind her knee, and drew her leg up over his hip, opening her to him. Rolling his hips, he slid his erection along her slick center. She was already wet for him.

Cat moaned. "I can," she said on a gasp, "because I've never felt like this before."

He palmed one of her breasts and pinched the tip as he continued to tease her with his cock.

She moaned again. "I didn't even know I *could* feel like this."

Yuri rolled her to her back and took her lips in a deep, devouring kiss. His tongue plunged inside to dance with hers.

Cat caught on quickly, giving as good as she got, ratcheting up his desire until he shook with the need to be inside her. Just the feel of her arms sliding around him and urging him closer . . . Imagining those small hands of hers sliding down and gripping his ass to urge him on as he plunged inside . . .

Yuri abandoned her breast and slid a hand down her soft, flat belly, buried his fingers in the dark thatch of curls at the juncture of her thighs.

She jerked and gasped when he touched her clit. He continued to stroke the sensitive nub and to apply rhythmic pressure with the heel of his hand as he slid his fingers lower still. She was so ready for him.

The hands at his back urged him closer as she squirmed against him.

Yuri dipped a long finger inside her sheath. So tight he could almost come just from imagining those warm walls squeezing him. Another long finger followed. She arched against him as he began to pump them inside her. He buried his face in her neck, listening to her gasps of pleasure as he drove that pleasure higher and higher until her tight flesh clamped down and spasmed around his fingers as a first climax struck her.

Cat cried out, stiffening and arching against him, her heart pounding beneath his chest. After a long moment, she collapsed against the covers, her breath coming quick. "What was that?" she asked, peering up at him as Yuri rose above her.

"Only the beginning," he said, settling himself between her thighs. He dipped his head and stole another kiss. "I wanted to taste you first, but—"

"You *are* tasting me," she said and kissed him back.

"Not like . . ." He trailed off, realizing that she had no idea that he meant he wanted to taste her everywhere his fingers had just stroked her. "Never mind," he promised with a kiss. "I'll show you next time. Now I just need to be inside you."

She nodded and locked her gaze with his as he positioned his cock at her entrance and slowly pressed forward. Her lips parted as she drew in a breath.

She was so tight, squeezing him with such delicious pressure.

"Okay?" he asked. Since she could clearly experience pleasure here in the dream realm, he assumed she could also feel pain and wanted to ensure he didn't cause her any.

She nodded. "You're so big."

Though he clung to control by his fingertips, he laughed. "You're so small."

She smiled. "But it feels good." Wrapping her arms around him, she urged him closer. "It feels *very* good. I like having you inside me, Yuri."

And that did it.

Those words and his name on her lips obliterated his control. Nearly withdrawing completely, Yuri plunged inside again. And again and again. Harder and faster. His lips finding hers. His hands exploring her curves with urgent caresses he hoped wouldn't leave marks. But he just needed her so damned much. Needed *this*.

Passionate sounds erupted from her lips as she threw her head back and arched against him, meeting every thrust with eagerness. Her hands slid down and gripped his ass, urging him on as he had imagined so often.

Yuri slipped a hand between them and teased her clit.

Cat called his name, her damp walls clamping down around him in a second orgasm, squeezing him even tighter.

So fucking good. Yuri stiffened above her as a climax ripped through him, so intense it almost felt like it was his first damned time.

Collapsing atop her, he tunneled his arms beneath her to hug her tight. The bulk of his weight propped on his elbows, he buried his face in her neck and just savored her as his racing pulse slowed.

His heart gradually ceased slamming against his ribs and settled upon a more sedate beat.

Cat wrapped her arms around him and held him tight.

He heard a sniff and started to rise, fearing he had hurt her and made her cry.

She wouldn't let him.

Rolling to his side, he let her burrow into him.

"I love you, Yuri," she whispered.

He eased back until he could see her face.

No pain. Just the love she had spoken. And the same joy he felt over what they had shared.

His own eyes burned as he pressed a gentle kiss to her lips. "I love you, Catherine."

And if this was the only way they could be together—the only way they could touch—it would be enough for him.

Chapter Six

Cat watched Yuri sleep in his bedroom in David's home. She wasn't sure what had yanked her out of his dreams, but his sleep was now too shallow for her to rejoin him.

And, truth be told, dreamwalking had left her weary.

Even *that* she welcomed, though. It felt so normal. So like the living.

Yuri stirred, rolling over onto his back, his large form sprawled beneath covers that had fallen to his waist.

Her pulse picked up as she recalled the feel of those large hands on her body. And the remarkable change she had undergone beneath his passionate explorations. She had become like Sarah. She had thrown her head back and moaned and done things to Yuri with her own hands that made her cheeks burn when she remembered them.

He sighed. His brown eyes opened, stared up at the ceiling, then widened. Rising up onto his elbows, he looked around until he found her standing in his reading nook.

The heat in her cheeks deepened.

He grinned, his handsome face lighting with triumph and pleasure. "You *were* there."

Though shyness did its best to overwhelm her, she nodded with a smile.

Yuri tossed back the covers and rose naked from the bed.

Cat supposed she should avert her eyes, but didn't, enjoying the play of his muscles as he approached her and stopped, mere inches away. She tilted her head back to look up at him.

He raised a hand, drew a finger down her cheek.

The mild warmth inspired by the touch she couldn't feel seemed a travesty compared to what she had experienced in his dreams.

"Thank you," he murmured.

Nodding, she reached up and curled her fingers around his wrist, already missing the skin-on-skin contact they had shared. "I wish it could always be so between us."

The same regret she felt darkened his eyes. "I do, too," he admitted. "But it's so much more than we believed we could ever have together."

"Is it enough?" she asked, unsure she wanted to know the answer.

"Even if *this*"—he nodded at where they appeared to touch, but didn't—"was all we could share, it would be enough for me."

She wanted to believe that, but thought it unfair to him.

"Having said that," he said, a twinkle of mischief entering his deep brown eyes, "will you come to me in my dreams again?"

She grinned. "Yes." And she already counted the hours until she could.

"Come hunting with me tonight," he implored with the eagerness of a young man wooing his first love.

"All right."

And thus began a pattern, a new way of life, for them both.

Cat accompanied Yuri and Stanislav on their nightly hunts, keeping them quiet company until they encountered vampires. Then she hied herself back to David's to avoid the freed vampires' spirits. As soon as Yuri and Stanislav returned, Yuri excused himself and went to bed early.

Cat always found him in his dreams, no matter where they took him. North Carolina. New York. Russia. Australia. Afghanistan. Norway. Peru. Brazil. Egypt. All the many places he had lived during his long existence. It was always nighttime in his dreams. Having lived so long without daylight, he no longer even dreamed of it, something that saddened Cat. She knew he missed the sun. But even as old as he was, he could only endure brief exposure without suffering damage.

No matter where his dreams took them, the two made passionate love, Cat learning as much about her own body as she did about Yuri's. The dreams were fleeting at first, like the first they'd shared, allowing them only enough time to make love. Then the time began to stretch until it seemed as though hours would pass in the dreams. Hours in which they had dinner at his favorite restaurant, then strolled through Central Park, holding hands and sharing tales from their pasts. Hours in which they swam naked and romped and played in the lake behind his childhood home. Hours in which they made love, shared a shower, then cooked dinner in his modern kitchen, Yuri showing Cat how to use the various appliances, their bodies brushing as they passed each other, stealing kisses here or there.

Dreams made all of those casual touches people so often took for granted possible for Yuri and Catherine. Dreams made it all feel real. She enjoyed them as much as Yuri did.

And yet worry soon crept in and impinged upon their happiness.

Yuri began to sleep more in an attempt to grab more of what he called *tangible time* with Cat. He stopped socializing with his fellow immortals, choosing to sleep and be with her whenever he wasn't hunting instead. When Cat cautiously remarked upon it, he shrugged it off and reminded her that he had always been a solitary sort.

But he didn't even read with Stanislav anymore.

The lovely immortal Lisette finally awoke from her coma.

The Immortal Guardians found themselves faced with the knowledge that one of their own—an immortal they had yet to identify—plotted against them, raising the new army of highly trained vampires equipped with tranquilizer guns capable of dropping an immortal in his or her tracks.

Seth, the ultrapowerful Immortal Guardians' leader, vanished for two days.

The terrifying and mysterious new winged immortal Zach insinuated himself into their group.

A lot was happening in Yuri's world, but he seemed distanced from it. Not unaffected, but certainly less affected by it than she thought he should have been.

In his dreams, Yuri remained charming and witty and passionate.

Awake, he often appeared distracted.

Cat feared such distraction proved dangerous when he hunted. He returned with more and more wounds every night.

The door to his room swung open. Yuri strode inside in full hunting gear. Cat greeted him with a smile that swiftly died as she got a good look at him.

A long, ugly gash began just below one ear and followed the line of his jaw to his chin as though his opponent had attempted to slit his throat and miscalculated. His coat bore numerous tears and glistened with blood. The hand that held a bag of blood to his lips bore a cut so deep she thought she could see bone. He limped badly, all but dragging his left leg behind him, and hunched over a little bit, favoring one side.

His face, lined with pain, lit with pleasure when he found her waiting for him.

Alarm struck. "What—?"

The door that had almost swung closed behind him flung wide, slamming into the wall as Stanislav stormed inside.

Scowling, Yuri swung around. His left leg buckled, nearly sending him to his knees. Dropping the blood bag, he threw out a hand and clutched the edge of a nearby dresser, barely managing to remain upright.

Stanislav slammed the door shut and faced his friend, his eyes blazing with amber fire. "What the fuck is wrong with you?" he roared.

Yuri frowned. "Nothing a little blood won't cure."

When Yuri bent to retrieve the fallen bag, Stanislav snatched it from his grasp.

"You think this is a joke?" Yuri's friend demanded, his face dark with fury. "You think this is funny? What the fuck happened tonight? Did you lose your fucking mind?"

Cat stared. She had never seen these two fight. They were as close as brothers and, in the time she had been observing them, were so alike that they could complete each other's sentences. They had never even disagreed over which audiobook they wanted to listen to or which movie they wanted to watch.

Irritation flitted across Yuri's face. "No. Would you just give me the damned blood. My leg hurts like hell."

Stanislav threw it at him.

Yuri fumbled the catch a bit, but managed to gain a hold on it. Raising the bag to his lips, he sank his fangs in and let them siphon the blood directly into his veins.

"Seth specifically ordered us *not* to engage any of the new vampires if we should encounter one," Stanislav snapped, voice rising with every word. "We were told to tranq the vamps, then call Seth. If one of the new vampires attacked us before we could tranq him, Seth told us to just kill the vampire as swiftly as possible. He said, and I quote, *Don't buy time and try to read his thoughts or emotions. Don't try to capture him or question him. Just* kill *him or* tranq *him. Period.*"

"I heard what he said," Yuri griped and tossed the empty bag in the rubbish bin.

"Then what the hell happened tonight?" Stanislav demanded, bafflement creeping into the fury that clouded his expression. "You knew as soon as we encountered those vampires that two of them were of the new highly trained variety. Why the hell did you engage them? Why didn't you just tranq them?"

"They were already drawing their own tranq guns. There wasn't time."

"Then you should have just killed the fuckers outright instead of trying to capture them!" Stanislav thundered. "And with five of the usual slacker vampires nipping at your heels? There was no way—"

"We need to know who the fuck is commanding them!" Yuri bellowed, his own eyes glowing now.

Cat held her breath. She had never seen Yuri so angry. Nor had he ever cursed in front of her, the values of his time too ingrained in him.

"How the fuck do you think we're going to do that if we don't capture one?" Yuri continued.

"Chris and the network are—"

"It's taking too long," Yuri interrupted. "We need to end this. Now."

Stanislav arched a brow. "Or die trying?"

Fear filling her, Cat looked at Yuri.

So she *wasn't* the only one who had noticed. He *had* been suffering more severe wounds of late. Was distraction leaving him careless? Or was he taking more risks?

"I was five hundred years older and five hundred years stronger than those vampires," Yuri gritted. "I had every reason to believe I could defeat them."

"Killing them is one thing. Capturing is another. Taking those bastards alive is proving to be impossible. As long as they breathe, they fight. And as long as they fight, you incur injuries. Just look at yourself! That's your third bag of blood and you still can't even straighten."

Yuri rose stiffly to his full height, wincing as he drew back his shoulders. "We needed information. I thought it worth the risk."

Silence fell, thick with unspoken accusations and rebuttals.

Stanislav studied Yuri. "Are you done with this existence, Yuri?" he asked, his voice soft with dread. "Is that it? Do you want to die?"

Cat stared at Yuri in horror. Was Stanislav right? Was Yuri taking unnecessary risks because he was ready to die? Was he . . . ?

He didn't want to die to be with *her*, did he? Had she done that to him?

Yuri glanced in her direction, but didn't meet her gaze. "I told you," he returned stonily, "we need information. And I thought I could get it."

"You didn't answer my question."

Yuri rubbed his forehead with long fingers smeared with blood. "You think I'm pulling a Marcus? You think I'm behaving recklessly because I have nothing left to live for?"

Stanislav sighed and sank down on the edge of the bed. "When you put it like that . . ." He shook his head. "I don't know what to think. I just know you've been different lately. Distant. Distracted. Have kept more to yourself." He shrugged. "What's going on, Yuri? We're brothers, or may as well be. Can't you tell me?"

Minutes dragged past, feeling like hours. The amber light faded from both men's eyes.

Yuri leaned back against the dresser, taking his weight off his injured leg. "I've met someone."

Stanislav's expression went blank with surprise. "A woman?"

Yuri laughed, then winced and grabbed his side. "Yes, a woman."

"Who?"

Yuri shook his head. "You don't know her."

Stanislav studied him a long moment. "You love her."

"Yes."

His friend mulled that over. "If she could be transformed and was willing to join us, I assume you would have already introduced me to her."

Yuri nodded. "It's . . . complicated."

"That explains the distraction."

Again Yuri nodded.

Stanislav quieted. "What about tonight?"

Yuri shifted and grimaced as he touched a hand to his side. "You know Lisette, Tanner, and I are sports buddies, right? We watch baseball together."

"Yes. I don't know how you can stand that shit. It's so boring."

Yuri rolled his eyes. "Which is why I don't watch it with you. Anyway, Tanner said something to me after Lisette finally awoke from her coma or whatever the hell it was that drug trapped her in. He said if the vampires upped the dosage of the tranquilizer even a little bit, the next immortal who was struck by a dart would likely die."

Stanislav swore. "I didn't think of that."

"Younger immortals like Lisette are more at risk than we, as older immortals, are. We aren't even certain the drug would affect you and me as strongly as it did Lisette." He shrugged one shoulder. "The other avenues we're exploring—Chris and the network doing their digging, Seth reading the minds of immortals to try to identify our betrayer—is taking too long. When I saw those two newbie vampires tonight, all that ran through my mind was that if we could capture them, Seth could pluck the betrayer's name from their thoughts and this would end. It would all be over. Lisette, the others, *you* . . . would all be safe once more."

Cat couldn't tell if Yuri spoke the truth or not.

But apparently, Stanislav believed him. He rose on another sigh. And Cat noticed for the first time that Stanislav moved with stiff, painful steps, too. "I'm not going to tell Seth about this."

"I appreciate that. He would hand me my own ass if you did."

"At the very least."

Yuri offered him his hand.

Stanislav clasped his arm instead and pulled Yuri into a hug, clapping him on the back.

Yuri grunted as pain flashed across his features.

When Stanislav released him and stepped back, he arched a brow, lips twitching. "That's for scaring the shit out of me earlier."

Yuri huffed a laugh, then grabbed his side again with a grunt. "Don't make me laugh, damn it. It hurts."

Stanislav crossed to the door. "I'll get you some more blood." He grasped the knob. "And, Yuri?"

"Yes?"

"I don't know what's going on with you and this woman you've met, but . . . if you ever need to talk, I'm here."

Yuri nodded. "Thank you."

Stanislav slipped out the door and closed it behind him.

Cat stared at Yuri, her mind a jumble of questions and fears, her stomach aching with dread.

He lowered his chin and leaned back against the dresser.

The silence stretched.

He avoided her gaze.

"Yuri," she said.

"Don't look at me like that," he whispered wearily.

The door opened. Stanislav leaned in and tossed Yuri two more bags of blood.

Yuri caught them deftly this time and thanked him.

Stanislav left.

"Was he right?" Cat asked when she could bear it no longer. "Are you . . . ? Do you want to die, Yuri?"

"I wasn't trying to get myself killed tonight, Cat," he

answered. "It was as I told him. We need information. I thought I could get it. I thought I was strong enough to capture those vampires, but the bastards wouldn't give up the fight. It was fight or die."

She heard no lie in his words, but he kept his head lowered. "You still haven't answered the question. Do you want to die, Yuri?" Just the thought of him giving up his life to be with her made her heart ache. "Is that why you've been coming home so battered and bloody lately?"

"Cat—"

"Don't lie to me, Yuri. I've seen your wounds. Far more of them than you used to incur when you hunted. There were nights when you would come home without a single scratch on you. And now . . . ever since we discovered we could be together in your dreams, ever since we made love that first time . . ." She shook her head. Tears clogged her throat. "You come home more broken every night, your wounds deeper and—"

"Don't cry, Cat." At last he met her gaze, his brown eyes full of remorse and . . . shame?

Was it true, then? Was Yuri trying to die so they could be together in more than just the dream realm? She couldn't let that happen. Couldn't let him sacrifice his life to be with her.

When he moved toward her, she backed away. "This was a mistake," she said, her voice choked with tears she couldn't prevent from spilling down her cheeks.

"It isn't what you think," he said.

She shook her head. "I'm not going to let you sacrifice your life for me."

"Catherine—"

"I'm not going to stand by and let you get yourself killed so you can be with me," she said, voice rising.

"I'm not trying to get myself killed," he insisted.

"I've seen the wounds, Yuri! So *many* wounds! What else—?"

"I let them wound me on purpose," he blurted, his features tight with frustration.

Cat halted. "What?"

Looking away, he swore softly. Seconds ticked past, during which she could almost see him mentally weighing his options. Then he resolutely met her gaze. "I've been letting the vampires I fight wound me before I defeat them."

Cat didn't know if that confirmed or negated her accusations. "Why?"

"I made sure the wounds were never fatal."

"Why would you let them wound you at all if . . . ?"

He reached for her arms, then swore bitterly when his hands passed right through her. Clenching his fists, he lowered them to his sides. "I sleep more deeply when I'm wounded."

"I don't understand."

"A couple of nights after you came to me in my dreams that first time, I fractured my femur while I was out hunting. Immortals tend to sleep deeper while recovering from more serious wounds and . . ." His shoulders slumped. "I discovered that the dreams last longer when I'm in a healing sleep."

Dread filled her. "Are you saying . . . ?"

"I've been letting the vampires wound me because I have more time with you in the dream realm when I'm healing."

Cat stared at him in horror. "That's why the dreams have been lasting longer?"

He nodded. "The more wounds I suffer, the longer I spend in the deeper healing sleep and the more time we have together."

She bit back a sob.

"Don't look like at me like that," he pleaded once more.

"You're hurting yourself so you can be with me!"

"Cat, I've been hunting vampires for five centuries. I suffer wounds all the time. They're nothing to me."

"You can barely stand!" she accused.

"I'm already healing. Look, it's closing, isn't it?" He pointed to the long gash on his face, which closed as she watched and became a dark pink scar.

"But you're in pain. All of these wounds . . . the cuts, your leg, whatever is wrong with your side and back . . . they *hurt*."

He said nothing.

"Yuri, they hurt, don't they?"

"Only until I fall asleep."

Then his body healed while he spent time with her.

"Look, I'm not sure why you're so upset about this," he said. "You saw me come home wounded hundreds of times before we even spoke. How is—?"

"Would you have fought those vampires tonight if you hadn't known the wounds you incurred would give you more time with me?" she asked.

"What?"

"Answer me honestly, Yuri. Would you have fought those two vampires tonight if you hadn't known the wounds you incurred would give you more time with me in the dream realm?"

"Yes."

"Would you have fought to kill or to capture?"

Lips tightening, he didn't respond.

Another tear slipped past her lashes. "I suppose I have my answer."

"It was a win-win situation, Cat. Can't you see that?"

"You risked your life, Yuri! You risked Stanislav's life!"

Guilt flickered in his dark eyes. "I knew we could take them."

"I can't be with you if you're going to keep hurting yourself like this," she choked out. "I was right. This was a mistake."

His eyes flashed amber as anger darkened his face. "Don't say that, damn it! I've waited five hundred years to find you. Five hundred years to love you. And you want to take that away because I got a little scratch and a sore leg?"

"It isn't just a scratch!"

"To me it is!" he shouted and raked a hand through his hair. "Cat . . ." He paced away, his limp less pronounced than it had been minutes earlier, then turned to face her. "If pricking your finger with a needle would give you more time with me in the dream realm, would you do it?"

"This isn't—"

"Just answer the question."

"Yes."

"If I took that lamp," he said, pointing to the lamp in his reading nook, "shattered it on the floor, and told you that you could spend more time with me, touching me and holding me, if you walked across the broken glass, would you do it?"

"I don't feel pain in this form."

"If you did, would you do it, knowing the pain would vanish as soon as you saw me and would be gone when you awoke?"

Yes, she would.

"You would, wouldn't you?" he pressed.

She nodded.

"Then this," he said, motioning to his battered body, "is not an issue."

"I don't want to cause you pain, Yuri."

He approached her slowly. "Then never again tell me that what we have is a mistake."

Nodding, she wished she could burrow into his arms and hold him tight. "Go take a shower. Eat something. And go to bed. I don't want you to hurt any longer than you have to."

"You'll come to me in my dreams today?"

"Yes," she whispered. "I'll come to you."

A faint smile tilting his lips, Yuri limped into the bathroom.

Yuri was so damned relieved to see Cat in his dreams that day. But their relationship changed. Despite his arguments,

Cat told him she would stop visiting him in his dreams if he kept letting vampires wound him.

Damn it. Why couldn't Stanislav have confronted him *before* they had reached David's home? Then Cat would still be none the wiser and Yuri wouldn't have to settle for whatever little time in the dream realm normal sleep allowed them.

And Cat insisted that Yuri start spending time again with the other immortals. For some reason, she thought that his wanting to spend more time with *her* impeded upon his *life with the living*, as she called it.

Yuri admitted he had been spending less time with his fellow immortals. But it wasn't as if he were a recluse like Roland used to be. He just enjoyed spending time with Cat more and couldn't speak freely with her in front of the others.

So, in the days that followed, he indulged her . . . to a point, spending an hour to two reading or watching movies with Stanislav as they had before while he sought some way to disabuse her of the notion.

And he stopped letting the damned vampires get in a few strikes when he hunted to keep his wounds to a minimum. He didn't like the way it restricted the tangible time he and Cat shared, but wanted to put her mind at ease.

Although he might just get a temporary reprieve.

"I trust you won't complain if I return riddled with wounds this time?" he said as he tugged on the rubbery suit the network had designed to protect immortals from daylight.

Across his bedroom, Catherine bit her lip. "No, but please be careful, Yuri. Don't take any unnecessary risks."

"I won't," he promised. He wouldn't have to.

The Immortal Guardians had finally located the new vampire army's base. Although Seth and the network still had not determined the name of their immortal betrayer, they *had* discovered—much to their astonishment—that the betrayer had given the vampiric virus and the sedative to a huge mercenary group, which had been infecting their own men.

An army of men with super-speed, super-strength, perfect night vision, and accelerated healing abilities that left them nearly unstoppable on the battlefield would bring the mercenary group billions of dollars. And this group didn't care who hired their vampire army. They would make the army available to the highest bidder worldwide.

It was a big-ass compound with countless well-trained vampires and humans with high-powered weapons. The Immortal Guardians—along with a virtual army of human special ops soldiers from the network that aided them—would descend upon it this afternoon, showing no mercy and ending the threat once and for all. They would discover, at last, the name of their betrayer so Seth could render whatever punishment he deemed suitable.

And Yuri was pretty much guaranteed to suffer enough wounds to put him in a long, deep healing sleep when he returned to David's place. He would have hours that would feel like days in the dream realm to hold and be with Cat. He couldn't wait.

"What do you think?" he asked.

"It sort of resembles a diving suit," Cat said. Her lips curled up in a slow smile. "And you look positively edible in it."

Laughing, he winked. "Maybe I'll wear one in my dreams tonight." While he packed on the weapons, Cat wrung her hands. "Stop worrying," he coaxed. "We've battled mercenaries before and won."

"But never on this scale. And never with highly trained vampires on their side."

Yuri waved off her concern. "Seth has brought in another elder to help us fight. And Zach will join us, too. Hell, Seth and Zach alone could probably raze the entire compound. We'll be fine."

"I'm going with you."

"*Hell*, no. I want you to stay here. All that blood and violence . . . I don't want those images in your head. And . . ."

He hated to say this out loud. "We're going to have to kill a lot of men today, Cat. So many spirits released at once . . . I don't think you should be anywhere near there."

Grudgingly, she nodded. "All right. But please be careful," she implored again.

"I will." Satisfied that he had loaded on enough blades, he grinned and picked up the mask that accompanied the suit. "See you when I get back."

"I love you."

"I love you, too." And couldn't wait for the day to end so he could spend that long healing sleep in her arms.

Chapter Seven

Yuri and his fellow Immortal Guardians made their silent way through the forest until they clustered together in the evergreens across the street from the mercenary compound's front gate. Thick trees and a bounty of chest-high weeds hid them from the guards' view and stymied the sunlight each time it tried to penetrate the dense foliage and hint at their presence.

An impressively large army of network special ops soldiers commanded by Chris Reordon lingered down the road, out of sight, ready to back up the immortals when they stormed the compound.

An attack like this in daylight carried risks. Once the battle began, all but the eldest immortals would have to take care to keep their masks on and to sustain as little damage to their suits as they possibly could to protect themselves from the sun's rays. They wouldn't burst into flames when exposed to sunlight the way vampires in movies did. They would rapidly sunburn instead, then blister. Things would swiftly go downhill from there. Yuri knew from experience that such could be incredibly painful.

But the mercenaries wouldn't see an afternoon strike coming. And the vampires slumbering in the large building that housed them would not be able to join the fray outside. This vampire army was too new to have developed the special suits the immortals now wore.

Yuri studied the compound's layout and compared it to the satellite maps Chris had provided them with minutes earlier.

The main building was just inside the gates on the right. Beyond it lay a helipad and runway, followed by two massive hangars. Seth had tasked Richart and Jenna with keeping the mercenaries out of those helicopters. The airplanes, too. Yuri suspected they would have their hands full. And they had no way of knowing just what vehicles the hangars contained. More airplanes and helos, certainly. But there were also likely tanks and other armored vehicles the mercenaries would do their damnedest to commandeer.

On the left lay two buildings Chris had estimated at about forty thousand square feet each. One housed the human mercenaries who slumbered after coming off the night shift. The other housed dozens and dozens of vampires.

One of the many training fields the mercenary compound— or global security company, as they called themselves— boasted began behind the housing buildings and continued out of sight.

Beyond *that* lay Yuri's target: the armory. The windowless brick building had only one door. And every mercenary on the compound would likely want to get inside it once they realized they were under attack.

Yuri and Stanislav had volunteered to man it. They'd have a wall at their backs to protect them and an endless supply of opponents coming at their front. Sounded like fun.

It looked like the two of them would have a straight shot back to it, but the men on the training field they had to pass would likely be armed, so bullets would fly until Bastien, Melanie, and Chris's special ops team closed in on them.

Okay, everyone, Seth told them mentally, *Chris is making the call.*

On Chris's mark, all cell phone reception would be disrupted and the landlines cut. Satellite phones would still function, though, so Yuri and the other immortals had been instructed to keep their ears open and prevent *any* calls from going out. The electricity would also be cut. Seth would take out the backup generators with several grenades.

Seth vanished.

Yuri slid his katanas from their sheaths.

Wonk! Wonk! Wonk!

The soldiers at the gate jumped when an alarm began to blare and gripped their weapons tighter as they tried to look in every direction at once.

Boom!

Flames and debris appeared to fly from four different locations as Seth teleported from generator to generator with lightning speed and tossed the grenades. The alarm ceased. Mercenaries ran helter-skelter about the compound, trying to figure out what the hell was happening.

Yuri saw two grenades skip across the ground toward the gate.

One of the guards caught the movement and looked down as the objects came to rest at his feet. "Ah, shi—"

The explosion that followed pierced Yuri's sensitive ears like needles and left them ringing for several seconds. Bodies and body parts flew. The gate blew open and broke apart.

Yuri and the others ducked as pieces of metal embedded themselves in the trees around them. Then they raced forward, David in the lead, to confront their enemies.

From the corner of his eye, Yuri saw Chris's network battalion surge forward in their armored vehicles.

Shouts rang out.

Mercenaries opened fire.

With Stanislav at his side, Yuri swung his katanas as he sped toward the armory, taking out every mercenary he could on the way.

The front of the main building exploded into chunks of granite and glass as Yuri and Stanislav passed it. Yuri saw David plow right through it—Lisette, Zach, and Marcus on his heels—and grinned.

He loved a good fight!

When Yuri reached the training field, bullets tore through the air like swarms of bees.

Yuri cut a swath through the mercenaries. Screams erupted. And the suit he so hated to wear stopped a hell of a lot of the bullets. Apparently, Chris and the network had made some improvements.

Yuri sheathed one of his katanas and yanked an AK-47 from the hands of one of the mercenaries. As he continued toward the armory, his pace never slowing, he sprayed the enemy with bullets.

Stanislav laughed behind him and soon followed suit.

The armory rose before them. Two stories. Larger than Yuri had anticipated.

What the hell did they store in there?

Most of the humans in sight ran toward it.

Yuri took out all he could with the automatic weapon, ran out of ammo, then grabbed another.

"I'll clear it out," Stanislav called and ducked inside.

Yuri planted his back against the wall on one side of the door and let the bullets fly. While guns had never been his weapon of choice, he *did* know how to use them.

By the time Stanislav returned, Yuri had run out of ammo again.

"Clear," Stanislav said and planted his back against the wall on the opposite side of the door.

The number of humans charging toward them dwindled as

the network's special ops soldiers swarmed the grounds, Bastien and Melanie in their midst.

Yuri dropped the AK and went to work with his swords.

Dmitry and Alexei, Yuri and Stanislav's Seconds, approached in a crouch, barely recognizable beneath their helmets and body armor. Automatic weapons spitting fire, they parked themselves at either corner of the building to keep mercenaries from sneaking up on Yuri and Stanislav from the sides.

A tank rumbled forth from one of the hangars.

Ah, shit. The mercenaries must have—

Two missiles struck it, launched by Chris's men.

Dmitry whooped.

Yuri grinned, then grunted as a bullet penetrated his suit where the material thinned under his arm. Another grazed his neck.

Beside him, Stanislav swore. "How many of these bastards are there?"

Good question. Yuri had slain dozens and they just kept coming, each and every one of them determined to get their hands on the weapons the two Immortal Guardians guarded.

Explosions pierced Yuri's ears periodically.

In the distance, flames spewed forth from the flame thrower atop one of Chris's Humvees as vampires opted to risk sun exposure and darted outside in an attempt to flee the blades of the immortals who had invaded their building.

Another bullet struck Yuri. Gritting his teeth, he swung his blades at two mercenaries who attacked his front.

Dmitry's weapon quieted as he hastily reloaded.

At least Yuri didn't have to worry about running out of ammo. His blades never failed him.

Breathing hard, he slew two more mercenaries.

Stanislav leapt to the edge of the building to take out a mercenary who crept up behind Alexei as Alexei fired like hell at mercenaries who must have been trying to come around the side of the building.

Mercenaries saw only one immortal guarding the door and seized the opportunity, rushing forward en masse. Those who were armed came with guns blazing.

Yuri took another bullet, then another and another as he held them at bay.

"Behind you!" Dmitry shouted.

Yuri spun around and found a mercenary aiming a tranquilizer gun at him.

The world went black.

Cat couldn't stand the quiet at David's house, couldn't take the waiting with nothing to do, so she hied herself off to network headquarters.

She knew the moment the battle began. The tension among the medical staff skyrocketed.

Soon Richart, the French immortal, began to teleport in members of the human network's special ops team who had been injured. Cat watched the dedicated doctors and nurses go to work, saving what lives they could. In very little time, a dozen patients filled the infirmary.

Was this what war was like? she wondered, her heart going out to a grim-faced Dr. Linda Machen when Linda couldn't save her latest patient.

By the time word came that the battle had ended, over a dozen more network soldiers fought for their lives.

Cat left the network and returned to David's home, happy to discover that no injured immortals had been teleported there for a blood infusion or treatment by the emergency medical staff on hand today.

A good sign. Yet Darnell and Ami, who had remained behind, still evinced worry.

Cat waited impatiently for the Immortal Guardians to return, nearly wilting with relief when their vehicles finally pulled up outside.

Thuds sounded.

The front door opened.

Cat stared. She had expected the warriors to return triumphant, tired smiles wreathing their faces as they congratulated one another on a job well done, pleased that they had defeated their enemies and eliminated the threat they posed. Instead . . .

Tight lips spoke no words as the Immortal Guardians filed inside, their Seconds with them. Shoulders slumped. Soot-stained faces bore clean streaks carved by tears.

Cat's heart sank. What had happened?

Her eyes searched each blackened face, looking for Yuri's, and failed to find him.

The front door closed.

Fear rose.

She searched again and found her gaze ensnared by Marcus's.

The British immortal stared at her with red-rimmed eyes. His Adam's apple rose and fell with a hard swallow. Then he shook his head.

Cat staggered backward. Surely he didn't mean . . .

Ami crossed to Marcus and hugged him tight.

Mouthing, "I'm sorry," Marcus buried his face in his wife's hair.

Denial gripping her, Cat looked for Stanislav and didn't see him either. Instead, she found Dmitry and Alexei, their noses red, tears streaming down their faces, and watched them walk numbly toward the back of the house.

Cat's eyes began to burn. Yuri couldn't be gone. He couldn't have fallen in battle.

Unable to believe it, *unwilling* to believe it, she went to Yuri's bedroom, sat down, and waited.

She didn't know how much time passed . . . perhaps an hour . . . before the door opened.

Heart leaping, she looked up, then swallowed hard when Marcus slipped inside and closed the door.

He leaned back against it, his expression telling her everything she knew he didn't want to voice.

Cat's vision blurred as tears rose.

"I'm sorry," he whispered. "He was killed during the battle."

She fought back the sobs that threatened to erupt. "Did he suffer?" she forced past the lump in her throat.

"No. He was tranqed right before it happened."

"What did they do to him?"

"It doesn't matter," he whispered. "He didn't feel it. And I don't want . . ." He looked away and swallowed hard. "It doesn't matter. He's gone."

"Stanislav, too?"

"Yes."

She did sob then, her heart breaking.

Marcus approached her slowly and crouched down in front of her. "Yuri loves you, Catherine. I wasn't there when it happened. I didn't see his spirit leave his body. And I don't know where he is now. I half expected him to already be here when we returned."

"Then why *isn't* he?"

"I don't know. But he loves you. If Yuri *can* find you, he will."

Cat did her damnedest to cling to the hope Marcus's words offered her. But days passed. Then weeks. And Yuri didn't come to her.

Had he crossed over?

Was he lost to her?

Cat lingered in his room. Touched his things to gain images of him from the past. Lay down on his bed. Drew in the scent of him left behind on his pillow. And wept until she couldn't anymore.

Dmitry came to Yuri's bedroom, packed his belongings up in boxes, and removed them.

The human male appeared as lost and desolate as Cat.

Nothing of Yuri remained in David's home now. Nothing she could touch and use her psychometric ability to see his handsome face and charming grin again. Nothing lingered save the memories Cat clung to as her despair grew.

Curling on her side on the big bed, she buried her face in his pillow for the hundredth time. All still considered this room Yuri's, though his personal possessions had been removed. Since none were eager to commandeer it, the bedding and towels had not yet been replaced.

Yuri.

"What the hell?" a deep voice spoke behind her. "I'm only gone a day and they ditch all of my stuff?"

Cat jackknifed up in bed and swung around.

Yuri stood just inside the door, clad in a black T-shirt, black cargo pants, and black boots. A scowl creasing his forehead, he looked around the room that was now devoid of his belongings.

His eye fell upon Cat. His scowl fell away. "Hello, sweetheart."

Leaping from the bed, Cat raced toward him.

Yuri grinned and opened his arms.

She hit him hard, his body as tangible to her now as it had been in his dreams. Sobs erupted from her chest as she hugged him tight.

Yuri wrapped his arms around Cat and squeezed her lithe form against him. "Shhh," he crooned when she burst into tears. "It's okay, Cat. Don't cry."

Her breath coming in harsh gasps, she wept into his chest.

Her hands fisted in the back of his shirt as she attempted to burrow even closer.

"Come now," he pleaded when she continued to sob. Easing back, he cupped her face in his hands and forced her to look up at him. "Why the tears?" He drew his thumbs over her wet cheeks, wiping away the moisture. "I didn't suffer, if that's why you're crying. And . . ." Dipping his head, he brushed a gentle kiss over her lips. "We can be together now. We won't ever have to settle for dreams again."

She curled her small hands around his wrists. "I thought I'd lost you."

He frowned. "Surely you knew I would come to you."

"I *hoped* you would, but it's been so long."

"What do you mean? I just died yesterday."

Her eyebrows rose. "What?"

"I just died yesterday. In the battle at the mercenary compound. I wanted to come to you as soon as it happened, but . . ." He swallowed hard. Moisture burned the backs of his eyes. "I heard them say the explosion took Stanislav and tried to find him. Or rather his spirit. I wanted to say good-bye."

"Did you?"

He shook his head. "There were so many other spirits released during the battle. I see why you never stayed after I slew the vampires when you joined me on my hunts."

She nodded.

"When I didn't find Stanislav on the battlefield, I thought I might find him at some of his favorite haunts." He grimaced. "Bad choice of words, I suppose. But it took me a while to get the hang of thinking where I wanted to go and ending up in the right place. When hours passed and I couldn't find him, I assumed he had crossed over or whatever it is spirits do when they don't linger here. I knew you would be anxious to see me—"

"Yuri," she interrupted. "It hasn't been hours. Or a day. The battle at the mercenary compound took place weeks ago."

He stared at her. "What?"

"You died weeks ago." New tears rose in her eyes. "I thought . . ." She shook her head. "When you didn't come to me, I thought I'd lost you. I thought that, like Stanislav, you'd crossed over."

"No," he murmured, stunned that so much time had passed. Drawing her to him, he rested his cheek on her hair. "No. I would never leave you, Cat. I love you. I'm sorry." He hugged her tighter. "I'm so sorry. I wouldn't have looked for Stanislav beyond the battlefield without coming here first had I known . . ." He shook his head. "For me, it feels like only hours have passed."

She nodded. "It was the same for me when I disappeared after Zach did whatever he did with that blast of power."

Yuri glanced around the room. "No wonder my things are gone."

"Dmitry came and collected them."

Sorrow filled him at the thought of his Second. "How is he?"

"Grieving. They all are."

Yuri felt the same sorrow, knowing he would never be able to speak to his friends again.

Well, except for Marcus, if he could convince his friend to abandon his no-communication-with-spirits rule.

"Did Marcus tell you what happened?" he asked.

"Only that you had been killed in battle and didn't suffer. He didn't go into any details."

Good. Yuri didn't want her to know he had been decapitated after he'd been rendered unconscious.

She raised her head. "*Did* you suffer, Yuri?"

He shook his head. "No, sweetheart. I didn't feel a thing," he was able to tell her with complete honesty. "One moment I was fighting mercenaries, and the next I found myself standing amidst the smoldering rubble of the armory." He grimaced. "I didn't realize I was dead until one of the network soldiers walked right through me. I can't tell you how furious

I was that I had let one of those mercenary bastards get the drop on me."

At last she smiled. "I'm sure you were."

He cupped her face in his hands. "And then," he told her softly, "I was filled with such joy, Cat. Such excitement. Because I knew we could finally be together. No restrictions. No limitations." He pressed a gentle kiss upon her lips. She felt so real to him now. As real as she had in the dreams. "I couldn't wait to get back to you. Had I not heard Alexei say Stanislav was dead, I would have been here sooner." He frowned. "At least, I *think* I would have. I still can't believe weeks have passed instead of hours. Did it really take me that long to figure out how to go from place to place?"

She shook her head. "It doesn't matter. You're here now."

He smiled. "And I'll never leave you again."

Rising onto her toes, she slid her arms around his neck and took his mouth in a scorching kiss.

When his heart began to slam against his ribs, Yuri broke the passionate contact in surprise. "I can feel my heart beating."

She grinned. "I know. I can feel mine, too. I can't explain it."

He kissed her again, loving the feel of her, the taste of her, so happy to be with her. Lifting her, he encouraged her to wrap her legs around his waist and prepared to topple her onto the bed.

"Wait," she whispered.

He groaned. "It's been weeks."

"For me. But only a day for you."

"I know. Far too long." His body already burned for her.

She laughed. "Put me down. I want to show you something."

Grumbling a bit, Yuri lowered her feet to the floor.

Cat took his hand and backed away. "Come with me."

Arching a brow, he smiled. "Where are we going?"

She tugged him through the door and out into the hallway. Eyes sparkling, she led him upstairs, through David's empty study, and pulled him through the wall.

Squinting, Yuri threw up a hand and winced as bright sunlight struck him.

Cat stopped and stood, smiling up at him.

Cautiously, Yuri lowered his arm. The sun's rays washed over him, bringing a startlingly tangible warmth.

No pain. No burning. No blistering.

"It can't harm me now," he marveled, holding out his arms and basking in the brightness he hadn't been able to enjoy for more than a moment or two in centuries.

"No," she confirmed, her brown eyes alight with love. "It will never hurt you again."

Yuri grinned, then leered as inspiration struck. "Have you ever made love outside with sunlight stroking your bare, beautiful body?"

Shaking her head, she backed away. One step. Two. "No."

He began to stalk her. "Do you *want* to make love with sunlight stroking your bare, beautiful body?"

She nodded, a playful smile toying with her lips.

His body hardened with anticipation.

Her hands gripped her skirts. "But you'll have to catch me first." Yanking the material up to her knees, she spun around and took off running.

Laughing in delight, Yuri raced after her.

Stake Out

Hannah Jayne

Chapter One

My design—an ultra-black slip dress with an asymmetrical hem and beaded bodice—hung on the model's thin frame like a sad sack, the elegant fabric catching on her angled hip bones and concave belly. I wished she would eat a sandwich, not just to do my design justice but because my stomach was growling and if I was going to have a nibble, I'd like to do it on someone with whom I couldn't floss my fangs. But I suppose all in all it was a good thing that this little pale wisp of a girl didn't whet my appetite in the least. I may have been six thousand miles from my home and my job at the Underworld Detection Agency, but I was still under Class-V contract, meaning if I even punctured a breather's vein—even just for the tiniest sip—I'd be tossed out of UDA on my ear and without dental coverage: A real bitch when you're a vampire.

The Underworld Detection Agency was my home, and what protection the agency offered—medical, dental, afterlife insurance for when one comes back to life, just to name a few—was indispensable and one of those things that made this country great for both one's life and afterlife.

And as long as we're being perfectly honest, it would be a whole hell of a lot harder to remain undead and unnoticed if I happened to occasionally nip the vein of those under my employ. I hadn't maintained my breather façade for a century plus by playing fast and loose. I sipped from blood bags rather than bodies and welcomed the beet smoothie craze— so much easier to hide a Big Gulp full of B Neg amongst all the other red-tinged cups. And, thankfully, my flawless, porcelain-pale skin was considered wear-sunscreen-chic rather than get-a-pulse passé out here in the fashion mecca that is Manhattan.

Though I had called San Francisco home for the better half of a century, I had gotten a bit of the wandering feet last year when I entered—and won, *natch*—a fashion competition out here. Granted, the win wasn't as sweet as it could have been as my competitors had the uncanny ability to drop out of competition by dropping dead, but that's really neither here nor there. Long story short, it's been a year and I've returned to the runways and maiden forms and put on my fashion designer hat once again. Hence the frustrated frown at the walking stick bug wrapped in haute couture before me.

I was considering a comment—maybe a nip here or a hem there to give the model some shape—when my cell phone pinged. I glanced down at the little pink alarm clock that bounced around my screen announcing that I had just two days to shape up everything and get my show and my models runway ready to expose Drop Dead Clothing to the world during New York's famed Fashion Week.

Fashion bloggers, hipsters, and celebrities everywhere were eagerly awaiting the debut of my whole collection. Right now, Drop Dead dresses were one-of-a-kind rarities which made them absolute necessities for everyone who was anyone who was (or wanted to be) in the public eye. I had a cult following that was growing by the social media minute, and I relished it. There was another cell phone ping and I glanced down again, grinning at the jumping icon of a sparkly pink stiletto— a new post by one of the foremost fashion insiders, probably popping up to gush about the sneak peek of a dress earmarked for a big celebrity—hush hush on the name, darlings—that had been "leaked" online. Little heart-to-heart: It was leaked by me, and the dress, though incredible, wasn't the one that would premiere on the red carpet. While the leaked dress was to be adored, the premiere dress was created to be worshipped.

I popped my finger over the icon and frowned at the dress that graced the top of the page. It was nice, but it wasn't mine. And if I had a breath I would have lost it when I read the site line: *New Mystery Designer Debuts a Stunner!*

> *Color this blogger stunned and positively chartreuse with envy! I was swilling champagne at the super chic-chic and incredibly exclusive Fashion Week Sneak Peek Cocktail Couture party and loving every chic piece that strutted by. As you all know, I've been counting the days to see the latest LaShay release from Drop Dead Clothing, the little black fashion label that could—and it didn't disappoint. It was a pretty charcoal gray little number with the perfect tiny tucks and pick-ups that the elusive designer is known for. The bodice work was impeccable and the stones inlaid in the filmy chiffon were genius. I was ready to scratch the model's eyes out and snatch that dress right off her when IT came into the room. Yes, it.*

> *I don't remember who the model was or even what she looked like—the dress was that fetching. First of all, it was short, which is practically unheard of for a Sneak Peek dress—a debut, no less—but it worked. The color was a soft mossy green and the stiches were so perfect and fine they looked like they were sewn by fairy hands.*

My stomach rolled over and I felt my upper lip roll up into a disgusted snarl. *Fairy hands?* First of all, fairies are bitches—don't let Walt Disney fool you. I worked with a clutch of them back in San Francisco, and if you ask them to do the simplest thing, like make a photocopy (which is far easier than laying a perfectly straight whipstitch, I assure you), you got nothing but grief and eventual retaliation from the whole lot of them. And second of all, who created this so-called masterpiece?

I scanned the rest of the article, willfully skipping over the stitch-by-stich narrative of the "it" dress just looking for a designer name. There wasn't one.

> *Of course I had to know who designed such perfection. The model told me it was from a new label called* Under the Hem. *When I asked who the designer was, she didn't know. I grilled her, Googled it, used all my sources, connections, and weepy doe eyes and . . . nothing. If anyone knows the mystery designer or proprietor of* Under the Hem *clothing, PLEASE let this blogger know ASAP! It's only fair.*
>
> *Bringing Couture to the Everywoman,*
>
> *xoxo Fashion Fish*

I was positively seething. My dress gets shown up by a no-name off-label? Impossible!

I Googled the "mystery designer" and there were a slew of similar blogger articles: *Who Is Under the Hem? Mystery Designer Steals Show! Under the Hem and Under Cover!* And as there always is from an event that is very specifically "no photography allowed," there was a cameraphone snapshot of the dress. It was slightly blurry and shot from the side, but even with the blemishes of the photo, the dress was unarguably stunning. It was skillfully draped, the dauphine fabric bias cut and sewn perfectly. Mossy green wasn't the right description of the color; it was closer to a deep ocean green sewn through with slick thread that looked like it was spun gold.

Spectacular.

I squinted at the model. She was in profile, her features blurred by the lighting. But she looked familiar.

I cocked my head to get a better view of the model on my runway; her name was something weird and exotic like Bathsheba or Honeydew, which made me that much more certain that she was probably an Anne from Nebraska who had parlayed her string-bean body and half-dead eyes into a high-paying career stomping down catwalks and staring vacuously into camera lenses.

She was the model in the picture.

I felt my jaw tighten and squelched down a low growl.

"One minute, please," I said, beckoning the model over. A puff of her perfume reached me before she did: It was something flower-scented, pungent and cloying enough to make my stomach churn. She followed behind the flower explosion, wide eyed and spacy looking, and I considered offering her a sandwich. Instead, I turned the phone toward her. "Is this you?"

She used her impossibly long, slender fingers to pull the face into focus and smiled thinly. "Uh-huh."

"Who were you wearing?"

She bopped her head from one side to the other, and my annoyance—and a pounding ricocheting through my skull—was growing.

"It's new. It's called Under the Hem."

I pinched the bridge of my nose and closed my eyes, trying to visualize puppies or snowflakes or bald monks—whatever it is that is supposed to bring you back to center. "I know the name of the line. It's the name of the designer I'm after. Who is it?"

The model chewed her swollen bottom lip. "I don't know. No one ever told me."

"Well, who dressed you? Who gave you the dress?"

Narrow shoulders went up to her ears. "I don't know. It was

on my rack when I walked in. I was supposed to wear Stella, but the organizer just said this is what showed up instead."

I studied her for a half second, decided that the vacuous look on her face wasn't an act, and sent her back to my runway, still trying to stifle a snarl. I was incensed that this mystery designer was stealing my fanfare, and I couldn't help but feel betrayed by a model whose name I hadn't bothered to learn.

There were three models in my studio; each one would be wearing two of my dresses for my Fashion Week debut. As I looked around at them, most already dressed in their Drop Dead attire, I gave myself a little pep talk—the dresses were gorgeous, the show was two days away, and the models were lovely. Everything was falling into place.

This so-called "mystery designer" would be old news by Tuesday.

I went back to watching the photo shoot, sitting in my little director's chair, sipping a fresh pint of O Neg from my Starbucks thermos. Everything was going to be fine. *Everything is going to be just fine*, I chanted to myself . . . even while a little spark of anger started at the base of my spine and gained fire with each passing moment I watched the exchange between my model and my photographer.

It wasn't that I hated models or felt a twinge of jealousy each time one of them slipped into a piece of haute couture that slipped through my fingers—well, that could have been a little bit of it—it was that I hated the way this one was pouting and thrusting her nothing-there hips in the direction of my boyfriend—not boyfriend, I refused to commit—male associate, who snapped every frame and didn't seem bothered in the least by the drab way she modeled my art.

"Stop!" I snapped, throwing up my hands.

Pike, a deeply bronzed, muscled god of a man who pissed

me off in all the right places, pushed himself up from his photographer's squat and sighed. "What now?"

"She's wearing that dress like a hanger," I seethed to him, and then, over my shoulder, "No offense, sweetheart, you're a dream, really. Take five."

The model nodded and stepped down from her perch, picking her way toward the craft services table where she probably had the other half of her breakfast grape stored.

"She's all wrong. The dress, the design—Drop Dead Clothing is supposed to be sensual and sexy. It should make your pulse race and your body hum when wearing it. The model should be sexy and curvy and"—I cut a glance toward Bathsheba/Honeydew—"not look like a baton wrapped in silk shantung."

"I think she looks fine, personally." Pike flipped through a half dozen digital images of the girl posing like a praying mantis. He was clearly entertained by the hip-out, pouty look, hip-in, pouty look the girl had mastered, and that made my blood—well, whomever's blood I was currently digesting—boil.

I don't consider myself a jealous person—seriously, I'm adorable—and after more than a century on this earth you learn that jealousy is a wasted emotion. Breathers are manipulated easily enough without me having to get all red-cheeked and huffy every time my beau looked at another lady. But this wasn't just any old beau. This was Pike, a delicious, carved, tropical coconut of a man, and though I've dated my share of beautiful men in the past, he was quite possibly the most beautiful. That skin, that hair, those eyes that were so intense and deeply dark that they could look through a girl and right into her soul if she had one.

Like me, he played the elusive card, which was as frustrating as it was sexy. After a brief but torrid affair that included a few deaths and dangerous situations last year, I had gone back to San Francisco and Pike had gone back to shooting photo essays. We tried to call, text, or make time for each other, but it never seemed to work. At such a great distance that was fine. The closer we got proximity wise, the more I felt the incessant need to bury my fangs in and never let go.

But, as is the case with every godlike breather dropped down from heaven, there were problems. Bird problems, mostly.

See, I hate birds. *Hate* them. It has nothing to do with my being a vampire or having an affinity toward bats or spiders or whatever foul creature modern media was intent on making you believe we like, it's that they're *birds*. Hollow boned. Flying rodents. Beady eyed with sharp little beaks just the right size for gouging out eyeballs.

Yes, I'm immortal. Yes, should my eyeballs be gouged out any which way, it wouldn't take but a few minutes to grow them back into perfect peeper form. But seriously, who wants to have a freaking bird gouge out their eyeballs? Not me. So, no birds.

Pike, on the very distant other hand, is a bird person.

Literally.

While my pre-vamp bloodline included a mansion in Paris and an education that centered around aristocracy and the arts, Pike was born in the island sunshine of Maui, where he learned spearfishing, probably the hula, and that his bloodline and his ancestors leaned more toward the winged.

Yes, I'm a hundred-and-twelve-year dead French ingénue, and he can shapeshift into a bird at will.

Oh, like you don't have a cross to bear.

But right now it wasn't Pike's penchant for poultry that was ticking at my last nerve; it was that vapid model, two days until Fashion Week, and a clothing line that was more stunted than stunning.

I chewed on my bottom lip while Pike reached out an arm

to me. "Relax, pecksie, everything is going to be fine. The pictures look great."

"The girl or the clothes?"

The edges of Pike's full mouth pushed up into a disgustingly sexy grin. "Both, actually."

I was considering laying a trail of bird-deterrent spikes across the floor while Pike crossed the room to our little kitchenette and began fixing himself a coffee or a pinecone covered in peanut butter or something. I was trying to count to ten and breathe deeply—a hell of a challenge when breath is in short supply—when my eyes landed on my little supermodel.

The little wisp of a thing had changed out of my dress and into the clothes she had showed up in—jeans that clung to her no-hips in an attempt to be skinny but edged away from her stick legs, and a tank top that slid over her tiny breasts that were mosquito bites more than A-cups. She had a business card pinched between her fingers and she was zeroed in on Pike, *my* Pike. She did a sexy little saunter toward him. I watched in horror as she pushed her chewed-to-the-quick nails through his lush, dark hair, moving the strands that forever fell into his eyes. She swiveled her hips in a laughable attempt at sexy, but the way she held her mouth made up for her stick-figure frame: Her lips were curved in a half pout, half scowl that oozed sex, pursed in that kind of grin that leaves everything to the imagination and sends it soaring into the sheets.

"It's Wendi," she was saying in a little singsong voice. "W-e-n-d-"—her eyes flashed into a mock-up of baby sweet innocence—"i." She blinked those doe eyes and dragged a corner of pretty pink tongue across her bottom lip, dropping her voice to what would have been a low whisper to anyone who didn't have vampire hearing. "Your girlfriend doesn't have to know a thing."

To his credit, Pike's spine stiffened before anything else on him did. His hand clamped around her wrist as she went to stroke his hair again. "I'm not interested."

"Why go vintage when you can go all new?"

Vintage?!

The word cut through me like a fang through flesh and I was seething, the rage thrumming like a pulse. I made a beeline for the kitchenette.

"Who are you calling vintage?" I roared, far louder than I'd meant.

Wendi's mouth dropped open to a little "o" of surprise. "Oh, Ms. LaShay. I didn't see you there." She licked her lips again and stared at me, her eyes full of faux innocence.

"Get out," I said, pressing my jaw together to regain a semblance of control.

Truth was, I wanted to pitch the bitch like a javelin, but I had worked too hard to get here—both as a designer and as a vampire posing as a breather—to blow it on this piece of insipid trash. Instead, I stepped forward, closed a hand around her upper arm, and told her in no uncertain terms that she was effectively fired from walking for Drop Dead Clothing, ever.

And I may have whispered something about her imminent death should she set foot near my man or my couture ever again. But again, that's beside the point—or at least it was.

I let myself into my apartment and my nephew Vlad was already there, stretched out on the couch as if he had done anything, *ever*, that required him to relax and unwind. His giant duster jacket was draped over my coffee table, his brocade Dracula vest on the floor, and his ascot was lying in a crumpled heap next to two empty blood bags and his boots.

While I got the fashionista gene in the LaShay pool, Vlad got the "movementarian" one and had become the front man for the Vampire Empowerment and Restoration Movement (VERM for short, and for annoying Vlad incessantly). The movement rallied against the modern concept of the vampire in media and strove to dash the image of sparkly, soul-having, friendly vamps and restore vampires and their detractors back to the days of old. Basically, VERM demanded its adherents re-create the image of the sexy, brooding vampire that terrified and mesmerized all breathers he encountered. And somewhere within those requirements was the "classic" vampire dress code that made Vlad and his cronies look like Count Chocula rejects rather than the terrifying bastions of hell they strove to become.

Vlad rolled over onto his side, pausing his Bloodlust game just as the cartoon vampire was about to feast on some busty brunette with wide anime eyes. He held his laptop steady with one hand and glared up at me like I was interrupting something in my own apartment.

I crossed my arms in front of my chest. "Surfing porn again?"

Vlad rolled his eyes —black as coal and a mirror image of mine—and looked suitably disgusted. "You're so gross, Aunt Nina."

"I've had a long day, Vlad," I groaned, dropping my things and heading for the refrigerator. "Want something?"

"Nah, just ate."

I rifled through the refrigerator that was half cold storage and half general bureau. Blood bags were kept on the top two shelves; batteries, nail polish, and a lone beer in the door should we have a visitor; and the crisper and meat drawers kept my selection of hats and scarves in pristine, if a little cold, condition.

Vlad kept his Doc Martens in the freezer.

I helped myself to a blood bag and pierced the edge with one angled fang, popped in a straw, and began sipping the thing Capri Sun–style.

"This is so good," I said, holding the viscous liquid on my tongue for a beat before swallowing it down.

Vlad wrinkled his nose. "I don't like the organic as much. They're always low fat. Can't you get the Trucker brand anymore? I like those. They have a bacon-y aftertaste."

"You buy what you like. Oh, that's right. You've been couch surfing for three and a half months and don't have a job. Or an apartment."

"I have a job," he huffed. "In San Francisco. I'm just here on an exchange program."

I slurped at the little stars of plasma stuck in the bottom of the bag. "Exchange of what?"

"God, Auntie! Why can't you just let me relax for like, five minutes? I'm tired. It's not like I didn't go apartment hunting today because I totally did."

I felt my eyebrows go up. Could it be true? I would soon have my *own* space, devoid of my dearest nephew and his bad attitude?

"You did? How'd it go? Did you find something?" I worked to meter my voice so my absolute excitement wouldn't be too obvious.

Vlad narrowed his eyes. "You don't have to sound so absolutely thrilled. It's not like I found one."

Crushed! "Oh no?"

"No. I hunted. You didn't expect me to find one right away, did you? Please. I have standards."

I felt my lip curling up into an involuntary snarl and cocked my hip out. "Standards? You? Really?"

Chronologically, Vlad was closing in on a century and thus should have had the grace and maturity not to annoy the crap out of me, to rent his own apartment, and to have actual standards. But, as his body was stuck at a perennial sixteen years old, somewhere along the line, dear old Vlad decided that his mind and maturity level should top out there as well. Which is why he had, once again, taken up couch surfing at my place, dedicated to his stupid Bloodlust video game while wearing socks that hadn't been washed since we both were in Afros and elevator shoes.

"Besides," he said, his eyes not leaving his screen. "You need me."

"I do, do I?"

"Word on the street is that you're down a model."

"And you're going to step in for her? Fabulous. Lose about ninety pounds, grow out that helmet you call a hairstyle, and practice your catwalk. In stilettos." I sucked at the little gelatinous pillows of plasma that floated at the bottom of my blood bag while Vlad let out an impressive groan and finally cut his eyes from his precious computer game.

"I was thinking that I could help you out. I know how busy and stressed out you've been. Fashion Week is, what? Two days away? You must have tons to do."

I softened. Family—actual bloodline, look-like-each-other *family*—is rare among vampires and I really was lucky to have Vlad. Granted, I made him. His poor mother, my little sister, had sought me out when Vlad had taken ill. I hadn't seen my family—actually, they hadn't seen me—since I'd been changed, but Lucienne came to me, her tiny face drawn and pinched with this little, this little *child* in her arms. Only he was sixteen years old. The disease had ravaged him so that he looked barely a day over eleven. I remember his dull, flat eyes, clouded by imminent death. The way his gaunt face caved in around his cheekbones, his cracked, swollen lips. And she had begged me.

"You can make him well," she had said to me in that small voice of hers. "You can make him live."

When Vlad and I outlived our family, all we had was each other. We are family and we need each other, we love each other, we'll be there for each other—for eternity, should we make it that long. All we'll ever have is each other.

"That's very kind, Vlad, I appreciate that."

He shrugged. "I figured you can handle all your sewing or

paperwork or ramp building or whatever, and I can interview model replacements."

All we'll ever have is each other.

Son of a bitch.

I smacked him hard with a pillow. "Don't you ever think with anything other than your bloodless little head?"

"Don't be gross, Auntie Neen." He opened his laptop once again, hitting the flashing red RESUME button. "Trust me. You'll need me."

Though I don't sleep, morning—the earliest, night fading into dawn morning—is easily my favorite time of day in every city that I've ever lived. In Paris, when I was new and would wander the streets all night long, fangs stained with the blood of snacks or meals or newfound friends, I would always stop on the Pont au Double and watch the fingers of light break through the city. There was nothing special or particularly beautiful about the view from the bridge, but it was the way the dawn broke and woke the city, a little at a time, that always gave me pleasure or hope or calm. It is these same stirrings of life that still give me pleasure whether it's the first commuters pushing their way through the San Francisco streets or here in Manhattan, when the night people switch to morning people, the beautiful partygoers scurrying away with the fading darkness, replaced by the smart office workers walking with purpose in the gray light of morning. There is something so fresh about a city, so hopeful in the mornings—which is why I was feeling particularly bright and cheery as I made my way to my studio. Winter was in the air, but fall was hanging on fiercely so snow flurries were still a welcome anomaly and the wool coats weren't out yet. I was in my mid-thigh-length angora-blend trench with the thick black whipstitch and skipping a little as I went.

Just because I was dead didn't mean I couldn't be happy.

I paused and admired my logo etched on the smoked glass doors of my studio door—Drop Dead Clothing, Designs by Nina LaShay—before sinking my key into the lock and throwing open the doors with a flourish and possibly a happy working song.

Except my door wouldn't open.

I checked my key and checked the lock—right key, lock rolling—but there was something holding the door shut. I fidgeted and jiggled and finally threw my shoulder against the wooden liner, and voila! The door lurched open a few extra inches only to stop and thud one more time.

I didn't need to see it to know what it was because I could smell it.

Death. Fresh.

Pinpricks of electricity walked down my vertebrae one by one. Something else hung in the air, too. Faint. Stale.

Perfume.

I edged my way into the studio vestibule, carefully allowing just enough wiggle room to sneak in. My breakfast was thrumming through my body, the blood pulsing at a dizzying pace. The hot, sour taste of adrenaline shot through me.

It was Wendi's perfume.

I looked down, and there she was in a pose befitting a supermodel. Eyes open wide, a clear, innocent-looking blue with pink-stained lips pursed in a sexy heart shape. She was bent at her impossibly tiny waist, her thighs pulled up against her, her long legs spread behind her as though she were ready to jump. And her hair . . . her long, honey blond locks still held some of the curl from the photo shoot I had sent her out of, but while the weak tea color flared out behind her, the hair close to her scalp was colored a heady, rusted red. The color of bricks. The color of blood.

A lesser woman would have trembled. A human who

didn't wear death like a second skin would have screamed cinematically, pressing her palms against her open mouth and lurching backward while ominous music blared behind her. And I wanted to do all those things, really, I did—but this was me, and in more than a century I'd had more than my share of dead bodies (though, admittedly, not all of them this pretty), so I simply sighed and stepped around her, sank down onto the next step, and pulled out my cell phone.

"Told you you'd need me" was Vlad's cheeky telephone greeting.

"I don't need you," I huffed into the phone. "Just come down to my studio, would you please?"

"Do you *need* me to?"

"You know, you're awfully flippant for a guy who could be stopped cold by a vegetable."

I could hear Vlad shift on his end of the phone. "Technically, garlic is considered a spice, and have you not checked the mirror lately? Because you have the same nonreflection that I do."

"Just get down your butt down here."

I stayed seated, thrumming my fingers on the step while I waited for Vlad. My instinct was to run upstairs and finish off the rest of my line; after all, it was now, I checked my phone, less than twenty-four hours from the kick-off of Fashion Week, and if I didn't get to my sewing machine, my four models—scratch that, three—would be stomping down my debut runway in various forms of haute couture undress.

I glanced down at Wendi and figured she wasn't going anywhere, then sprinted upstairs, plopped myself at my sewing machine, and got to work on a three-quarter-length body-con dress with a flouncy little peplum. The ensemble was a near replica of something I had worn back in the early days of jazz and blues in the back-alley clubs of Chicago.

Decade after decade, I always made a splash.

"Hey, you know you got a supermodel lying on the floor

downstairs? The least you could do is prop her up with an Open sign in her hands or something."

I spun around to face Vlad, my lips pressed together in an unamused pout. He grinned, showing a toothy mouth.

"You're hysterical. Now help me. I—I don't know what to do with her."

Vlad followed me down the stairs and we stood over Wendi.

"I don't know," Vlad said, itching his chin as though he had suddenly sprouted a ZZ Top beard. "We could just eat."

I stomped one Via Spiga peep-toe bootie. "You know we can't do that! Not just because of UDA bylaws but because—and may I remind you—we're *trying* to fit in here?"

Vlad, ever the obnoxious and unruly teen, slumped against the door and shot me a look of pure disdain. "Whatever."

"I suppose I should call the police." I pinched my bottom lip, remembering the last time I found myself with the dead and law-enforcing living—it wasn't pretty. "Look, Vlad, everyone in my studio yesterday heard me fire Wendi, and I'm not sure if the fact that I threatened her with death was as private as I thought it was."

This amused Vlad and he glanced back down at the body. "Go, Auntie. Finally got a little bite in your bark."

I stomped my foot. "I didn't kill her! But it could look a lot like I did. I did threaten her and now here she is, dead in my building." I frowned. "All signs point to me."

Now, this is the point in the story where I have to break in and remind you that I'm a vampire. While I don't have any discernable body weight or a soul and can burst into flames on one overly bright day, I do have a modicum of feeling for the freshly dead—especially if their lives were cut short due to someone else's whim, and yes, even if the dead at hand was rather vapid and annoying in life. Death is death, and in a lot of cases, it's forever.

He snorted. "Talk about fitting in here."

"What's that supposed to mean?"

"We've been here two years, and how many dead bodies have you rolled across?"

I stepped around Wendi—gingerly, again, my belief in respecting the dead even if I threatened them with death in life. "I didn't roll across her. I opened my door and she happened to be here." I pointed down to the body sprawled on my hand-laid vintage subway tiles. "And here."

"Just like you opened your sewing cupboard and your biggest rival just happened to fall out on you—wearing your scissors as an ornamental chest plate. Never bothered you before if bodies dropped, whether or not all flesh wounds pointed to you." Vlad grinned smugly and I felt my nostrils flare.

"Sometimes you've got to grow up, nephew. Now, are you going to help me with this or not?"

He snapped his jaw. "I told you what I'd do."

I was about to fly at Vlad, say something about his dorky new ascot that made him look like Count Chocula on speed, but my cell phone rang, shooting out a tropical little ditty that made Vlad's smug grin positively glisten. I glowered at him and answered.

"Hi, Pike."

Vlad rolled his eyes and whispered, "Ukulele music for your Hawaiian boyfriend? Isn't that a little racist?"

"Piss off," I mouthed back.

"Everything okay?" Pike wanted to know.

Vlad rolled his eyes and waved, then turned on his heel and slunk out the door, a little cold puff of air popping into the vestibule behind him. Then I looked down at the ruined Wendi, her pale skin looking waxy and slightly sallow, her puckered lips rimmed with an icicle blue.

"Not exactly." I worried my bottom lip. "Would you mind coming over to the studio? Like, now?"

"Sure. Why?"

I did my best to explain about Wendi, then hung up the phone and waited for Pike to arrive. In the interim, I bit the proverbial bullet and dialed 911.

"Nine-one-one, please state the nature of your emergency."

I turned my back on Wendi, not wanting to face her broken body for another second, and started to pace. "Uh, murder?"

"I'm sorry, ma'am, what was that?"

"There's been a murder. Here, at my studio. A model I work with has been killed."

"Is she breathing?"

I glanced over my shoulder as though I needed the reaffirmation that Wendi was indeed not breathing—and the phone went clattering to the floor.

"Hello? Hello? Ma'am? Ma'am?" The 911 operator's nasal voice filled up the vestibule and mingled with Wendi's ragged breathing as she fought to push herself up. Her hair swung around her and I could see now that the gash at her hairline was topical—certainly not what killed her. No, that would be the gaping flesh wound that started just behind her left ear and ended a half inch above her collarbone.

"Son of a bitch," I huffed as Wendi blinked at me, the life in her eyes hazy but relighting.

She patted her head. "What happened?"

I clapped a hand to my forehead, feeling something in there start to throb. The only thing worse than supermodels hitting on my boyfriend? Supermodels who've had their throats nearly torn out, but not enough to kill them.

Suddenly, I was dealing with a vampire. Supermodel. A vampire supermodel.

If I wasn't damned before, I certainly was now.

Chapter Two

"Well, Wendi, it seems that you've been . . ." I was picking my words carefully, trying to come up with the best way to let the little half-dead twit know that she was hovering in that odd space between undead and underdead. If I could get a hold of her and just keep her under wraps and out of vein view for the next twenty-four hours, she would lapse into an honest, soul-to-heaven or Buddha or whatever the religion du jour was death. It would be a tragedy for sure; I could already see the headlines blaring, *Beautiful Supermodel a Victim of Homicide*. But if I let her go and find someone to feed off— or worse yet, gave her the half-second thought of feeding from me—I would have borne a new vampire—one whose obnoxiousness in death could only be compounded in her afterlife.

I couldn't let that happen.

I watched as she straightened. Even flat-footed, she was a whole head taller than me. Her size, combined with even a few drops of the superhuman strength we vamps possess— and she wasn't full-fledged, not by a long shot—could be enough to put a flush on my cheeks if we came to blows and would be more than enough to overpower a regular human being.

Wendi opened her mouth and pressed her fingers against

her teeth like a kid with a loose tooth. I saw her run the faint point of one of her emerging incisors under her index finger, the skin catching and slicing open neatly. Instinctively, her tongue went to the cut and lapped up the tiny bubble of blood that appeared and instantly, her eyes appeared slightly brighter, her cheeks that much less pale. She was drinking her own blood and she obviously liked the taste. Each sip stole away an inch of her life, but shored up her afterlife. It was an odd, unnatural dance, but it happened this way when a breather became a Halfling—literally a half-bred vampire hovering in the spot between life and death, obsessed with drinking the one thing, the only thing that could save their life. The Halfling becomes a vampire when they choose life force—blood—over their own soul.

I saw the afterlife twitching in Wendi's facial features and remembered my own becoming. It was like going to sleep in a black-and white world and waking up in Technicolor. Everything was brighter and louder and sharper; smells were more pungent, sweet, and engulfing. It was like being a child—all the wonder, the hunger, the lust—while being old enough to appreciate it. At that point, you see the body was a shell: Your skin goes from warm and pink to hard and cold with a marble-like sheen. There's no heartbeat, no breath, but whatever is inside is thrumming at a frenetic pace, awakened to a plain of—of *otherness* that didn't exist before. It was intoxicating—and terrifying—but at some point I envied Wendi, envied her these moments of newness when everything beckoned and thrived. Being damned seemed like a sweet, sweet gift then, but after years, then decades, then centuries, the colors fade, the smells are sickening constants, the sounds reminders of a life you can emulate but not actually live.

"I feel so good," Wendi said, her lips stained strawberry red with her own blood. "Everything seems so different." She reached out to touch me, as if making sure I was there, but I dodged back.

"It is different," I said to her.

"I feel alive."

I moistened my lips and started again. "You're not alive, Wendi. You're dead."

Her eyes snapped to me and flashed with hard anger. "I'm not dead. I'm standing right here, right here with you." She paused, suddenly smiling. "You look so bright."

I knew her eyes were refocusing, recalibrating the veil that hangs over all breathers. We exist—we vampires, plus all other manner of demon, werewolf, troll, or other—amongst breathers and we always have. It is simply a magical veil and a breather's logic that makes us "disappear." You don't expect to see a Minotaur directing traffic and so you don't. Your eyes tell you it's simply a burly police officer and you should lay off the caffeine. Ditto with the paper "boy" whose backward hat and surly disposition hide a pair of horns and the horrific stench of troll.

Now Wendi was seeing the world for what it truly was.

"Everything is different," she breathed again, holding up her own hands, touching her own skin in wonder. "Why is it so different?"

I pinched the bridge of my nose wondering how I was going to explain the whole thing and toss in the "thanks for playing, but it's time to go home" phrase when the clatter of the front door stopped me. I spun on my heel and did a mental head slap.

Pike.

"What the—?" He paused in the doorway, eyes scanning the pooled blood on the tile, then taking in me and Wendi. She licked her lips, her newfound hunger palpable, throbbing with every audible beat of Pike's heart.

"Pike . . ." Wendi's voice was a near growl, sexy and dripping with want. She took a step toward him and her whole body arched forward, ready to close the distance. I immediately held out my hands, palms pressed outward—one against

Pike's firm, warm chest while his heartbeat thumped against my palm, the other hand on Wendi, her chest lukewarm but hard as granite, her heart struggling to beat from somewhere deep inside, layers under the change.

Wendi's eyes went to my hand, to my outstretched arm. There was confusion and something like hurt in her eyes. "I want Pike," she said, her voice like a spoilt child.

"Get out of here, Pike. She's a vampire."

Pike stumbled backward a few inches. "She's a what?"

But the word was snatched out of the air by the sound of Wendi launching herself from the bottom step right across me and directly to Pike. I saw her mouth open, saw the budding edges of those two new fangs cutting through her bright pink gums, her own blood pooling and dribbling over her chin.

I've been a vampire longer than I've been anything else, and so our speed is more than second nature to me. I sliced in front of the newbie, landing an elbow to her chest with such force that she snapped backward, her bony model back hitting the wall with a solid smack. She slid down the wall in a crumple that lasted only a few seconds. Then she was back on her feet, a blur of blue jeans and bloodstained hair as she whipped by Pike and disappeared out the front door and into the Manhattan morning.

"What the fuck just happened here?"

"I would like to know the same thing," I said. "But, in a nutshell, someone attacked Wendi and left her for dead. Or undead. Now we have to go find her."

"Wait. A vampire attacked her?"

I cocked my head, looking at the smears of dried blood that had oozed into my once-gleaming grout. "I'm not sure. The attack may have happened first, the vampire second. If it was a complete vampire attack, there wouldn't be this much wasted blood."

I hated myself for it, but my eyes stayed locked on the blood, the little pools that had dripped into low spots in the tile beginning to congeal. I had eaten already but my mouth started to water.

"Nina?"

I snapped to attention. "Yeah, sorry. We've got to go, Pike. We have to find her."

I pushed Pike aside and went to the door, but he stopped me with a hand on my arm. "Hey, she's a vampire on foot. How far could she have gotten? It's not like she can fly."

The smugness in his voice didn't go unnoticed, but being the bigger person and the better of two supernatural creatures (and vampires are quite fast, let me assure you), I let it go. Instead, I pushed open the door and gestured to the deserted street. "She can be halfway to Brooklyn by now. Come on."

"Why is it so important we find her? Isn't she just going to, I don't know, run out into some sunlight and self-combust?"

I narrowed my eyes. "It's a wonder your mother didn't toss you out of the nest when you were hatched."

Pike let out a slightly audible growl, his eyebrows going low. "I wasn't hatched. I just meant that aren't new vampires meant to be a little squirrely?"

"Squirrely, not stupid. And she can do a hell of a lot of damage. We need to find Wendi before she attacks anyone else or goes back to her sire. People can't just go around making vampires willy-nilly. It's against the rules."

"Rules?"

I shook my head, going for the door. "It's complicated."

Pike clapped a hand on my shoulder, pulling me back into the vestibule. "No, that's complicated."

I glanced to where he was pointing and groaned. I had been so preoccupied that I must not have heard the sirens and now, a police car was stopped in the middle of the street, flanked by a fire truck and an ambulance. I watched in horror as car doors flung open and uniformed officers jumped out, all poised and ready to move, each with guns at the ready.

"How did they know?"

Pike leaned down and snatched my cell phone from the floor. "Nine-one-one?"

"Crap." I pasted on a sheepish smile and pushed open the smoked glass door just enough to shimmy out but not enough to expose the smears of blood undead Wendi had left behind.

I batted my eyelashes and kept to the shade of the awning over the building's large windows. "Is there a problem, Officer?"

I hoped my smile didn't sink, but my heart did when I saw the officer who was striding toward me.

"Oh. Officer Moyer."

Now, I have nothing against cops. Though I prefer fire-fighters (mainly for their calendar potential), I have a soft spot for cops, too—I just wasn't all too keen on running into the same handful of officers over and over again, particularly at crime scenes. Tends to make a girl look suspicious, and the last time I had the good fortune to chat with Moyer, he was examining a pair of wardrobe shears that belonged to me . . . and that were firmly implanted in the chest of one of my biggest rivals.

He really got the wrong impression of me.

If Officer Moyer recognized me, he didn't comment on it. He was all business. "We received a call about an incident here. Someone called nine-one-one?"

I forced a blush. "I'm so very sorry, that was me. I—it was a scare. I thought I saw someone, turns out I was wrong."

"You told the nine-one-one operator, and I quote," Moyer started, pulling out his every-cop-everywhere-has notebook, "*There's been a murder here at the studio. One of the models that I work with.*" His eyes flicked from the notebook back to me, one eyebrow cocked.

"Yes. Right. I did call and say . . . that, but it turns out she was just sleeping. She had fallen asleep and I thought she was dead. Whoops!" I clasped my hands and did one of those silly-me looks and giggled. "Wendi's quite the hard sleeper. Supermodels, huh? Who knew?"

I angled myself just enough to block the giant bloodspot while giving myself a sweeping view of the street. I thought perhaps I could spot Wendi banging her head into a plate-glass window or trying to feed off a fire hydrant (the girl wasn't exactly a brain surgeon in life), but no such luck. The street was empty and there wasn't a single clue as to which direction she might have gone.

Moyer took a step toward me, his giant cop head blocking my view, his eyes narrowed as though I would throw myself at his feet and confess any and every trespass I'd ever made. I held his gaze until he broke away, edging a chin toward the door behind me.

"That Pike?"

Pike had a history with the NYPD as an occasional crime scene photographer. My mind was ticking, thinking how best to use that to my advantage. All I came up with was a tiny tremor of annoyance that Pike hadn't come striding out to save the day with some sort of inside joke or doughnut or something.

"Yeah, of course. We're friends. Acquaintances. We do business together. We're friends." I was happy to steer the conversation away from Wendi. So happy that I babbled like an idiot, apparently.

Moyer nodded. "Was he here when you called in the murder?"

I bit down hard, working to keep my expression light and pleasant. "When I called in what I thought was a death? No, no, he just got here. You know, on time, ready to work with Wendi."

"Why don't you go ahead and send Wendi and Pike out here, just so I can get everything squared away."

"Of course I can send Pike out. I'll do that right away."

"And Wendi."

"Wendi." I blinked, then focused directly on Moyer. I could feel my glamour—a sexy little vampire superpower that is occasionally used (responsibly, of course) when one might need to sway the opinion of a breather in the vicinity—start to ramp up. Immediately, Officer Moyer's shoulders relaxed, dropping a half-inch from his earlobes. His belly eased out and his back swayed the slightest, his eyes getting the telltale glaze of being wholly under my "spell."

"I would like nothing more than to send Wendi out to you, Officer, but she's inside getting ready for her photo shoot. We're on a really, really tight schedule." I accented all the right words, seeing Moyer's jaw go slack each time my lips moved. I kept my eyes on him while I straightened his collar, my long, pale pink nails striking against the blue of his shirt. His eyes followed my every motion, and his breathing went low and ragged. "So you see, I could send her out, but it would really make things hard on me, cutting into my precious, precious time an' all."

Moyer swallowed, eyes still wide as saucers, Adam's apple bobbing slowly in his throat. "That's fine, then."

I held the glamour until he turned on the heel of his department-issued boot and locked himself in his squad car, starting a parade of first responders down the street and out of my life.

"Whew," Pike said, coming up over my shoulder. "Glad that's done."

"Yeah, thanks for stepping in."

Pike didn't back down, which grated on my nerves but kicked my body into sexual overdrive. "You look like the kind of girl who can handle her man."

"Oh, I can handle a man. Any man. But now I'm more concerned about a lady. Are you coming with me to find Wendi or not?"

Chapter Three

I dialed Vlad and he picked up before the first ring had even completed. "Another dead breather drop in your lap, Auntie?"

"Turns out Wendi is a lot less dead than previously thought."

"What?"

"Halfling," I said. "She came after Pike and then took off."

"Did she feed?"

"Not on Pike, but she took off."

"You let her go?" I could hear the incredulity in Vlad's voice.

"No, I didn't just let her go, she took off."

"Well, on the one hand, no one is going to suspect you of being a murderess since there was technically no murder." He seemed pleased.

"And on the other hand, I've just allowed a hungry Halfling to take Manhattan."

Vlad paused. "Yeah, that's going to be a rather significant problem."

"So we've got a Halfling to kill. Be outside. We're on our way."

I hung up the phone.

"We're going to kill her?" Pike asked incredulously.

"Technically, she's already dead. Let's go."

Vlad was waiting outside for us—shaded by the awning for the Hungarian bakery that covered our first floor, of course—by the time we pulled up to the apartment. He stepped out from the shadows and Pike and I both started, mouths dropped open.

It's obvious that I got the LaShay fashion gene both by my career and by the fact that my nephew, by all accounts, dresses like a cross between Bela Lugosi and the Count from *Sesame Street*. The brocade vests and ridiculous ascots are a throwback from the time of vampire empowerment, before the vampire was raped in modern media, when people feared and revered us. A time far before people painted us as emotionally abusive sparklers or overly broody jackasses who routinely went ashes-to-ashes at the hands of a spunky blond slayer. However, this was beyond Vlad's normal poor clothing choices.

He pulled open the car door and settled himself in the backseat. Both Pike and I swung around.

"Are you really carrying a bow and arrow?" Pike asked him.

Vlad looked down at the bow in his hand as though it were the most normal accessory on earth.

"I'm just carrying the bow. The arrows are in my quiver."

He turned sideways, showing off a clutch of feathery arrows bound in what looked like a FedEx tube. He grinned. "Let's get vampire hunting."

Pike leaned forward, hands spread in front of him. "Wait, wait, so you guys are used to this? Isn't vampire hunting like cannibalism?"

I cocked an eyebrow. "Don't birds eat their young?"

He threaded his arms in front of his chest and glared at me. "No, but they have been known to attack random others."

"Guys, guys," Vlad said, trying to edge between the two of us from the backseat. "Please dispense with the foreplay on your own time. We need to find the supervamp."

Now I glared.

"What? Supermodel vamp? Vampmodel? I'm looking for a catch phrase here, people. I think I could get a reality show."

I rolled my eyes. "You can't be seen on film."

"Always the negative one, aren't you, Auntie?"

Pike started the car. "Okay, where to?"

I pulled out my phone and started to navigate. "We should probably start at Wendi's apartment. There's a good chance she'll go back there, especially if she hasn't fully realized what's going on yet. Make a left up here."

"So does this kind of shit happen often?"

I bit my bottom lip. "No, not really." Then, "Probably more often than it should. Three more blocks, then it should be on the right."

"What happens if she's not here?" Pike wanted to know. "Is there like, some kind of vampire community meeting house or something?"

"Oh, you mean our clubhouse? Yes. We all meet under the folds of the Statue of Liberty's dress."

Vlad snorted but Pike glared. "No need to be all snarky. Where I'm from, we're pretty much the only otherworldly creatures around."

"Yeah," Vlad said with a nod. "Lotta sun in your neck of the woods. Tends to be bothersome with all the bursting into flames and stuff. And also, vampires can't swim."

"They can't?"

Vlad and I both shook our heads. "Nope."

"Fascinating."

"I can't believe whoever sired her left her there. It's just bad form," Vlad said, shaking his head.

"Why do you think we're after her?"

Pike slammed on the brakes and gaped at me. "Wait. We're risking our lives to take down a snappy little vamp because it's bad form to leave her?"

"Vampires have a very strict honor code, Pike. There's a certain social code by which we all must abide in order to function in society."

Vlad leaned over the seat back. "And also, a single Halfling or vampire left to her own devices can decimate whole towns in a matter of hours."

Pike stepped on the gas again, though more slowly this time. He looked pale. "Hours? Really?"

Vlad nodded. "Absolutely. I speak from experience." He broke out in an ear-to-ear grin and chucked me on the shoulder. "Remember that one girl? Three towns and a water park. That little thing was fast. Slipped right through my fingers."

Pike swallowed and scooched up in his chair a half inch.

"We're close," I said.

"Can you sense it or something?" Pike asked.

I held up my phone, Google map illuminated on the face. "Yeah. I can sense it. It's right here."

Pike pulled the car to a stop in front of a squat, soot-colored building nearly set right on the curb. I recognized the stop instantly; I had dropped a few of my models there in the past. It was a little hovel in an ancient building that rented solely to artists and models. The place was run-down, with threadbare carpets and a single, broken-down cargo elevator. The fading wallpaper was yellow with nicotine stains, and the scent of cigarette smoke was as much a part of the scenery as anything else. Mail was strewn around the front hallway, a litany of fat, glossy fashion magazines, over-due bills, and tear sheets.

I glanced down at my phone. "She's on the second floor."

We walked up the stairs single file and stopped in front of Wendi's door.

"What do we do?" Pike asked. "Do we just knock, like, 'hello, we're here to rightfully kill you' or something?"

Vlad drew a ridiculously long arrow from his quiver and fumbled it against his bow.

"You're both a bunch of asshats. Let me do the talking."

I knocked and waited, running through possible introductory lines in my head: "Hey, Wendi, sorry about the firing yesterday, and by the way, you're a little too undead for my taste. Please present your chest so that my idiot nephew can drive a wooden stake through it."

It was as good as anything else I could come up with.

"Hello?"

The voice was small and meek and coming from behind us. We turned as the strange motley crew that we were and stared down the speaker. She was tiny, five foot one at best, with ink black hair that fell into enormous deep-set green eyes. They were trimmed with enviably long lashes and when she blinked, she looked even more innocently sweet, like a Disney character ready to burst into song or ask us on a quest at any moment.

"Can I help you?"

"Uh, we're looking for Wendi," I said. "She lives here, right?"

The girl nodded. "Yeah, she does. I'm her roommate, Celeste."

Celeste cut directly through us and sank her key into the lock. We followed her into the house. "Wendi? Some people are here for you."

"I'm her boss, actually, Nina LaShay." I offered a hand. "Well, I was her boss. And these are Pike, our photographer and"—I narrowed my eyes at Vlad, who swung his quiver and bow behind him—"Robin Hood."

Vlad was so adept at slipping into glamours—and he did have the uncanny ability to make mere mortal girls swoon with just the ruffle of his ascot even without the glamour. Whatever it was, it was working on Celeste, and her eyes inched open even wider before her lips pressed together into a tiny heart shape.

"It doesn't seem like Wendi is here," I said, stepping between Vlad and Celeste and breaking the spell.

Celeste frowned. "She should be. She called me twenty minutes ago and said she was waiting here for me."

A protective instinct washed over me. Celeste was small enough to crush with my pinkie, and those leaf-green eyes were so warm and trusting. I knew why Wendi wanted Celeste to come to her, and I knew the second she sucked the life out of those wide green eyes that Wendi would turn into something darker, something awful . . . something that lies at the pit of us all: evil. New evil, evil sucked from innocence, is deep and unwieldy and cannot be tamed.

It can only be killed.

"You need to get out of here," Vlad said, and I knew he saw the vulnerability in her as well.

Celeste cocked her head, her eyes genuinely puzzled as she went from Pike to Vlad, and back to me. "No. Wendi is probably just in her bedroom."

She had the door open before we could stop her, and the scream she let out was raw and primitive, the kind of blood-curdling that needled into your brain and hung there long after the screamer had stopped.

"Oh, my God."

Pike was in front of me, striding into the room. It seemed to be about the size of a matchbox, but I'm not sure if that was because of the three disheveled twin beds shoved against the walls or because of the arc of blood splatter that covered them all. It was still dripping and fresh, and the raw-meat smell of torn flesh was overwhelming. I saw in my periphery Vlad taking a step forward and I pushed him back. "Wait," I growled.

"Call nine-one-one," Pike yelled. He was hunched on the floor, and once I tore my eyes from the blood, I saw that he was cradling a young woman. Her eyes were open and cloudy, but her eyelashes fluttered and she was still breathing, each breath ragged and painful sounding. Her hands were pressed up against the gaping wound at her neck and she held something there, too—a blood-soaked pillow or crumple of bed sheet. She was trembling and a light sheet of sweat broke out over her thin body. Her eyes were terrified, skidding from Pike to me to Celeste, a single tear pool and dripping over her cheek. She opened her mouth but Pike shook his head. "No, don't speak. We're going to get you help."

Vlad appeared behind me again, a wisp of ice-cold air coming off his body.

"Ambulance is on the way."

"Allison! Allison, what happened?" Celeste was in the room, the soaked carpet making a squishing sound as she fell to her knees. "Who did this?" Her little body was racked with tears and I folded down next to her, pulling her to me in my best effort at a comforting hug.

Pike shot me a glance and I knew what he was thinking: There was no way Allison would survive until an ambulance came. Allison herself looked up at us as if she knew, too, her head lolling to one side, her lips working, nothing but tiny, ineffectual gasps of air.

"Wendi," she finally said, her breathy voice nearly inaudible. "It was Wendi." Allison's whole body spasmed and her trembling finally stopped. Her hands fell from the wound at her neck and flopped down behind her, the piece of cloth still balanced in her clawed fingers.

We shut the door behind Allison while we waited for the ambulance to catch up with its siren.

"So Wendi killed her roommate?" Pike whispered to me. "Why? Why not a stranger?"

"Opportunity," I said. "Trust. And maybe she's trying to ruin my runway show."

Pike groaned.

"What? People kill for less every day."

Celeste was standing in the center of the room, utterly lost. I guided her to the couch where she crumpled, instantly curling herself into Vlad, who had abandoned his quiver and bow and stretched an arm across her shoulders. He snuggled Celeste close and cooed to her, the motion so natural and full of concern that it made my heart hurt, made me wish that Vlad could really feel, could really love someone like Celeste and have her love him in return.

"So that's what a Halfling can do, huh?" Pike's face was drawn and slightly ashen.

"That's only the beginning," I said, feeling my own stomach start to turn. I glanced back at Celeste, who was crying, her tiny shoulders shuddering, her hands pressed against her eyes. She pulled her feet up underneath her, Allison's blood dried in smears up her naked calves. "We have to find Wendi."

I knelt in front of Celeste, placing my hands on her knees. She jerked from me. "Sorry. Your hands are so cold." She glanced up at Vlad. "Yours, too."

"Circulation problem," Vlad and I said in unison.

I pressed my hands into my pockets while Vlad tried to unwind himself from Celeste; she just snuggled closer to him. "It's okay," she whispered.

"Celeste, where do you think Wendi went?"

"Wendi?" She blinked. "Why?"

I tried to think of how best to word "your roommate is an undead bastion of hell who will tear the throats out of anyone in her wake." Turns out, there's just no good way. "If Wendi did this, she might do it again."

Celeste shook her head, her dark hair swirling around her shoulders. "She couldn't have done this. Not Wendi."

"Please. Can you just tell us where you think she may have gone?"

"I don't know. I don't—she wasn't working, so . . ." She worried her bottom lip. "Maybe Ruby?"

"Who's Ruby?" Pike asked.

"Ruby is a place. It's a bar. She has been there almost every night. She met some guy there. His name was . . ." Her eyes rolled upward as though the answer might be on the ceiling. "I can't remember. Oh, I think the ambulance is here."

I could feel my cheeks flush—a feat seeing as I hadn't eaten since breakfast—when I thought of Moyer showing up again, finding me and Pike *again*.

"We should go."

Celeste's eyes grew. "What?"

"Uh, we should go downstairs and tell the paramedics what apartment you're in." I stood, Pike following behind. "Vlad?"

He looked from Celeste to me. "I'll stay here and take care of," he paused, his eyes flicking toward the bedroom, "things."

Just before we were about to leave, Vlad joined us at the door and dropped his voice. "Ruby is a lounge up top. Rouge is the lounge on the bottom. I'll stay here with Celeste and make sure that Allison . . . stays dead."

I nodded, and Pike and I disappeared down the stairs.

"So, lounge on the bottom?"

"Underground," I clarified.

"That's what we're looking for, huh?" Pike asked as we got into his car.

"Yup. If it's underground, it's underworld."

Chapter Four

We were at Ruby right at lunchtime, when the sidewalks swelled with admins power walking in sneakers, fancy types ambling to three-martini lunches, and tourists trying on every iteration of sunglasses and hat. The neighborhood was bustling with energy but the doors of Ruby were firmly locked. I shielded my eyes with my hands and pressed them up against the floor-to-ceiling windows. It was dark inside, chairs on industrial-chic tables, not a single breath of movement from the inside.

"They don't open until five," I said with a frown.

"Well, at least we know where she isn't."

I rolled my eyes. "Great, so we can scratch one place off our list of thirty million."

Pike held up two fingers. "Technically, two. We know she's not at her apartment."

"You're not helping."

"Yeah, well, you're on fire."

"What?" I glanced down at a lazy swirl of smoke coming from my shoulder and started slapping at it. "Oh! Crap! Geez!"

Pike's arms were around me in an instant, warm and fleshy, and I relished the protective feeling as he gently steered me to the shade. "That better?"

The fire was out, but the sickening smell of ash hung in the air. "Thanks."

"Well, we know another place Wendi won't be."

"Where's that?"

"Outside. Unless Halflings don't have the tendency to burst into flame at seventy-plus degrees?"

I plucked my sunglasses from my purse and slid them on, careful to stay in my little umbrella of shade. "After that scene? I don't think Wendi is a Halfling anymore."

"So . . ."

"So it's only going to get worse." I pressed my fingers to my temples. "I can't think out here. It's been a long time since I was new. It's hard to think about where I'd go."

My cell phone pinged and the little alarm clock icon let me know that there was now less than twenty-four hours for me to gather up the scraps of fabric and recruit a new model for my runway show. There was also a new tweet from Fashion Fish—@FashFish01: *Mystery designer kills it w new gown. Who is this phantom fashionista?*

The tweet set my teeth on edge.

"Something about Wendi?"

My head was starting to throb. "No. I'm just running out of time to get my line finished and there's this new mystery designer who's stealing all my thunder."

Pike swung his head to me and I held up a silencing hand. "I know, I know, a young woman is dead . . . ish, on the verge of decimating an entire city block, and all I can focus on is fashion. It's my afterlife, Pike, my livelihood. I'm not completely callous, but this is important to me."

"I wasn't going to say anything."

I softened. "Really?"

Pike nodded, then abruptly stopped. "Well, I was actually going to say that all of this sounds like it could best be solved with a cheeseburger and a side of fries."

I quirked an annoyed eyebrow and Pike scoffed. "What did you think I ate? Birdseed?"

We started to walk. "So, a mystery designer, huh?"

I nodded, the annoyance seeping into my every vein. "No one knows who she is. She just popped on the scene"—I snapped my fingers—"Like that."

Pike stopped and looked at me. "And you don't find that odd?"

"I find that exceptionally odd, actually. I mean, this designer comes out of nowhere and bam, not only on the fashion scene but adored by Fashion Fish? Fashion Fish is a legend in the fashion blogging community, and I was her favorite find." I felt my lower lip push out, my sadness all encompassing.

Pike looked skeptical. "I think by definition 'legend' has to be something that's older than the Internet and not a fashion blogger. That's not what I meant, though. I meant, this mystery chick comes to town, is getting all this great press, and yet still decides to remain hidden? And then a supermodel is mysteriously dumped on your vestibule floor and turned into a vampire? Maybe the designer is a vampire, too."

I put my hands on my hips, ready to scoff at his theory—but it wasn't all that crazy.

"Okay, sure, *possibly*. But why would this other vamp drop one of her bodies at my feet?"

"Obviously, she knows you're a vampire, too. Maybe it was like, a peace offering or a sign of respect or something. Don't you guys do that?"

I narrowed my eyes. "Like when a cat leaves a dead bird on its owner's pillow?"

Pike glared at me. "I'm just trying to help."

We ducked into a tiny, dingy café—one that I was sure hadn't been there yesterday but had enough grease buildup and dried mustard stains to prove me wrong. The beer-bellied man at the counter looked like he'd been standing behind that counter longer than I've been made. After Pike ordered his burger, something disgusting and gluttonous with one slab of animal flesh packed on top of another, the counter man looked at me and snorted when I said just water would be fine for me. We sat in a booth at the back of the restaurant, me taking in everything and everyone while Pike drummed his fingers along the cracked Formica tabletop.

"So since Wendi"—he grimaced—"fed off Allison, that makes her full-fledged, then?"

I nodded. "More or less. She's still got a while before she gains her full strength, but yeah, for all intents and purposes, Wendi's V-card has been punched."

Counter guy dropped a plastic basket piled with fries and Pike's burger just as I finished my statement. He kind of smirked, his forehead shiny with spits of hamburger grease.

I expected Pike to unhinge his jaw and swallow his burger but he just stared at it for a beat before speaking. "Is that what happened to you?"

I was taken aback, a wave of prickly heat racing down my spine.

"When you . . . you know."

"No. My sire I—he—" It was the vampire equivalent of the "when did you lose your virginity" conversation, only much more prickly as I couldn't flippantly mention a case of Pabst Blue Ribbon, senior prom, or the back of some guy's Chevette. We couldn't share the war stories, the awkward first moments, the silent moments afterward when everything needed to be said, but nothing ever was. We couldn't swap stories about how underwhelmed we were, about how we thought everything would somehow be different.

Being bitten—being changed—wasn't something universal. It was definitely a becoming, a changing of everything—body, mind, spirit—couched with the unyielding knowledge that you will never belong again. You'll never be *right* again. This was the chasm that divided me from lovers for a hundred years. It kept my breather best friend at arm's distance and it kept me on my guard, constantly.

And it was exhausting.

"No. I was made by another pure vampire. That means that the person who changed you knew what they were doing. They bite, and while you hover in that state between life and death, you feed from the sire. It's a circle."

"Like the circle of life," Pike said, picking up a French fry.

"More like the circle of death."

I watched Pike eat his fry, then pause and look up at me. His eyes were serious. "Did it hurt?"

I blinked.

"You know, when it happened. Do you remember? I mean, we turn—become shifters when we hit puberty. Kind of stereotypical, you know, but that's how it is. But I remember. We had a ceremony and a . . . kind of a party. I guess that really wasn't the case with you."

I thought about a thirteen- or fourteen-year-old Pike, celebrating his ascent into manhood, and bird-hood, I guess. I imagined him on some beautiful Hawaiian black sand beach with a clutch of family members whose dark, caramel-y skin mirrored his, all of them dancing, celebrating, exultant that Pike now shared the one characteristic that made him one of them—a familial tie that could never be severed.

"No." I shook my head, surprised at how soft my voice had gotten. "There weren't any parties. And yes . . . it hurt."

I thought I was going to die.

I heard the skin breaking—it was a sharp, quick, popping sound—and then his fangs sank deeper and deeper into my flesh. Searing heat raged from the wound site, and each time he sucked it was like he was tearing out a tiny bit of my soul. His body was pressed against mine, his fingers digging into my flesh as I struggled and tried to turn away. I knew what he was doing. I knew what he was. I knew what I was going to be.

"Non, monsieur. S'il vous plaît." *My voice sounded like it came from somewhere below me, like I was floating above, watching the scene—and I was. I could see my head pressed back, the milky white of my virgin flesh being stained a rich, velvet red. I could see the wound he created each time his lips, glossy with my blood, broke from my flesh. The skin was ragged and torn, puckered and swollen.*

His voice was as dark as the night. "Boire de la vie, mon amour."

Drink of life.

When he was on me, lips pressed against me, the pain exploded through every inch of my body. But when he tore away, the ache was unbearable—pieces of me breaking away, dying.

I wanted him. I needed him. I craved him.

A single drop of blood escaped his hungry mouth and made its way across my throat. I felt it pool in the hollow at my collarbone, then slide across my breast. It stained the pure white of my bodice a heady ruby red, the spot making its way through the lace, spidering through the thread pattern until it was more red than white.

He broke away and I whimpered, the ecstasy of pain thrumming through me. Then my hands were on him, digging at his marble-hard flesh, clawing at his clothing. I had to have him near me. I had to have him in me. I buried my head in the crook of his neck, smelling his sweet night scent, dragging my tongue across his perfect white flesh. And then I bit . . .

"The pain didn't last long, though. So I guess that's the good thing."

Pike pushed his hamburger and fries away, his voice low. "Then what happened? Maybe Wendi will do the same things you did after. Did you go home? Is there like—"

"Like did we all get in a V-formation and fly? Hold hands and sing AC/DC songs? No, that's not how it works," I snapped.

Pike looked hurt and I immediately felt bad. I wasn't mad at him.

"Sorry, I just thought maybe we could get some insight."

I reached out and laid my hand over his, the sheer warmth from his hand shooting goose bumps through me. The feeling was so foreign.

"I'm sorry, I'm just—just nervous is all. About finding Wendi. What did I do after?" I tugged at a lock of my hair and tried to pretend that I was thinking, trying to remember. But I never could forget.

It had been an unseasonably hot summer that year, and the heat and this newfound life pulsing through me made me restless. I roamed at night with Luc, my sire. We waited in his darkened flat until the sun dropped low in the sky, when twilight tinged everything orange and cast long shadows on the Parisians as they walked, our unwitting prey. We paced the windows like caged animals until we found one that we liked, and then we pounced.

A dashing young couple walked by one evening, elegant as petit fours. He well-dressed in an impeccably tailored suit, she in a dress resplendent with exotic spun silk, and I could see Luc's jaw tighten, the way it did when he lusted for something.

We stole into the shadows until the lovely couple had come to the river's end. Luc, mesmerizing, stepped out and began talking to the man. I hung back at first, watching. There was something more to the couple and

I could feel a nagging, like a shard of memory I was missing at the back of my head. There was a longing, too, something that I hadn't felt since I first sucked Luc's blood. I broke from the shadow and the woman sucked in a surprised breath when she saw me. The man looked shocked—and then smiled.

"Sister!" he said.

Everyone had become prey. My brother, my sister-in-law, reduced to sustenance. I reached for Victor—I so wanted that human connection—but the animal in me was greater. I could hear his heart beating, could hear the sound of Cora's blood as it rushed through her veins. I knew Luc could hear it, too.

The memory sickened me and I shook my head, the smell of Pike's burger and the lifetime of restaurant grease pungent and nauseating. "Vampires don't go home."

Pike continued to pepper me with questions, each time revealing a bit more of himself and his story. I was surprised when the overhead lights clicked on in the restaurant and the darkness began to settle outside.

"Looks like it might be about time."

Pike nodded. "Let's go."

Ruby was throbbing before we even opened the door. It was already packed, the music low but the bass still a chest-thundering thump. Pike pulled open the door and I stepped into the place, immediately wincing at the cacophony of sounds. There were the usual high-pitched squeals of almost-drunken girlfriends swilling cosmopolitans and mango-tinis, the low rumble of men more coifed than I was telling strange women how beautiful or mysterious they were while tinkling the ice in their gin and tonics, the roaring, overbearing laughter of a group of uncomfortable office drinking buddies clinking beer glasses to some success or other. Every sound was intense on its own, but massed together and echoed within the industrial-chic décor—shellacked cement floors bursting with bright swaths of Jackson Pollock-on-crack paint, slabs of reclaimed steel pounded into irregular (and therefore "stylishly upcycled") bar tables, and walls covered in corrugated steel, polished to a gaudy shine—it was ear-splitting.

My head was aching with the pulse and energy in the bar, and Pike's cologne—which was faint to everyone else, I suppose—was choking me like I had chugged the entire bottle of eau de-whatever-the-heck-it-was. I pressed the back of my hand up against my nose, doing my best to blot out the cologne, the comingled scents of human bodies, and the acrid smells of mixed spirits and hops. It wasn't working as Pike leaned into me, wiped a tear from the edge of my eye, and held it on his thumb.

"Your eyes are watering."

I blinked furiously and worked to paste on a dazzling, this-is-my-kind-of-place smile. "I'm fine."

Pike put his hand on the small of my back, the vibration of his living, breathing warmth sending delicious little shock waves all the way through me—so much so that I forgot for a brief moment that we were on a reconnaissance mission. I wanted to slump into him, to curl up and listen to the sure, steady beat of his heart and nothing else. When his fingers walked down my spine and reached the few inches of bare skin underneath my filmy blouse, the hot versus cold, him versus me, living versus dead was almost too much to bear. I bit my lip, the edge of my fang digging into my own flesh, a blossom of blood sliding onto my tongue. My knees weakened.

The high-pitched squeal of a female patron pulling a hideously shiny pink negligee from a gift bag snapped me back into unfortunate reality.

"This can't be the right place."

I strode into the bar, careful to leave a slight distance between my bare skin and Pike's oozing sex appeal, and took a seat in front of the polished wood. Pike plopped down next to me and scanned the place, then leaned into me.

"How can you tell which ones are"—his eyes flashed and he dropped his voice—"vampires?"

I arched an eyebrow. "You just know."

He held my gaze a beat before nodding, a knowing smile cutting across his face. "Oh, like vamp-dar or something?"

My nostrils flared, a little bubble of annoyance welling up inside me. "Something like that."

"Well, which ones are they, then?"

I did another precursory scan and frowned. "None of them. Well, that girl over there." I jutted my chin toward a chubby girl sitting next to the bachelorette with the negligee. "She's not a vampire per se, but she's definitely dead. Well, undead."

Pike's honey brown skin paled slightly, his lips pulling down at the corners. "She's dead."

"Undead," I corrected, narrowing my eyes. "She's—" Knowing, like a stone hot and heavy, sank in my gut. My saliva soured. "She's Nephilim. A half-breed. No good."

"What's a Nephilim? Are they water-based?"

"Water-based? Pike, we're on land. In a bar."

He cocked an eyebrow and I could see a hint of amusement playing at the corners of his mouth. "Manhattan is an island. And this is a wet bar."

I rolled my eyes.

"Nephilim. Neptune? Aren't they from the same . . . phylum or whatever?"

"Okay, quick little lesson. Neptune is the god of the sea. He's also not real. Nephilim, superbad eggs. No relation even though they sound the same."

Pike held up both of his hands and blew out a sigh. "Sorry, I didn't read my latest edition of *Mythical Creatures Monthly.* But at least I'm trying."

"Are you implying that I'm not?"

"I'm implying that you've been biting my head off for

the last day and a half. I don't have to be here, you know. No supermodels dropped dead, then came back to life again on my watch."

Pike took a few steps back, and that was all it took for the crowd to part, then swallow him whole. I was annoyed and angry—and frankly, a little scared. I hadn't gone up against a newbie vampire in thirty years, and I hadn't been on my own in even longer. Now here I was, about to come face-to-face with a wild-eyed predator, and Vlad was with Celeste and Pike was done with me. It was just me and my haute couture.

Maybe next season I could create a lovely line of bejeweled wooden stakes.

"Pike, wait!" I cut through the crowd and got to Pike just as he slipped out the front door. I stepped out after him and was immediately surprised at the quick drop in temperature.

"Hey, I'm sorry," I said. "I don't—I'm not usually so jumpy or short-tempered . . . anymore."

"I get it—a little. You're after someone who could, according to you, tear your throat out and/or decimate this entire island in a single episode of *American Idol*. That's a little scary."

I looked down at my shoes on the damp concrete. "It's not just that."

Pike took a step closer to me and I could feel the live heat wafting from his body. "What else?"

My tongue flicked over the point of one of my fangs. "Look, vampires—we—we're not great with emotion. Feelings, you know."

Pike's eyebrows went up. "And you have feelings?"

Suddenly I was a step closer to him. I wasn't sure if I closed the distance or if he did. "I do."

"About what?"

"Whom," I corrected. "About whom."

"Me?" He seemed genuinely surprised, and it endeared me to him even more.

Until he kind of snort-laughed that "as if" expression.

"What was that?"

"You have feelings for me?"

I looked away. "Maybe."

"And that's the way vampires show their affection for someone? They treat them like shit, constantly bite off their heads?"

I narrowed my eyes, crossing my arms in front of my chest. "No," I deadpanned. "Usually we bite. Now let's go get Wendi."

Chapter Five

I went back into Ruby, my head a tumbling fog of vampire-in-love, vampire-annoyed-with-love, and vampire-hunting-vampire. I was honest when I told Pike that we vampires aren't great with emotion. We're spectacular at hunger and thirst; but love, longing, need? Not really our bag. It had taken me just over a hundred years to recognize that I still had the ability to consider love—or need.

We found a spot at the bar.

"Can I get you two anything?" A hipster bartender with a shoulder span the size of my left foot stood in front of us looking uninterested.

"What are your specials?" Pike asked with a wide, annoying grin.

"Kumquat Manhattan. Vodka martini with fresh stinging nettles."

Pike swung his head back to me. "Stinging nettles? You still think this is the wrong place?"

"We're looking for something else," I said, my gaze intense. "Something with a little more energy. Something that'll make my friend and I here feel"—I dragged my tongue slowly across my lower lip—"alive."

I could feel my glamour—the little something extra that we vampires have when we need to get our way—begin to work on the bartender. His shoulders relaxed slightly as he leaned in toward me. The unaffected expression was gone, the dull look in his eyes vacated and replaced by a mesmerized spark that shone behind his glasses.

"Alive?" His eyebrows went up over the thick black frames of his glasses, his lips rolling over and over the word as though tasting it for the first time. "Alive."

Pike thumped my shoulder with the back of his knuckles as though we were childhood chums—it irked me—but I followed the jut of his chin as he aimed it toward the clutch of bachelorettes. The chubby one was excusing herself; she had a stiff British accent.

"She's probably going for a pee," I hissed at Pike, then swiveled back to my bartender, who looked like his bones had suddenly gone oozy and soft. "So, do you have some information for me?" I pasted on my most beguiling smile and the bartender smiled back, his lips looking cartoonish and plastic with puppy-dog love.

"I can make you a Bloody Mary."

I fisted my hands, about ready to fly over the stupid steel bar and shake the hipster like a rag doll when Pike's hand closed around my arm, tugging me from the bar stool and steadying me in my Via Spigas.

"Come on," he said, his voice throaty against my ear.

I straightened, letting the reverberation of his voice thunder through my every vein. It was a sexy, delicious feeling but not quite enough to quell my annoyance.

"What are we—?"

But Pike had already threaded an arm around my waist and practically had my feet off the ground as he strong-armed me, commandeering a path through the crowd of beautiful people as we followed the chubby Brit.

She walked as though she knew the place but avoided eye contact with every head that swung to take her in. Her chin was hitched and she walked with purpose, cutting down a hall that led to the restrooms. I shook myself loose from Pike. "See? She's going to the bathroom."

Pike's eagle-eyed expression didn't change and he gave me yet another soft shove forward. "Follow her."

I whirled in a huff and stomped down the soggy-carpeted hallway, coming up just against the girl's shoulder as she slowed in front of the ladies' room. She turned to face me, trying to act casual, trying to paste on one of those "ladies always have to pee, huh?" kinds of expressions.

"After you," I said pleasantly.

Her smile was staid. "I insist."

"I don't actually have to use the loo," I said, my voice conspiratorial, low. "I was just going to fix up my makeup."

As a vampire, it is always easy for me to tell the "others" in the room, both because of a sort of unspoken language that we all speak—darting eyes, slight glances that result in one of us suddenly mimicking the action of a breather in the room, or because of the smell.

Everything has a smell.

As I mentioned previously, breathers stink of everything from general body odor to bitter coffee, and everything in between—Tide, shampoo, high-end cologne, fear, stale noodles, fried onions, wanton sex appeal (à la Pike). Non-breathers have their scents, too: Werewolves smell like wet dog even in the driest climates, zombies reek of moist soil and rotting flesh (a huge reason why vampires and zombies are rarely, if ever, in closed quarters together). Succubi smell like a three-day-old sex shop and buttered popcorn, and your run-of-the-mill Wiccan or witch always smells like a mishmash of herbs and citrus rinds. But the Nephilim have absolutely no scent.

They do, however, have the same uncanny ability to spot the undead.

The chubby girl licked her waxy lips and her friendly smile slid into a smirk. "Care to borrow my mirror?"

We held each other's gazes for what seemed like a millennium until Pike clattered down the hall and cleared his throat loudly.

"So, everything straightened out?"

The Nephilim's eyes widened as she took Pike in; I could see the light in her eyes change to something hard and dark and seductive as she undoubtedly peeled off his clothes in her mind.

"My name's Liv," she said, offering Pike a hand.

I stepped between the two, arms crossed in front of my chest, our little dance of the undead suddenly tiresome.

"Where's the real club?"

"Club?" Liv's eyebrows disappeared into her hairline. "I'm sure I don't know what you mean."

"Look, Liv, I don't care what your deal is, but the two of us"—I thumbed to Pike and myself—"are just looking to get out of heartbeat alley before something goes"—I licked my lips, making certain that she could see the hard edge of one of my fangs—"wrong."

"Wouldn't have pegged you for the type to care," she said, cocking out one hip.

"I don't. But if my stomach keeps growling like it is, I just might rip the throats out of your little bachelorette party, and I have a feeling that no one, not even you, wants that."

Liv's eyes flashed back to the booth where the girls were seated. She seemed to consider their demise by vampire for a second before relenting with an annoyed sigh. "Follow me."

I turned to Pike, who offered me an impressed smile. We followed Liv through a door marked Employees Only and then down another dark hall. I felt Pike quicken his step so that his chest was pressed against my back, one hand clapped protectively over my hip bone. I had only a half second to enjoy the sensation before Liv pushed open a door to the "real" club.

She glanced over her shoulder at us. "You're on your own, kids." Then she disappeared into the throbbing vortex of low lights and black leather.

"Ugh," I groaned, edging my way through a team of vampires trussed up in latex like sexy turkeys. "So stereotypical."

"So what are we looking for in here exactly?" Pike asked, yelling over the music.

My eyes were scanning the crowd, and I guess Pike didn't think I heard him. He stepped closer still, now his belt buckle pressing into the small of my back, his stiff angles fitting into my curves. Electricity shot up the back of my neck and it was like every hair on my head was standing on end as static crackled through my mind. I felt alive, tip to tail, sex and need pulsing through me as Pike's warm breath broke over the back of my neck.

"What are we supposed to do here?" Pike said again, this time his voice low and throaty as his lips traced my ear.

"Blend in. Listen. Look for Wendi. If she's not here"—I glanced around, taking in the scene of beautiful people and thinking back to the disheveled Wendi, her face stained red—"which I don't think she is, someone will be talking. Someone will know there is a new vamp in town."

Pike nodded, his eyes scanning the crowd.

Sex hung in the air and everyone in the club moved together like one single throbbing body, pulsing and grinding and gripping, eyes closed, faces obscured by the low light. Someone thumped against me and Pike's arm was there again, snaking in front of me, pulling me into him protectively.

His hand tightened on my hip, pulling me closer, now grinding his pelvis against my backside, either out of necessity or desire, I couldn't be sure—nor did I care. The sensation was so tantalizing, like Eve with the apple, and every inch of me wanted to forget these supermodels and disappear into Pike, let him swallow me whole. He used a rough hand to push my hair away from my neck and his lips were there again, slightly moist, his breath breaking in little sexy bursts against my ice-cold skin.

"I know we're technically on a stakeout, but damn, there ain't a girl in here that I'd rather be with."

His voice slid through me like melted chocolate and I was humming, the music pulsing through my empty chest.

"Is that so?"

I leaned back against him, moving slowly with the music, and Pike growled, the sound reverberating through my skull. His other hand traced its way down my arm, his fingers lacing through mine, and I was thrust back to Paris, to Luc, to the way we lay, bodies intertwined as we waited for night to fall, as we waited to assuage our hunger. The image shook me from loving the feel of Pike's body against me and I stumbled forward, breaking the spell.

"I'm going to the bar."

I could see Pike in the mirror behind the bar; he was one of the few people that had a reflection and his face was drawn, confused for a brief second while he looked after me. I didn't look back—though it took all my willpower—and what seemed like a lifetime later Pike slunk into the shadows, hugging the soft velvety walls, scanning the crowd.

"Highball of O-Neg, please," I said to the bartender.

She looked me up and down, her dark eyes made darker by the heavy cat's-eye makeup she wore. Like mine, her skin was milky pale, and she was corseted into a red damask bustier that brought her boobs to her chin.

"Haven't seen you here before."

I sat down. "I'm new."

She poured my drink and slid it to me. "How new?"

"Just to the area," I said, palming my highball glass. "You get a lot of newbies around here?"

The bartender studied me and I could tell she was considering how much to tell. "Not really. If so, they show up with regulars."

I took a casual sip, the liquid warm as it went down my

throat. Just the smallest bit was like swallowing a light that ran through every inch of me. "Anyone interesting?"

She leaned in, a grin slicing across her face and exposing her fangs. "Honey, we're all interesting. I'm Kat."

"Nina."

"What are you after, Nina?"

"I'm looking for a newbie. Made. Or the one that made her."

Kat's eyes darkened. "I'm not sure what you mean."

I was about to answer when I felt Pike's hand close around my arm. "We've got to go," he whispered.

"I'm talking to Kat."

He swiveled me on the bar stool until I was facing him. His eyes were set hard, his lips pressed in a thin line. Without taking his eyes off mine, he slapped a few dollars down next to my drink and said, "Now."

We were on the sidewalk in record time, but it took another minute or so for the din of music and conversation to die down in my head. "What's going on?"

Pike still held my arm and was nearly dragging me along with him. I snatched my arm away. "What?"

He held up his cell phone as if all the answers were there. "Allison's death is all over the news. They don't think Wendi's responsible, of course, but they do think she's in trouble."

"If they only knew she was the one causing the trouble."

Pike slid a button on his phone and a cackle of static filled the air before Vlad's voice came on the line. "Hey, Pike, it's me, Vlad. Sorry to leave a message on your phone but Auntie Nina isn't picking up. I hope you two aren't—oh, geez, no, gross. Okay, I'm going to erase that image out of my head . . . and maybe cauterize my brain. Anyway, I kind of ran into someone when I was leaving Celeste's apartment this afternoon. Her name is Rose. Rose Carmichael?"

"She's one of my models," I said to no one in particular.

"Yeah. I guess I didn't so much run into her as nearly run over her. But don't worry, I didn't. I didn't hurt her . . . she was already dead."

Something sank inside me. I yanked out my own phone to see that I had six missed calls, all from Vlad, all within the last thirty minutes. I speed-dialed him and waited, nerves welling up in my chest.

"Finally."

"Vlad! I'm sorry, we were following up on another lead that didn't really pan out."

"Bad sex? Yeah, that happens. So while the rest of the team—a.k.a. me—was diligently working, I found Rose."

"How did you even know it was her? You've never met her."

"You mean how do I *know* it's her? Because although she is currently sans attire, her purse was shoved underneath her. I pulled out her driver's license."

"Currently sans attire? Are you there with her now?"

"Yeah. I mean, I went across the street and got a drink—"

I felt the blood I had just drunk sink to my feet. "Vlad—"

"Geez! Not from her. There was a bloodmobile. Then I came over here to look after the body until you could stop whatever depraved thing you and Birdboy were doing and call me back."

"Wait. Did you move her to get to her purse? Did you touch her? Are you touching her now? Stop touching her!"

Vlad snorted. "Because I have matchable fingerprints? Yeah. Maybe in 1873."

"Where are you? How did you find her?"

"I'm just around the corner from Celeste's place and I let my nose lead the way. She smelled robust."

I felt my jaw tighten. "If you even think of nicking an artery before I get there, I will stake you myself."

"Rule follower," Vlad huffed.

Chapter Six

It didn't take long for us to find Vlad and Rose—and Vlad was very right—even without her heart pumping, Rose's blood gave off a robust, vibrant odor. My mouth started to water despite myself.

"Oh, Vlad."

Other than a pair of white panties and a soiled bra, Rose was naked. Her lean body looked spider-like; her arms and legs were outstretched at odd angels. She was balanced on a load of black trash bags and general debris. She wasn't a victim of the same bloody destruction that Allison was. She was battered, severely, then her carotid artery was punctured. I could see where Wendi's fangs went in, and it looked like she raked a bite down, tearing the flesh halfway down Rose's neck. Judging by the bruises on her hands and arms, her fingernails ragged and torn and the blood drying on her fingertips, Rose had put up a hell of a fight. Though no matter how hard, it would never be a match for Wendi's newfound strength.

Pike winced when he saw her. "You think Wendi did this?"

"Hard to imagine there's another supermodel-killing vampire out there."

"Well, someone tried to kill or unkill Wendi."

I nodded, considering. "So you think this might be the work of the sire?"

Pike shrugged and looked at Vlad. "What do you think? And is she"—he waggled his hand toward Rose's still-staring eyes and dropped his voice to a low whisper—"all dead?"

Vlad carefully plucked Rose's bony wrist between his two fingers and let it drop again. It flopped unceremoniously back against the garbage bag it was resting on. "Yeah, I mean for now."

Pike grimaced. "What exactly does that mean?"

"She's *dead* dead for now, but Wendi could always come back—if that's who sired her—and give her the old two-fang revival."

"Thanks, Doctor. He means that a sire can come back even to a body that's completely dead and revive her by having her drink his blood."

"Or hers and hers." A slow smile spread across Vlad's face. "That's hot."

Pike was openly gaping now. "A vampire can bring back a corpse at any time? That's sick and awesome. Is that why everyone keeps seeing Elvis?"

"Pike . . ."

"Forty-eight hours at best," Vlad clarified. "They still have to have their own blood and all their factory parts." He held up a finger. "Not bagged. They need to be as organic as possible."

"How . . . responsible of you."

I snatched Rose's purse from Vlad and tucked it back in the garbage pile, trying to figure out how to make a Dooney & Bourke shoulder bag look natural on a corpse and a pile of trash bags. I gave Rose one last glance, eyes trailing over the wounds on her neck. "It does look like Wendi's handiwork."

Pike crossed his arms in front of his chest. "But why leave her naked? Is that normal for you guys?"

Vlad cleared his throat. "First of all, I would prefer not to be lumped in with 'you guys.' Wendi's a newbie, and whatever she does should *not* be the benchmark for the rest of us."

"Okay, okay, sorry, geez. I'm still learning."

I glared at Vlad. "Chill out, nephew." Then something just over his left shoulder caught my eye. I sighed and went to it, crouching down. A heap of fabric, blood soaked and balled together, was halfheartedly stuffed behind the Dumpster. I pulled a pen out of my purse and used it to poke at the wad.

"Well, I think I know why Rose is nearly naked."

Pike crouched down beside me. "What is all that?"

"The jeans and T-shirt that Wendi was wearing yesterday. She must have been covered in Allison's and Rose's blood."

"Great. Now we know she's relatively clean, well fed, and has a taste for supermodels. I would say that helps us not at all," I said with a groan.

My cell phone pinged and I swiped it on, then groaned a little louder. The cheery old-fashioned alarm clock icon was vibrating all over my screen, reminding me that there was now only one day left until the start of fashion week. With all due respect for the dead, I was now down two models and not a lick closer to stopping the bloodthirsty one.

"I'm going to head back to the house," Vlad said. "I can throw out some emails and see if any of the Empowerment members know anything about Wendi or her sire."

"I can give you a ride," Pike told him. Then, to me, "You ready? We can call the police in the car and give them an anonymous tip."

I glanced back at Rose, nodding. Even from this distance I could see the little pops of blood where the vessels in her eyes, hands, and around her mouth had burst. She had fought.

"No, actually, you guys go on ahead. I'm only a few blocks from the studio and I should see who I can pull together. You'll do all you can, right? And call the police?"

Pike and Vlad both nodded and disappeared out the end of the alley. I could see Pike pulling out his phone and beginning to dial. I didn't want to leave Rose, dead, exposed, tossed away like garbage at the hands of a predator—at the hands of someone like me. But I couldn't stay with her. I couldn't cover her lest I ruin any evidence. I didn't want to think of all the wrecked bodies I'd left behind in my past.

"Ms. LaShay, we meet again."

Detective Moyer surprised me, his cruiser pulling up to the mouth of the alley just as I turned to leave. Until that moment, I had never realized how dumb "we meet again" sounds when it's not coming from a superhero's arch nemesis.

I cleared my throat and nodded. "I was just going to call you."

His bushy eyebrows raised up to where his hair should have been. "You were going to call me on yourself?"

"I don't understand."

"We got a call in saying there were three suspicious persons hanging around the alley back here."

"And you came out for that?"

"There's been a rash of robberies around this area, Ms. LaShay. You wouldn't know anything about that, would you?"

I took a small step back toward Rose, suddenly protective. "Of course not."

"Were you one of the three out here? Caller said it looked like a woman and two men. Possible vagrants."

That tore it. "Vagrants? This, sir, is Oscar de la Renta. Vintage. Hand sewn. Impeccable." I spun, giving him a full look at classic design genius, my black hair perfectly complementing the charcoal gray as it swirled over my shoulder. "Vagrant, ha!"

Moyer just stared at me as if every word that came out of my mouth was nonsensical and I could feel my nostrils flare, annoyance flaring up in my stomach.

"There's a body over there, Detective. We came across it. Her name is Rose Carmichael."

Moyer got out of the car and followed me to where Rose lay, his eyes going big. He pulled his radio from his shoulder, mumbled a few numbers and words, and looked back at me, face slightly ashen. "Who were you with?"

"Pike and my nephew, Vlad."

"And you just came upon . . ." He waved his hand toward Rose and I nodded.

"What exactly were the three of you doing out here?"

I was caught off guard and my mouth fell open just the tiniest bit. "Jogging," I blurted quickly. "We jog. Together. This is our route."

Moyer's head bobbed as he looked up and down the length of the alley. "You jog here?"

"Totally," I said nonchalantly.

He pointed a stubby finger toward me. "So you go jogging in that vintage Oscar de la Hoya dress? With the, uh, good sewing and whatnot?"

Everything inside me told me to nod silently and just let him think what he wanted.

But I've never been one to follow best practice.

I put my hands on my hips. "Vintage Oscar de la Renta, not de la Hoya. Hand stitched. No whatnot. Isn't the murder of this poor, innocent ingénue more important than my choice in sportswear?"

I could hear the rest of the units pulling up, the sounds of car doors opening and closing. Moyer glanced over his shoulders and beckoned the first responders over toward us. I began edging away but he snapped back with a speed that shocked me and pinned me with a glare. "I'm going to need you to stay right there."

I pressed my hand over my nose, trying to daintily block the stink of rapidly expelling gases that Moyer and the other breathers wouldn't be able to smell for at least twenty-four more hours, while trying to look properly affected like an actual human would. I shifted my weight, growing slightly impressed as Moyer directed the cops and paramedics with a fair amount of authority. I tried not to look at my phone, tried to keep my eyes from the alarm clock alerts telling me exactly how little time I had left before I was expected to show a full fashion collection to the world.

Moyer finished barking orders to his officers and to the gentleman I assumed was the coroner based on his sensible black business-tennis shoes and the paper thin nylon jacket he wore, the word CORONER stenciled in white lettering on the back. Moyer came back to me and whipped out the same cop notebook he had earlier today and did one of those weird lick-the-lead of his pencil things before dropping into inter-rogational mode.

"So you just happened to come across this body on your jogging trip this morning?"

I cocked my head, wanting to point out that in a city of 8.4 million people where just about a murder a day is the norm, Detective Fire Plug and I meeting up twice in one day wasn't that statistically significant. But I decided against it.

"Yes." I nodded simply.

"Because you and your buddies run around here regularly."

"Yes." Another nod.

"You weren't stunned to see a dead body?"

I am a dead body. My mind was screaming out all sorts of irrational one-liners and I shifted my weight, pressing my teeth together before answering, "Of course I was."

"But not one of you thought it would be a good idea to call nine-one-one? To call the police?"

"My nephew was on his way to do it right as you pulled up."

Moyer's eyes cut to the cell phone in my hand and then back up to me. "Any particular reason you didn't use that phone right there to make the call?"

"Um. Nope." I paused. "Because I was stunned. So much.

I was so stunned by seeing the dead body that I guess I forgot that I had this cell phone right here in my hand."

"Because you just stumbled on her."

I hated the way Moyer was finishing my sentences, but when I glanced at him, he raised his caterpillar eyebrows, his flat eyes challenging. I felt an instant growl roil through me; challenge wasn't something from which I was used to backing down.

I wanted to tell him that I couldn't "stumble" on Rose's body if she was covered in thirteen pounds of stinky trash and I had a Google Street View pointing to where she lay. The scent of death is so distinct and strong, it's like a natural homing beacon to the supernatural crowd. But of course, I couldn't exactly spout that out to dear Detective Moyer without getting tossed in the loony bin or having to make the very unladylike (and un-UDA-acceptable) decision to eat him, lest he try and arrest me.

"So, Ms. LaShay, you find our victim here and don't call the cops because you're too"—his eyes flashed toward mine, the disbelief in his obvious—"stunned. Or was it that you thought perhaps this one was taking a nap, too?"

I was pretty sure that steam was welling up inside my hollow gut, and I immediately regretted signing my UDA afterlife insurance policy, because some people just need a good throat-ripping-out.

"I was fairly certain Rose was dead."

"Because you come upon a lot of dead bodies—while you're jogging, while you're working."

"Are you trying to ask me something, Detective?"

Moyer's expression fell to one of pure innocence. "I'm just trying to figure out what happened to this poor girl just like you are, Ms. LaShay. And I'm just trying to find out what exactly it is that you have to do with it."

I pressed my palm to my forehead and closed my eyes,

doing a mental count to ten and reminding myself that a man this thick probably tasted like old gym mat.

"Are you saying that you suspect me of something, Detective Moyer? Do you want to ask me something specific? Because if that's the case, I would prefer a proper interrogation including a trip downtown and a cup of that legendarily bad NYPD coffee."

And that's how I ended up in a squad car that smelled like urine and regret, speeding through the city streets while Kenny Rogers reminded me to "know when to fold 'em" from the radio in the front seat.

Detective Moyer kept assuring me that I wasn't "technically" being arrested, but he continued to give me that stare-down-his-nose look of disapproval as he "escorted" (his word) me to a small, cinderblock square excuse for an office. There was a couch lined up against one wall, the whole thing made up of one giant circus-orange cushion that was probably teeming with more bacteria than a Times Square toilet seat. I was relieved when Moyer ushered me to a tiny laminate round table surrounded with plastic chairs, less so when he set a steaming Styrofoam cup of what smelled like the most horrific mix of burnt coffee and tire fire ever created.

He actually smiled and I actually felt sorry for him. I could see that his eyes were sunken and his cheeks had deflated over the year. The brackets around his mouth dipped straight down, giving him a droopy dog sort of look, and I found myself wanting to pet his thinning hair and assure him that everything would be all right.

"Look, Ms. LaShay, I'm just trying to get to the bottom of Ms. Carmichael's murder, and lo and behold, here you are. Tell me the truth. We both know you weren't out jogging dressed like that."

And for a split second, I wanted to tell him everything.

Not that Vlad had called and had been the one to find Rose, not that Allison had been viciously murdered by Wendi, but *everything* everything. Sitting down in that hard plastic chair in that nondescript square of cinderblocks made me realize how tired I really was. My phone was throbbing, letting me know in hourly animation that my dream of being a premiere Fashion Week designer was slipping away because in my life, the dead and the undead were far more normal than dreams and eternal bliss.

Moyer took my reflection time for insolence. "Still not going to talk, huh?"

I was about to answer, apologize, even, when the door cracked open and a pup officer poked his head in.

"Sorry to interrupt. Can I see you, please, Detective?"

Moyer's eye went to the pup cop and then to me. He sighed and stood. "I'll be right back. Stay here."

The door clicked shut behind him with a slight echo and I leaned forward, resting my head on my arms. I figured I should probably just pack up my studio and head back to San Francisco. As much as I thought I could create a fairly normal afterlife after all this time, I was beginning to realize that would never happen.

I glanced up at the clock, each minute ticking by with a maddening click. I glanced at the door, willing it to open, willing Moyer to walk in, say "forget this whole thing," and usher me out.

I kept waiting.

I wasn't sure what was supposed to happen next, but I seriously hoped it wouldn't be a full booking. Fingerprinting I was okay with—even the new high-tech "roll your thumb on this track pad" was fine with me—fingerprints don't change, even in the afterlife, and mine were completely normal. It was the mug shot I had an issue with. Obviously photography was not any government agency's strong suit; I had seen enough DMV photos to know that. (Mine, however, was rather spectacular despite the fact that the wonderfully grinning woman in the photo wasn't me.) But it wasn't my vanity that the photo would be awful that steered me away from mugging for the police camera; it was the knowledge that there wouldn't be any photo at all. Just the little ticker tape telling the world how tall I was (or wasn't) and the identification box floating in midair. It's no legend that vampires can't be seen on film—it's fact. And under the watchful eyes of the New York City Police Department, it would be a little difficult to explain.

Or a lot difficult.

Sure, I knew that the whole of my conversation with Moyer was being recorded (he had to tell me for legal reasons, as if I hadn't seen enough cop television to know), but I wholly expected to be out the door and far away before that recording was ever viewed and my presence—or lack thereof—was discovered.

I sat there in that little interrogation room turning my Styrofoam coffee cup around and around in my hand, waiting for Moyer to come back. I knew that he was doing that "make them wait" thing, probably hoping to squeeze a little bit more information out of me . . . and frankly, I was beginning to crack. Despite the whole "vampires sleep in their coffins" lore, I wasn't really one for confined spaces.

It was probably only a minute more, though it felt like a millennium, when Moyer clicked open the door and, without actually crossing the threshold, shoved his big head in the room and said, "You're free to go, LaShay."

I perked up, eyes wide. "I am?"

He waved the thick manila file folder he was holding in my direction as if trying to shove me out. "Yeah. We've got something else going on. But you're not in the clear yet. I still have some questions, so don't leave town."

I pumped my head and jumped up, practically knocking the plastic chair I was sitting on onto the floor. "Yeah, sure, no problem." I fished a card from my purse and pressed it in his hand. "Call me anytime."

I pressed through the doors of the New York Police Department ready to throw the hat I wasn't wearing up in the sky and do one of those Mary Tyler Moore "I'm going to make it after all" montages. Instead, I kicked open the door, threw my hands up, and immediately felt them start to singe.

Sometimes an afterlife can be a giant pain in my Broadway-bound ass.

I was huddled in the sunless safety just outside the police station when Detective Moyer and a few other officers gathered on the other side of the glass doors. I chanced a glance and saw Moyer's face, the edges of his lips pulled into a deep frown, his dark eyebrows two thick bars over his eyes. He had one arm crossed in front of his chest and was holding his chin in his hand.

"Bodies don't just disappear. It's not like she got up and walked out of there," Moyer barked.

". . . Just gone," another officer was reporting. "I didn't believe it either, but the drawer was empty. The bag was empty."

"The press is going to have a fucking field day with this," Moyer again.

"At least she went missing in the coroner's custody, that's technically not ours."

"It's ours."

I slunk into the shadows, laying low the entire way home.

Chapter Seven

When I pulled open my own front door, Vlad sat bolt upright and glared at me. "Pike and I have been trying to get a hold of you for hours. We checked your studio and everything. Were you off getting a manicure or something while we went after Wendi?"

"Did you and Pike find her?"

Vlad's eye twitched. "No. When Pike was dropping me off, we heard that a Red Cross worker had been attacked leaving work, so we turned around and went right over there. I tried to call you."

I glanced down at my cell phone to see three missed calls from Vlad, another alarm clock ping, and a throbbing pink stiletto letting me know that Fashion Fish had posted another blog entry.

"So what happened?"

"We couldn't find you."

I slapped a palm to my head. "Obviously. I mean what happened with the Red Cross lady. Did you get over there? Was it Wendi?"

Vlad gave me one of those supremely teenage expressions and wagged his head. "Nope. When we got over there, the police had just arrived and the lady was saying that she had been mugged. It was a guy and he just took her purse. The whole Red Cross thing was just a co-inky."

"Anything after that?"

He let out the longest sigh I've ever heard, his whole expression letting me know how much this conversation was taxing him. "We tried to call you again, went by the studio thinking Wendi had taken you out, realized you weren't there . . . Then I realized how hungry I was since we kept talking about the Red Cross thing, so I got a pint and Pike got a pulled pork sandwich."

"So you thought maybe Wendi had killed me and then you went and got something to eat?"

Vlad shrugged. "Your studio looked fine. Wendi does more damage. We figured you were probably fine."

I threw down my purse and slid out of my coat. "My heroes. I was actually not fine. Detective Moyer dragged me down to the police station and started interrogating me."

Vlad looked me up and down, his coal black eyes scrutinizing. "Did you get a prison wife?"

I helped myself to a blood bag and ignored my nephew.

"It was weird, though. Moyer was all over me about Rose and then suddenly, he just let me go. You and Pike didn't hear of another death or anything, did you?"

"Pike didn't say anything if something came across the scanner."

I took a giant, life-giving gulp from my bag. "I don't know what it could have been. And then Moyer was talking to his guys about someone going missing. He was really worried that the media was going to pick up on it and put the PD through the wringer."

Vlad leaned over, picked up the remote control, and unmuted the television. "Think that could be it?"

Detective Moyer was standing behind a podium, his hands gripping the sides. He was looking at the crowd, waiting for them to quiet, and though he looked authoritative in his pressed uniform, his face showed his discomfort.

I glanced down at the headline splashed just below his belly: *Murdered Model Disappears from Morgue.*

Moyer cleared his throat and the cacophony of camera snaps and media chatter died down.

"It has come to our attention that model Rose Carmichael, who was discovered dead several hours ago, has disappeared from the county morgue."

There was an explosion of chatter, and Moyer held up one of his meat-hook hands to silence the crowd. "I understand that this information has already been leaked via social media and I can assure you, despite what you may have read online, the New York Police Department is working to find Rose's body as soon as possible. We are working on several leads."

"Detective, Detective!" A brunette with a severe cowlick raised a microphone in the detective's direction. "Is it true that the likely culprit is one of the officers who escorted the body down to the morgue, and that pictures of Rose's naked body are already popping up on eBay?"

Moyer pressed his lips together for a half beat. "No, ma'am, it is not."

Cowlick was undeterred. "Isn't it true that this is the third body the coroner's office has lost in as many months?"

Moyer's chest seemed to puff out a little more, his shoulders broadening. "As of right now, those previous cases have no link to this one. This press conference is over." He stepped away from the podium, and the assembled media started throwing out questions and accusations at his back.

". . . black market organs!"

". . . mob involvement!"

". . . true you have no leads whatsoever?"

". . . necrophiliac sex perpetrator since all the bodies have been female?"

My stomach turned at that last one and I clicked off the TV. "Well, I guess we know where Wendi went after she left."

"Why wouldn't she just have made Rose then and there?"

I shrugged. "Maybe she got interrupted."

Vlad narrowed his eyes. "There's something weird there. I mean, you saw what Wendi did to Rose. She did real damage and she didn't have to. She could have overpowered Rose even with her half strength."

Rose's face, her cracked lips parted, her skin a mottled purple and red, and her accepting stare flashed in front of my eyes. "Usually when you sire someone, you don't actually want to kill them. Could have just been a power thing."

"I'm thinking the reporter with the necro-sex-perp theory might be on to something."

I was thinking that maybe Wendi wasn't our problem—maybe her sire was the one who was setting up the supermodels and taking them down—when Fashion Fish's throbbing stiletto pinged again. I couldn't help myself. I glanced down at my phone and thumbed open Fashion Fish's latest entry.

Mystery Designer Can Do No Wrong!
The blogoverse is a buzzing with the first peek of Under the Hem couture! Though snapping at Cocktail Couture is a faux pas of the highest high, the leaker's punishment has been overlooked due to the gasp-worthiness of the dress.

The picture of Rose was reposted in this article, significantly cleaned up and cropped so the dress was the star. Rose's head was cropped off, leaving only her elegant bare shoulders and the dress on display.

I skimmed through the rest of Fashion Fish's gushing until she got to the designer details—

*There is still no word on the actual designer/proprietor
of the Under the Hem line. Calls go unanswered, and
it seems like the designer himself made some sort of
deal with the devil—or Google Earth, at least—as the
address given of "headquarters" is shielded by a
giant van in every image. Doesn't San Francisco have
parking laws?*

The blood I had just drunk pulsed in my veins. The mystery
designer was from San Francisco? *My* San Francisco?

I flipped through a few more lines before getting to two
new pictures: One was of a cocktail-length dress that was
structured like the rings of Saturn—and the result was breathtaking. The second was a slightly longer dress in a radiant
purple that was one of the most dazzling pieces of clothing I
had ever seen. There was something so drastically different
about each piece, but there was something faintly familiar
in them, too. My need to know was like a mosquito buzzing in
my ear, and I physically felt the need to itch.

Each of the dresses was modeled by a different girl. I had
a faint recollection of the first woman—she had been in fashion magazines and stomped a few runways—but the second
woman was absolutely familiar.

"Celeste!"

Vlad flopped his head in my direction, slightly interested.
"Huh?"

"This picture. That's Celeste modeling this dress."

I turned the phone to Vlad and he nodded. "Yeah. Huh. I
didn't know she modeled, too. Not surprising since everyone
else in that place did."

"Vlad, someone has knocked off three supermodels. The
last one happened to be wearing a dress from this mystery
line. Celeste is wearing a dress from this line. Either she
knows more than she's telling us, or she's next on the chop-
ping block."

"Do you think this designer guy is killing off his models?"

"He wouldn't kill off his own models. What would his reason be?"

"Like no guy would want an army of vampire supermodels at his disposal."

I cocked an eyebrow. "Ew, and no more Cinemax for you. And honestly I don't even know if the designer is a male or female. He or she is supposedly from San Francisco and has just been laying low. Even his models don't know who he is."

Vlad's eyebrows went up. "San Francisco?"

"Here's what we're going to do. Go get Celeste and bring her back here. We can keep an eye on her, at least until this is cleared up. Call Sophie in San Francisco on the way; maybe she and Alex can find something out about the designer. I'll grab Pike and we'll try to track down Wendi or Rose. Maybe at the very least we can figure out what Wendi's grand plan is and stop it before"—I gulped, bat wings flipping through my stomach—"tomorrow's debut."

"Yeah, I'm on it," Vlad said, grabbing his keys. "I'll be back with Celeste in a little bit."

"Tomorrow's debut," I murmured again. "Oh, God, there's a gala tonight!" I glanced at the clock and groaned. I had less than thirty minutes to wash off twenty-four hours of dried blood and cop rot, secure a date, finish my dress for the evening, and get down to the Met.

Excellent.

I had my phone in hand, finger hovering over the speed dial, when the screech and cackle of a couple of birds fighting over a French fry on my fire escape startled me. My phone crashed to the floor and I glared out the window, narrowing my eyes. There were two small blackbirds pecking at the fry and a giant, beady-eyed crow staring directly at me.

I had to remember how hot Pike was in human form just to approach the window. Again, birds—definitely not my thing. I threw the latch, squinted again to make sure I wasn't about to let a bunch of random winged hellions into my home, then pulled the window open. Bird Pike hopped from one hideously clawed foot to the other before ducking his head and stepping onto my windowsill. I didn't even have the window completely relatched before he was human again.

He had grown very conscious of my disdain for him in any form other than human.

"I was just going to call you."

"I figured you might. I heard about Rose's disappearance. Does that mean Wendi got to her?"

I filled Pike in on my and Vlad's conversation and sweetly asked him to be my date by saying, "I have to go to a gala and you have to be my date."

He cocked his head. "Uh . . ."

"I know, killers on the loose, no idea what's going on overall, and—"

"And we're going to drink champagne and eat tea sandwiches?"

"We just need to make an appearance. It'll actually be a good thing. Maybe the mystery designer will be there and we'll know for sure if he's the sire."

Pike nodded.

"And the models are supposed to be there, so maybe Wendi will show up."

"But she's dead!"

I shook my head. "No one knows that except us."

Pike looked down at his clothing—black jeans, black T-shirt, and back up at me. "Not exactly gala attire."

"Go home—or fly home or whatever—get a suit on. I'm going to the studio to finish up my dress and I'll meet you at the Met. Thirty minutes, okay?"

Pike, looking confused and stunned, turned on his heel and threw the window open. I grabbed my black Louboutins and headed out the door.

I opened my studio door and tried to avoid the swish of

Wendi's blood that had dried on my floor. The sight of it
annoyed me; if my Fashion Week debut went poorly due to
Wendi and her newfound bloodlust, I was going to kill her,
bring her back to life, and kill her all over again—her and her
irresponsible sire. The Underworld Detection Agency never
had to know a thing.

I rumbled up the stairs and opened the door to my studio,
feeling a sense of calm that I hadn't felt since this whole
debacle began. I grabbed my dress in progress and sat down
at my sewing machine, letting the humming sound of the
machine soothe me. I suppose I was too lost in that sound to
hear the studio door open and close. And of course, as we
know, vampires have no discernible weight, so I wouldn't
have heard Wendi's footsteps anyway.

Chapter Eight

"Hello, Nina."

I spun in my chair just in time to see the hungry sparkle in Wendi's eyes and her Cheshire-cat grin. Her fangs were still smallish, but they were sharp and she was ready. She sprang and I dodged her. She moved quickly but was still unsure of her power, so her half-second hesitation was more than enough time for me to step aside, grab her by the back of her head, and ram her lovely model face into my desk. She howled, immediately learned from her error, and twisted from me and on me. I stumbled backward, shocked by Wendi's strength, when her hands closed around my neck, her thumbs pushing against my windpipe. She was fully on top of me and paid back my smashing of her face by repeatedly slamming the back of my head into the blond hardwood.

Unless we've eaten recently, vampires are impervious to pain. Unfortunately, I wasn't one to starve, so Wendi's bongo-drumming of my head was causing me quite a bit of discomfort.

But the fact that the incessant shaking was also ruining my hair was pissing me off more.

I spun and we changed positions, my hands on her neck. Much to my pleasure, she winced. She had just eaten, too.

"Why are you doing this?" I hissed at Stringy Supermodel.

She grinned again and stared directly into my eyes. "You fired me."

I pulled my hands from her neck and sat back on her chest. "Not this, this. I pretty much get this," I said, gesturing from her to me. "I mean overall. Why Allison? Why Rose?"

Wendi dragged her tongue over her lip and I could see the faint tint of bloodred still there. "She told me to."

"She who?"

But Wendi furiously bucked and I toppled right off her, taking a long, hard slide across the room and crashing into my sewing table. The leg wobbled once before it split down the center, and my sewing machine—dress still locked under the presser foot and pinned down by a European 110 needle—came raining down on me. I was blinded by layers of black linen gauze, pinned underneath them by the weight of my Singer.

"Whore!" I screamed.

"Hack!" she barked.

I felt Wendi's fingers tear through my tent of dress and close around a handful of my hair. She yanked and my scalp felt like it was on fire. I let her pull me and used her own strength to come at her, walloping her squarely in the chest. I heard the "oof" as she hit the floor and I leapt over her, diving for the door. I was on my belly, just about to reach up for the knob when I saw the flash of silver. By the time I looked over my shoulder, Wendi had plunged my shears deep into my calf. We both watched, momentarily mesmerized by the deep red blood that pooled around the blades that stuck straight up from my flesh.

I could see the hunger. I could practically see her mouth watering. She paused and bent, fingers outstretched, reaching for the bubble of blood. I let her get close, then kicked as hard as I could. Wendi took a Louboutin to the temple and flopped backward unceremoniously.

Intellectually, I knew that I should stake Wendi with the splintered wooden leg of my desk, or at the very least secure her in one of the wardrobes. But it was T minus ten hours until Fashion Week and I was already late for the gala, and my Cinderella brain took over. I reached over Wendi and snatched my dress from my toppled sewing machine, blocking out the loud rip the fabric made as I pulled it, and yanked it over my head. I worked off the clothes I was wearing while simultaneously straightening the dress and taking the stairs two at a time—I can do things like that, I'm a vampire.

And because I'm a vampire, certain things *shouldn't* have been happening: Large chunks of my hair shouldn't have been coming out in my hands as I tried to work what remained into some semblance of a topknot or chignon. My nose shouldn't have been bleeding and the vision in my left eye shouldn't have been growing blurrier by the minute as the skin around it swelled. Of course, when one has fresh blood coursing through their veins, one is subject to the wounds of humanity—it doesn't even matter if the blood is yours or not.

I still made it into my clothes and down six blocks in record time, rounding the corner just in time to slow to a demure trot and toss a smile at Pike.

He was dressed in his very sexy deconstructed tuxedo, holding a glass of champagne and lounging on the steps of the Met. With the slice of yellow light from the party inside reflecting out on him, he looked a scene right out of a romcom—and there I was, his lovely Cinderella, rushing toward him, jumping into my perfect heels.

Pike stood when he saw me, and I expected him to greet me with open arms, because I lived with my ex-roommate and best friend Sophie Lawson too long, and she lived the majority of her life in romance vignettes and *Lifetime* movies.

Apparently, it had rubbed off on me.

"I thought you said thirty minutes," Pike said, his tone annoyed.

I stopped, my mouth dropping open. "Seriously? That's how you greet me? Look at me!"

"There's a hole in your dress. There's a lot of holes in your dress. Is it supposed to be like that? I'm not saying that it's not nice . . ."

"Pike!" I stepped into the light and Pike's eyes widened.

"Oh my Lord, Nina, what happened to you?"

I pressed my fingers to my sore eye and thankfully felt that it had stopped swelling. "Wendi. Wendi came into my studio and attacked me." I looked down at my dress and felt a lump in my throat. "And she ruined my dress."

That made the edges of Pike's lips twitch into a smile that he fought. I should have been mad, but the reality of the day finally hit me and I realized how exhausted I really was.

"What happened to Wendi?"

"I locked her in the studio."

"Is that going to hold her?"

"It'll do." I grabbed Pike's arm. "Besides, I have to make an appearance."

"Baby, please. Don't take this the wrong way, but you look like you've gone through a wood chipper."

I paused. "Take off your jacket."

"Excuse me?"

"Take it off."

Pike did as he was told and I proceeded to rip the sleeves and pockets off and slid into it, using a length of linen gauze that was currently hanging in a sad loop around my ankles to secure it at the waist.

I undid my topknot and brushed through my hair with my fingers, glad to feel that the new hair was already growing in. "How's my face?" I asked.

"Beautiful. Your black eye is already going down." He

pulled a hankie from his back pocket and wiped the tiny trickle of blood from my nose, his other hand gently cradling my chin. "That whole vampire super-healing thing is pretty cool."

"Yeah, well, you can fly." I smiled. "We're just going to go in and make an appearance, then we can go back for Wendi and make her talk."

"You didn't ask who her sire was when you were with her?"

I narrowed my eyes. "It wasn't exactly a tea party." I stomped in front of Pike, who grabbed the back of my dress, leaned over, and yanked the shears from the back of my leg.

"I think you might want to consider giving up your accessory line."

As expected, the incredible works of art all around us were wholly ignored by the influx of coifed celebrities, fashion powerhouses, and models. Everyone fluttered around each other with champagne in their hands and benign smiles pasted on their faces, moving fast enough to not look static but slow enough so that each attendee could be scrutinized and, hopefully, idolized for their fashion choices and daring hairstyles. I immediately felt myself straighten, throw my shoulders back, and pop my statuesque stance, doing all three quickly enough so that people could take me in, but not have enough time to take my picture. Pike played the perfect counterpart, his hand moving to the small of my back, the sensation from the simple move sending shock waves through my body. I tried to quash down the inappropriate sexual feelings as we made our way through the crowd, smiling and nodding and nodding and smiling. Pike rescued two glasses of champagne, handed me one. He leaned in, his lips next to my ear.

"So what exactly are we supposed to be doing here?"

"We'll split up and do a quick go round the room. You keep your eye out for Rose."

"And if I find her, I take her by any means necessary?" His eyes raked over me, over the slices and tears in my dress and, presumably, the eye that just a few seconds ago was in danger of swelling shut.

"How about just corralling her by any means necessary?"

"And what exactly are you going to be doing while I'm fighting the good fight?" Pike asked, finishing his champagne and taking mine.

"I'm going to sniff out this super-new mystery fashion designer."

He cocked a disbelieving eyebrow. "I thought the whole stopping supermodel vampire thing was 'our' responsibility. And when I say our"—he made finger quotes—"I mean *your*."

"You know as well as I do that this mystery designer"—I made the obnoxious finger quotes right back to Pike—"is likely Wendi's sire. Or possibly. At least the timing is right."

"So you do think so."

I cut my eyes, taking in the assembled group. "It's a possibility. Think about it—the killings started at right about the same time that designers started coming into town."

"But you said he had no motive. Why would he pick off his own models?"

I knew that whatever I said about the sire's motives would reflect back on me, but life and afterlife was on the line, so I didn't have time to be coy.

"A vampire—especially one who sires—doesn't need a motive. It's about hunger, want. Sometimes need. Sometimes nothing. A vampire sees something she likes, she takes it."

Pike held my eyes for a beat; I'm not sure if the intensity exchanged in that three-second glance was based on the sexual prowess of a vampire taking what she wants or based on the realization laid in front of him that I was no different from the sire.

I was a being moved by hunger. By want. And I was ashamed.

Pike stepped closer to me, his hands on my shoulders,

squeezing gently. "We are all beings moved by hunger, Nina. We're all moved by want."

In a heartbeat the distance between us was closed and my mouth was on Pike's, my lips pressing hard against his until he gave in, his mouth opening slightly. My body shattered against his and his arms slid from my shoulders until he was holding me against him.

"Geez, get a room, you two."

We pulled apart, the electricity between us waning, turning into a dim anger when I saw Vlad, dressed in the finest they had to offer in 1875, his arm around Celeste's dainty waist. She was a vision in a vintage whisper-pink Givenchy gown, her long locks brushed into a lovely side chignon that seemed to accentuate her enormous doe eyes.

"'Get a room'?" I hissed. "You couldn't come up with anything original in your century or so?"

Vlad's eyes widened and I realized that we were in the presence of a breather. There was just something about Celeste that made me forget that. . . . A niggling suspicion traveled up my spine and I wondered why I hadn't felt it before. Celeste must have noticed my scrutiny as she backed away a step, half hiding herself behind Vlad's ridiculous cape.

Sadly for me, his cape and her hint of 1930s glamour worked and heads were turning to stare at them. I cleared my throat, shook off the delicious taste of Pike, and took control.

"Celeste, you were in an Under the Hem gown. Do you know who the designer is?"

She shook her head. "No. The dresses just showed up on our racks. I was supposed to wear one tonight, but Vlad told me I shouldn't."

"Did you call Sophie, Vlad? Did you find anything out?"

"Well, you know how fashion forward Sophie is. . . ."

As I mentioned, Sophie Lawson is my former roommate, my very best friend, the other woman Vlad openly sponges from, and she has the fashion prowess of a spinster librarian crossed with a Mennonite. Maybe I didn't mention that last part.

"I checked in with her, but she obviously didn't know anything, so I set Lorraine to work on it."

I opened my mouth and then closed it again when Vlad held up his phone and continued. "She's calling me back."

"Okay. I'm going to see if I can get any information on Under the Hem, you guys keep your eyes out for Rose."

Celeste's eyebrows went up. "I heard about Rose on the news. Isn't she—"

My cheeks burned, Vlad's eyes went round, and Pike's mouth dropped open just the tiniest bit. "A different Rose," the three of us lied in unison.

Celeste nodded and Vlad steered her away, depositing her at the bar. Pike went the opposite way, moving into his charming stealth mode, shaking hands and grinning, moving quickly through the crowd. I went directly through the middle.

If I hadn't had so much on my mind—Wendi, Rose, Under the Hem, getting my own designs done—I would have been paying more attention to the lovely dresses swishing by me and to the crowd through whom I was jostling. I would have noticed that two models slipped right by me. I would have noticed that there was a short, roundish woman directly on their tail.

I would have noticed when she turned and stared at me that she was a vampire.

Chapter Nine

I continued twirling through the crowd, listening in on snippets and bits of conversation. The identity of the Under the Hem designer was the center of at least every other conversation, but everyone seemed to know just as little as I did—supersecretive, from San Francisco. One man was assuring the women that he entertained that the Under the Hem designer was in fact a man and that they were exceptionally tight. I leaned in until I heard the girls twitter and giggle when the speaker invited each of the ladies back to his suite to see some of the sketches his "buddy" had loaned him. No designer in his right mind would loan sketches to a buddy with a comb-over and a set of brand-new blue-white veneers that made his mouth look so unattractively horse-like.

"Um, Ms. LaShay?"

The woman was right behind me, wriggling her way between a statuesque blonde starlet and her slightly sweaty manager.

"I'm Sasha."

There was something vaguely familiar about Sasha. She was about my height, but the enormity of her stuffed-in-her-dress breasts threw it off. And she was wearing Wendi's "it" Under the Hem dress.

Slight alterations had been made—a hemline dropped, a slight curve to the bodice to scaffold her ample cleavage—but it was definitely *the* dress.

I pointed. "Where did you get that dress?"

The woman grinned ear to ear. "Do you like it? It's an original design."

"I know, by Under the Hem."

Sasha's face clouded, the anger evident in her snarled lip. "No, *not* by Under the Hem. By me, Sasha Pierce."

"You're the Under the Hem designer?"

Sasha bristled. "No. Under the Hem doesn't exist. These are my dresses, all of them."

I had heard the spiel before. There was always someone with a fistful of drawings claiming that their "originals" had been scooped by the bigwigs. Don't believe me? Google conspiracy theories and click on fashion. It's there.

I was initially curious how she was able to get her hands on a dress so shockingly similar to the original, but then I remembered the leaked photograph and realized that any detail-oriented nutter could probably whip out a decent facsimile given some time.

"I would love to talk to you about some design ideas that I have." Sasha went for her pocketbook. "I even have some photographs I'd like to show you."

I pasted on a quick, appeasing smile. "I'm so sorry, miss. I would love to see your designs and help you out, but now isn't the time."

I whirled on my heel and caught Vlad out of the corner of my eye. He was clear across the room, beckoning to me with wide, manic eyes. I tried to make my way through the crowd, but in the span of ten seconds it seemed to swell and double in size, bodies going shoulder to shoulder and wall to wall. I tried to look for Pike, but he was swallowed up as well, and I could feel a strange sense of panic edging up my spine.

And then the lights went out.

There were a few halfhearted screams and a ripple of laughter before the lights flared up again and the music pulsed so hard I could feel it in my chest. I saw Pike zigzag through the crowd and wrap a protective arm around me.

"What's going on?" His lips were at my ear and yet I could barely hear him.

I shook my head and glanced around when I was hit with a waft of ice-cold air—it was Vlad and Celeste and, directly behind Vlad, Sasha. Her eyes were narrowed and a beady ice blue; I couldn't tell if the disdain in them was aimed at me or the impromptu runway that popped up with the lights.

I gaped when the first model came out. She stomped down the makeshift runway with the sure, confident gait of a seasoned professional, the unaffected expression on her face precise for haute couture and for the mid-thigh-length dress she was wearing. It was an Under the Hem design.

Vlad's hand was on mine, tugging at me. I could see his lips move but couldn't hear a thing over the pulsing bass and the roar of cheers that went up with the second model. Another Under the Hem dress, another design so stunning it was breathtaking. Vlad shook me hard and started to sign, pointing to his phone and furiously mouthing something that looked like "leave." I glanced over my shoulder toward the door and saw Sasha. She was incensed. Practically panting. Her hands were clawed and then fisted.

I knew what I'd missed. I knew why the air around Vlad was so exceptionally cold.

Sasha was a vampire.

She dove over us with lightning speed and clobbered the third model just as she burst from the curtain. I thought she was going for the poor girl's neck, but she went directly for the dress. A vampire who overthrew blood for fashion was like a we-have-no-soul mate, and I warmed to her, instinctively holding Pike and Vlad back with my arms.

It was a woman so moved by couture she felt the need to act. It was beautiful.

"These are my designs!" Sasha screamed in an earsplitting screech. "Mine! You're *my* models!"

The girl underneath her was clearly terrified by the woman holding fistfuls of her wardrobe—especially when that woman turned as if just noticing she was in front of a packed house, and the glint of one pointed incisor flashed under the stage lights.

"I'll rip out your throat!"

Maybe it wasn't beautiful, after all.

Vlad, Pike, and I acted in unison, Vlad shuffling the other startled models offstage, Pike surprising Sasha and yanking her off the model. Sasha was still clawing and grabbing at air, still hysterical. Finally her eyes focused on me and she stopped flailing so hard.

"You! You should be as angry as I am! We were supposed to be fashion legends! We were supposed to rule the industry! We would have had a team of perfect models who never aged, never changed, never gained or lost an ounce. We would be in complete control!"

Her arms flopped down by her sides and I noticed the pin she had used to gather the bodice of the reconditioned dress: It was a single, pink, sparkly high heel.

"You're Fashion Fish?"

She grinned a weird, maniacal grin. "The pulse of the fashion industry. Don't you see? I was setting it all up for us. Your designs would be the darlings and then mine. We would have the fashion rivalry to end all rivalries, but we would be partners." She dragged her tongue over her teeth. "Forever."

I was reeling and ready to tell this big-breasted, supermodel-vampire-creating hack that just because we shared the same orthodontia, we were never going to be partners when Sasha snapped her head toward the curtain and hissed, "But then he came along and ruined everything."

"Oh, good God."

Peeking out from behind the curtain at just about hip level were two beady yellow eyes I would recognize most places and a stench I could never forget. The curtain swished open and Vlad ran out, effectively blocking the tiny-eyed guy.

"Steve is behind Under the Hem!"

Steve, a three-foot-tall troll who smelled like the most unholy combination of blue cheese and feet, proudly stepped out—only after making sure that Pike still had a secure hold on Sasha.

Steve was a San Francisco native and did contract work for the Underworld Detection Agency—none of it fashion related. The bulk of his fashion sense came from doing his smarmy best to look up the skirts—oh, "Under the Hem," ew—of every lady he ran into, most notably mine and Sophie Lawson's. He was sleazy, sex starved, and annoying, and the apple of his yellow-tinged eye had always been Sophie—until he met Sasha.

"You were a paramedic, weren't you?" I gaped.

Sasha nodded, anger and hate lining her face as she glared at Steve. "That was only supposed to be until I made it big in the fashion world. But then I met Steve. . . ."

Steve apparently didn't care or didn't know that he was *thisclose* to being torn limb from moss-covered limb by a busty, irate vampire.

"Shouldn't we not talk about this here?" Pike cut his eyes to the crowd, who were desperately focused on the exchange going on. Luckily for us, our voices were lost in the bump of the music; luckily for them, the preternatural veil only allowed them to see four full-sized humans and one half-sized one having a very passionate conversation. Even so, someone must have called the police, because the sirens were already upon us and there was Detective Moyer, looking like a Lego cop amongst the sea of statuesque beauties dressed to the nines. He beelined directly for me and clamped a clammy hand on my wrist.

"What are you doing?" I yelled, trying to pull away. "She's the one you want. She's the crazy one!" I jabbed a finger toward Sasha, and Moyer took his sweet time looking over at her. He didn't take his hand off my wrist, though.

"I got a call that someone attacked a supermodel, and you know what they say, if it sounds like horses, don't go looking for zebras."

"I don't even know what that means but it's her, she's the one who attacked! She's the one who killed Wendi, Allison, and Rose!"

Moyer looked to Pike for confirmation and Sasha started to sag. "I was doing it for us," she breathed.

"We don't even know each other!" I shot back. "I met you once when we were pulling my best friend from the clutches of a Snuggie-wearing madman."

The detective's glance cut back to me and I shook my head, not wanting to give him any more fodder for his report. "It's not like it sounds."

Sasha straightened up, her eyes glistening. "Don't know you? Nina, I've followed you and your fashion line since you were working out of your little closet room in San Francisco. You're a legend. You have been for decades."

Once again, it wasn't hard to warm to the misguided vampire. What can I say? Vanity is a LaShay trait.

"I started Fashion Fish for you. I wanted everyone to know your name."

"So that you could ride on her coattails," Pike put in.

"On my coattails," Steve clarified.

"You are not the designer," Sasha screeched. "I am the designer! You were just supposed to be the face behind the line, the cash behind the line."

My eyebrows went up and I pointed to Steve. "That was the face you wanted for Under the Hem?"

Steve puffed out his little barrel chest, his stubby gray fingers tugging the lapels of his jacket. He grinned a wide, mostly toothless grin that just made his potato-shaped head look even more misshapen and unattractive. I was waiting for him to smooth down the three mossy hairs that made up his coif, but he didn't.

"Sorry, Sasha. You and I just don't share the same idea of what is attractive. Thanks for the shout-out in your blog, though."

I gave her a finger wave while Pike explained to Moyer what happened. Apparently, Pike had a great deal more credibility because two other officers flanked the detective while he put Sasha in handcuffs. I slumped down in a chair in the makeshift "backstage" area and let out a long sigh. My phone did its little ping thing, and there the icon was again, letting me know that I was mere hours away from my debut. I had no clothing, no models, no hope, but I did help end a sire from taking on the Manhattan fashion world.

It didn't seem like enough.

Vlad came over and locked me in a rough half hug. "I can't believe you want me to move out. We make such a good team."

I couldn't help but grin up at my idiot nephew. He kissed me on the top of my head and slipped back into his jacket.

"Where you going?"

Vlad backed toward the door, beckoning for Celeste. She came running over like a doe-eyed spaniel and tucked herself under his arm.

"Is that a sewing kit in your hand, Celeste?"

She nodded. "I'm a really incredible seamstress."

"We're headed over to the Fashion District. I hear there's an amazing fashion line that's supposed to debut tomorrow, but the designer has been out chasing killers, so she hasn't been able to finish . . ."

I felt a wash of mist go over my eyes and I swallowed

down the lump in my throat. "Really? You guys are going to help?"

Vlad shrugged. "I told you you need me."

He and Celeste disappeared out the door and Pike walked over.

"Well, it's over," he said, pulling another chair and then pulling me into his arms.

I shook my head. "No. We still have to deal with Wendi."

Pike pushed a lock of hair behind my ear. "After this, stopping one half-made vampire seems like cake."

I smiled slightly. "I wonder how she is with a needle and thread."

"Speaking of sewing, apparently, Sasha thought her plan would go off without a hitch. She figured if she could get the models wearing the dresses on her side—literally, on her side—she could create some sort of undead fashion army to take it over. Then I suppose she thought the two of you would run off into the sunset—"

I cocked an eyebrow.

"Into the darkness, and rule the fashion industry by iron fang."

"Sounds heavenly," I said, "except for the whole thing about *us* ruling the fashion industry. I work alone."

Pike narrowed his eyes.

"Sort of."

"Better," Pike said, rubbing his thumb over my lip.

I knew there was work to do. I knew that on some level, I should remind Pike that all vampires weren't the same and all of us didn't turn into couture killers no matter how gorgeous the gown was. But all I wanted to do was kiss him—so I did.

Drop Dead Clothing Wakes the Dead!
*Nina LaShay and her Drop Dead runway show was
all anyone was talking about for the whole of fashion
week! Though this blogger is new on the scene, she was*

*able to score a front-row ticket (courtesy of the now
defunct Fashion Fish) to the show of the millennium!
Not only are LaShay's designs gorgeous, but she pulls
from fashion through the ages—everything from
French pre-revolutionary coats and jackets to funky 70s
jewelry and eyewear to the exact thing they'll be
wearing in Milan next week. LaShay is the epitome of
fashion respect. But if it wasn't the clothing that stole
the show, it could have been LaShay's choice of models.
Since Drop Dead is known for an edge toward the
macabre, the designer made sure each girl looked
suitably vampiric—pale, statuesque, with white marble
skin and coal black eyes, each girl with a fresh coating
of blood-red lipstick. This blogger has never seen
models Allison Hunter and Rose Carmichael look more
stunning. And they say runway fashion is dead!*

xoxo Celeste